D1521959

CROWN OF SHADOWS

CROWN
OF
SHADOWS

BOOK 2 OF
THE SEVENTH KING SERIES

BY
MAGGIE FORBUSH

2024

A Note on Content:
This book is not suitable for everyone. It includes adult
themes, violence, and strong language. A non-exhaustive list of
potentially upsetting content may be reviewed at my website for
those so inclined: www.maggieforbush.com/content-warnings

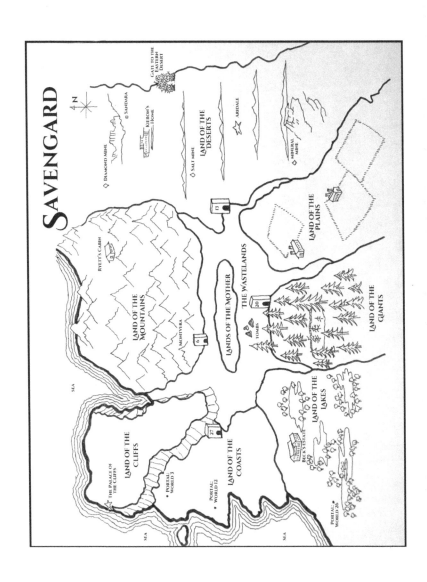

SAVENGARD

N

SEA

LAND OF THE MOUNTAINS

RYET'S CABIN

MONIVERA

6

13

DIAMOND MINE

SAMDARA

KIERON'S HOME

SALT MINE

LAND OF THE DESERTS

ARIDALE

MINERAL MINE

GATE TO THE EASTERN DESERT

LANDS OF THE MOTHER

THE WASTELANDS

20

TOMBS

LAND OF THE PLAINS

LAND OF THE GIANTS

LAND OF THE CLIFFS

THE PALACE OF THE CLIFFS

PORTAL WORLD 3

PORTAL WORLD 12

LAND OF THE COASTS

27

LAND OF THE LAKES

BECK'S ESTATE

PORTAL WORLD 26

SEA

SEA

PART 1: THE KING OF SHADOWS

CHAPTER 1

Genevieve

The sun was setting against the red cliffs. I stood on the red stone patio looking out across a pool of water whose edge disappeared against the desert. My magic did not hum under my skin anymore, it only seemed to sputter and flicker like a flame that was running out of fuel.

I walked towards the edge of the pool and without dropping my clothes or even stepping out of my shoes, I stepped into the water. It was cool, but not cold. The perfect temperature to keep you comfortable on a scorching hot day. I took another step into the water and felt it soak my pants up to my knees.

I took another step and another. The calm water rippled as it lapped against my waist—then against my chest. The water did not get any deeper. I took one last slow blink, soaking in the sunset. Then I dunked my head below the surface.

I felt my hair become weightless and flow around me. I let bubbles of air release from my lips and float up to the surface. I opened my eyes to stare into the nothingness and the salt water stung. A last bubble of air floated up.

My lungs fought me. *Breathe. Don't breathe. Breathe.* My muscles involuntarily flexed and twitched, begging for air. All I had to do was put my feet down and stand up. But I wouldn't. There was nothing in my mind but the silent command to suck in a breath.

The water rushed around me and strong hands yanked me above the water. I fought against them crying and screaming. Hands planted firmly on either side of my face.

"What the fuck? I am not letting you die here. Especially not on your first day, maybe your second, but not today." Kieron's voice was gruff and nearly yelling, his face was inches from mine. "Do you hear me? Not today!"

My body shook with my sobbing. Kieron pulled me against his chest, cradling my head and body against him, and safely above the waterline.

Hours Earlier.

I slipped quietly from the bed Ryett and I were in. His deep breaths told me he was still sound asleep. *Good.* He needed to rest. I closed the door to his room with a soft click.

The halls of Beck's residence were quiet, but I could see a guard standing alertly at the end of the hall. As I approached he spoke, "Beck is in the dining room. Kieron has not returned yet."

"Thank you." I replied softly and headed down the stairs to find Beck.

Just as the guard said, I found Beck in the dining room, sitting at the head of the table with untouched food in front of him.

"Thank you, Beck. Thank you for helping us and letting us stay here." I said in greeting. Ryett had successfully restored the twenty-seventh gate, but when Vossarian had shown up to kill him—well, I was the one who had done the killing. I had killed Voss. I balled my hands into fists trying to erase the feeling of the axe handle against my palms and the impact it had sent through my hands when I chopped off Voss's head.

Kieron had been separated from us with Voss's arrival, but he had somehow found Beck and convinced him to help us. Beck had shown up just in time to save Ryett and me from burning to death and he had held up his offer to help. All of us had gotten out alive thanks to him. My thank you to him was sincere.

"Of course," he replied with an idle hand wave. "I assume Ryett is still asleep."

"Yes." I sat down in one of the chairs and took a deep breath, bracing myself for what I was about to tell Beck. "Kieron is bringing someone back with him. Or at least he should be. She has been kept captive under Vossarian and his father, Luther, for somewhere in the ballpark of two hundred years."

Beck stiffened and his eyes were sharp, "Go on."

"Her name is Rachel. She is Ryett's lover from early in his life. He thought she was dead all this time." My chest tightened at the words. It was hard to swallow. Hard to breathe. I continued, "Luther told me about her when I was in the twenty-seventh world. He found her and kept her captive as an eventual bargaining chip with Ryett. When Ryett started business with Vossarian he continued to keep her a secret in case Ryett ever turned on him. Voss tried to play that card before I killed him, but I already knew where she was. Kieron is bringing her here."

To Beck's credit his face was calm and neutral, "I will send for Esmay." Esmay was Beck's healer of choice. She had seen to Sarla and me when we tumbled through a portal from my world, the twenty-sixth world, and into Beck's kingdom. She was the best of the best.

"Thank you." I said and reached for the small carafe of coffee. I poured myself a cup and cradled it in my hands as I stared blankly at the food on the table.

Kieron strode through the glass double doors into the dining room. The female who trailed him was beautiful. She was thin, but had curves in all the right places. Her skin was creamy white and her lips full. Her eyes were a piercing emerald green and she scanned the room as she followed Kieron. Her red hair hung in gentle waving curls just past her generous breasts. She tucked her hair behind an ear—a nervous twitch I noted—and I saw the slight point to the tip of her ear. She was indeed not from Savengard.

She was all the things I was not—delicate, gentle, ethereal. My body tingled as I forced down every emotion that welled up within me.

"You must be Rachel." Beck stood as he greeted them. "Come. Sit and enjoy some food."

She nodded gracefully to him and Kieron pulled out a chair for her to sit.

"Rachel, meet Beck, The King of the Lakes. This is his residence. Also, meet Genevieve, you can thank her for your liberation from captivity." Kieron introduced us, his voice calm and even.

"It is nice to meet you." I said as calmly as I could and forced a smile. "Kieron, can I have a word?"

I stood and followed Kieron into the hall. "I did as you asked and did not tell her about Ryett. She claims she has not been harmed and the servants where she was kept also said she was well taken care of." He explained.

"Good. Thank you. Beck will send for Esmay to have her checked out anyway." I took a deep breath and ran my hands down my face. I was going to throw up. Or explode into a million pieces. "I need to go tell Ryett."

"Are you sure? You don't have to. You certainly do not have to do it yet." Kieron pressed me. His voice was gentle—concerned. "I can keep her safe until you are ready."

"No. Waiting will not make it easier." I countered. It would not. And I could not look Ryett in the eye knowing I was hiding his long lost and thought to be dead lover from him. "I will tell him when he wakes up and he can decide if and when he wants to see her."

"And what about you?" Kieron asked, his voice suddenly hard.

"What about me?" I said dismissively and turned to go to Ryett's

7

room. Kieron did not say anything more as I left him standing in the entryway. I walked down the guest wing and it never felt so long. Never felt like the wide hall or tall ceilings were closing in on me like they were now.

I quietly entered Ryett's room and found him awake and sitting in one of the chairs. The color had returned to his face and he looked surprisingly well. He stood and crossed the room to me in a few strides. His lips met mine as he wrapped his arms around me. My legs were weak.

"What's wrong?" Ryett whispered, "Is everyone okay?"

"Everyone is okay." I murmured, "But Ryett—" He kissed me again. "We found Rachel."

He pulled back from me, "What are you talking about?"

"Rachel is alive. She is here." Confusion and pain and guilt all crossed Ryett's face. I continued, "When we were fighting Voss, he sent me to the twenty-seventh world. His father was there. Luther was there. He told me many things, one of them being that he had kidnapped Rachel to use as leverage against you. He also told me where they kept her. Kieron brought her here this morning."

"But she is dead." Ryett breathed.

"Red hair, green eyes, pointed ears?" Ryett's eyes grew wide as I spoke, "She is alive and in one piece. We have not told her about you. I wanted to tell you first."

"She is alive? She is here?" Ryett asked slowly, his face beginning to pale again.

"Esmay, Beck's healer is coming to examine her and make sure she is unharmed, but I can bring her here first if you want to see her. If you are ready ..." Pieces of me felt like they were flaking off and floating away as I spoke. Ryett seemed to be pulling further and further away with every heartbeat.

"Yes, I would like to see her." He finally said. I could see tears building in his eyes.

"Of course." I breathed. "I will go get her."

This fucking hallway was too long. I did not know what to say to Rachel as I led her down towards the room I had left Ryett in. I had only told her someone wanted to see her. We stopped outside the room and I swallowed, my mouth was dry. My throat was tight and burning. I reached out and turned the door handle, pushing the door in as I entered the room and held it open for Rachel to follow in after me.

My head went completely silent as I watched Rachel run for Ryett. As Ryett wrapped her in his arms and held her. As he pushed back her hair and stared into her eyes. I stepped back into the hall and closed the door behind me. I did not need to witness this. I had seen enough.

Somehow my feet took me back to the dining room where Kieron and Beck still sat, food untouched.

"So it is really her?" Kieron asked.

I gave a quick nod of confirmation as I walked past them to the small sitting area near the fireplace and sat down. I stared at the low table in front of me and into nothingness.

I did not know how much time had passed, but Ryett's voice

jerked me from my numbness.

"Esmay is with her now." Ryett said as he entered the room, "Thank you, Kieron."

"Don't thank me. My vote was to kill her for good, but your soulmate convinced me otherwise. I am still not sure I agree." Kieron's voice had a bite to it.

Beck's head snapped up to look at Ryett, then me. "You two are soulmates?" He blurted out.

Ryett ignored him, "Genevieve—"

"Let me guess, you failed to mention that significant detail to Rachel, didn't you?" Kieron cut in.

"Kieron, don't." I said flatly. It did not matter. I stood and looked at Ryett. I fished inside of myself for the humming in my magic. The electricity that Ryett always brought out in me. There was nothing. I grasped for the invisible bond that tied us together, like a rope always pulling me towards him. I only found a slack line and when I pulled it, a cut end wound up in my hands. I had my answer. I had let myself open up to the potential and possibility with Ryett —of a new life here in Savengard. An opportunity to move forward. To be happy. I felt my heart ache. Felt my chest cave in as that possibility was ripped from me.

Ryett's face was pained as he spoke, "Genevieve, I can't just abandon her—"

"I know, Ryett. I understand. I just can't stay." I responded, my voice soft, but surprisingly steady.

"What do you mean?" He breathed, his eyes growing wide.

Kieron cut in, "Okay, now that *that* is settled, G and I need to get back to the Deserts. I have a kingdom to get under control."

"Genevieve is not going with you, Kieron, what are you talking about?" Beck said sharply.

"Oh, she is. You asked what I needed and I need someone to ensure you two do not stab me in the back once I leave here. Plus you two need someone you trust to report on me. Genevieve fits both." Kieron explained casually.

"Take anyone else." Beck gritted out.

"My mind is made up." Kieron crossed the room to me and put an arm around my shoulders.

"You can't." Beck was stepping towards us, the air flowing around him as his magic built.

Kieron threw up a shield around us, the air rippling like heat above the desert sand.

"He can." Ryett breathed.

"What?" Beck snapped.

"That's right, Ryett, I can. By law Genevieve is still my possession. Do not make me call in on that inter-kingdom law." Kieron said, almost sounding bored. Beck was fuming, "To bring you up to speed, Beck, since clearly you missed out on the gossip, Genevieve here was carrying my child. Obviously it didn't work out, but by law she is still mine."

Beck's face paled. Ryett looked like he might throw up, "If you hurt her—" Beck gritted between his teeth.

"I know, I know. If I hurt her then our alliance is over and you come and rip me and my kingdom to shreds. But don't worry, I won't even touch her … unless she wants me to." Kieron said mockingly. Then the room disappeared around us.

I was dressed too warm for the heat of the desert, but I did not

11

care. I just stared at the pool that stretched into infinity in front of us. Kieron was saying something, but I could not hear him over the roaring in my ears. He had done everything I had asked him to. I did not think it would feel like this though. That every reason I had come up with to fight for this life would slip away like sand through my fingers. I stepped towards the pool.

CHAPTER 2

Kieron - Months Earlier.

"You two will not believe who I stumbled upon in Beck's woods." Vossarian sat lounging on his plush velvet couch. Why Voss had summoned Rook and him, Kieron did not know. Vossarian chuckled darkly, "No guesses? I will give you a clue: Both of you died the last time you saw her."

Kieron's eyes flashed, but he quickly schooled his features to be neutral. After over four hundred years of dealing with Vossarian's bullshit he was a master of deception and lies—and pretending like not a damn thing irked him.

"Which bitch, Voss?" Rook looked almost ravenous. His need for revenge and to mend his wounded ego after their unfortunate failed assassination of Sarla months ago had turned him into an even bigger prick than usual.

Vossarian let out a dark chuckle, "Her name is Genevieve."

"And what was Beck's female doing out in his woods alone?" Kieron leveled the question at him, faking boredom. Inside, Kieron was screaming. *Genevieve. Her name is Genevieve.*

She had been unexpected and the only reason he had failed killing Sarla was because he had lost his fucking mind when he looked into Genevieve's eyes that day by the river. Afterwards, he had dreamt about her for months before his spies reported that Aada, Sarla, and an unknown female were spotted out to dinner in Beck's kingdom. He knew it was dangerous—careless even— but he had immediately gone to see for himself. He had hidden in the shadows and watched as the females left the restaurant. Sure enough, it was her. She was even more beautiful than he remembered.

"Frankly, I don't care." Voss replied, "But the game has changed. Beck will bow before me to get her back. Now I just need to break her."

Rook was practically drooling, Kieron noticed. He could not let Rook get his hands on her. The two of them were the deadliest assassins in the history of Savengard—or any world—and their skill sets also included various forms of torture. Rook's brand tended to lean towards permanent damage or death—he was hot headed and not well practiced at containing his emotions.

Kieron was doing everything in his power to not speak first. This was a game of patience and intelligence—two things Rook lacked.

"You both know the drill. So who wants her?" Voss tossed out the opportunity.

Just as Kieron expected, Rook nearly fell over himself, "I'll break her in no time."

Vossarian nodded at Rook's enthusiasm with a dark smile on his face.

"No. She's mine." Kieron growled. He would not let Rook touch her. He had felt her magic even as the bullets she had shot him with had entered his body and killed him—temporarily, but she had still killed him. "Sarla took you down, she took me down. She is mine."

Kieron noticed the change in Voss, he looked intrigued. Kieron had never demanded to be involved in breaking prisoners or slaves, he had only ever been ordered to—and did it with unmatched expertise—but he had never volunteered. Then again, he had not lost a fight in nearly four hundred years either.

"You make a good point. She is yours, Kieron." Voss said with a glint in his eye. Rook started to object, but Voss raised a hand sharply. Rook bit his tongue. Voss continued, "Let's go see if she is awake."

Kieron was going to lose it. Genevieve had of course been given the magic suppressant drugs in her food and water and would continue to get them the entire time she was here. It was standard protocol, but Voss had decided she would get the other drugs too. Kieron hated the other drugs. He stood just inside the doorway and watched as the two female servants dressed Genevieve—if one could consider it clothing. They had basically wrapped her beautiful naked body up like a fucking present. His cock pulsed and he shifted on his feet to relieve the pressure in his pants.

He had to get her out of here. He had an overwhelming urge to fuck her, yes, but that was not the only reason. He had to get her out of here because she did not belong as a prisoner. The magic he had felt emitting from her—she was a queen. And not Beck's queen either.

Those golden brown eyes rimmed in a ring of blue gray steel met his briefly as she was brought to the cage. *Fuck she was already so high, what dose of drugs had Voss given her?* It did not matter. There was nothing Kieron could do about it as he lifted her into the cage and secured her in.

Genevieve had blacked out minutes ago, Kieron noted as he stood against the wall watching the crowd dance and Voss lounge on his throne. At some point Voss would notice too and signal Kieron to take her back to her cell. He would get his chance to at least get her away from the groping hands. He had never cared before, never cared with the hundreds of other females he had done this same game with. Sure he hated it, but he had never *cared*. He had also never met another being with powers that matched his and *that* was what this was about.

He had heard the other assassins and warriors talk about the primal and animalistic pull they got when they had found their match, but of all the females he had fucked he had never felt it himself. Until now. And she was a prisoner in the lethal game Voss was playing. That he was playing.

Holy fuck. She just spat at him. Kieron was lurking outside the door to Genevieve's cell, waiting to see if she would continue to comply or eventually tell Voss to fuck off. Tonight it was the latter. Voss did not take disrespect well, but his response had been surprisingly reserved tonight.

"I do not care if you beat her or fuck her or both. Just break her. Oh and I guess leave her in one piece. I would not want any permanent damage on that pretty body or face of hers." Voss seethed to Kieron as he stalked out of the cell. Kieron could do that and it was exactly why he had demanded that she was his. Except now he would have to do something beyond his wildest nightmare. He took a deep breath. He was her only chance at surviving this and even if she never forgave him, he would do this so she could live. He was going to have to torture his soulmate.

Kieron's knees almost buckled as he closed the door to Genevieve's cell. He had felt a piece of his soul leave him every time he had struck her. And it took everything in him to not ravish her when she had finally begged for him to give her pleasure. The way her sharp taunting words had cut into him ... he could thank four hundred years of practice for being able to keep the evil torturer act up because damn did it turn him on. She was beautiful and smart and he knew she would not break. She had seen far worse things than this disgusting dungeon could offer. Now he just needed a plan to trick Voss into thinking she was breaking long enough to get her the fuck out of here.

"How tight was her pussy." Kieron froze at Rook's question.

He had been so caught up in trying to get back to his rooms without being sick at what he had done he had not heard the assassin sneak up on him.

"None of your fucking business, Rook. She's mine, find some other prisoner to beat off to." Kieron replied with venom. Then without waiting for a reply he simply folded into the air and appeared in his bedroom. In six steps he was into his bathroom and on his knees, vomiting into the toilet.

CHAPTER 3

Genevieve - Present Day.

Everything was numb. My body. My mind. All I knew was that I was breathing. I rolled over in bed and opened my eyes. Kieron was sitting in a chair staring at me, "How are you feeling, sweetheart?"

"I'm not." I whispered and rolled over again so I was facing away from him.

"I am happy to change that for you. Just say the word and I will make you feel whatever you want." His voice was low and deep. Teasing.

"Go away." I responded flatly.

"Uh uh." He said and I heard his feet on the floor. The bed shook as he sat on the edge and leaned over me. His hand grasped my chin and jerked my face towards him. I tried to pull away, but he held firm. "You do not get to tell me to go away after I have just done everything you asked. I put my kingdom in jeopardy for you, G."

I averted my eyes. I had just relived my worst nightmares, killed Vossarian, and watched Ryett let me go like I was nothing. I just wanted Kieron to leave me alone.

"Look at me." He growled. I didn't. "Look. At. Me." A butterfly fluttered a wingbeat in my chest at the tone and I lifted my eyes. "Good girl." I swallowed and clenched my jaw. I hated when males said that. *Good girl*. Like I was some pet. Kieron continued, "What's going on in that head of yours? Talk to me."

"There is nothing to say." I gritted out between my teeth.

"Get up." He released my chin and ripped the covers off of me. "You are not sitting in bed all day feeling sorry for yourself. Get up."

I reluctantly pushed myself up to a seated position and threw my legs off the side of the bed. That was when I remembered the only thing I was wearing was one of Kieron's shirts. I did not pack anything before we had left and I had soaked all my clothes in the pool when we arrived yesterday. I forced myself to stand up. Kieron was standing a step back with his huge arms crossed over his chest. "Happy?" I asked sarcastically.

"Not at all." He responded, his eyes burning into mine.

"This was a mistake." I bit out, "I should not have asked you to take me with you."

"So what? You just want to sit around the Mountains and wait for Ryett?" His voice was filled with anger now.

"I could have at least had a conversation with him about it before running off like a child." I met his anger with my own.

"You think he is not fucking her?" Kieron yelled back at me, "They probably fucked all night long and you are supposed to do what? Just supposed to be okay with it? To wait for him to get it out

20

of his system and choose you? Then just pretend it didn't happen? I would not have brought her back if I knew you were going to do this to yourself!"

"What was I supposed to do? Keep her a secret? She lived as a captive for *two hundred years*. The only thing keeping her going was knowing that Ryett was still alive and still out there and she might get to see him again. And he *lost* her. She *died*. The female he chose died and he had to live through that. I would give *anything* to know my family was alive." I screamed back at him. Tears were streaming down my face.

"And what about you? What do you get? Where is your happy ending?" Kieron pressed, his voice low and stern.

I was breaking into a million pieces. My voice was shaking, "I do not envy Ryett. He thought she died—he would have kept searching for her if he had known she was alive. But then she comes back after he has found his soulmate and now he has to choose. There is no winning for him. He loses and hurts someone whatever he decides. I am trying to support him and not destroy myself in the process. It sucks for both of us, but it is better than lying to him."

Kieron let out a sigh. His voice was calm as he spoke, "He made his choice, Genevieve. Get dressed. I will be in the dining room." And with that he left the room.

Whatever emotions and feelings Kieron had just brought up in me dissipated. My body went completely numb again. Ryett *had* made his choice. He had chosen Rachel. I glanced at the clothes from Beck's that I had been wearing and simply walked after Kieron in nothing but his shirt.

This home was large by my standards, but probably cozy for

kings and infamous assassins. It all stretched across one level with a beautiful red stone courtyard at the front and a pool that disappeared into infinity in the back. Between the two were the kitchen and dining spaces along with a gloriously cozy and oversized lounge area with cream colored cushioned couches and chairs. The two halls that stretched away from the center of the home had countless doors that must certainly lead to more bedrooms and suites.

Every finish, floor, piece of tile, cabinet knob, and linen was coordinated with the extraordinary red desert that surrounded us. It created a clean, natural, and calming aurora for the home. Had I not been so numb, I would have appreciated the beauty of it more.

Kieron stopped in the middle of the great room. "I said get dressed. We have company coming."

I stared at him with my dead eyes and lifted my hand. A glass filled with water appeared in it and sloshed water on the floor. *Damn. I had actually done it.* Kieron's eyes gave a quick flash of surprise before they returned neutral, "They will be here any minute." He continued gruffly.

I took a sip of water then poured the rest down the front of the shirt I was wearing. Wet cloth stuck to my skin as it pebbled against the cold. The soft cream fabric was now nearly transparent. I set the glass on the table. "Oops." I said sarcastically and, as if on cue, I heard two sets of footsteps behind me.

Kieron gave me a look of annoyance and I glared back before I turned to meet whoever it was Kieron had invited over.

I could not help the quick inhale of breath I took and I was shocked I did not cry out in surprise. Two of the most beautiful and horrific males were strolling across the room towards us from the entryway. They were both honed with muscle and armed—heavily. One appeared to be much older and the other around my age—or whatever age that would be here.

But that was not what had my knees nearly shaking. Both males' faces were painted—no—tattooed into an image of the bones that lay beneath their skin. It was a thing of nightmares and yet so shockingly beautiful at the same time.

I should have put some fucking clothes on. What was I even doing? Pouring water on myself? What the actual fuck? I straightened my back and turned to Kieron. "Well. I think I am going to go for a swim." I said as casually as I possibly could. "Don't worry, I won't pull any shit like last night."

Before he had a chance to say anything or introduce me I walked away towards the open glass doors that spanned across the entire room. As soon as I crossed to the outside patio I peeled the wet shirt I was wearing up and over my head. Then I dropped it with a loud smack onto the patio. I continued walking in nothing but my bare skin across the patio and directly into the pool.

Kieron

"So that's Genevieve." Orion stated in a painfully neutral tone.

Fuck this female is going to ruin me. Kieron could only turn back to his two oldest friends and give them a look that he hoped conveyed an 'it has been a day' message. Then he clasped each of their forearms and pulled them in one by one to an embrace. He had missed his friends. They should both be dead—he should be dead—but they had covered for him and earned the tattoos and banishment to the Eastern Desert reserved for traitors of the crown. Kieron's face should be tattooed also. The guilt of it ate at his heart.

"You have no idea how glad I am to see you both." Kieron breathed and he gestured to the chairs at the table. "Let me get you up to speed."

Genevieve

I pulled myself from the pool and walked inside still naked— dripping water everywhere. It was almost physically painful for me to know I was making such a mess, but I tried to pretend it did not bother me. I stopped a few paces away from the three males who were huddled around a map laid out on the table. Kieron's head raised slowly and he looked at me. "Yes?" He asked tightly.

"Give me one day to be completely fucking miserable. One day." I said it without emotion.

Kieron paused, staring at me, considering. His eyes somehow managed to stay above my neck. "Okay. Anything else?"

It was my turn to make him wait. I counted to five, "I pissed in your pool." I said, then I blew him a kiss before walking back to the room he had put me in the night before.

Kieron

Kieron swallowed and rolled his neck. *This fucking female.* It took every ounce of him not to burst into laughter at her comment. She knew how to play games and he loved it. Plus how she had just walked in completely naked ... and that ass as she walked away ... the things he wanted to do to her. Sure they had fucked, but he had not done what he really wanted to. No. That was reserved for when there was trust, not for when she was a prisoner or when they were hiding from beasts in a cave after almost becoming monster meat. He needed a second—or third—chance with her.

"I see why you like her." Orion chuckled once Genevieve had disappeared behind the door to her room. Nothing else was said on the topic as they dove back into planning.

CHAPTER 4

Genevieve - Many Years Ago.

The skin on my hands was nearly raw and cracking from all of the dishes I had been scrubbing. I was assigned an unending sentence of dish washing duty after mouthing off to one of the Sergeants. Like most of the Commanders and Sergeants here, he was a total pig and deserved a fist in his face. He had been assaulting and abusing other females in my unit for months now and I just could not take another female stumbling back into the barracks crying with her clothes torn. Instead of outright punching him, I had decided to fight another way and settled for what I did best: using my snarky comments to push his buttons until he snapped.

His attention had quickly shifted off of the others and on to me. He tested me on every skill we were forced to learn here—cleaning, sewing, dancing, how to host parties, etiquette, etcetera, and he had even put a loaded gun to my head while he forced me to play the piano. When I had not made a mistake, and he looked completely furious, I simply asked him if he wanted me to ride his cock while I did it again. Then he snapped.

Thankfully he did not break any bones when he beat the shit out of me, but my face was still shades of purple, green, and yellow. He was promptly removed from duty and sent to some other location. At least he was far away from us.

"Genevieve." I nearly dropped the dish I was rinsing at the snap of my name. "Stop what you are doing, the general wants to see you."

General Chad Johnston had never asked to see me. This probably had to do with the Sergeant. Maybe not. Either way, seeing the general probably was not going to be a good thing. I had only seen him during orientation. The other females whispered about his good looks as he gave some speech about serving our people or some shit—I was not really paying attention. Sure he was good looking, but more in that 'I spend a lot of time lifting weights in front of a mirror' kind of way. It was good looking not by nature, but by pure vanity and time and money spent. I placed the clean dish on the drying rack and did my best to dry my hands on the damp towel that was slung over my shoulder. I turned and followed the male who had come to fetch me.

It felt like eternity following the male down corridors until we reached the center of the building. We approached handsome wooden double doors and the male knocked a sharp tap. "Enter." A voice replied. The male opened the door and pointed for me to enter. He apparently was not coming in with me.

I stepped into the grand office of the general. The wood was a rich mahogany and every seat and painting and piece of furniture was extravagant and rich with color. I swallowed and stood at attention as I waited for the general to speak.

"Genevieve ... I have heard a lot about you the last few days. How are your injuries healing?" The general was standing and looking out the window. He was not as old as I thought he would be, still probably fifteen years my senior, but I think I expected him to be older up close. His muscles clearly were not made for function, but just like the way his hair was styled perfectly, they were built for looks. There was an obvious difference if you knew what you were looking at.

"I'm healing fine, Sir. Thank you, Sir." I said as I turned my eyes straight ahead.

From the corner of my eye I saw him turn from the window to face me, he leaned back and sat casually on the windowsill. "I hear you have excelled at every skill this facility trains in. Perhaps you feel you are too good for us?"

"No, Sir." My heart was pounding in my chest. He still had not revealed why he had summoned me to his office.

"Come here." He said flatly. My eyes flashed to him. He was staring straight at me. I did as I was told and walked to him until I was a few paces away and stood at attention again. "I am in need of an assistant and I would like you to serve the position."

"Yes, Sir."

CHAPTER 5

Kieron - Months Earlier.

Kieron had been up most of the night trying to figure out two things: First, how to make sure Voss would believe Genevieve was breaking, and second, how he was going to get her out of here without losing his head. He would lose his head if that is what it took.

He had a plan. Step one was to make sure he had more time with her. How that fit his end goal he was not completely sure, but he needed it—he had convinced himself it was because he needed to learn more about her limits to better help him ensure she did not get killed.

Step two was to convince Ryett to come for a visit. Which would be exceptionally hard considering Ryett had made it extremely clear that Vossarian was on his shit list after he had ordered the hit on Sarla. An unfortunate hurdle, but Kieron had dealt with worse.

Part one of his plan was about to take place. Kieron was waiting outside Genevieve's cell when Vossarian arrived. *Let's see if she fakes it or fights it.* Kieron thought to himself as Voss strode into her cell, waking her.

"It's time to come play." Vossarian coaxed. She did not move. He continued, "I can send Kieron back if you would rather."

Well that answered my question. Kieron watched as Genevieve took the pill Voss gave her. He continued watching as she was washed and dressed by the female servants. She walked towards him and the cage. *Good, she knows the drill already.* Kieron thought to himself. As she reached him, Kieron lifted his hand to her face, brushing her hair back from that delicious neck of hers. *Focus.* He reminded himself and he ran his fingers around her neck. Oh the things he wanted to do to her … he felt his cock bulge in his pants as he leaned down to her ear and whispered, "I am disappointed. I thought you would be more fun to play with. Maybe it is just an act. Or maybe it was just that easy to break you."

The look in her eyes was exactly what Kieron was hoping for. She was going to fight. Not now, but soon. *Good.*

◆ ◆ ◆

Vossarian was all too eager to take the bet Kieron made with him. "I do not know what it is about this female, Kieron, but I like this side of you she is bringing out." Voss taunted Kieron.

Kieron again had four hundred years of lies and deceit to thank for the cruel grin he flashed at Voss, "I guess I just needed the right prisoner to play with."

Dark amusement crossed Vossarian's eyes as they stopped outside Genevieve's cell. Then he opened the door and strode in. Kieron instantly knew he had won the bet. Genevieve backed against the wall and defiantly told Voss 'No.'

Voss was pissed as he gave her one more chance. The way she looked when he released her and she fell helplessly to her hands and knees ... but Kieron's thoughts were interrupted by Vossarian's exit, "You were right, I owe you a hundred coins. I will be back in a few days. I don't care what you do, just leave her in one piece." Then Voss paused and his voice dropped to a whisper, "You know what, I do care what you do. No drugs and fuck her senseless. Make sure she is ready to be shown off by the time I am back."

Kieron placed the same chair in the middle of the room and removed his shirt. The way she had eye'd him last time—fuck, he wanted those eyes raking over him again. He wanted a lot more than that and he knew he was going to get it. Voss had given his orders and this was going to be worse than Kieron had been planning.

Kieron sat in the chair and looked at her beautiful body standing against the wall. If getting caught did not kill him then what he was about to do to her surely would. It would at least ruin him. He wanted it—not like this, but he wanted it. Wanted *her*. He also knew she was a prisoner. She did not want it. She would hate him for this. It was a sacrifice he was willing to make.

Genevieve's naked body rested against Kieron's bare chest and he slid his hand down her stomach. Her breath caught—he could feel her nervousness. Her fear. She had held out longer this time when he had beaten her—she had even fought back more—but the fear that crossed Genevieve's eyes when he told her again she would not get drugs tonight had almost ruined him right there. His fingers dipped between her legs and Kieron took a deep breath—he wanted her so badly, but this ... this was *wrong*. He stroked her gently and she flinched. He held her body firmly with his other hand and stroked her again. Then he slowly slid his finger into her. Her entire body tightened, "Breathe." Kieron said gently into her ear. She only turned her head away from him.

Kieron racked his brain for any way that he could get out of this. For any way that he could stop right this moment. They would be hunted if he did. Genevieve would be killed or far worse if she was caught and he would not be able to save her. He let himself stroke his finger inside of her. This was the only way he knew how to get them both out alive—he had to keep playing the game.

Just as her body began to relax for him, Genevieve shoved his hands away and jumped off of his lap, backing away towards the wall. Kieron just watched her, she was shaking and tears were streaming down her face. He had done this to her. He was hurting her. Kieron slowly stood up and licked the finger he had inside of her—*fuck, that was the wrong decision, she tasted so good.* He had to pause and gather himself. *Focus.* He took another step towards Genevieve, "We are not done." Kieron said flatly.

Her fist connected with his jaw and his head jerked to the side.

32

"Fuck." She gasped and he saw her cradle the hand she had just punched him with against her chest.

Kieron raised his fingers to his mouth and when he pulled them away there was blood on them. She had a good punch and he definitely deserved that and far worse. "Here is how this works," he said to her calmly, "You get pain until you beg for pleasure. Then you get pleasure. If you resist or fight back at any point, we go back to pain until you take your pleasure without resisting. Then we start all over again. When I am satisfied you will completely submit to what I tell you to do and continue to take pleasure without resisting, then we will be done." Genevieve just glared back at him. "Now let me see your hand." He said and reached out his own in an offering.

Genevieve continued to cradle her hand close to her chest and took another step backwards. He stepped forward quickly and grabbed her wrist. She winced as he ran his fingers along her knuckles and the bones in her hand. "You broke a knuckle, but you will be fine." He said and released her wrist. "Now that you know the rules, I will give you a choice. We can return to pleasure or go back to pain."

"Does it matter? It seems like you get off on both." Genevieve said through her teeth.

"I don't get off on any of this." Kieron responded quietly. He never had and certainly wouldn't start with her. He had once been completely sickened by it, then he became entirely numb to it. If anything, this was just as painful for him as it was for her—no it was definitely worse for her. There was no comparison. "I would recommend choosing pleasure." Kieron said as he stepped towards her.

He saw the slap coming, but did nothing to stop it. His cheek stung where she had struck him. "Go fuck yourself, Kieron." Genevieve spat at him.

He let out a slow breath. "Pain it is then." Kieron said before hitting her with the back of his hand and sending her sprawling to the floor.

He watched Genevieve try to push herself up, but her arms were shaking too badly. Kieron walked back to the chair in the middle of the room and sat down. "I will give you a moment to reconsider." He said as he watched her tremble on the dirt floor. It took everything in him to stay seated, to not rush across the room to hold her and tell her she would be okay.

Eventually, she slowly pressed herself into a seated position. Then she stood up. Kieron watched her slowly walk back to him. He patted his thigh indicating for her to sit. She shook her head no. He narrowed his eyes on her. "No foreplay. Just fuck me already." She said with a bite to her voice.

"That isn't—"

"For this first time just fuck me and get it over with." She held his stare as Kieron considered her request. He had planned to ease her into it, to try and make it as gentle on her as possible. *"Please."* She whispered.

A moment later he had her pinned on her knees on the dirt floor. Her chest and cheek were pressed into the dirt by his hand between her shoulder blades. If this was her request, he would do it. Kieron's hand undid the fastenings on his pants and he freed himself. He was large enough he knew this would hurt her. She cried out as he buried himself inside of her.

Kieron had never felt such pleasure and disgust at the same time. He was raping her. Even if she had just told him to fuck her, he was raping her. He was hurting her unforgivably. He pounded into her and she cried out with each thrust. He hated himself for how much he liked hearing her cry out. His climax was already threatening to release. Then Genevieve let out a scream and it sent him over the edge. "That's it." Kieron grit out and he thrust to hilt as he spilled into her.

Kieron was breathing heavily as he slowly pulled out of Genevieve. He had never finished so quickly in his life and he could feel her trembling beneath the hand he still had on her hip. He lifted his hands off of her and she collapsed, curling up on the dirt floor. Kieron felt like his heart was being completely ripped out of his chest as he stared down at her shaking body.

He summoned a warm wet towel, "Let's get you cleaned up." He said gently as he reached for her.

She smacked his hand away, "I can do it myself." She said softly, but not weakly. Then she pushed herself up and held out her hand for the towel. Her other hand, with the broken bone, she still cradled close to her chest.

Kieron handed her the towel and summoned a small bottle of oil. "Put a drop or two of this on. If I had to guess, you have probably torn and this will help it heal." She just looked down blankly at the bottle. "I will go get something for your hand." He said as he set the bottle of oil on the floor next to her. Then he left her in her cell.

His mind was spinning as he made his way to the healers' room. He would have to do this to Genevieve again and again until she became completely submissive. It would just get worse each time. But the way she had just demanded he get it over with—no one in his four hundred years of doing this had responded the way she had. He was going to lose his fucking mind and that would not help her. He had to focus and get through this. Get her through this. Then he would get her out of here for good.

Kieron waited in the frozen clearing. He blew warm air into his hands. *This fucking cold.* He cursed to himself. After two days torturing and fucking Genevieve, Kieron had sent a message to Zain. It was not the usual message from Vossarian that Ryett and his court was used to receiving. It was a private request to meet. He hoped the deviation from normal procedure would be enough to convince Zain to come. If he did not, Kieron would try again and again until something worked.

Zain, thankfully, appeared moments later. Zain was possibly the only being that terrified Kieron, but he would never admit it. Zain was ancient and more than just this world's magic rolled beneath his skin. That was what scared Kieron, that he could not get a full read on what Zain was capable of. Or *what* he was.

"Want to enlighten me as to why you were so insistent on this meeting?" Zain grit out between his teeth.

"We have new slaves you need to see." Kieron responded coolly. "Vossarian's temper tantrum aside, Sarla is alive, and even though he might be willing to hold a grudge, I know what shipments you prefer. Consider this an apology offer."

"We are considering other partnerships." Zain countered. "Why should we continue business with you when you broke our agreement?"

Shit. Kieron had known Zain would bring up exactly this issue, but all of his rehearsed answers now seem lacking. *How honest could he be without giving away the real reason?* He had to try, "Maybe this should be your last deal with us. I would not blame you if it was, but I promise you this is a *special* batch. You will not be disappointed."

Kieron had to get Ryett to come back for one more potential deal and then he had to get Genevieve in front of him. She was either from the Mountains and this might start a war or, if she was not from the Mountains, she had at least saved Sarla before they had gone through the portal and Ryett would owe her. Ryett might have been one of Voss's best partners, but he did at least seem to have some standards. He would not leave Sarla's friend in Vossarian's dungeons.

Zain eyed him carefully, his face was infuriatingly neutral. "I will let you know our answer." Then he was gone.

If Kieron believed in the gods—any god—he would have said a prayer.

Kieron returned to the warmth in the palace in the capital city of the Deserts, Aridale. He remembered Aridale when it was full of life—art and music and laughter. In the last century the city had turned dirty and ruthless. There was no pride in the city any longer, only greed. Vossarian had done that to his beautiful city. Voss had let it wither and die and be overrun by filth while he handed out drugs and surrounded himself with wealth and sex.

When Kieron reached the door to his rooms he found Vossarian waiting for him.

"Your work is like art, Kieron." Voss drawled as he leaned against the wall smirking at Kieron.

"What do you need, Voss." Kieron asked warily. He was in a foul mood and did not want to deal with Vossarian's bullshit.

"I mean it. I think watching you break Genevieve has been my favorite experience to date." Voss continued as Kieron opened his door.

"My rule is that I don't want to hear about it unless you are displeased. So are you displeased with something?" Kieron replied sharply.

"The opposite, Kieron. What made it so great is that I actually saw you enjoying it ... I saw her enjoying it too. And the way she asked you to fuck her ... Mmm." Voss kissed his own fingertips before tossing them dramatically away from his lips in praise of Kieron's work. Kieron stepped into his rooms, but did not offer for Voss to follow him. He gave Voss a withering stare. "Remind me to give you a raise or something." Voss said offhandedly as he turned on his heels and walked away down the hall.

Kieron closed his eyes and took a deep breath as he slammed his door shut. *The disgusting fuck had watched.* It made Kieron's stomach twist into knots.

CHAPTER 6

Genevieve - Present Day.

I spent the afternoon summoning my clothes from Ryett's chateau. Most of them were not appropriate for the weather in the desert, but they were the only things I owned. I was exhausted and summoning one piece at a time was taking all of my concentration. I knew I had asked Kieron for one day to mope about, but that did not mean I needed to lay in bed all day. It meant I needed one day to gather myself and I would move forward tomorrow. I had suffered far worse heartbreak than being ditched by some male ... even if I had allowed myself to imagine I would spend the rest of my life with him.

I finally succeeded in summoning my pack. I opened it to see if everything was still inside and ran my finger along the folded inner seam. My fingers felt the two barely there lumps—my rings—and I let out a breath. The important things were still here. I closed the pack and tucked it carefully under the bed before starting to hang everything in the walk in closet. My things only took up a few feet of space and the top drawer of the dresser.

Out the window I could see that it was already getting dark. My stomach growled with hunger, but I had no intention of eating today. I had spent long enough half starving to death that a day without food did not bother me. I stepped into the bathroom and washed myself before crawling into bed. Tomorrow I would have to move forward. Ryett had chosen Rachel. He had severed the bond between us and I had to accept it. He deserved happiness. I would not take that from him even if I was envious.

What is with these males lurking in my room when I wake up? I had opened my eyes to find Kieron lounged in the chair he was in yesterday. It irked me, but I had promised myself I would clean up my attitude. He needed to regain control of his kingdom and I had promised to support him in doing it. *How?* I had no idea, but here I was anyway.

"Good morning." I said brightly as I pulled back the covers and swung my feet to the side of the bed. At least I had worn pajamas last night.

"Good morning." Kieron replied. His voice was smooth and so sexy—*What is wrong with me?* "How are you feeling today, sweetheart?"

"Much better, thank you." I replied. It was a lie, but I would fake it until it was true. I walked to the bathroom and closed the door behind me. Once I had relieved myself and freshened up a bit I returned to the room. Kieron was still sitting in the chair. I glanced at him, doing nothing to hide my annoyance, and started to make my way towards the closet.

He stood slowly and walked over to me, blocking my path. "You do not have to lie to me. So tell me, how are you feeling?"

I looked up at him, "Much better, thank you." I lied again.

"Uh uh. This is not how this is going to work. You are going to tell me the truth, always." There was a slight bite to his voice now.

I rolled my eyes, "Why the fuck do you care, Kieron? I am fine and promise to be on my best behavior." I stepped to the side to walk around him, but Kieron grabbed my arm. Before I knew it I was pinned against the wall with his body leaning over me. One hand still firmly held my arm and his other hand pressed against the wall next to my shoulder, caging me in.

"Try lying to me again. I will not tolerate that between us." Kieron growled, "I care more than you know. So I am going to ask you one more time. How are you feeling?"

What the fuck was actually wrong with me? My entire body quivered and warmed under Kieron's touch—at the way he just scolded me. I was at least feeling *something*, but it was not what I expected. "I feel like shit, but I am trying to suck it up and move forward with my life." My voice was calm even though my body was anything but.

"See? Was that so hard?" Kieron said with a small smirk as he ran his thumb across my lower lip. I felt my entire body heat at his touch.

He released me and stepped back. I watched him walk to the door and leave me in my room alone. It took me a good two minutes before I had calmed myself enough to step away from the wall to walk into the closet and find something to wear.

When I walked into the great room, Kieron and the two tattooed faced males were seated at the table enjoying breakfast. The three of them were grinning and chatting and did not bother to glance at me until I walked right up to the table. Kieron stood and pulled back the chair next to his for me to sit in. I sat and did my best not to blush. I acted like a fool in front of these males yesterday and now I would have to live with it. "Good morning. My apologies for my rudeness yesterday, my name is Genevieve."

"Nice to meet you, Genevieve. No apology necessary. I am Orion and this is Zealand." The older of the two replied with a kind smile.

"I think you made quite a good first impression." The younger male—Zealand chimed in between bites of his breakfast. I blushed.

"Orion and Zealand are two of my oldest friends. They were marked and banished to the Eastern Desert by Luther and Vossarian for committing treason. They have come back to help us regain control of the kingdom." Kieron told me as he spooned food onto a plate and placed it in front of me. "To get you up to speed, Rook has announced himself the new ruler of the Deserts, so when we return to the palace in Aridale we will get the pleasure of removing him."

I started to eat. "Last time I saw Rook his brains were all over Beck's wall."

"He was not too happy about that either." Kieron said, amusement flickering in his voice.

"So how did he get away from Beck?"

"When you are immortal you learn not to announce you have come back to life until after you are able to jump to safety."

"Hmm. That is unfortunate." I said under my breath.

"Very, considering Voss was able to keep Rook leashed and my little side trips to make sure you were safe allowed that animal to move in and take the throne. From what little information we have, it was a bloody event." Kieron's tone had changed from amusement to a sharp seriousness.

I swallowed down my anger and stared down at my plate as I spoke. "So that is what you meant when you said you put your kingdom in jeopardy for me? That it is my fault Rook is the new ruler?"

I watched Kieron's hand ball into a fist where it rested on the table, "I did not say that." He said tightly.

Before Kieron could continue, Zealand cut in, "Rook has been a piece of shit for centuries. Even if you had been there Kieron, there would still have been bloodshed. Rook is the worst of the worst. He has always been hungry for power and always believed the Deserts should rule all of Savengard. If he remains in power, not only will he bring down the Deserts further than it has already fallen, but he will likely create the next great war. We know he was the one behind Voss's plan to control the beasts of the Wastelands and use them against the other kingdoms. I do not want to find out what other schemes he has been dreaming up."

I watched Kieron from the corner of my eye. He blinked one long blink and his fist released as his finger spread out on the table. It was like he was forcing himself to calm down. Rook had always seemed awful—evil even—but to hear he would likely start a war? And Kieron blamed me? "Do you have a plan?" I asked, willing my voice to be steady.

Orion set down his fork, "We will gather the other Undead and return to the palace. Hopefully, we can remove Rook with little bloodshed, but he does have significant support. Even if some of it is likely out of fear. If Rook refuses to step down then there might be more bloodshed than this kingdom has seen in centuries. Regardless, we do what is necessary to take back the throne so the True King can rule." He nodded towards Kieron with his last words.

"Undead?" I had not even considered that Kieron taking control of his kingdom might create an internal war. I guess I thought we would just walk in there and say 'Here is your True King' and be done with it.

Zealand pointed to his face, "We are the Undead. All of us who have been marked and banished. We have been working with Kieron behind Vossarian's back for a century to create an army to remove Voss from the throne. Many of us believed Voss was not the True King of Savengard and probably not even worthy of ruling the Deserts, but we could not do anything to prove it and did not know who would replace him. We knew that someday it would become clear and we needed to be ready."

"How many of you are there?" *They had a whole army? What had I gotten myself into?*

"Nearly one thousand. More than enough." Orion shared. "Zealand and I will leave here after we eat to prepare everyone and we will see you in the Eastern Desert as soon as we can get agreement for your visit."

I looked at Kieron, he nodded in confirmation. "I hope you are ready to make good on your end of our deal, Genevieve, because we are both about to be thrown into the fire."

"Of course." I replied as calmly as I could. Kieron had promised to find Rachel and bring her back to Beck's for me. He had also promised to get me out of there and give me a place to live if things went poorly after Rachel arrived—if I could not bring myself to stay. In return, if I indeed needed to leave, I had promised I would help Kieron in any way I could as he took back control of his kingdom. He needed people he trusted and I somehow made the short list. This might not have been the best bargain to make— agreeing to work for the male who had tortured and raped me, but I could not hang around the Mountains as Ryett lived out his happily ever after with Rachel. It was just too much for me. At the time, this seemed like a better option.

Orion and Zealand finished their meals and they politely said goodbye to me. Kieron escorted them to the front courtyard. I could see them all through the open doorway as they discussed final details. Then Orion and Zealand folded into the air as they disappeared.

Kieron strolled back into the room. He pulled the chair next to me out from the table and faced it towards me. Kieron sat, then leaned over to grab my chair. He turned it so I was facing him. Then he pulled my chair closer to him across the terracotta floor. We were so close my knees were nearly touching the front of his chair and his legs were spread, feet planted on either side of me.

He leaned slightly forward. One arm propped on the table next to us. "I have rules." He said, his eyes piercing into me. "This is my kingdom and if you want to survive it, you will follow my rules."

The nerve. Here I thought we were helping each other. *Was this how things had really been going between us?* He had helped me and Ryett and all of Savengard by working together, not demanding things. "Hmm, I thought this was more of a collaboration." I said with a little more snark than I meant to.

"Oh I respect you and value your opinion and contributions, but that does not mean there aren't rules." Kieron replied.

Damn the way his eyes were looking over me. I might as well have been naked. And that command in his voice ... I could not help the way my body was reacting even if I wanted to. "Let's hear these rules." I responded tightly.

"First, you will trust me completely." He paused. I only raised my eyebrows. He continued, "Second, you will never lie to me, and third, you will always do as I say."

I choked on my own laugh, "You are kidding me."

"No, Genevieve, I am completely serious. I promise I will always have your best interests in mind and I will do everything to keep you from harm, but these are my rules. I suggest you agree and we can move on with it." His face was dead serious.

"No." I scoffed. He had lost his mind. "I am not agreeing to that." I tried to stand, but his hands slammed me back down into the chair.

"If you want to go back to the Mountains or the Lakes just say the word and I will take you back. But, if you are staying in the Deserts,

I do not want you to die. If you think the Wastelands are bad, the Eastern Desert is worse and returning to the capitol might even be worse than that. You either agree or you stay here in this house." He kept his hands on me as he spoke.

I swallowed. I did not want to go back to the Mountains or the Lakes. I couldn't go back. Not right now. "Fine."

"Say you agree." He would not let me go until I did.

"I agree." I said through my teeth. *How bad could this be?* But I already knew first hand how bad this could be.

Our eyes were locked. Staring at each other. "Good girl." He finally said as he let go of me. *Ugh.* I wanted to smack him. I had trusted him and I definitely did not think he was like *this*. Maybe I *should* leave. Maybe I should go back to— "Do I want to know what that look means?" He asked, an amused smirk on his face.

"Probably not, but I just agreed to never lie. So that *look* means I want to smack you." He laughed at my response. His deep, hearty laugh. That laugh he laughed when we were sitting on the beach after he had saved me from the esurim in the Wastes. The laugh that made me think he was not really like *this*.

"Good. Stand up." He finally said as he stood and looked down at me waiting. I just glared at him. He inclined his head in warning.

Fine. I stood and his hand wrapped behind the back of my neck. His head dipped close to mine as he sucked in a breath like he was breathing me in. Then he let out a soft groan. *Was this why he agreed for me to go with him if I needed to leave Ryett? For sex? And these rules?* I didn't know if I was frightened or angry or completely turned on by the way he was handling me.

"Ryett made the wrong choice." He whispered in my ear. My

skin pebbled. Then he stepped away from me and his demeanor completely changed. "Is fifteen minutes enough time to get ready for some training? I need to see what combat skills you actually have."

I slowly nodded and he left me standing next to the dining table. *Damn him.*

CHAPTER 7

Kieron - Months Earlier.

Kieron waited by the gates to Aridale. They had received a message that Ryett would be coming and wanted to look at a shipment of slaves. Kieron's conversation with Zain had worked. A moment later Zain and Ryett, The King of the Mountains, were standing in front of him.

"I hope you are not wasting our time, Kieron." Zain said in greeting.

"I can assure you, I am not." Kieron responded and turned to lead them into the not so secret tunnels that connected the gates to the palace. Both males were more heavily armed then they usually were, but that was to be expected after their last interactions with his kingdom. He would have been disappointed in them if they did not show any signs of wariness towards their visit.

As they approached the doors that opened into the lower levels of the palace Kieron threw out one last seed to be planted, "I know you usually skip the festivities, but I recommend you partake tonight." He could feel the disgust from both of the males and did not blame them. Vossarian's parties were more of a dirty and drugged orgy than they were a party.

"Why is that?" Ryett asked between his teeth.

Kieron did not even bother with being discreet. They had already made it here and he was not going to miss any chance to let Ryett see that Genevieve was being held captive. He turned to look the king straight in the eye. "Vossarian has a new pet."

Kieron left the cage in the middle of the dance floor like Vossarian had instructed. Genevieve was barely conscious tonight, but she was still alive. She had been playing the game well—so well Kieron was starting to wonder if she had played this game before. But what Kieron was focused on tonight was that Ryett had agreed to come to the party. Kieron would soon find out if his plan was going to work. He made his way back through the crowd and people parted for him as he walked to where he usually stood by one of the doors.

He leaned his back against the wall casually and tried to steady his pounding heart. If Genevieve was from the Mountains this room could get bloody quickly. He was ready to swoop in and get Genevieve out of there if he had to. But nothing had happened ... yet.

He forced himself to glance to where Voss and Ryett were seated. That was when he felt it. The pulsing of magic. The rage and anguish leaking from Ryett. The invisible bond that stretched out from Ryett and straight towards Genevieve. Kieron forced a swallow and his fingernails dug into his own arms where he held them crossed over his chest. *Oh you have got to be fucking kidding me.* Not even the pain of his nails breaking skin could steady the wild pounding in his chest. Nothing could calm his own magic rising inside of him and beating against his skin to get out—his pure dark and lethal magic threatening to meet Ryett's magic and put an end to him.

Kieron's breathing grew heavier as he forced air in and out through his nose. *Genevieve was a match to Ryett. They were soulmates, too.* His back was pressed hard against the wall in every effort not to show his anger or start a fight himself. He should kill Ryett right now. He should grab Genevieve and escape with her. He should ... he should do nothing. *Nothing.*

Kieron now paced his rooms. It had taken every ounce of restraint not to cause a scene as he had pushed his way out of the party. He had asked Ryett to come here to save Genevieve, but he had not known they were soulmates. He knew he had no chance of being with her after what he had done, but he did not think he would be handing her over to another match. And Ryett *knew* she was his soulmate, too.

Kieron pressed his fisted hands against the countertop in his kitchen. Then he turned and slid down to the floor. He leaned back against the cabinets and stared unseeing at the cabinets across from him. Maybe he had hoped things could eventually be different. That one day, after all of this was over, he could find her and explain himself to her. Explain why he had done it and beg her for forgiveness. Now there was no chance. He had to live with it. Just like he had to live with what he had done. At least she would be safely far away from Voss ... from *him*.

CHAPTER 8

Genevieve - Present Day.

I found Kieron outside and past the pool that seemed to stretch into infinity in what appeared to be a training ring. It was circular and framed in red stacked stone walls of various heights. The ground was red sand. I froze before I even made it into the ring. "I thought Savengard did not have guns." I said. There were six guns laid out on a table.

"Savengard does not, but I have collected a few from my travels. I thought you could show me some of your skills and I wanted to see if you could help me figure out why some of these won't work." He picked up one of the guns and looked down the barrel.

In a few strides I was into the training ring and taking the gun from his hands. I set it back down on the table, "Just because you can't die unless your head is cut off does not mean you get to be an idiot." He raised his eyebrows at me, "I *can* die, so if you are going to have guns out here you are going to handle them properly. Rule one, do not point it at anything you do not want to kill."

"Understood." He said and raised his hands in submission. I quickly and efficiently removed the gun clips and cleared the chamber of each gun.

"These two need to be cleaned before you do anything with them." I said pointing to two of the guns. "This one has the wrong type of bullets in it and these three should be good to go."

I looked up at Kieron who had a smirk of satisfaction on his face. "How about you show me how to use them?" He said and gestured towards the cliffs. I looked out and realized he had six targets made up of bottles and wood placed at various distances. "How many of those can you hit with that gun?" He said and pointed to one of the guns I had told him was ready to be used.

In less than ten seconds all bottles were shattered and wooden targets splintered. I ejected the clip and cleared the chamber, setting the gun back on the table.

When I looked back at Kieron his eyes were wide, "I think I completely overestimated my ability to win the fight at our first meeting." He breathed.

"Had I known you both were immortal I would have aimed for your heads." I said.

"Why wouldn't you anyway?"

"The body is a bigger and easier target. In my world the average person dies or is disabled enough when they are shot in the torso."

He just stared at me and heartbeats passed. Finally he spoke, "I am starting to think I do not know very much about you, Genevieve." *He had no idea.*

"I will help you clean up the guns and teach you how to use them, but considering you are the most feared killer in all of Savengard, how about you teach me a few things first?" I countered.

"Fair enough." He said and with a wave of his hand the guns and table disappeared. "We will start basic and work up from there."

We did start basic. Foot placement. How to throw a punch. How to block a punch. How to move my body and use the right muscles, breathing, and momentum. All things I knew, but let Kieron guide me through anyway. He made slight tweaks to my form and I was not surprised that I saw instant improvement.

"How do you move so fast?" I asked when we were stopped and taking a short break.

"A combination of how I am made and my magic." He responded casually. "You, for example, seem to be operating under constraints. I am guessing in your mind you have an idea of what your limits are with strength and speed, but your body has changed since being here. It is faster and stronger. You have seen it in action when you have been under pressure, but you do not know how to access that speed or strength whenever you wish. Does that sound about right?"

Another surprisingly accurate assessment. "Yes, that sounds about right." I responded.

"I thought so." He smirked. "Let's try a few things to see if we can break that mental block."

I swallowed and nodded.

An hour later Kieron told me we were done and led me back inside to the great room. The table was covered in a spread of food for lunch. I was beyond hungry. Kieron had patiently put me through a series of exercises designed to push my body to show its maximum strength. When I had nearly sobbed with exhaustion or defeat, Kieron had given calm and direct words of encouragement. His belief in my ability to handle more was unshakable and we had not yet found my physical limit. Eventually, he had just given me a huge grin and told me I had done more than enough for the day.

I shoveled food into my mouth and gulped down water, trying to quench the thirst I had developed from being out in the hot sun. Kieron leaned back in his chair and crossed his huge arms over his chest. His eyes were searching me, but I just ignored him and continued to shovel food into my mouth. Finally he spoke, "In Voss's dungeon, you never begged me to stop. Why not?"

"I don't know what you are talking about." I leveled back at him and took another bite of my lunch.

He stood slowly and walked around the table, moving the chair next to me and sitting on the edge of the table. "I am going to give you one warning for breaking rule number two. Tell me the truth. Why did you never beg me to stop?" Kieron said in a lethal calm.

I set my spoon down slowly and raised my eyes to glare up at him. "Well now you can tell me off for breaking rule three, too. I am not lying, I am just not answering you." I replied defiantly. It did not matter that he had easily broken down my mental barriers during training. It did not matter that he had done it all while being kind and calm. It did not matter that he was seriously gorgeous—I stopped myself. No. I was not going to take this bullshit from him about his stupid rules. "And while we are at it, your stupid rules ruined any trust I had—"

I didn't even have time to blink before I was out of my chair and bent over the table, my cheek and chest pressed into the wood. Kieron's hand connected with my ass as he spanked me. I cried out in shock. The sting brought water to my eyes. His hand rubbed the spot he just smacked. His other hand was holding me down on the table.

"Try again." He demanded.

My fingers wrapped around one of the knives on the table. "So you get to lie about not touching me unless I ask for it, but I have to tell you everything? Fuck you, Kieron." I spit venom back with my words. I would not let him treat me this way.

A small cry released from my mouth as Kieron spanked me two more times in quick succession. As his hand gently caressed my ass again I stomped my foot down on his. I pressed up off the table enough to slide off and drop to my knee as I sunk the knife deep into Kieron's thigh.

His hand around my neck yanked me from my knee and into the air as he slammed my back down onto the table. Kieron's body leaned over mine as his hand around my throat held me down. My hands were wrapped around his forearm as we glared at each other. "Harder." I breathed.

Hungry amusement lit Kieron's eyes as he looked over me. "There she is." He growled. His hand tightened and my body involuntarily opened for him as he cut off my airway.

"There is more than one way to ask for something. Your words, your eyes, your body, your feelings. One of my various skill sets, sweetheart, is the ability to sense other people's feelings. If they are lying, angry, scared, aroused, etcetera." His hand loosened slightly and I sucked in a breath. Then with his other hand he pulled the knife from his leg and buried it into the table next to my face, "It is quite easy to torture when you have direct insight to how your prisoner is actually doing."

My head was completely spinning. I was so angry at him for laying a hand on me and at the same time infuriatingly aroused. He continued, "Like right now, your body is oscillating between being enraged and extremely turned on. It is practically begging me to spank you again just so it can make up its mind." One of his hands dropped to my hip and he guided my leg up so he could caress my ass. Then his hand lifted from me and my body tensed in anticipation. He only chuckled and gently returned his hand to my ass. "But knowing how you feel does not explain the 'why.' So I will ask you one more time: Why did you never ask me to stop?"

What the fuck was wrong with me? I guess he was right because instead of answering I gritted out between my teeth a solid, "Fuck you."

He spanked me again. I do not know if I cried out or moaned, but now I was panting beneath his firm grip on my throat and trying to calm my breath. *What the actual fuck? I guess aroused was the right answer.* Kieron's eyes looked over my body hungrily, "So you do

58

like that." It wasn't a question. He pulled his hand back again and paused—waiting to see how I would respond.

I could feel my underthings were soaked with my arousal. It was just a matter of time before I soaked through my tight shorts. And with him already between my legs—this was getting out of hand. I decided to finally answer his question, "It was an oversight. I know how torture goes. I knew I could just obey Voss and get drugged every night until he got bored of me or believed I was broken enough to do whatever the next step in his plan was. I did not want to wait that long so, I decided to speed up the process of making him believe I had broken. I invited everything you did. Expected it—and worse."

Kieron's hand on my throat loosened more, "Good girl. Was that so hard?"

"If you knew how I was actually feeling during it all, why didn't you go harder?" I managed to ask. I had once told him he sucked at torturing me.

He sat and pulled me onto his lap, his hand slid up from my throat to grab my jaw and turn my head towards him so he could look me in the eye, "It was intentional."

I stared at him in silence. Disbelief. *He had intentionally gone easy on me?* Then I finally said, "So I have to give the whole truth, but you don't?"

The corner of his mouth twitched up, his hand released my face and the back of his fingers stroked down my arm. "Vossarian offered the honor of torturing you to me and Rook. I demanded it be me. Rook has a tendency to lose control and leave permanent damage or kill his prisoners. I needed to buy us time to figure out how to get you out of there, but I also had to go through with it. Voss was disgusting and sadistic and would often watch prisoners be tortured through a spelled mirror in his chambers. I had to actually torture you in case he was watching and hurt you as little as possible at the same time. My intentions behind it do not make it any less abhorrent."

"What do you mean get me out of there? Why did you care? You did not know me. Did you do that with everyone you tortured?" He had also helped me in the Wastes and then helped us free a shipment of enslaved children—

"I did not do that with anyone else. They were all innocent casualties in a war they did not know was being fought." I waited for him to continue. To actually answer my questions.

He let out a deep sigh, then continued, "I am guessing the version of soulmates you were introduced to was the version where a soul is split in two and then they meet again?" I nodded. *Where was he going with this?* "That is not the only belief. Different kingdoms have different ideas of what causes the same phenomenon. Here we believe that your magic finds its match and pulls you towards it. You might have more than one match, but you choose who you want to build that bond with. You can release that bond if you do not want it—like what Ryett did. I felt that bond break between you two, just as you did. You were a match to Ryett *and* you are a match to me."

His eyes scanned my face. I just stared back at him in complete shock, trying to process everything he was saying. I felt his thumb caress the back of my hand as he spoke, "I choose you and I hope you will choose me too. I will not hide or pretend to be anything

I am not. I am a monster and will continue to be one in order to change my kingdom into something better. I value you, your brilliance, your power, and I want you standing next to me."

I shoved his hands off of me as I stood and quickly walked across the room. "I need a minute." I mumbled. *How could this be happening? This could not be happening.*

"Do not walk away from me." There was a bite to Kieron's voice.

"I am not walking away! I need a minute to process what you just said." My heart was pounding. Nothing was ever as it seemed in this world. I was used to a more black and white life. This was every shade of gray imaginable. My entire body tingled and I could not catch my breath.

Kieron crossed the room to me in a few strides and took my face in his hands. I tried to push him away, but he just wrapped me against his chest. "It's okay, G. I am not asking you to make a decision now or until you are ready. You asked for the truth and I gave it. I will not apologize for telling you what I want."

I did not know why I was shaking, but I was. I did not know what to say. *He had beaten and raped me and now was claiming we were soulmates? Was I just supposed to believe him?*

"Talk to me, what are you thinking?" He whispered.

I could not process what he just told me. I had trusted him enough to ask him to give me some place to live outside of the Mountains. The last thing I expected was any of ... this. I felt everything inside of me going numb again. "I promised I would help you. I will help you, but I don't have an answer for you otherwise." I finally responded.

His arms loosened and he let me go. I felt a pulse of warmth in my body as his fingers trailed down my jawline and his thumb caressed my lower lip. He stepped back from me, "That's okay, baby. Just try to give it a chance."

CHAPTER 9

Genevieve - Many Years Ago.

Things with General Chad Johnston started out exactly as I imagined they would. He was demanding and continuously kept me on my toes by asking me to complete a wide variety of tasks with little explanation. I always figured it out, but it was infuriating. The only thing I could not figure out was if he was pleased or not that I was actually completing all of his bullshit tasks.

Then things started to change. He started complimenting my work. He even went as far as getting me little presents when I did something exceptionally well. Then he started leaning in closer to me when looking over my shoulder or touching my arm or back while he talked. I did my best to shake him off, but he just became more persistent.

That was what was happening now. He was leaning over my

shoulder as I showed him another report. I could feel his warm breath on my cheek and his fingers gently adjusted the way my hair laid down my back. "Has anyone ever told you how smart you are, Genevieve?" He said smoothly as he rolled my chair back from the desk and sat on the edge of it in front of me.

"Thank you, sir." I said simply as I looked up at him.

"Stand up." He replied gently. I did. "Beautiful and smart. The perfect combination." He said as his eyes looked me up and down. I could feel my cheeks heat with embarrassment at his compliment. I guess it was nice to be receiving compliments from the general, but why would he ever be interested in me? I was a nobody.

He stood up from the desk and stepped close to me. "I am going to kiss you now, Genevieve." I stepped back. *No, he was my commanding officer, this was against policy.* He only stepped with me. "I am going to kiss you because I have wanted to taste you for months now. You aren't like the other females. You are perfect and I want you to be mine." In my shock I let him kiss me. Then I kissed him back. It was not a bad kiss. It was actually a very good kiss. "Good girl." He whispered as he pulled his lips from mine. *Good girl? Damn did that turn me on.* I did not know what to say back to him.

I watched the corners of his lips turn up in amusement, "You are going to start accompanying me each day."

"Yes, sir." I breathed.

I was now The General Chad Johnston's shadow as he oversaw

combat training and firearm training along with a variety of meetings. I tried to melt into the background, to stay unnoticed, but I also paid attention. You could learn a lot just by watching and listening and as far as I was aware, females were not trained in these skills. When we drove between stops together in his armored truck, Chad would explain to me what I had just witnessed and what he was going to do at his next stop.

When we were in front of the other officers and service members he acted as if I was not even there, but when we were alone together Chad made me feel like the most important person in the world. He made me feel smart and pretty and *wanted*. He even moved me from the group living quarters to a private room near his office. I later realized he did this because he wanted even easier access to me at night, but I was not complaining.

One day on our trips to visit the various units during their training day, we stopped at the shooting range. No one else was there. That was the day Chad taught me how to shoot. His eyes lit when I had turned out to be a surprisingly good shot. When we had returned to his office at the end of the day he made love to me on his desk and then informed me he would be training me further— whatever that meant.

CHAPTER 10

Kieron - Present Day.

Kieron watched Genevieve from his large glass patio doors in his room as she slipped into the pool. Her ass was still beautifully pink from where he had spanked her. When he had felt her arousal it had taken every ounce of him not to tear off her tight shorts and feel how wet she was. She was absolutely perfect for him, she just did not want to admit it.

He had hoped the conversation would have gone better, but Genevieve had pulled away from him after he told her she was his match. She had completely shut down. But he could be patient. He had even resigned to letting Ryett have her before—turned out to be a mistake—but he could wait for her to come around. She *would* come around.

◆ ◆ ◆

Hours later Kieron was standing on the patio in front of a small table set for the two of them. The stars were already bright. He had convinced himself he could be patient, but that did not mean Kieron was not going to do everything he could to move things along.

"What's this?" Genevieve's voice came from behind him.

"I thought we could have a nice evening together." Kieron responded as he turned. He laid eyes on Genevieve and realized it would be hard for him to get through dinner without tearing her clothes off. He forced himself to continue, "I don't know how many nights we have before things might get really rough for a while. I thought we should enjoy ourselves while we can."

"I should have dressed more appropriately." Genevieve said as she stepped back and gestured towards her room as if she would go change right that minute.

"Don't even think about it. Come sit." Kieron replied with a smile. She was perfect exactly how she was. Her hair was still damp from her shower and she was wearing a pair of those small tight shorts that Kieron loved her in. Under her oversized sweatshirt she clearly had not bothered to put on a bra as he could see the peaks of her nipples through the fabric.

Kieron pulled out her chair for her to sit, then summoned a blanket for her legs. The night was already starting to cool off. "Thank you," She said quietly as she tucked the blanket around herself.

Kieron took a seat himself and suddenly could hardly think of what to say. Maybe he had pushed her too far today. Maybe his rules and rule enforcement was not the right thing to do. Maybe he had been too rough with her ... but he had felt her arousal when he spanked her ... he had seen the look she had given him when she told him to choke her harder. She just seemed so distant from him now. He probably should not have dropped the news that she was his match the way he did. He could kick himself. That was it. He had just dumped it on her. He should have saved that information and done something more ... romantic with it. At least waited for her to be ready to hear it. Not after she had felt the need to stab a knife into his leg. No wonder she was so withdrawn.

"Why are we waiting around here before going to the Eastern Desert ... and why aren't we just going straight to the Desert's capital and taking the throne from Rook before he gets comfortable?" Genevieve finally asked.

Kieron shifted in his chair and cleared his throat, "Rook put a bounty on my head, so as good as I am, I can't just go walking back into Aridale when everyone there will want to collect the payment." He watched Genevieve's throat bob as she swallowed. Kieron felt a flash of something like concern or shock from her, but the feeling was gone an instant later. He picked up the bottle of wine and poured her a glass before pouring himself one too. Then he continued, "I have made good progress with the Undead, many of them will support me as king, but there are still some who will require some convincing. Orion and Zealand have returned to the Eastern Desert to prepare them for us to visit. Obviously, they also want to make sure we aren't walking into a trap. We will see how much convincing I have to do once we arrive."

"So you are building an army of traitors to help you?" Genevieve asked blatantly.

"It is more complicated than that."

"Okay," Genevieve took a sip from her wine. "When do we leave?" She was sitting stiffly with her back straight.

"As soon as I get word back from Orion that the counsel of the Undead will meet with me. It could be days or weeks." Kieron responded.

"And my role is to be what?" Kieron could not help but smile to himself at her question. Genevieve was all business tonight.

"Your presence shows them that both the Mountains and the Lakes, along with their allies, will back me as king. I have been talking of rebuilding the Deserts into something better than it is and having strong allies is a part of that. To show the Undead and then the people of Aridale I have support will only encourage them to join me too." Kieron watched Genevieve, trying to get a read on her, but she showed no emotion, he could not feel anything from her. So he continued, "I also need you to stay out of trouble and alive. These are dangerous people, Genevieve."

She chuckled, "Kieron, all I do is deal with dangerous people." The look she leveled at him had fire in her eyes.

"Good." He said and summoned their food to the table.

Genevieve slowly turned her eyes to look down at the food, "Who makes all the food?"

Kieron laughed, "Zed does. He lives here and takes care of the place along with cooking most of the meals."

He watched amused as Genevieve's cheeks reddened, "Zed? There is someone else who has been here and I haven't even met them?"

She looked absolutely mortified and it only made Kieron laugh harder. "Don't worry, he would prefer it that way. He likes to stay behind the scenes, but if it would make you more comfortable I can ask him to come out here so you can meet him."

"Is he ... a slave?" Her eyes were burning into him.

"Zed!" Kieron hollered, "Come out here for a second!"

A moment later Zed strolled out from the hall behind the kitchen and onto the patio. Zed was wearing his usual flowing pants and shirt with his long hair tied into a bun on the back of his head. He was thin, but still strong, and he was always calm. That was something Kieron loved about Zed's company—the tranquility of it.

"How is everything, Kieron? Genevieve?" He asked.

"Everything is excellent, Zed. Genevieve here is concerned you are my slave." Kieron had to have a little fun with this.

Zed burst out laughing, "Oh Kieron pays me quite handsomely. Plus I like that he is gone most of the time."

"I am sorry, I had to ask. It is so nice to meet you, Zed." Genevieve composed herself quickly and gave Kieron a glare, "I would have thanked you much sooner, but Kieron failed to mention he had someone here who took such good care of him."

"Don't worry about it, Genevieve. Let me know if you ever need anything, I am at your service." Zed said as he gave an exaggerated bow.

"Thanks, Zed. Everything really is fantastic. Enjoy your night." Kieron said with a smile and Zed turned and left Genevieve and Kieron on the patio.

"Was that necessary? You could have just told me without summoning him out here!" Genevieve hissed.

"Oh, but it was fun to see you squirm a little." Kieron chuckled back. Genevieve gave a huff and rolled her eyes. Kieron loved the fire and sass she had.

Both of them dug into their meals, eating in silence.

"How do you feel about being king?" Genevieve finally asked.

Kieron snorted, "I never wanted to be king."

"Well congratulations, it's happening. So how do you feel about it?" She replied.

"I want the Deserts to be better. I want my kingdom to flourish and be a safe place. It is far from flourishing and further from being safe. Sure the ruling and wealthy families have flourished for centuries, but I want the people to flourish. I knew for that to happen, Vossarian and his family had to be removed from the throne, but I did not think I would be the one to take over."

"Tell me more." Genevieve pressed.

Kieron took a deep breath, he had never really discussed this with anyone. "I always knew I had more power than Voss, but Luther and Orion taught me to keep it muted. I never understood until I was older and realized Voss would kill anyone who threatened him. I have spent most of my life secretly building a network of others who want something better for the Deserts also. I have sleeper spies in every piece of Voss's slave network. They are all ready to act when I tell them to. I never understood why Orion and Zealand did so much for me ... including taking the fall when we got caught by Voss. They were marked and banished, when it should have been me. I could not understand why they would subject themselves to that or why others had before them. I think you telling me I am the True King of the Deserts just made a lot of pieces fall into place. And I think others knew it and did not tell me."

Genevieve was quiet for a few moments, "You feel guilty about it." It was not a question.

"Very." Kieron responded. "I owe them my life." It was something Kieron would never be able to repay. They had done so much to protect him, including sacrificing themselves.

"I think you will get to repay them by changing your kingdom for the better, Kieron. It sounds like that is what they want too." Genevieve said as she took another bite of food. Kieron smiled to himself, she understood.

"I still wish I could have done something to stop them from being hurt." He whispered.

"I know." Genevieve replied under her breath. They sat staring at each other for heartbeats.

Kieron finally cleared his throat and shifted in his chair again, "Any other questions?"

Genevieve sat back in her chair and took a long sip of wine before she spoke, "Aren't the rules a little much? Is it really necessary to set those rules? Or are you just so used to being in control you can't give it up?"

Kieron leaned back as well, cocking his head to the side and studying her. His eyes narrowed. "Are you really that concerned about giving up some of your own control?" He watched her chest rise with a deep breath, but she did not reply, "Genevieve, I like being in control and I like when you let go of your control and give it to me."

"I do not do well with rules or giving up control, Kieron." Genevieve replied without breaking his stare.

"Well you agreed to the rules so you might as well give them a try. I think you are already surprised how much you like it." Kieron leveled back at her before he took another sip of wine.

"And what sort of things fit under rule three—doing what you tell me to? Are there any limits or am I completely at your mercy?" Genevieve asked tightly. He watched her fingers tighten on the base of her wine glass.

Kieron considered his answer for a few heartbeats, "Anything and everything is fair game." He watched her throat bob as she swallowed. "I will not hurt you again, Genevieve."

"Hmm. Rule one—trust you. I guess we'll see. Thank you for dinner." Genevieve replied and she pushed her chair back to stand up.

"One more thing." Kieron stopped her, his heart beating strongly. He had already pushed her too far today, but this was important. He had convinced himself this was important. "From now on you will be sleeping with me." The look on Genevieve's face could nearly kill him. "Sleeping in my bed, I mean—"

"Absolutely not." She cut him off.

"Rule three—"

"What? Are you going to hit me until I agree?" There was fire in her eyes as she questioned him.

He schooled his face to calm amusement, "Hitting you and spanking you are two very different things, sweetheart."

"Is it now?" She snapped back sarcastically.

"And I do not trust you to be alone." He could feel her anger building.

"Oh so I have to trust you blindly, but you don't trust me?"

"I did not try to drown myself in the pool when we arrived here." He countered calmly. She chewed the inside of her cheek as she glared at him, but she did not respond. "You can talk to me about that whenever you are ready." She still glared at him so he continued, "And once we leave here we will be heading into part of my territory that is filled with some of the deadliest warriors and assassins and they have been deprived of female company for far too long. I will not be letting you out of my sight. So you will be sleeping in my bed starting tonight."

Genevieve stayed tense, "As you wish, Your Grace."

"Don't call me that." Kieron responded more gruffly than he had intended. He had always felt 'Your Grace' was a title reserved for bratty princelings who grew up knowing they would one day become king. The types who were pampered and coddled. The types who shit on everyone around them because they thought they were better than everyone else. To Kieron, it was an insult.

"My King?" She countered, raising her eyebrows at him. The way she said it had Kieron's cock pulse—had him imagining her moaning the words as he fucked her.

He tilted his head to the side, "I think I might be able to get on board with that one."

"Then it is 'My King' if you promise to never say 'good girl' to me ever again." Genevieve leveled back at him.

Kieron bit his lip as his eyes searched her face, "You are being such a good girl for me?" He finally suggested, his voice a deep whisper.

Kieron watched Genevieve's breath catch and he felt her pulse of arousal. Just feeling her arousal had him on edge. Then she shook

74

her head and rolled her eyes, "Nice try, but no."

"Hmm. Well I can't make that promise." Kieron leaned casually back in his chair as he watched her, "Especially because you don't want to admit you actually like it."

Genevieve ignored his comment as she took a step away from the table, "I prefer to sleep naked, do you think you can contain yourself?"

"I will not touch you unless you want me to." Kieron replied coolly. He did not know if he *could* contain himself. He had already been imagining lifting her shirt over her head and sliding her out of those tight shorts. It had been hard enough when they reeked of the Wastes and sea and were both clothed—even then he ended up buried inside of her. Genevieve just stared unwaveringly back at him. She was tormenting him in response to his rules. Testing and teasing. He could play that game too. He liked that game. "Let's go then." He said with a small smirk as he stood. She followed him to his room.

Kieron watched her from the corner of his eye as she summoned a small bag with personal care items to his bathroom. She washed her face and cleaned her mouth before closing the door behind her when she went to the small toilet room. By the time he had finished getting cleaned up from the day she was already laying in his bed, her bare back to him and a single sheet draped over the rest of her body. He could almost taste her desire in his mouth. The nervousness and want. Kieron's cock hardened and he was grateful she was facing away from him as he dropped his clothes and climbed into the big bed.

They lay there in silence for a while. Finally Kieron spoke up,

"Either you can take care of yourself or I can do it for you, but your arousal is going to keep me up all night." He would have to take care of himself soon if her feelings did not change. That was the worst part about this skillset. He sometimes could turn it off and sometimes he just could not. Tonight he could not.

"Sounds like a personal problem, My King." Genevieve replied sarcastically.

Kieron rolled over to face Genevieve's back. He watched her body tense as he stroked his finger slowly down her spine. "Here's the thing, baby. I said I would not touch you if you did not want it. Your body is begging me for it and your mouth is telling me no. So you are breaking rule number two. When your body and mouth say the same thing, I will listen to what your mouth says." Kieron moved her hair from her bare shoulders and felt her shudder beneath his touch. Her skin pebbled as he ran his lips along her shoulder and kissed the back of her neck.

The way she tasted has Kieron restraining himself. He kissed her again and she let out a barely audible moan. He could not resist ...

Genevieve

Kieron's hand grabbed my hair and yanked my head back. I was ruined and I knew I would be as soon as he said I would be sleeping in his bed. My mind had been offering me conflicting thoughts ever since getting here, but my body—even as it was numb—only wanted one thing. *Him.*

I felt his teeth nip at my neck and moaned again. I tried to turn, but his hands kept me facing away from him. He pulled the sheet off of my body and grasped my breast before pinching my nipple between his thumb and forefinger. I sucked in a breath at the small hurt as he gave it a small tug before releasing it. His hand continued down my body and caressed my ass. "Do I need to punish you for breaking rule number two?" He whispered, his breath warm against my ear.

My head was still cranked back by his hand in my hair and I could only whimper. I gasped as his hand smacked my ass then rubbed over the sting. *What is wrong with me?* I was so turned on by this I was almost embarrassed. His hand smacked me again, "At some point you will learn not to break my rules, but until then, I will punish you for breaking them." His finger dipped between my legs and gently stroked my center. Then he released my hair and rolled me onto my stomach before straddling my legs. His hand smacked my ass again and I buried my face in the pillow as I cried out.

Then I felt his weight lift off of me and his hands grabbed my hips, "Get on your hands and knees." He commanded. I let his hands pull my hips up and I pushed up to my hands. I looked over my shoulder in time to see him strike me again. I cried out at the pain of it. Then his finger found my center again and stroked my wetness. "See baby, I knew you would like to give up control." He said with a low chuckle.

He smacked my ass again and slid his finger deep into me not a second later. "Oh fuck!" I gasped at the pain of his spank and the pleasure of his finger inside of me. His finger pumped into me and

I felt my inner muscles involuntarily clench. I had never been so close to climaxing so quickly.

He leaned over me and I felt his breath against the back of my neck, "That's it, baby." He whispered against my skin, his voice deep and smooth. "You are being such a good girl for me." My breath shuddered and my body completely opened to him. He was right. I did not want to admit how much I liked hearing Kieron call me his good girl. It had me completely and involuntarily surrendering to him. Then his finger slowly slid out of me. He rolled away from me across the bed and pulled the sheet up over himself—leaving me breathless and naked on all fours. "Good night, sweetheart. Now you are just as frustrated as I am."

You have got to be fucking kidding me. I pressed my face into the sheets and took a deep breath. Games. He was playing games. I could play games too. I lowered myself down and turned away from him as I pulled the sheet up to cover my naked body. *Good fucking night to you too.* I thought and willed myself to go to sleep.

CHAPTER 11

Genevieve

Kieron was not in bed when I woke up, but I heard the shower running in the bathroom. *Perfect.* I got out of bed and let myself into the bathroom. Kieron was indeed showering. It took everything in me to not just stare in awe at his powerful body as I ducked into the small toilet room and relieved myself. When I was done, Kieron was still in the shower, ignoring me. So I opened the glassdoor and stepped into the steam with him. I could feel him tense slightly. *Good.* Then I turned on the second shower head and stepped under the water.

I had not even gotten my hair fully wet before Kieron's body pressed me against the wall and his mouth was against mine. I could feel his huge hard cock pressed against my pelvis. I kissed him back and threaded my fingers into his wet hair. His hand kneaded my breast and I moaned into his mouth as I pressed my hips into him. He pulled back his mouth and stepped away from me. I leaned my head back against the tiled wall and met his hungry gaze. He reached over and turned off the shower head he was using. "Enjoy your shower." He said with a smirk and he stepped out of the shower door, pulling a towel from a hook on the wall to wrap around his waist.

I most certainly will enjoy my shower. I stepped back under the water and let the droplets pelt my face.

I did not know what I was doing with Kieron, but it was a good distraction from the fact that for a brief moment in time I thought I was going to spend centuries with Ryett. I did not blame Ryett for his choice—I understood it, but just because I understood it did not mean it didn't hurt. Caught in lust—or whatever *this* was—with Kieron kept me out of feeling completely numb from how things ended with Ryett ... or terrified of what we were going to have to do to get Kieron on his throne. Maybe it was messed up, but I just didn't care.

I pulled on the skimpiest training clothes I had and told myself I was doing it because of the heat—if I was being honest I really wanted to make Kieron sweat. I knew I had made a good choice when I walked barefoot across the terracotta floor in the great room and saw Kieron's throat bob as he looked up at me. "Good morning!" I said cheerfully and sat down in the seat next to him, pulling the lids off of the dishes scattered along the table and helping myself to breakfast.

"Did you sleep well, sweetheart?" Kieron asked in an infuriatingly neutral tone.

I propped my elbow on the table and rested my head on my hand as I looked at him next to me. I let my eyes wander over every beautiful inch of him before I spoke. "You know, I slept surprisingly well." I was not even lying this time. I had. I felt rested and refreshed. "How about you?"

"Took me a bit to fall asleep." He responded, his eyes burning into mine. Neither of us were going to address what happened between us last night or in the shower this morning.

"Hmmm." I responded as I licked my lip and let my eyes wander over him again. Then I turned back to my breakfast.

◆ ◆ ◆

Kieron

Kieron had waited until Genevieve's breathing was deep and even before he had silently slipped out of bed and into the bathroom to find release for himself. It had taken four hundred years of discipline to not fuck Genevieve last night. Maybe he had been wrong to insist she share his bed. When they were in the Eastern Desert, yes, but here? He must be a masochist. The way she completely surrendered and opened to him had almost pushed him over the edge.

Then she tested him in the shower and now again sitting next to him at breakfast. Kieron did not know what the extent of Ryett and Genevieve's relationship had been, but based on how they looked before Ryett had restored the gate, Kieron assumed it had been serious between them. Maybe it was not as serious as he thought.

Yes, she had tried to end herself, but there seemed to be more to it than just what had happened with Ryett. Then after a single day of being miserable she slipped right into taunting him.

He had never been able to shake the connection they had in the Wastes. Maybe she hadn't either. The way she had wanted him. No one had ever shown desire towards him like that. Sure he had fucked hundreds of willing females, but most were terrified of him or trying to climb the social ladder. They wanted him for his reputation and were willing to give their bodies to him in hopes they would be the one who stuck and could live a life of luxury as the partner to the king's right hand. None of them stuck. Few of them made it to more than a one time thing. And the couple that turned into what one could consider a relationship—well it was hard to maintain a relationship when most of your life was lies and secrets. None of them lasted.

Kieron had a completely primal urge to claim Genevieve and make sure no other male ever touched her again. He had made up his mind that she was his, now he just had to keep drawing her in until she was just as convinced as he was. But after last night he promised himself he would not force himself on her again. That was why Kieron had stepped away from her in the shower that morning. He could not undo what he had done to her, but he could make sure he never did it again. Her body and mouth would both need to say yes for him to take her again. She had to be completely sure she wanted it. Wanted him.

Unfortunately, this was all terrible timing. Instead of focusing on conquering his rivals and taking his rightful throne, he was too busy focusing on conquering the female who had promised to help him. He had to get his priorities straight.

Kieron watched Genevieve devour her breakfast. "How much of your magic can you use?" He finally asked her.

Genevieve pushed back her plate and twisted her body to look at him. "I can summon things. I used other magic when I killed Voss, but I don't know how to do that again."

"It's a start. We will practice today. If you are done eating, we should get started." Kieron leveled a look back at her. She only shrugged her shoulders and Kieron decided that was a good enough answer as he pushed back from the table, "Let's go before it gets too hot." *Before I lose my good sense and take you on this table* was what he really meant. He aimed for the outdoor training ring and Genevieve trailed behind him.

Genevieve

"Explain to me what happened when you killed Voss." Kieron requested. I had already spent the last fifteen minutes showing Kieron I could summon various items and explaining how I had left the twenty-seventh world with the wolves.

"My entire body was glowing and it was like I had a permanent shield around me. Anything he threw at me just … deflected. Then when I threw my axe, it was like my magic stayed with the axe and broke through any defense he had." I explained. *Wow, I sound like a crazy person.* But Kieron was just chewing his lip, deep in thought.

"I guess Ryett showed me how to throw knives while willing my power to stay in the knife ... I am assuming that was what happened when I threw the axe."

"And you have never done something like that before?" Kieron asked.

"Nope. Kieron, I did not know I had magic until I was living in the Mountains."

"Really?"

"Yes, really."

"Hmmm ... What were you thinking or feeling while it happened?" He now sat on the edge of the rock wall and crossed his arms across his broad chest.

I looked up at the sky and rubbed a hand down my face. I was trying to remember, but also it felt like there was a huge floodgate of emotion that I was about to open once I remembered the answer. "Well ... all I was thinking is that I had to save someone I loved. I was feeling ... love. That sounds so crazy ..." My voice trailed off and my throat burned as I tried to swallow the emotions that were rising in me.

"It is not crazy. Tell me what you mean by that. That you were feeling love?" Kieron pressed.

"That I was loved. That I had felt love and given love and in spite of all of the pain from my losses that there was still love in me. It just radiated out of me." I felt my cheeks heat as I blushed.

Kieron smiled, "That is beautiful."

"It was also terrifying, Kieron ... there was this rage behind it." I said softly.

"There is nothing wrong with feeling rage. Do you think you can summon those feelings again?"

"I am not sure I want to."

Kieron shifted slightly and he took a deep breath, "We are about to head into the Eastern Desert. I have spent a century working with the Undead to build an army, but that does not mean all of them want to or will support me as their king. Some of the Undead are good people who were caught up in bad situations and some of the Undead are bad people who have done extremely heinous things. They are all males and I assume you can imagine what they are going to be thinking about when a female shows up. I will protect you, but I also need to know you have some means to protect yourself."

"So I need to be able to shield myself?"

"That. And probably a few other things. I know you *can* do it, I can feel it in your magic, but I do not know if you are *willing* to." He responded.

"What does that mean?" I asked, completely confused.

"The Undead are not just called that because of the tattoos. They are called Undead because death has been taken from them. No one knows the details of how it all started, but the myth is that a male was given the gift of immortality from the beings in the twenty-seventh world and that he could give that same gift to others. He became known as The Death Taker. One day, while he was away, his family suffered a terrible death at the hands of another male. The Death Taker hunted down the male responsible and tore death from his body. He then locked him into what is now known as the Eastern Desert for all of eternity as a sentence for his crimes. After this, The Death Taker himself stayed in the Eastern Desert to ensure the punishment was lived out.

"Many centuries before I was born, The Death Taker made a deal with The King of the Deserts. The king could banish any male he saw fit to the Eastern Desert and The Death Taker would deal out the sentencing. And before you ask, there are no female Undead. Anyone banished was sent through the gates to the Eastern Desert. They then have to survive the desert as well as the creatures within the desert while they search for the Palace of the Undead. If they are able to find the Palace of the Undead, then The Death Taker will make them immortal and oversee their sentencing and punishment.

"Only those who have been made Undead know what happens during the process. All that Orion and Zealand have shared with me is that it is something they would not wish upon any of their enemies.

"What we do know is that there are only three ways to kill someone once they become one of the Undead." He stood up and summoned a watermelon to the small table next to him, "First, blood rain." The watermelon exploded into a million droplets. "The other options are to be killed by a Great Wolf or Esurimagicae. You are not a Great Wolf nor Esurimagicae, so you must learn to turn someone into blood rain."

I swallowed. "We can't just cut off their heads?"

"No." Kieron's voice was hard, "An Undead body will just search for its head until it finds it and if it does not find it, both pieces will continue living until they are reunited."

"Blood rain it is then." I breathed.

"Are you okay with killing? If not, maybe I need to rethink

bringing you." Kieron asked.

"I am not staying here while you go off on your own. And no I am not okay with killing, but clearly I will do it if I have to." His offer to just leave me here frustrated me. I was getting sick of all this protection bullshit from these males, "Show me how to do it. The blood rain."

He stared at me for heartbeats before he spoke. "Blood rain is dark magic. Dark magic, unlike other magic, has its own set of rules and limits. Using it will deplete you significantly and should only be used as a last resort. Of the few beings who have the ability, most can only turn one other being into blood rain at a time and it might nearly kill them. It is as if the magic knows it is too terrible to be used limitlessly. Across the kingdoms it is considered a terrible crime to use dark magic against another being like us, not to mention it is extremely dangerous. You must only use it as a last resort and know that you will likely have no magic reserve after you have done it. Do you understand?" There was a seriousness in Kieron's voice I had never heard before.

"I watched you turn all those beasts into blood rain. How did you do that?" When Ryett was restoring the twenty-seventh gate Kieron had battled the beasts that had been coming for us. I remember watching dozens turn into mist.

"My magic leans towards the killing kind and I have been training for centuries. I knew exactly how many beasts I was killing and how much magic reserve I would have left. I am also the only one I know of who can use blood rain to kill more than one being at a time and not kill themself in the process." He looked away from me and summoned another watermelon to the table.

"How much reserve did you have left?" I asked.

"Enough to find Beck."

"And how many people have the ability to do this?"

"Very few." He said softly.

"So it is extremely hard to do, but you somehow think I can do it even though I barely know how to use my magic?"

"No. It is not hard. Very few people have the type of magic that *can* do this. You are one of them." I was processing what Kieron said as he turned back to me, "You can't bring someone back from this."

"Obviously." I replied, my voice a whisper. "Teach me how to do it."

"And how do I make sure I do not kill you while I am trying to kill the watermelon?" I asked as I stared at the watermelon still on the table.

Kieron chuckled, "Send your magic out and wrap it around and into the thing you are trying to kill. You will be able to feel it— its essence, its heartbeat if it has one." I stole a nervous glance at Kieron. He reached over and took both my hands in his, turning me away from the table to face him. "Here send your magic out to feel me first. I am not worried about you killing me quite yet." He teased me. I let out a nervous laugh. "Close your eyes." I did. Then I let my magic ripple out from my center and I imagined it gently wrapping around and into Kieron. "That's it ... Good. Do you feel my heartbeat?"

I nodded slowly. This felt completely invasive. I could feel the beat of Kieron's heart echo through my magic and into my own body. I could feel his kindness and—I let my magic stop. Then I opened my eyes and looked up at Kieron staring down at me. I carefully pulled my hands from his and turned back to the table. "Okay. Let me try the watermelon." I said absently before he could say anything.

I had turned a table full of watermelons into nothing but juice that now soaked the red dirt beneath and around the table. "Very good." Kieron said, his voice hard. "Looks like you will be coming to the Eastern Desert."

"Good." I responded. "Are we done here?" I needed to get out of here. I obviously was not *leaving* leaving, but I needed to get out of this training ring. I had just learned how to completely obliterate someone and instead of feeling scared or drained like I should have, I only felt my magic thrumming in my blood as if it was growing and pushing to get out. It terrified me.

"Yes, we are done." Kieron responded, I felt his eyes watching me as I hurried from the training ring and into the house. I aimed straight for the pool and jumped into the cool water without taking my clothes off.

CHAPTER 12

Genevieve - Many Years Ago.

It was late in the evening when Chad told me to follow him. He gave no explanation and I did not ask for one. The room Chad brought me to was in the basement of the building. It was cold and damp and there were two people tied to chairs. One male and one female. Both of their heads were covered. A chill ran down my spine. *This was wrong.* Whatever was going on here was wrong.

"Genevieve. This is your first lesson." Chad spoke as he unbound a leather satchel and rolled it out on the table exposing the various knives, pliers, and instruments inside. "You will do exactly as I tell you to and if you do not, she will pay." He pointed a knife at the female. She let out a small sob.

I felt like I was going to throw up. "Chad, no—" I started to protest.

"Genevieve, Genevieve. This is not a discussion. This is a

command." He replied and held out a knife to me. I took it. "Good girl. Now I want you to slice a three inch horizontal cut above his right knee."

I just stared at Chad in horror and shook my head no. In four strides he was across the room and slicing a cut across the female's leg as she screamed in pain. He then ripped the hood off of the male. It was the Sergeant who had beaten me. "Does this make it any easier?" Chad asked darkly.

The Sergeant was dead. I had killed him, but the female had not received another scratch. My entire body was shaking and there were tears streaming down my face. "Good girl." Chad said as he took the knife from my hand and set it on the table. The female was crying quietly under her hood. "You are mine, Genevieve. *Mine*. Do you understand?" Chad asked as his hand caressed my cheek. I only nodded. "Good girl. When I summon you, you will come. Do you understand?"

"Yes, sir." I whispered. *What had I done?* The Sergeant was a pig, but I was not sure he deserved any of what Chad had me do to him.

"You will not question me. Ever." Chad continued as he walked over to the female and stood behind her. "Do you understand?"

I nodded.

Then he snapped the female's neck and her body slumped in the chair. She was dead.

We had just finished shooting practice. I had hit every target. Easily. As I pressed up from my stomach to my hands and knees Chad stopped me, "You have one more lesson to complete today. Lay back down." I only sighed and did as I was told. "Five hundred yards out. Pick one and drop them."

I froze and looked at Chad's face. He had the spotting scope up to his eye. I settled into position and looked through my scope. Six males walked in a line, all of them had hoods over their heads. "Pick one, Genevieve. I am waiting."

I hesitated. They were all wearing our uniforms. They were our people. "What did they do?" I asked tentatively as I aimed, trying to steady my breath.

Shots fired from somewhere nearby and I watched all six males drop to the ground. All of them were dead. "Do not question orders. Do not hesitate. When you hesitate, people die, Genevieve. Only one of those males had to die today, but your disobedience caused them all to lose their lives." Chad said.

It was the second and last time I hesitated.

Chad had summoned me to his office that evening and now I stood staring at a skimpy dress, heels, and a bag of cosmetics. "Get dressed, Genevieve, I am taking you out tonight." Chad said as he shuffled papers on his desk.

I only took a deep breath and picked up the pile before slipping into the bathroom attached to Chad's office to get changed. I had gotten used to never questioning Chad's orders. Eventually my emotions just dissipated and were completely replaced by numbness. I was merely a ghost going through the motions of living.

When I emerged, Chad looked me over and the corner of his lip turned upwards in approval, "Let's go." He said and took my arm.

The bar he took me to was crowded. I recognized many of the patrons as others currently serving their military service. All of them recognized Chad. A hostess took us to a private table in a section of the bar that was roped off. I sat gingerly on the fake leather couch next to Chad. A bottle and glasses were delivered to the table and Chad poured me a drink. I shook my head no. "You will drink what I tell you to drink. If you do not, all of the people in this bar will find themselves going home in boxes."

My stomach dropped. *He was willing to kill all of these people if I didn't take a fucking drink.* I knew better than to test him. I stretched out my hand and took the drink from him. A few drinks later and the room was nearly spinning. I had never drank so much in my life. Chad had his hands all over me tonight and I did not dare refuse, but finally I did have to excuse myself to the bathroom. Chad gave me a stare that threatened violence if I tried to pull anything over on him. I wouldn't dream of it. I staggered to the bathroom and found myself vomiting into one of the toilets a moment later.

When I had emptied my stomach, I staggered back to the sinks and tried to clean up. I glanced in the mirror. I looked awful. My makeup had smeared, my face was oily and sweaty. "Here, let me help you get cleaned up." A female voice said from beside me, "Drink this." A water bottle was shoved into my hands.

I gladly accepted it and gulped down the water. "You're with Chad aren't you? Are you okay? Do you need us to help you?" A different female said.

I swallowed and turned to see three females hovering around me. "I think I drank too much. Could you help me get cleaned up so that I don't look like such a mess. I am so embarrassed." *Yes! I need help!* I wanted to scream, but I knew they would be killed if I said anything.

I was in a fog as they whipped cosmetics from their bags and helped me straighten myself up. I asked their names and tried to commit their faces to memory. When I looked back in the mirror again the room was not spinning as terribly and I looked significantly better.

"Thank you all so much." I breathed.

"You just give us a wave if you need us to come rescue you. The general seems to be getting a little handsy and you do not have to put up with it even if he is the general." *They had no idea.*

"I am fine. Really. Thank you." I said and I slipped out of the bathroom and made my way through the crowd back to the table where Chad was waiting.

His eyes burned into me as I slid onto the seat next to him, "That took quite a while." He said between his teeth as his hand found my leg.

"I'm sorry, I was a complete mess and needed to freshen up. You deserve someone looking their best when they are next to you."

I said carefully. He gave me a sly grin and slid his fingers under the hem of the dress he had ordered me to wear. Then he placed another drink in front of me.

By the time Chad told me it was time to leave I had no idea how I was still able to stand. I prayed he would ditch me in the room near his office he had decided to make my living quarters, but he led me past the door and towards his office. The building was empty and dimly lit at this hour of the night.

He pushed open his office doors and led me in. A single small lamp was still on in the corner and it cast shadows around the room. "Good, I was hoping you would be here already." Chad said. A male stood from one of the chairs in front of Chad's desk. I hadn't even seen him. I had been solely focused on standing and not blacking out or throwing up.

Chad led me to the other chair and deposited me in it. Then he walked around his desk and sat in his chair, "You better make this good." He said and leaned back as he undid the fastenings on his pants.

The male stepped towards me, "Stand up." He said gruffly.

I glanced back at Chad, he was just watching. Waiting.

I stood up slowly and had to hold on to the chair to keep from falling over after all of the alcohol. The male's hands guided me to turn around and his fingers brushed my hair around one side of my neck. Then I felt the zipper on my dress tug. I took a quick step forward away from him and spun around.

My head cleared as my body panicked. The male stepped for me and I backed further away. *This could not be happening.* "Chad, please!" I begged. I did not know what I thought Chad would do.

He had arranged this. Before I could do anything else the male had grabbed me and ripped the top of my dress down. He spun me and pressed me against the wall. I threw my elbow back and it connected with his nose. He swore and released me long enough for me to duck away from him and make a run for the door.

Just as my hand hit the door handle I heard Chad's voice, "Eloise. Rebecca. Mia. Those were their names right? The females who helped you at the bar?" I froze completely. *Those were their names. How had he known?* "Now come back here like the good girl I know you are."

Chad had groomed me into a mass murderer, a personal pet, and his very own fuck doll for himself and whoever he wanted to watch fuck me. There was not a drop of innocence left in me. I had stopped counting when my kill count hit twenty-six. I wish I could say there were only a few more after that number, but there were a few multiples of that number instead. I was a ghost. A coward. A monster. But I still had so much rage. All that was left was rage. He had taught me how to kill and lie and manipulate—I guess he thought I would never turn on him. That I somehow loved him. But I didn't. I just hated myself too much to do anything about it. Not any longer. I was done playing his games. I would play games of my own.

Over the next month I carefully adjusted the End Date of Service for Eloise, Rebecca, and Mia. The reports I gave Chad only showed released servicemembers the Monday after they were sent home. The three females would be long gone before Chad knew they had left.

To be safe I doctored the reports and only included one female at a time weeks after they had all actually left. Eventually, the Monday came for the final doctored report. Just as I had planned, all three females had been released and had left weeks earlier. I set the report on Chad's desk along with the other Monday documents.

An hour later Chad called me back into his office. "Come here." Chad commanded as he slid his chair back from his desk, indicating that he wanted me between him and his desk. I obeyed and sat on the edge of his desk in front of him. He stood and caressed my face. I forced myself not to pull back from his touch. He leaned close. "Did you really think you could lie to me? That I would not notice you doctored the reports? That I would not find out your three friends were released from service early?" Chad growled softly in my ear. My body tensed, but I did not move. "Just to make this absolutely clear for you: You are *mine*. This is your home. *I* am your home. And even when you leave here, if I ever summon you home, you will fucking come. Do you understand?"

"Yes, sir." I whispered. He lifted my chin and kissed my mouth. Then he beat me unconscious.

CHAPTER 13

Genevieve - Present Day.

The first thing I realized was that my body was soaking wet. There were beads of sweat rolling down and dripping between my breasts. The next thing I realized was that there was a strong hand on my shoulder. I flung myself from the bed and turned to look at the room. My chest heaved as I sucked in breaths. I felt the cool terracotta tile under my feet and saw the soft cream drapes gently swaying in the breeze with the soft glow of the starry night behind them. *I am in Kieron's home. I am in his room. I am safe.*

"Genevieve, baby, what is going on? You were screaming." Kieron's voice was strained. He was halfway across the bed as if he was in the middle of following me off after I had jumped up. He asked again, "G? Are you okay?"

"I'm fine." I managed to whisper. I rolled my shoulders and a chill ran down my spine, "I was having a nightmare. I didn't know where

I was."

Kieron climbed off my side of the bed, "Shit, the sheets are soaked." He breathed. Then with a wave of his hand, fresh sheets were on the bed. I was still standing feet from the bed, my body trembling. "Genevieve …" He touched my arm gently. "Do you want to talk about it?"

I shook my head, no. I did not want to talk about it. I wanted to forget about it. "I am going to shower off before I ruin another set of sheets." I said quietly and stepped past him, moving quickly into the bathroom. I wished I could wash away every memory. Every terrible thing.

Before I could close the glass to the shower behind me, Kieron braced his hand against the glass and stepped into the shower with me. He reached out and turned the shower on without saying a word. Then he gently pulled me close and into the warm water. "I am fine, Kieron—" I started to protest.

"Shut up." He whispered as he brushed my hair back. He held me in his arms and under the gentle stream of water until my body stopped trembling and my breath matched his—slow and even. Then he slowly turned me in the water, making sure my body was fully rinsed. His touch was firm yet gentle as he helped me rinse off. *Not that I needed help*, but his hands calmed me. The sheer panic and fear slowly faded from my body.

I was standing with my back to him. His hands gently rubbed my shoulders. "Please do not ever ask me to kill anyone for you." My voice was nearly a whisper.

His hands stopped moving. "I am capable of doing my own killing." Kieron replied.

"I mean it. Do not ever ask me to." My eyes were brimming with tears as I turned and looked up at him.

His eyes searched my face before he responded, "I promise I will never ask you to kill anyone for me."

"Thank you." I breathed and I let my head drop to rest against his shoulder. His arms wrapped around me and he held me close. I let my tears fall from my face and wash away in the water.

Eventually, he turned off the water and reached out of the shower to grab us towels. He shook one out of its neatly folded state and wrapped it around my shoulders. Then he wrapped a second towel around his waist.

When we crawled back into bed I rolled over to face away from him. "Uh uh." He said and rolled me back, pulling my body close to his and tucking my head into his shoulder. I lifted my leg and draped it over his, tucking my foot so it rested along his shin. The palm of my hand found its home on his chest over his heart and the scar I had given him.

Neither of us said anything more. Eventually his heartbeat and steady breathing lulled me back to sleep.

CHAPTER 14

Genevieve

I had to peel my face off of Kieron's chest when I woke up and I was pretty sure I had drooled on him. "Hey sweetheart, did you get some sleep?" His voice was gentle this morning.

I pushed myself up so that I was sitting, the sheet draped around my waist, as I wiped my face and the corner of my mouth. His hand gently rested on my naked hip and his thumb stroked my skin. "I think I drooled on you." I responded.

He only chuckled, "I don't mind." *What was actually wrong with me?* Looking down at Kieron laying in bed with the morning light filtering through the curtains—I stopped myself. Only days ago I was with Ryett. Maybe I needed to stay away from all males for a while—even if Kieron demanded I sleep in his bed.

I got out of bed and headed to the closet to find some clothes to throw on. Then I slipped into the bathroom to freshen up. When

I came out Kieron had already left the room. I found him at the dining table with a letter and a book in front of him. "It's for you." He said and held them out to me.

The envelope just had my name on it and I moved it to see the book: *Passion's Sweet Surrender*. I raised my eyebrows and opened the letter. It was from Sarla.

> *Genevieve,*
>
> *What the actual fuck! I am so mad at Ryett I cannot even see straight. Are you okay? He just let you leave with Kieron? Tell me what happened. He isn't sharing much and just returned home with some redhead—who by the way completely sucks—and barely even acknowledged that you were not with him. Now the two of them are planning a union ceremony and I think all of us might murder one or both of them before it happens. Zain will not even speak to Ryett and has basically been impossible to find the last few days. I need to know that you are safe and okay. Write back.*
>
> *Sarla*
>
> *P.S. I just finished this book and thought you might like it too.*

I dropped the note and the book on the table and walked outside without saying anything. Kieron was right. Ryett *was* done. I had known it—kept telling myself it, but maybe I had been holding onto hope that none of this was actually happening. That it was a mistake. It wasn't a mistake. He was going to marry her—join in union or whatever the fuck they called it here.

"What are you thinking?" Kieron asked from behind me, "I can feel your rage, but what are you thinking?"

"He just dropped me like I meant nothing to him. I fucking chose to come back to *save him*. I could have been done with all of this. But I came back to save *him* and he just dropped me. I did not expect him to choose me over her—I knew he would choose her—I mean fuck! Did you see her? They are perfect for each other. I just didn't think I would be discarded like I meant nothing. Without even a thank you." My rage was sizzling beneath my skin.

"Is this why you tried to drown yourself in the pool when we arrived here?"

I slowly turned to face Kieron. "I could have moved on from this life when I was in the twenty-seventh world ... I *wanted* to move on, but I came back so Ryett could live. So he could have happiness. He got what he wanted—I just wanted to get what I wanted too."

I saw the sadness in Kieron's eyes. I could see him trying to think of what to say next. "You didn't love him?" He finally asked.

Had I loved him? "Ryett is genuinely ... good." I started, then paused. I had just started allowing myself to think that I *could* love again. I guess I had *loved* him in a way, but I had not allowed myself to consider if I could be *in love* with him. I took a deep breath before continuing. "He showed me I could live again, that I could have another life. I thought it could be with him—I thought it was going to be with him. That I could love him. That maybe he could love me. But Kieron, I have already had love and the bar is high. This hurts like hell, but it is nowhere close to the pain I have already been feeling. This pain will pass. I am not sure the other pain will ever leave me."

I felt Kieron's hand on my arm and snapped, "No!" I took a step back from him. "No. You do not get to just swoop in when I am broken and expect to sweep me off my feet. You already have all your fucking rules. You have a kingdom full of slaves, if you want someone to do exactly as you say, go get one of them. I need some space right now."

I turned and stormed back into the house. I needed some privacy. I needed to bury my head in a pillow and scream. I had just made it to the hallway when I heard Kieron's footsteps behind me, "Leave me alone!" I shouted over my shoulder at him.

His hand wrapped around my arm and he had my back pressed against the wall a moment later. "You are hurting, I get it, but that does not mean you get to take it out on me." His eyes were hard.

I opened my mouth to spit venom back, but felt a gentle warmth pulse through my body. I closed my mouth. He was right, I was being awful. This was not like me to yell at someone who did not deserve it. Kieron did not deserve this. I had said awful things to him and he was only trying to be there for me. The rage fizzled out of me like a fire that was drenched in water. "I am so sorry. You are right." I breathed.

"Apology accepted." He said, but did not let me go, "And I do not want a slave, I want you. I wanted you before all of this and if you would stop being so stubborn maybe you will start to understand that my rules are to protect you." Then he released me and walked back to the great room. Leaving me standing in the hallway.

I took a deep breath. *Okay then.* I needed to write Sarla back and focus on following through on helping Kieron. I was not helping him by throwing tantrums.

"Do you have paper and a pen I can use to write Sarla back?" I asked softly as I reentered the great room. Kieron had made himself comfortable in a chair at the table and was already eating his breakfast.

He waved his hand and paper and a pen appeared on the table next to him, "So what is the deal with this novel Sarla sent?"

I took a seat next to him and pulled the paper and pen to me, "She got me into reading trashy erotic romance novels." I said simply and I began to write.

> *Sarla,*
>
> *I am safe and I am being well taken care of. I promise. I want to be here in the Deserts right now. I do miss you though. Please try to give Rachel a chance. Cut Ryett some slack too, they have been through a lot. Let me know the date of the union ceremony and I will be sure to arrange a major interruption solely for your amusement. Thank you for the book—please send more when you find other good ones!*
>
> *Genevieve*

Kieron was flipping through the pages of the book laughing to himself when I finished my note to Sarla. "How do I send this back to her?" I asked and ripped the book out of his hands.

He snapped his fingers and the letter disappeared. "Sent." He said with a smirk.

We just sat there for a few minutes before I spoke. "I need to ask you some questions." I set the book down on the table and faced Kieron.

"Anything."

"You said I am your soulmate … or a match? How do you know? When I was around Ryett, I felt my magic respond to him. I saw … things …" I willed myself to stare at Kieron.

He straightened in his chair and then turned it to face me, "I can feel it. I felt it when I looked into your eyes the day you killed me by the river in your world. It is actually why you were able to kill me, I completely froze."

"But why can't I feel it?" I countered.

"You hesitated when you first saw me, when you were going to shoot me, didn't you?" Kieron asked. I stared at him. *I had hesitated.* I gave him a questioning look, "I imagine being attacked and then tortured and raped by me was not a great first impression. Your brain is telling you I am *not* someone to be trusted. But I also know that you are drawn to me. Why do you think you willingly gave yourself to me when we were in the Wastes? Or why do you think your body responds the way it does to my touch?"

Good points. I had been feeling things for him, but only wondering what was terribly terribly wrong with me that I would want him after all of *that.* Wondering how I could feel so conflicted. My brain told me I should stay far away from him and my body wanted the exact opposite.

The corners of his mouth twitched upwards, "So you do not deny that you are drawn to me?"

I laughed and stood up from the table, "You made some good points, Kieron, and no I am not denying that I am drawn to you."

I tried to step away and go anywhere but here, but his hand grabbed my wrist. "I have told you what I want, but I would not blame you if you could never forgive me, G. What I did to you was horrific." I could hear the pain in his voice.

I looked down at him sitting in the chair. I had already forgiven him. I had forgiven him in the Wastes when he had chosen to help me. I had forgiven him again when he had explained why he had hurt me. He was not the first male to have done terrible things to me, but it just *felt* different. *He* was different. He had been trying to save me the only way he thought he could. I forgave him because it was what I hoped for myself: Forgiveness for the terrible things I had done. How could I hope for that forgiveness, but not be willing to give it? "Sometimes doing terrible things is justifiable, Kieron." His grip on my wrist loosened. "I forgive you." I said and left him sitting at the table.

CHAPTER 15

Kieron

The letters from Ryett and Beck just kept coming. Both kings demanded he send Genevieve back and their letters continued to contain more and more threats. Kieron had hoped that Genevieve writing back to Sarla would shut the two kings up for a while, but apparently it had not. This morning he had finally sent back a strongly worded letter telling them to both fuck off—he did not use those exact words, but his next letter might. Genevieve knew if she wanted to leave all she needed to do was ask. It was her choice. Not any of theirs.

Kieron had responded to the letters before breakfast and was in a bad mood all throughout eating. Now it was time for training with Genevieve and he still had not been able to shake off his annoyance and anger. They would start today with a workout—maybe that would clear his head.

Genevieve

"Have you ever used a sword?" Kieron asked. We stood in the training ring after he had just put me through an almost unreasonably tough workout. A rack of swords was set against one of the walls.

Have I ever used a sword? I wanted to laugh. No. Sword fighting sounded so ... ancient. "No, I have not used a sword." I responded. I could not help my eyeroll. Knives? Guns? A variety of other weird killing and maiming instruments? Yes. Axes? Yes. Swords? No.

He tossed a sword to me and I stepped out of the way as it fell onto the dirt. "You were supposed to catch that." He said, not hiding his annoyance.

"Warn me next time." I snapped back at him. Apparently we were both grumpy this morning. He had been silent and stewing at breakfast and by the workout we had just done I was pretty sure he was trying to get his mind off of something. I thought we had made good progress together. I had at least made progress, but here he was, being a total ass this morning.

I was not sure what was wrong with him today. Maybe it was because we continually undressed each other with our eyes, but neither of us had made a move. Maybe he was finally getting run down by the taunting. But this was the game we were playing—at least it was the game I was playing—how turned on could I get him before he snapped? He had not snapped yet. Today was looking like it might be the day. Maybe it was bad, but I kind of hoped it would be the day.

"Pick it up." He said slowly. I could tell he was forcing himself to stay calm.

I pressed my lips together to stifle my smirk as I bent down and picked up the sword. He was glaring at me when I stood back up. "Which Kieron do I have today?" I asked. His eyes flashed confusion at my question. "Do I have the dominant Kieron who has to be in control by any means necessary? Or do I have the Kieron who is calm, kind, and compassionate?" I watched his jaw muscles work as his eyes burned into me. I turned my eyes to look over the sword in my hand, turning it this way and that. "I just want to know who is training me today. I would also like to know who the real Kieron is."

"And if I am both?" He said in a low growl. "Do you have a problem with that?"

I let my eyes scan slowly over his body. No, I did *not* have a problem with that. I bit my lip as I settled my eyes back on his, "Well then. Let's get on with it."

"Fucking asshole!" I grit out through my teeth as I dropped my sword and pressed my hand over the wound Kieron had just inflicted.

"Block better next time." He responded with a smirk. "And that mouth of yours—"

"Oh shut the fuck up." I bit back. "Don't pretend swearing

bothers you."

He chuckled, "You *are* kind of cute when you swear." I glared daggers into him and he calmly wiped my blood off of his blade and onto his pant leg. "Now heal yourself."

I carefully lifted my hand from the wound to peek and nausea rolled through me. I could see down to the bone where his blade had sliced through meat and muscle. I pressed my hand back down and quickly sat in the dirt before I passed out and fell over. A string of four letter words left my mouth.

Kieron came and crouched in front of me. "Heal yourself." He said again calmly.

"I don't know how." I said through my teeth as I glared back at him. I still could not believe he had nearly taken my entire arm off.

"Deep breath. Send your magic into the wound like you are pouring water into it." His hand was now gently, but firmly, on my leg as he stared into my eyes. *Fuck I would let him cut me again if he continued to look at me like that.* "Deep breath." He coaxed. I took a deep breath. Then I willed my magic to trickle out of me and sent it into the wound. The pain slowly subsided. "Very good." He said, his low voice felt like a hand caressing down my body. *I was seriously messed up to be thinking about his hands on my body after what he just did.* Then his hand peeled mine away from the wound. I looked down—*I had done it.* The skin was still bloody, but there was no wound. Not even a scar. I grinned and looked back at him—only to watch him stab a knife into my thigh.

My other foot connected with his chest as I swiftly kicked him. He fell backwards and I ripped the knife from my leg. I was on top of him with the knife pressed to his throat a moment later. "Doesn't feel great does it?" He asked with a smirk on his face. *Fucking asshole.* I sunk the knife into the sand next to his head and rolled off of him. I quickly healed my leg the way he had just shown me and stood up, heading towards the house. I was done with training today.

"We aren't done." He called from behind me.

"Yes we are." I responded, then collided with his chest. He had jumped in front of me, blocking my way.

"No, baby. I didn't say you could stop." His voice was smooth and teasing. I could only swallow as I looked up at him and he looked down at me. I knew he could feel my feelings and that made it even worse. I could see it in his eyes—that he knew how badly I wanted him right this moment and that he also knew I would not admit it outloud.

"I respond better to positive feedback." I said between my teeth. My breasts and between my legs were tingling and aching. *This was ridiculous. He had just stabbed me and I still wanted him.*

The corners of his mouth turned upwards, "Oh, you seem to be responding very well to this type of feedback." I planted my hand firmly on his chest to shove him out of my way so I could go inside. His hand wrapped my wrist, stopping me. "I know exactly what game you're playing, sweetheart. You are doing well, but you forget I have been playing these types of games for centuries."

"If you are as good as you think you are, why haven't you won yet?" I managed to bite back.

He chuckled, "Maybe because I like to play the game. Now get back in the training ring. We are done when I say we are done."

My breath caught as his eyes burned into me. "I am done for the day." I said and pushed him aside. He let my hand slip through his and I heard him laugh as I walked away.

CHAPTER 16

Kieron - Months Earlier.

Kieron hated the Wastelands, but at least when he was out there he was far away from Vossarian and his disgusting habits. He had not yet decided what he would do if he found Ryett out here, Voss seemed to think Ryett had been bringing slaves to Aveline, the Queen of the Cliffs. Which seemed somewhat crazy because Aveline had taken a very strong and public stance against slaves. Either way, Voss had become so paranoid about Ryett and Beck being buddies that he sent Kieron to keep a close eye on whatever it was Ryett was doing.

Kieron brushed a spider from his sleeve as he saw the line of slaves led by Sarla and Ryett snake between the trees. None of them were shackled. *Interesting.* Maybe Voss was right to be suspicious. His eyes followed the line and his heart stopped as he saw Genevieve near the back with Alias. *Why the fuck did he bring her out here?*

He moved silently through the trees following them for a few hours before deciding he had seen enough and slinking away from their group. He still did not know what he was going to tell Voss. He would have to consider what the truth would do to his plans. Maybe it would be better to lie. Maybe he had a new ally.

His thoughts were interrupted by screech that silenced the already quiet Wastelands. Beasts had found them. He should leave —quickly—but that fucker had brought Genevieve out here. He had not risked his neck to free her and then swallowed his pride as he handed her over to Ryett for her to be killed out here. When he had realized Ryett's magic had matched hers, it took everything in him not to rip Ryett's head off. It was an almost uncontrollable urge that he had quickly shut down, convincing himself that she was better off far away from him and further away from Voss. Now she was out here and in danger. He blew out a deep breath and turned back towards the sound.

It was worse than he could have imagined. Alias and Genevieve were separated from the group and Alias was laying unmoving on the ground. Kieron sized up the two esurim as he circled in —he was going to have to move quickly if he wanted to live. It would be a miracle to survive a fight against these monsters and who knew how many more were on their way. Kieron was not keen on learning what death by magic eater felt like—at least it was something he likely would not come back from and have to experience a second time. He watched in horror as Genevieve threw her knife directly into the chest of the bigger esurim—*damn that was a good throw*—but she was trying to draw the esurim away. *Fuck.* Kieron took off running as the esurim chased her. He kept one eye on Genevieve and one on the forest ahead of them as they sprinted through the thick and dying woods.

He was gradually moving closer. Maybe he could get between the esurim and Genevieve and she could get away. Kieron's heart stopped as he watched Genevieve stumble and fall to the ground. Without even thinking he was next to her hauling her to her feet and screaming at her to get up.

"Faster." Kieron yelled, "We have to make it to the cliffs and jump." He was nearly dragging her through the forest at this point. She was fast, but he was faster and he needed her to move faster. "Run, dammit! Your choice is to run and jump with me or be eaten by those things." They had broken from the forest onto open ground. The cliff's edge was getting closer, "Jump as far out as you can, then pull your arms to your chest and keep your legs together until you hit the water." Kieron bit out between breaths. This could end very badly, but it was the only chance they had, "Jump far!" Kieron yelled as they leapt off the cliff's edge. He was acutely aware that the esurim were way too close as they both plummeted down towards the sea.

Genevieve looked half drowned, but she was alive. Kieron watched her try to catch her breath. He had no idea what to say to her. He did not know if he could trust Genevieve yet and he was not willing to risk centuries of work even if she was his soulmate. He had to keep playing the game—and in this game he was the assassin who had tortured and raped her. "Have you been missing me? You seemed to enjoy our time together."

"Did I? I didn't think you were that memorable." *That little—* but Genevieve spoke again before Kieron could finish his thought, "Thank you. Thank you for saving me ... How did you ... Why? Why did you help me?"

Oh, she is good. Kieron smiled to himself as he replied, "Here I thought you might have actually missed me and would want to see me again." *And that eye roll.* What he wanted to do to her when she showed him that side of her.

"Considering the alternative was to be eaten, yes, I am happy to see you." Genevieve replied, the relief was clear in her voice.

"Don't be too happy. I'm taking you back to Vossarian." His mind was already racing with what he would tell Voss. What he would have to say to keep her out of Voss's dungeon. Maybe he would just bring her to his private residence and not tell Voss he had her.

"You should have let me be eaten by the monsters." The dread that leaked out of Genevieve was strong. She had kept herself together well while she was a prisoner, but Kieron could feel she would rather die than go back. It was his private residence then. Just another huge risk in the game he was playing.

"That seems like it would have been the better choice." Kieron said as he took off his boot and dumped water onto the rocks. "But here we are, so you are coming back to the Deserts with me. Voss is not going to be happy to find out Ryett has been freeing his slaves."

"Why does it matter what Ryett does with his slaves? He paid for them, he can do what he wants with them." She countered. *Good point.* Kieron thought, one he agreed with, but he also did not condone slavery so he was biased. There was just something about the way she defended Ryett ...

"Does he do what he wants with you?" There was a bite in Kieron's voice. She defended him and Ryett had left her to be eaten by the esurim. Ryett should have been there. Ryett should have been protecting her.

"Oh let me guess, you are jealous he doesn't have to drug me or beat me in order to fuck me?" She said sarcastically. Kieron didn't respond, but his body tensed. She had just insinuated that Ryett had already bedded her. He saw red and forced himself to take a breath. Then she continued, "What do I have to do for you to not tell Vossarian?"

Kieron could not help the laugh that burst from his mouth, "You'd have to kill me and we both know you can't do that."

"I will do anything. Give you anything. Name it." She actually sounded desperate. She hadn't broken, but she really did not want to go back. She was willing to bargain *anything* to keep this secret. Maybe she could be trusted.

But now was not the time to find out. Kieron reminded himself that to her he was just as bad as Voss. He had to keep playing the part. "Clearly I went too easy on you for you to be offering *anything* to keep this a secret."

"Oh please, you're a terrible torturer!" Kieron couldn't hide his shock. *That was unexpected.* She continued, "I didn't even have to sit in the pain of my injuries for days on end. Do you know how easy it is to manage pain knowing that at the end you will get a magic salve rubbed on you that numbs and heals everything? You definitely fucked that up."

He watched in disbelief as she turned to sit facing the water. He had sensed that she had been through worse things than Voss's dungeon, but he was not expecting her to be able to talk so nonchalantly about what happened to her. "If you really wanted to torture me you should have brought me flowers and a fancy dinner with too small of portions so I would still be hungry after eating. Add in a private string quartet to play for us while we eat and you have a winning combination for a terrible time. Then to really top it all off, fuck me gently, but only in missionary, and ask if I'm doing okay every five seconds. Bonus points if you can finish in under two minutes. Now *that* would have been torture. Dominated in a dungeon and pounded by that huge cock of yours? That was practically living out a sexual fantasy."

Kieron blinked back his surprise. Then his head tipped back as he howled with laughter. *That* was definitely not what he expected her to say. He loved how smart and quick thinking she was. A smile was still on his face when he finally regained some of his composure, "I think I *have* met my match."

Then he watched her give him a wink before she turned and vomited onto the rocks. "Swallow too much sea water?" Kieron asked tauntingly.

"I think I am pregnant." Genevieve whispered.

Kieron felt like he had been smacked across the face. "You think you are what?" He blurted.

"Pregnant. The baby could be Vossarian's or ... yours." Genevieve responded softly.

No. Fuck. No. There was no way. He took a contraceptive ... No ... He spent two days with her in the dungeons. He had forgotten to take it the second day. *He had fucking forgotten to take it.* He had done this to her. *How could he have been so careless?* But he also could not shake the sheer joy that was filling his heart. *A baby.* "Voss never slept with you. You are pregnant with my child? How far along are you?"

"I don't know. I have not had my cycle at all since coming here. I just started getting symptoms. I do not know how pregnancies work in this world, it is different where I am from." The words just fell out of her mouth.

Kieron's joy turned to complete panic. "What do you mean you do not know how pregnancies work in this world? You're not from Savengard?" He managed to get out.

He had brushed off the crazy old male in the city when he had nearly chased Kieron down in the street all those months ago. The male's ramblings came flooding back to him. *A baby with a female from the twenty-sixth world ... oh your daughter will die in the womb, but the mother... save her and she will be your salvation. The salvation of all of Savengard. The only hope for the True King.*

Kieron scrambled to his feet and backed away from Genevieve. *Please don't let this be her.* "What world are you from?" He was going to explode.

"Does it matter?" Genevieve replied.

"Tell me." Kieron's demand was nearly a growl.

"The world you first saw me in, the one you were in when I shot you. What does it matter?" She snapped back. And with her response his entire world tilted. *What had he done?*

"We have to get you back to Ryett." Kieron was going to throw up. He couldn't keep her. She was going to save Savengard and the baby would not live. *How could he be so selfish to keep her?* He would take her back to Ryett. That was surely the safer option. Not only had he tortured and raped his soulmate, but she was pregnant and going to lose the baby. Even if it killed him, he had to do the right thing and let her go.

Kieron retrieved the pack he had tucked into the corner of the cave and unfastened the bed roll and blanket. He laid it out on the dirt for Genevieve. "Here, you can sleep on this, it is not safe to move through these woods at night. Tomorrow we will find Ryett."

"What about you?" Genevieve asked as she sat down on the bedroll.

He pulled out the little bit of food he still had left and tossed it onto her lap along with a canteen of water. Then Kieron fished out his flask. "I will be fine." He said and he took a swig of the liquor. It was the cheap stuff, but that seemed to work the best at keeping him warm. He would need it tonight and unfortunately he could not risk using his magic to warm them.

Kieron made himself as comfortable as he could sitting with

his back against the cave wall. He watched Genevieve eat the food before laying down and wrapping the blanket around herself. He tried to only think about one thing—keeping her safe until she was back with Ryett. It was proving difficult to keep his mind from wandering to all the questions he wanted to ask her, how he wanted to get to know her. He also could not stop thinking about running his fingers along her skin and tasting her. He bit down on his own tongue hard enough for the pain to get his thoughts in check as he closed his eyes.

Kieron watched Genevieve run to Ryett. It took everything in him to turn away and disappear into the Wasteland forest. He knew if he lingered it would cause an altercation. An unnecessary altercation. They had all been through enough.

As the forest rushed past on either side, Kieron was not even sure where he was running to. His heart just ached. It ached harder with every step he took away from her. With every thought that raced through his head reminding him of how he had hurt her. She was so beautiful. So smart. So perfect. Kieron did not want to leave her, but it was the one good thing he could do. She had even let him fuck her. Twice. She had wanted it. Wanted him. He had felt how much she wanted him and he did not understand it, but he was not going to question it. It felt incredible to be inside of her. To feel her touch him and kiss him. The way she had looked at him as if she actually saw him, as if she understood him on a level no one else did …

Finally Kieron slowed and took in his surroundings. His magic thrummed inside of him. It was muted, but it was still thrumming. It still pulled on him to turn around and go back. To go back to Genevieve. Even in the Wastelands, where magic was stifled, he could feel Genevieve's magic calling to him. Her magic was like his—he had never met someone with magic like his—dark and powerful and capable of causing mass destruction and death. Maybe that was why they were a match.

CHAPTER 17

Genevieve - Present Day.

Kieron had summoned the rack of swords again this morning. "Since yesterday was cut short, I thought we would start with some more basic sword training." He said casually as he flipped a sword over in his hand and extended it to me. *Cut short?* Yeah, cut short by him nearly cutting my arm off and then stabbing me in the leg with a knife. I slowly extended my hand and took the sword from him without saying a word. I had ignored him the remainder of the day yesterday and even when we went to bed. He had just looked completely amused by it all, which only pissed me off further. I wasn't in the mood to test him this morning either. He at least seemed to be less grumpy today.

Kieron walked me through more basic movements and watched me practice them over and over again. Swords were much heavier than I imagined they would be and I was soon sweating in the brutal heat. "You are doing great. Now one more combination." Kieron said. I raised my eyebrows, he was being almost painfully kind today. "Slice and thrust." Kieron said as he demonstrated the movement again.

He stopped and nodded for me to try. I did. "Beautiful, again." I did it again. "Good. Now you are going to do the same thing as I block the slice, then you will thrust into me."

"I'm sorry what?" I said as I stood up straight and let the sword fall to my side.

He gave me a dark grin, "You are going to stab me through with that sword. Slice and thrust." He stepped in front of me and motioned for me to take my fighting stance.

"No. I am not going to stab you with a sword."

"Do I need to get you a smaller sword to use? You seemed perfectly fine stabbing me with a tiny dinner sword the other day at lunch." He countered. He was not wrong. In my defense, he had provoked me. I guess after being sliced and stabbed myself yesterday I was not in the mood to stab anyone let alone Kieron. "You need to know what it feels like to stab someone through with a sword and fortunately you can practice on me without me dying." He gestured to his torso.

"I think I am sufficiently aware of what it feels like to injure, maim, and kill someone. I do not need more practice."

"Are you now?" He said almost curiously.

"And I am most certainly not going to stab you. Just because you can't die, does not make it okay to stab you." I said as I set the sword carefully on the rack. Then I walked over to the small table with our water canteens on it. I picked mine up and drank from it.

"Rule three." He said simply. I put the canteen back down and turned back to him.

"I am not going to stab you with that sword or any other sword." I said firmly back to him.

"Rule three. Do what I say. I let it slide yesterday, so today you are going to pick up that sword and do what I say." He was slowly walking towards me as he said it. The way he moved was predatory.

"Then spank me because I am not going to stab you." I turned and placed my hands against the stacked stone wall, bending over slightly.

Kieron's hands wrapped my waist and slid down to my hips. I heard him take a deep breath before his hands dropped to my ass and lifted and separated me gently like he was going to do something other than hit me. Then his hands slid back up to my hips and one continued up until it wrapped around my tied up hair. He gently pulled my hair, forcing my head back and to the side as he leaned into me. I felt his hips and his hard cock press against me. I pressed back into him.

"Are you ever going to tell me what made you this way?" Kieron asked, his voice a smooth whisper in my ear.

"How do you know this isn't just who I am?" I countered quietly.

"Because just like me you have two sides that are fighting each other. One you were born with, the other was made. Sometimes, you just forget which is which." I swallowed. Maybe it was his special skill set of feeling others emotions, or maybe it was just that we were so similar. I had shown him so many different sides of myself and he had not backed down from any of them. Maybe that was why I just wanted more of him. He let me be who I wanted to be and exactly who I was. I did not have to hide any side of myself from him.

"Are you going to punish me for breaking rule three or what?" I finally responded.

His hand took mine off of the wall and he turned my body around to face him. I looked up at him. His body was so close to mine. I would never hurt him—even if he could not die—but if he ordered me to do *anything* else I would. My heart pounded in my chest and my breath caught as his hand raised to my face. I watched him lick his lips as he gazed at me. I wanted to taste his lips again. I let my head lean into Kieron's hand as my body arched closer to him. My mouth opened for him as his thumb stroked over my lower lip. "I think *not* spanking you is the punishment today, sweetheart."

I think he was right.

CHAPTER 18

Genevieve - Many Years Ago.

"You signed your release papers?" Chad screamed as my door banged open. I turned to him only to take his fist to my cheekbone and fall backwards against my dresser. *That would definitely leave a mark.* My hand raised to my face where it throbbed as blood rushed to the injury. He crouched in front of me and tore my hand away to inspect where he had just punched me. "I told you to ask for a fucking extension. What happened?" He growled at me.

"I signed the release papers." I said quietly. It had been a calculated risk. Either I would indeed get released or Chad would kill me—either way I would be done with this place. Done with him.

"Why would you do that?" He hissed. His hand now held my jaw and forced my face up so I had to look at him.

"Because I have served my time." I managed to bite out.

His eyes flashed rage. I knew what came next. First he would beat me. Then he would fuck me. Then he would act as if I was the most precious thing in the world to him. I was only bothered by the fact that it did not bother me any more. That I was so completely numb to it.

My knife's tip was whittling a small hole in the bar as I spun it under my finger. The bartender was not going to say anything about scaring his bartop. He had given me a glass and the entire bottle of whiskey when I asked for it, then he stayed on the far side of the bar serving the other patrons and only occasionally glancing my way.

I stared at the blade as it spun and reflected the few lights in this place. No one had approached me—it was either the fact that I was spinning a very large hunting knife on the bar, the bottle of whiskey in front of me already half gone, the black eye and split lip, or the 'fuck off' that was clearly written all over my face. Any one of those would have been sufficient on their own, but I had always been an overachiever.

The narrow brown envelope next to my knife held my service release papers. *I was out.* Chad had completely raged when he found out I had signed my release papers and not requested at least an additional year of service. He had been coaching me to stay for months. Trying to manipulate me to choose to extend my time in the service. To choose to stay with him. *Fuck Chad.* Even *The Great*

General Chad Johnston was not powerful enough to keep me there. He had made it very clear by the way he had beaten and fucked me when he found out that he still considered me his—that I would never truly be free from him. I poured another glass of whiskey.

"So what are we celebrating?" A male's voice said as his body slid onto the stool next to me. I stopped the spinning knife and let my eyes glance over at him. He had dirty blonde hair and an impressively full beard. There was a scar above his left eyebrow and a tattoo snaked up his muscular arm. I watched as his finger tapped the bar top. I would have told him to find another seat, but he also had that look in his eyes—that one like he was dead inside.

I reached over the bar and grabbed another glass before pouring some of my whiskey into it and sliding it in front of him. He lifted it in a salute and downed the glass in one gulp. I poured him another.

"Cheers." He said this time and held up his glass to me. I finally turned to face him as I lifted my glass. His eyes caught on my face —on my black eye, then my split lip. "And how does the other guy look?" He asked as he clinked his glass against mine.

"I definitely look worse." I said and turned back to face the bar.

"Well shit." He said and sipped his whiskey.

We sat in silence for long enough I had nearly forgotten he was there. Then finally the male spoke again, "You just got out, huh?"

"Was it the papers or the celebrating that gave it away?" I responded flatly.

"It is the look in your eyes." He said simply. "It gets better. Whatever you had to do to survive it—I just want you to know it does not matter now. You are out. It is okay to start fresh and pretend like it never happened." Then he finished his glass and pulled some money from his pocket. He set the money on the bar.

"The drinks are on me." I said.

He slowly picked the money back up. "Then how about tomorrow night the drinks are on me?"

***

His name was Eli. Why I had agreed to meet him tonight I was not quite sure. I could see his tall frame standing on the street corner he suggested we meet at. I was still a block away. I could turn around right now—no—he waved as he saw me. I took a deep breath and continued walking towards him.

"Hey." I said as I approached.

"Hey yourself." He responded with a small grin. "Have you eaten?"

I shook my head no. I was planning to drink my dinner tonight. You know, completely ensuring I could not feel a single thing. I was supposed to feel happy. Feel free. But I just felt empty.

"Good. I have the perfect place we can go to get something to eat. I know the owner, his name is Jacob and he makes a very good sandwich."

After our third night spending time together I only knew I wanted to be around Eli more. I was feeling like myself again—the person I was before. Eli had been a commander in the service and had gotten out only a few months before me. He never pressed for details of what I had experienced and he rarely if ever offered any of his own. He firmly believed that I did not need to tell him about myself, I just needed to show him who I was. And I let him do the same. He quickly became someone I loved.

There were no ups and downs with Eli—sure life still had its ups and downs—but Eli was always my rock. I never had to guess at who he was or if he would be there for me or not. I had not intended our little chance meeting at a bar the night I had been released from service to turn into a relationship, but we both could not get enough of each other. Six months later Eli was asking me to move in with him. And six months after that, we were getting married. It was the only thing I had ever been one hundred percent certain about in my life. Eli was my person. He would always be my person.

CHAPTER 19

Kieron - Present Day.

"Today we are going to play a game." Kieron said as he and Genevieve entered the training ring. She just looked at him. He tried not to smile to himself as he felt her nervousness—he fucking loved playing with her. Kieron led her to the far side where the training area opened to some of the trails. "This trail splits into multiple trails that all lead to that plateau," He pointed to where he was talking about, "I am going to give you a head start and you are going to run. If I catch you before you reach the white flag at the base of the plateau, you will either answer a question for me or do something small for me. We keep going until you figure out how to use your magic to run fast enough to reach the flag before I can catch you."

"You're not even going to show me how to run fast before we start?" Genevieve leveled back at him.

"No. It will be more fun to watch you figure it out." He said with a smirk. She just rolled her eyes at him and grumbled something under her breath. "What's that, sweetheart?"

Genevieve glared at him, "I said, lucky fucking me."

Kieron only chuckled, "Are you ready? I will give you a ten second head start."

"I am not getting out of this am I?"

"No, baby. This is what we are doing today." She let out a sigh and readied herself. "Go when you are ready and I will start counting." He watched her shake her head, then she took a deep breath and tore off down the trail. She was surprisingly fast for not knowing how to use her magic to help her yet. "One. Two ..." He yelled down the trail. When he reached ten, Kieron took off after her.

Kieron caught her in less than six seconds. She let out a small scream as his hand wrapped her arm and he stepped around her, pulling her to a stop. She cursed as she stepped back from him. "You are going to have to try harder than that." He said.

"Ask your question." She panted and tossed her hand in the air, clearly annoyed.

"Why Beck? Everyone seems to love him and he is just such a prick. How did he get you? Why him?"

The look she leveled at him was pure fire. Then Kieron watched her swallow it down and take a deep breath. "I had been alone for a while and he was actually very kind to me when I first ended up at his estate. Plus have you seen him? His eyes? Males should not look like that."

Kieron laughed at her response, "So you are just another female who fell for the pretty boy, huh?" She rolled her eyes at him and he grabbed her arm before jumping them back to the starting line. This was going to be more fun than he initially thought. "Again."

"Can you at least explain to me how to use my magic to run faster?" She asked, annoyed.

"Let it carry you. Now go. One. Two." She shot him an annoyed look and then took off down the trail.

This time it took him eight seconds to catch her. "How serious was it with Ryett? Why did you ask me to take you with me if he picked Rachel?"

"That is two questions." Genevieve responded as she put her hands on her head and sucked in deep breaths. Kieron narrowed his eyes at her and tilted his head. He had to know. It was not his business, but he wanted to know. She continued, "I will never be good enough for Ryett."

"No, do not say that. You are more than good enough—" Kieron started.

"Hey." Genevieve snapped back, "Do you want my answer or not?" Kieron gestured for her to continue, "I will never be *good* enough for him. Every person Ryett has had to kill has haunted him. It does not matter if it was a bad person who deserved it or if it was someone who maybe did not deserve it, it haunts him as killing someone should. Ryett does not know what it is like to actually enjoy killing and I hope he never finds out." It was Kieron's turn to be speechless.

They just stared at each other. *What had Genevieve gone through to make her like this?* There was more to it than just avenging her family's deaths. Kieron knew first hand that the satisfaction of revenge and the enjoyment of killing were two very different things. Finally, Kieron reached out and took her arm, "Let's go again." He jumped them back to the starting line. "Whenever you are ready." He said flatly. Her eyes scanned him, then she took off back into the desert.

It took Kieron twelve seconds to catch her this time and she dodged his first attempt to grab her. She was getting faster. She was figuring it out. "Why don't you want me to say 'Good girl'?"

Genevieve let out a big sigh, "'Good girl' used outside of the bedroom? Gross. I am not a dog. It feels degrading and disgusting. In the bedroom is completely different ... *but* it implies a level of possession that you certainly have not earned."

"So how many males have earned that level of possession?" Kieron pressed, he was not actually sure he wanted the answer. He could already feel himself getting territorial—his magic rising to eliminate anyone who threatened him being with her—and they were in the desert alone right now.

"Earned? One and he did not use it." She replied simply.

Okay. He could live with that answer. His magic cooled as it washed through his veins and settled. "So no one has used 'good girl' with you in the bedroom before?" Kieron asked with a smirk.

"I didn't say that."

"Oh? But you didn't like it?" He chuckled as he teased her.

"I didn't say that either." She responded, her voice even and serious. She did not even break eye contact with her response.

Kieron's eyes narrowed as he looked over her. This was a different side of her—she was competitive and she was actually answering his questions. "So what if I say 'You are being such a good girl for me?' or 'That's my good girl?' or how about 'Be a good girl and—'"

"I have already answered more than one question." She leveled back, interrupting him.

Kieron stepped close to her as he prepared to jump them back to the start again. His cheek brushed her temple as he leaned in. "Answer my questions." He whispered in her ear. Her body shivered.

"If you can catch me again, I will answer them." Genevieve responded with a slight quiver to her voice. Kieron smiled to himself as he jumped them back. That was definitely a yes.

Genevieve sprinted away almost as soon as they appeared at the starting line. Kieron caught her in only four seconds this time—he could not let her get too comfortable thinking she was running fast enough. He did not let her go as he looked down into her eyes, "Say 'Yes, daddy.'"

She shoved out of his arms, "Hard pass."

Kieron burst out laughing, "You can not blame me for trying."

"Hard pass." Genevieve repeated and rolled her eyes, but she reached out her hand so he could jump them back to the starting line.

Kieron watched Genevieve look over him like she was about to say something. When she didn't, Kieron finally said, "Whenever you are ready, baby."

Genevieve sighed and turned back to the trail. She rolled her shoulders, then she sprinted away. She was actually doing it this time. Her magic was carrying her.

It took Kieron twenty seconds to catch her and when he did, she dodged him twice before he tackled her into the red dirt. She laughed as she pushed herself back against a large rock and leaned back to rest with her knees up in front of her, "I thought I had it that time."

"You were doing it. I am just faster." Kieron said.

Her chest rose and fell as she caught her breath. Kieron crawled across the dirt, moving in front of her. "Open your legs." He said as he stared into her eyes. He wanted to watch her reaction—a little bit of shock. *Perfect.* "Open your legs for me." He repeated, his voice low.

Kieron watched Genevieve swallow as he lifted his hand and used one finger to push on the inside of her knee. She gave in and her legs slowly opened. He leaned down and sunk his teeth gently into the skin on her knee. "Now touch yourself."

"That is two requests." She said back quietly, not breaking eye contact.

He stroked his fingers up her leg as he rested his chin on her knee and stared into her eyes. "Be a good girl for me and touch yourself." *Yes. She loved this.* Kieron could feel it. He could feel the involuntary wave of arousal as it pulsed through her body.

Genevieve snapped her knees closed and rolled away from him. "If you catch me again, I will." She said with a smirk as she reached out her hand to help him stand up.

Kieron grasped her hand and she helped haul him to his feet. He let his thumb caress the back of her hand before he jumped them back to the starting line. "Ready, set, go." He whispered, then he let go of her hand.

Genevieve

The ground ripped past beneath my feet as I sprinted through the desert. I was running faster than I had ever run. It was not even hard. When Kieron had said 'Go' something in me just flipped and my magic took me. I finally saw the white flag—I had been wondering if there even was a white flag out here—and dared a glance over my shoulder. The world was ripping past and was in slow motion at the same time. I could see Kieron, but he was not going to catch me. I let out a laugh as I crossed the flag and skidded to a stop.

Kieron stopped in front of me a moment later, "That's my girl." He said with a huge smile on his face.

CHAPTER 20

Genevieve

I continued to train with Kieron every morning while we waited for word from Orion and Zealand that it was time to travel to the Eastern Desert. Some days it was more combat and fighting skills and some days the focus was more on teaching me how to use my magic. Kieron had me constantly trying new things with my magic and I had to admit it was getting quite fun. I could now summon nearly anything I wanted. My shielding still needed work, but I could at least shield on command—sometimes it was just bigger than I expected.

Even Kieron marveled at my shield. It shimmered with an eerie glow. It was not the kind of light that brightened its surroundings, nor did it cast shadows. Instead, as it radiated from every pore in my body, it seemed to absorb the very essence of illumination, wrapping the air around it in a strange, velvety darkness. When

I gazed upon it, there was a sensation of being drawn into a void —yet there was warmth to it and a faint, comforting hum. The light itself seemed to drink in the world. Kieron tested it again and again with weapons and magic and everything he could think of— nothing broke it. Now I just had to practice controlling it.

The one thing I had made absolutely no progress on was jumping, but Kieron assured me we would keep practicing until I got it—that I would eventually get it. I tried to believe him.

My favorite new magic skill, however, was the ability to move objects. To throw a knife into a target then have it zoom back into my hand like it was in reverse was significantly more satisfying than summoning objects. I practiced this skill often by slowly and ever so slightly moving things Kieron was using. Was he dipping chips to eat while reading? The dip moved between each chip and he dipped into thin air before looking up to aim his chip again. Were we using the weights during morning training? I swapped which weight was where while he did his reps and he would inevitably pick up one too heavy or too light for his next workout and have to search for the right one.

Today we were eating lunch in the great room like usual. Kieron seemed to be lost in thought as he ate. It was not odd for us to eat in silence and my thoughts were fully focused on moving Kieron's drinking glass so that he had to constantly recheck where it was before he could drink.

I pretended to sip my water as I slowly and subtly let my magic reach out and slide his glass two inches to the left. Kieron reached out to grasp it and completely missed. I had to bite down on the rim of my own glass to keep from laughing. He looked up at his glass confused before grabbing it and lifting it to his lips. He set it down again and dug back into his food. A few moments later I started to move the glass again.

Then I saw Kieron's eyes dart up to his glass while it was still in motion. I stopped moving it and pretended I was not paying any attention to him. My heart pounded in my chest as I slowly raised my eyes to meet Kieron's fiery gaze. I felt my lip twitch as I willed myself not to smile or laugh. I watched as Kieron slightly tilted his head to the side, not breaking eye contact with me. Then in one swift movement he ripped me out of my chair and threw me over his shoulder. He tickled me mercilessly and I squealed and giggled uncontrollably.

"No! No! No!" I yelled and struggled in his arms as Kieron strode out towards the pool. He tossed me into the pool and I gasped as I stood up in the cool water. I was splashed by a wave of water as he jumped in after me.

Kieron emerged from the water laughing. "How long have you been messing with me?" He asked as his hands grabbed me to tickle me more.

I squirmed out of his grasp and splashed water at him. "Days and days!" I laughed. I could not stop laughing.

"What else did you do to me?" He chuckled as he grabbed me again and pulled me close to his body, guiding my legs to wrap around his waist before he sunk us up to our necks in the water. One hand held my body against his and the other caressed my cheek.

I let my head lean into his touch and I did not stop my own hand as it reached up to brush Kieron's hair back from his face, "Oh I

mostly moved things you were eating ... I also moved the weights."
I admitted as his eyes lit with amusement.

"I thought I was going completely mad!" His body shook with
laughter as he spoke, "That is very impressive, baby. You are getting
quite good at using your magic."

"Thank you." I whispered. My eyes were locked in his and my
cheeks hurt from laughing. I was also acutely aware of how much I
liked my body being wrapped around his.

The next morning was like all the others. Kieron and I ate
breakfast and then made our way to the training ring. Most days,
after we worked on my training together we would eat lunch and
then have the afternoon to ourselves. I typically found more ways
to push my body to build my strength and stamina. Just because I
could use magic to assist me while I was fighting did not mean I did
not want to be at the top of my game. If there was an altercation
I would probably be fighting someone who had hundreds of years
worth of training. Today Kieron said he would be teaching me to
put it all together—to fight in close combat while also using my
magic—but first he was putting me through a grueling workout.

"G. Baby. Sweetheart. What's with the nicknames?" I gritted out
as I completed my exercise reps. My quads were burning.

"I got the impression you liked it."

"What gave you that impression?" I countered. I was not sure
when I had noticed the pet names, but they almost felt normal.

Familiar.

Kieron paused in the middle of his set, "You melt for me when I use them. Your shields come down and your body opens up for me." *Did it really?* My cheeks heated as I blushed. "I will stop if you want me to." He offered as he tilted his head and bit his lip.

Did I want him to stop? Oh that look he was giving me ... "No. Don't stop." I breathed.

"Okay, baby." Kieron gave me a sly smile, "Two more reps. Let's go." He was right—my body ached for him when he called me baby. I had to blink and blow out an intentional breath before I could finish my reps.

"Good work. Now it's time to practice your ground game before we add in magic." He said and stood, removing his shirt and taking position in the ring. *Of course he had to remove his shirt.* By ground game he meant wrestling. If an enemy got me on the ground, what we were practicing was supposed to get me out of it.

Kieron pinned me again. His skin was damp with sweat as his body pressed against mine. He was holding me in a position I definitely was not getting out of. He smelled faintly of something like citrus and eucalyptus—whatever it was had me wanting to press my lips against his skin. To run my tongue—

"Are you even trying?" He asked, his voice frustrated. I was trying, but I was also distracted. He was asking me to roll around on the ground with his half naked, muscular body—of course I was distracted.

He let go of my arms and I reached my fingers out to gently touch the bullet scar that rested on his skin above his heart. The scar that marked where I had shot him. "Did it hurt?" I asked quietly.

Kieron sighed and sat back into the dirt, pulling me with him so we were seated facing each other with my legs bent over his. It was an intimate position. "Yes. Every wound hurts just the same as if I were mortal. Usually the wound hurts, but the dying part does not."

"How did you become immortal like this?" I questioned. He had never explained it. The others had theories, but no one seemed to know for certain.

"Voss received a gift when he was in the twenty-seventh world. He wanted to be immortal and so it was gifted to him. He also asked that if anyone were to swear a blood oath to him, they would also become immortal as well. So he was able to build an army of assassins and warriors who were immortal and who also could not kill him because of the blood oath." Kieron explained.

"You took a blood oath to Vossarian?"

"I did. I was young and it was expected of me. So I was gifted immortality and I was chained to him. I would have killed him centuries ago had I been able to, but the magic behind a blood oath removes that option. He, however, could have killed me whenever he wished."

"What happens when you die? I don't mean if your head is cut off, but if you are killed in a way you will come back from." I whispered. My finger gently touched the scar I had given him again. I had killed him with that wound.

"Nothing. There is just nothing until I wake back up. It is like waking suddenly from a deep sleep." He explained.

"How many times have you died?"

"Quite a few. I stopped keeping count ages ago." I just looked him in the eyes, then scanned over his body again, my finger tracing the lines of other scars, "I can heal without scarring, these are just the scars I have chosen to keep."

My hand stopped moving. "Why would you keep them?"

"Reminders."

I touched the two bullet scars I had inflicted—the one over his heart and the other on his shoulder. "And why did you want to remember these?"

"Because it was the only piece of you I had and knowing you were out there gave me enough hope to continue fighting." Kieron said as he tilted his head to the side. He was trying to read my reaction. I had shot and killed him and the scars somehow did not remind him of the violence we had inflicted on each other. He had *chosen* to keep them to remember *me*. His match. To give himself the hope he needed to keep going. I could only swallow. His eyes scanned my face. "Alright, let's get back to it. You are not done training for the day."

CHAPTER 21

Genevieve

We were getting ready for bed when I realized my cycle had started. It was the first real cycle I had had since coming here. I summoned the underthings Sarla had given me to the toilet room. Then I summoned a pair of my luxurious pajamas that I never wore.

Kieron watched me from the bed as I exited the bathroom and climbed under the sheets. "Are you going to start wearing pajamas now?" He asked. I detected a hint of disappointment in his voice.

"Pajamas? These are luxury sleepwear." I teased back as I lay down.

"Well excuse me." Kieron chuckled, "So are you wearing luxury sleepwear to bed now?"

"My cycle started. I did not want to bleed all over the sheets." I said simply and snuggled into the bed. Kieron sat up slowly as he stared at me. "Don't tell me you banish females to mud huts or some shit when they are on their cycles."

"Why in the world would we do that?" Kieron asked, sounding confused.

"You would be surprised what some cultures do." I responded.

"Well we don't do that. Do you have everything you need? Supplies?"

"Yes, Sarla got me some things when … when I lost the baby." I said softly.

Kieron scanned over my body before speaking again, "I will have Zed pick up some more supplies for you and tomorrow you should sleep in. We won't do our regular training."

I raised my eyebrows at him and my cheeks heated. Males had the tendency to ignore female cycles in my world. It was just something that was not talked about. "Zed does not need to get me anything and I am bleeding, not sick."

"I am aware. This is also your first cycle here isn't it?" I nodded and he continued, "Well stop being embarrassed. Zed and I have both been alive for centuries and cycles are not something to be embarrassed about. We might have some backwards laws about females here in the Deserts, but a female on her cycle is something celebrated. It is a beautiful thing. Many believe sex with a female on her cycle gives a blessing for future fertility—"

"Don't you dare get any ideas about that." I cut him off. "Maybe I do need to find a mud hut to go sleep in."

Kieron just laughed, "No ideas here, sweetheart. But tomorrow we will do something different. You have earned a few days of rest anyway." Then he settled back under the sheet. His hand reached out to settle on my leg.

The next morning I woke to Kieron sitting on the edge of the bed with a mug of tea in his hands. "Well now this is getting weird." I said in greeting as I pushed myself up to a seated position.

He handed me the mug with a chuckle, "Get used to it. You are going to have a relaxing morning and then we are going for a walk before lunch."

"Okay." I said and took a sip of the tea.

Kieron stood and backed towards the door. "No working out this morning. I mean it." I rolled my eyes at him as he shut the door.

When I got out of bed I found a wicker basket on the bathroom counter filled with a variety of female supplies. I might have felt a little awkward about it, but I could get used to being taken care of like this. It was thoughtful and a welcomed change.

Kieron

Kieron filled his pack with lunch for himself and Genevieve. He was planning to take her for an easy hike today—they needed to rest from all of the training they had been doing and Genevieve getting her cycle was a good excuse to take a few days off.

MAGGIE FORBUSH

Kieron looked up as Genevieve entered the great room. He could only think about how much he loved having her here—in his home. In his life. She had not given him an answer to whether or not she wanted to be with him—or if she was even willing to try to be with him—but he would settle for any minute she was willing to spend with him. "So where are we going for this walk?" She asked as she eyed his pack.

"It's better if it is a surprise." He said and slung the pack over his shoulders. "Are you ready?"

She nodded and he led them outside past the training ring and to the trail that would take them into the desert and up to the top of the plateau that was on Kieron's land. From there they would have a spectacular view of his property and the nearby town. He was not sure if he was nervous or excited to share this with Genevieve. Zed, Orion, and Zealand were the only other people he had shown this property to. Now he was sharing it with Genevieve.

Genevieve followed Kieron as they strolled along the trail. He smiled to himself as he watched her crouch down to examine different plants or rocks. She soon had a handful of rocks she was inspecting as they walked along. "What month and day is it?" She asked as she tossed a couple of the small rocks back onto the trail.

"It is the thirteenth of August." Kieron responded. They were starting the ascent up the plateau. The trail was winding and not very steep—it made for a pleasant walk even with the heat of the sun.

"Hmm." Genevieve responded and she bent down to pick up another rock.

"What is with the rocks, G?"

"Do you know what this one is?" She held out a soft white shard with long, prismatic crystals. Kieron shook his head. He had no idea what the stone was. "I was hoping you did. It's very pretty."

He laughed to himself and turned to continue hiking. Eventually, they found themselves on the top of the plateau and Kieron led Genevieve to his favorite overlook. There was a tall tree that provided good shade and from there they would be able to see every corner of his property. He dropped his pack and pulled out a blanket for them to sit on. "I hope a picnic lunch is sounding good to you." Kieron said as he took a seat on the blanket and patted the spot next to him. She sat and tossed aside a few more stones. She still had the soft white crystal in her hand.

"A picnic sounds great." She said as she looked out at the view. "This is gorgeous up here … is that a town I am seeing?"

"Yes, that is Sandara. It is a few days north of Aridale and a very beautiful place." Kieron responded as he pulled out the food and drink he had packed.

"Around your home … there is nothing else for miles."

"That is because all of this is my land." Kieron said simply. He looked out at it. He loved every inch of it. The quiet. The space. "I needed my own freedom, so I tried to buy it using the blood money I was paid with. Zed, Orion, Zealand, and now you are the only other beings who know where my private residence is."

Genevieve was quiet for heartbeats as she scanned the land below them. Then she finally spoke, "I think I would have done the same thing. This property is magnificent. You should not feel bad about wanting your own freedom."

He did feel bad. He had done horrible things throughout his life to earn the money he used to buy this land with and some days he felt so selfish for wanting something that was his own.

Genevieve looked down at the crystal in her hand, "Do you mind if I keep this?"

Kieron snorted, "It's a rock, be my guest."

"Thanks. Do people give presents for birthdays here?"

Kieron stopped what he was doing and looked at her. She was turning the crystal over between her fingers and gently scraping away dirt with her nail. "No. Typically people do not give gifts for birthdays, but they do throw parties."

"Hmm." She said, her mind clearly deep in thought. Then she reached over Kieron to grab herself one of the sandwiches he had pulled out from his pack.

She had asked him what day it was and then asked him about birthdays ... "Is it your birthday?" Kieron blurted out.

"Apparently it was two days ago." She said and bit into her food. Then she saluted the sky with her sandwich, "Here's to thirty-four."

"Genevieve! We should celebrate. I can't believe you did not tell me—" Kieron was kicking himself. He would have done something for her. *How had he not asked her when her damn birthday was?*

"It's okay. I have not done anything for my birthday in a few years now. I haven't even known exactly what day it was for a while now anyway. Last year I just guessed when my birthday had passed based on the seasons." Then she tossed the rock in her hand, "Plus I just got myself a present."

"Do you give gifts for birthdays in your world?" Kieron asked.

"Presents and cake. Sometimes a party, but always presents and cake."

"Well I guess I owe you presents and cake ... and a party. You have to celebrate in true Desert fashion."

She patted his thigh, "How about next year. Today ... this hike ... this view ... It's a gift in itself. And this sandwich sure tastes like a cake to me." Kieron just watched her. Watched the little wisps of hair that had fallen from her ponytail and now blew gently in the breeze. Watched her chew and swallow her food as she looked out at the view. Watched her roll her shoulders and straighten her back. He was lost in noticing the little things about her when she spoke again, "So where exactly does your property end."

He leaned over and extended his arm to point out the landmarks that marked the edges of his property. She scooted closer to him and leaned into his shoulder to better see where he was pointing. Kieron rested his cheek against her hair, getting lost in her scent for a moment before continuing.

CHAPTER 22

Kieron - Months Ago.

Kieron jolted awake to screaming, but his rooms were silent. His heart was pounding and his breathing heavy as his eyes adjusted to the dim light in his bedroom. There it was again—pain and fear and screaming. It was not in his rooms and it was not in the palace. It was inside of him—it was pulling on him. *Genevieve.* It was Genevieve and something was wrong. Very wrong. Without thinking he tore out of bed and threw on his clothes. A moment later he was folding into the air and following the tug that pulled on him.

The air was cold and the forest silent. Kieron had nearly stepped out of the forest's edge and onto the exposed lawns around Ryett's chateau in Montvera as he blindly rushed towards where the pain and fear were pulling from. His hand braced against a tree as he tried to calm his breathing and gather himself.

He scanned the chateau and saw warm light flickering from one of the rooms—it was not a light from a lamp—it was light from magic. The fear he was feeling was leaking from that room —from Genevieve in that room. Slowly the fear dissipated and was replaced with a hollow and empty sadness.

She had lost the baby. It was the only explanation. If there was another threat there would be more commotion at the chateau. The others would not just be standing around outside. Kieron watched Alias, Jax, and Zain pace the patio, their shadows flickering against the chateau's stone walls from the light of the fire that lit the fire pit. Eventually, Ryett joined them. They all turned to him and his head dropped as he shook it. Alias pulled Ryett into an embrace as Jax walked a few paces away, turning away from the building and running his hands down his face. Zain just sunk into a chair. They all looked devastated.

But she was still alive. He could still feel Genevieve's grief. Her pain. *She was still alive.* Kieron fell to his knees as sobs shook his body. The seer had been right. His daughter had not survived long enough to come into this world. He had hoped and prayed to any god that might listen for it not to come true. For him to wake up from this nightmare he was living. To erase the guilt he had for doing this to Genevieve. For her to not have to go through a loss like this. But once again, his prayers were not answered.

Slowly Genevieve's pain faded and Kieron could only feel her sadness and grief remaining. He wrapped her feelings in his own sadness and he held on like he was holding on to her. Like he could wrap her in his arms and tell her how sorry he was. Like he could hold her and tell her it would be okay. He leaned against a tree as he continued to cry.

A warm weight pressed next to Kieron's hip and thigh. He stopped breathing—his heart pounded as he slowly turned his head. A huge black wolf sat next to him. Golden eyes met his and then the wolf laid down, resting its head on Kieron's leg. Normally Kieron would have been terrified to be anywhere near a Great Wolf, but right now he did not care if the wolf killed him. Maybe it would kill him. He deserved it. But if the wolf was going to kill him it would have done it already, not laid down next to him. And certainly not rested its head on his leg. Kieron did not try to stop the tears that fell from his eyes. He let his head fall back to rest against the tree again.

The light faded from the room in the chateau and a dim light from a lamp lit the next window. Eventually, that light faded too. Then he watched Ryett return inside. Sarla emerged onto the patio and everyone made their way back to their cottages.

The wolf slowly got to its feet. Kieron did not move as he turned his eyes to the wolf. It only looked back at him with sadness in its golden eyes. Then it took a few steps onto the chateau's lawns before disappearing into the air. Kieron stayed where he was at the edge of the forest and held on to the feelings he felt leaking from that room in the chateau. He sent a gentle pulse of his magic into the room. It was all he could risk. No one could ever know he had been here.

Kieron continued to stay in the cold night air, leaning against the tree, until the sun started to rise. Then he wiped the tears from his eyes and folded into the world around him, returning to his rooms in the palace in the capital city of the Deserts.

CHAPTER 23

Genevieve - Present Day.

I had convinced Zed to let me cook all of us dinner. It took some sweet talking, but after I had shown great interest in and gushed over his garden and storerooms he finally gave in. His garden was beyond amazing and it was not hard to find nice things to say as I wandered through it after him and he pointed to all of the different vegetables, fruits, and herbs he grew. He even helped me select lettuce and tomatoes and a few herbs to go with dinner. Then he pulled out the other ingredients and meat I had requested and I sent him on his way with a glass and bottle of wine.

I settled myself into the kitchen and began prepping food for dinner. The last week and a half here had been wonderful. I realized I was actually enjoying myself. I was enjoying learning. I was enjoying the quiet. I was enjoying the desert climate. Kieron continued to surprise me with who he was. I actually felt ... *good*.

I had not felt good like this in a long long time. I opened a second bottle of wine and poured myself a glass.

Kieron found me singing to myself and dancing while I was chopping yams into thin slices. I chucked another handful of sliced yams into a bowl and grabbed the bottle of wine, pouring Kieron a glass while I continued singing. He narrowed his eyes at me as I handed the glass to him and twirled back to the counter where the cutting board was waiting for me.

"You know I pay Zed a lot of money to do this for us." Kieron said over my singing.

I raised the volume of my voice, pretending to ignore him before I burst out laughing. "I know. I convinced him to take the night off. You have a beautiful garden by the way."

"Did you have to bribe him?" Kieron asked, with an amused chuckle.

I continued slicing the last yam, "Only with compliments."

"So what are you making?"

I drizzled oil over the yams and sprinkled in salt before tossing them with a large wooden spoon, "Burgers and fries."

Kieron scrunched his brow, "What is that?"

I laughed, "You people here in Savengard are severely deprived when it comes to food. You will like it, I promise." I dumped the yams onto a metal sheet pan and spread them around before sliding the tray into the oven. I still could not quite figure out how the oven actually worked. Zed had set it up for me and it clearly was not electric, but whether it was wood or gas fueled I still did not know. "You also are lacking in technology, but I guess the magic makes up for it."

"Technology?" Kieron asked as he slid into one of the stools at the counter.

"Electricity, communication channels, screens to watch things on, vehicles ... There has to be other worlds besides mine with these things." I cracked two eggs into a bowl with the ground meat Zed had fetched from the cold room.

"Yes, some of those things sound familiar. The worlds are all different. It is interesting to see what developed the same in some worlds and what developed differently." Kieron said and he took a sip from his wine.

I added spices and herbs to the bowl and plunged my hands in to mix and make the burger patties. I smiled to myself as Kieron just eyed what I was doing with a hesitating look.

"I know you have music here, but do you have music *here* or do I need to keep singing?" I teased as I placed the first formed patty on another metal tray.

"I will put on some music." Kieron smirked and a moment later music started playing. I guess by *putting on some music* he meant he would use his magic to turn it on. I continued making the patties and swayed my body to the music—at least he had good taste.

Soon I was washing my hands and grabbing a towel to pull the tray of buns from the second oven. They had turned a perfect golden color. "Well those smell good." Kieron said as he eyed the buns.

"Hopefully they taste good too!" I said as I hopped up and sat on the counter next to where Kieron was sitting on the stool.

"Why did you want to cook us dinner?" Kieron asked.

I leaned over and pulled my wine glass over from where I

had abandoned it. "To me, the kitchen is the heart of the home. It is where everyone comes together to talk and enjoy food and enjoy good company. I have so many good memories cooking and drinking in kitchens with the people I love. It is also calming and a small way I can say thank you to you and Zed ..." My voice trailed off and I took a sip of wine just to fill the silence.

"All of that sounds really nice." Kieron said as he studied me, "Does that mean I am the good company tonight?"

I laughed, "Only if you dance with me before we put the burgers on the grill." I hopped off the counter and stuck out my hand for Kieron, singing along with the catchy chorus of the song that was playing as I moved my body. Kieron stood just as Zed wandered in from the patio. I saw him pause and turn on his heels, "You too, Zed! Come dance!" Zed raised his hands in surrender and joined us in the kitchen.

Kieron

Nothing else mattered to Kieron at this moment. Not that he was a king. Not that they were about to go raise an army of the Undead. Not that he would have to fight another deadly assassin along with thousands of his own warriors in order to gain control of his kingdom. He did not care that he still kept receiving letters from both Ryett and Beck begging him to send Genevieve back. No, in this moment the only thing to him that mattered was the smile on Genevieve's face as she danced with him and Zed in his kitchen.

She was barefoot with the cuffs of her tight pants rolled up and wearing one of her many slouchy shirts that hung off of one shoulder. Her hair was messily tied up and she sang to the music as her body moved to the beat. It was the happiest Kieron had ever felt. *This* was the life he had dreamt of for himself.

The song changed and Genevieve laughed as she stopped dancing. "Okay boys, grab the wine, it is time to go grill the burgers."

They followed her out to the grill and Kieron watched Zed show her how to get the grill fired up as he topped off everyone's wine. With a wave of his hand he had a small table by the firepit set with seats and place settings for the three of them. "Kieron, I do not need to invade your dinner." Zed said in protest when he turned around from the grill and saw the table.

"Nonsense, Zed. You are family, join us." Kieron said with a smile. Zed had been with him for centuries. At times Zed was the only one Kieron could confide in.

Meat sizzled on the grill and Genevieve scooped up her wine from Kieron's hand, "How did you end up here working for Kieron, Zed?" She asked before taking a sip.

"I was one of the first slaves Kieron liberated from the crown." Zed said simply as he settled down into one of the chairs. "He has tried to send me on my way to go get my own life multiple times, but I quite like it here. So, sorry Kieron, you are stuck paying me a ridiculous salary to take care of this place for you." He raised his glass in a salute.

Kieron returned the gesture. "I am fortunate that you actually put up with me, Zed." Kieron had smuggled out hundreds of slaves to freedom and Zed was one of the firsts. Then the slave trade had gotten much larger and he had been promoted to a position that had too much scrutiny for him to actually get away with sneaking people out. That was when he switched tactics and started infiltrating the network with sleeper spies so that one day they could completely collapse it.

Kieron looked at Genevieve as she flipped the meat on the grill. He could not read her emotions right now, but the look she gave him was one of respect. "Do you have a partner, Zed? Or a lover?" She asked and turned her attention back to Zed.

"Still working on finding the right one." Zed replied. "I am not sure if I am the crazy one or the people I meet are the crazy ones."

Genevieve laughed, "When you find the right person they will be your specific brand of crazy, Zed. Don't give up."

"I think I am just done trying to change myself just to find someone to be with." He said.

Genevieve removed the meat from the grill, placing each patty neatly on the platter. "Good. You should not have to change yourself at all." She paused. "Alright, let's go build our burgers."

Kieron and Zed did as Genevieve instructed them to do—heaping their plate with fries and dressing their burgers with the toppings she had selected. Then they all found themselves back out on the patio to eat. Whatever this was Genevieve had made, Kieron could eat it everyday. He looked at Zed, "I am going to need you to figure out this dinner so you can make it for us, Zed."

Zed laughed, "Way ahead of you, brother. This is fantastic, Genevieve!"

When all of them had finished eating they made their way over to the couches by the pool and continued drinking and chatting. Zed shared his life story with them and Genevieve asked questions —both about his life and about how it was to work for Kieron.

Zed eventually laid down on one of the couches and shortly after, started snoring. Genevieve had moved from the couches and laid down with her back on the stone patio looking up at the stars. "Come look at these stars with me, Kieron." She said quietly.

He eased himself down next to her and followed the line of her finger as she pointed up towards the stars. "Those three stars there were called The Hunter's Belt in my world. The western most star represented the warriors who once ruled the part of my world where I lived." She explained. "I think it is the only constellation I can reliably pick out and name."

Just then hundreds of comets shot through the sky. "Do you make wishes when you see shooting stars?" Kieron asked. His wish was for at least one more night just like tonight.

"I never have." Genevieve breathed.

"What would you wish for?"

She was silent for heartbeats. "I am not sure, Kieron, but I think I really like it here."

He had wanted Genevieve since the moment he had laid eyes on her, but this—this was so much more than that. He could not get enough of her. What had started as a pure physical and primal reaction of wanting to claim his match had completely turned into what he could only describe as—*love*. He loved her exactly as she was. He loved who she was and who he was around her—

A snort from Zed shook Kieron from his thoughts. Genevieve

laughed softly, "Do we need to move him?"

"No, I will get him a blanket though. Doesn't hurt to sleep under the stars now and then." Kieron responded as he raised himself from the patio. He summoned a blanket and gently draped it over Zed. "Come on, we should head in too." He said and offered a hand to Genevieve.

They headed into the kitchen. Kieron wrapped his hands around Genevieve's waist and lifted her onto the counter. "You sit right here and keep me company while I clean up." He said and turned to the plates from dinner that still sat next to the sink.

"I did not cook you dinner so that you would have to clean up, Kieron. Let me do it." Genevieve protested, but Kieron's hand shot up to stop her.

"Don't even think about it."

◆ ◆ ◆

Genevieve

I sat on the counter and watched as Kieron quickly cleaned the remaining dishes from dinner. I was not sure if it was the wine or just how the night had gone, but I was tingling with desire. My body was warm and aching for him to touch me again. When Kieron finished he dried his hands on a towel and tossed it on the counter next to him as he leaned back against the edge and faced me. "Thank you for tonight." He said, his eyes raked over me and my breath caught.

"You are welcome. I am glad you enjoyed it." I responded softly. "You were great company if you were wondering."

"Was I?" Kieron asked with a teasing smile.

"Most definitely. I think I could get used to more nights like this." I ventured. It was bold, but I believed it. I loved it here. There was just something about the red desert that surrounded Kieron's home that seemed to heal my soul. I loved every detail of his home too. The quiet. The coziness. And most of all, I was *really* enjoying the company. The more I learned about Kieron the more I wanted to be around him. He was kind and compassionate and charming and confident and fun and damn was he sexy. His teasing and taunting was starting to get the better of me—especially with me sleeping naked next to him every night. I wanted nothing to change and everything to change at the same time.

"I think I could get used to more nights like this as well." He said as he gently pushed my knees apart and stepped between my legs. His hand raised and wrapped firmly around my neck. His thumb forced my head to the side and he ran his lips up my neck before turning my head back to him and kissing my lips. He pulled back from me and gazed at me as my breath caught. I loved being kissed by him. His eyes scanned over me—like he was deciding where he would plant his lips next. Then his mouth dropped to my exposed neck.

The way he handled me made me ache for him more. His touch was firm and he was clearly the one in charge. I could not help but submit to him. Let him do whatever he wanted to me.

"I want you so badly." He whispered against my neck and I felt his teeth bite gently into my skin, sending a chill through my body.

"Do that again." I breathed. He chuckled and obliged. My body melted for him. I wanted *him* so badly—"Why don't you just command me to have sex with you?" I found my mouth asking.

He paused and his hand around my neck loosened. "Genevieve —"

I cut him off, "We both know I couldn't stop you." *What was I doing? Why was I saying this? I did not want to stop him. I wanted him to take me right here on the counter.*

I felt his warm breath on my neck and shoulder before he pulled his lips back from me and looked me in the eye. "You are right, I could. I could command you to or I could just take you right now and there is nothing you could do to stop me." I was trembling as he spoke, "But I won't. It does not matter how much I want you, or how hard it is for me to hold back and contain myself, I will never force you to do that again. I will taunt you and tease you and push you to your edge, but I will never force you. I want you wanting me so badly it hurts. I want every piece of you aching for me. Only then will I take you again. And when that happens, you better be damn sure you want me too because I will never let you go."

He ran his thumb across my lower lip before he completely stepped away from me. Then he turned and walked towards his bedroom, leaving me breathless and sitting on the counter. If this did not count as every piece of me aching for him then I did not know what did.

CHAPTER 24

Genevieve - A Few Years Ago.

Harlowe's tiny fingers wrapped around my forefinger as we walked down the dirt road. Our dog, Rex, was running back and forth—sniffing and pissing on nearly everything. I reached out my free arm to wrap it around Eli's waist and pulled him in close. He planted a kiss in my hair and his arm draped over my shoulders.

"I don't think it gets better than this." I said. The sun was setting and the forest was filled with the gentle whooshing of the breeze in the leaves and the chirps of the birds.

"I don't think it does." Eli responded. We had sacrificed so much to build our family and to escape to this quiet corner of the forest. Harlowe, our son, was now nearly three and I had loved every minute of being out here and away from the chaos and stress that came with living in town. Our town and territory was filled with good people—and ruled by bad ones. How we thought bringing a child into this dying world was a good idea I wasn't sure, but Harlowe's smile and laughter made everything feel okay. It gave me hope.

Harlowe bent down to pick up another rock and offered it to me. I had to extract my arm from around Eli's waist to accept it. "Oh this one is cool, buddy." I said as I crouched down to examine it with him.

"Babe," Eli said, his voice distant, like he was deep in thought. "If something ever happens to me, I want you to find someone new."

"Don't even say that. Nothing is going to happen to you until we are both very very old." I responded absently as I picked up another small rock and handed it to Harlowe to inspect.

Eli stopped and waited for me to look at him. "I hope that is the case. But I am just saying, if something does happen, you deserve to be happy. Don't you dare settle, but find someone who makes you happy. That is what I would want for you."

I swallowed and Harlowe tugged on my finger, pulling my gaze away from Eli again. I blinked away the tears that were starting to gather in my eyes. "The same goes for you, Eli, but we are dying together when we are old and wrinkled. Okay?"

"Okay." He breathed. Then he whistled for Rex and we continued our evening walk down the road.

CHAPTER 25

Kieron - Present Day.

It had been a long day and Genevieve had been unusually quiet and compliant during their morning together. Kieron had not seen her since lunch and Zed had informed him that she had taken dinner early and alone. It was not like her. She had never taken dinner alone. He was starting to worry. Maybe something was wrong. Maybe he had moved too fast. Kieron found Genevieve lounging on one of the couches next to the pool. A fire was lit in the fire pit. Kieron paused and admired the way she sat, with her legs tucked up and a book in her lap. Her slouchy shirt exposed her skin along her neck and collar bone. His mind wandered to running his mouth along that skin again—to the way she tasted.

Kieron finally summoned the courage to step onto the patio and invite himself to join her. "How is your book?" He asked. He did not know if she wanted to be left alone, but he just could not do that.

Genevieve slowly lowered her book and lifted her eyes, "Absolutely filthy."

Kieron chuckled and sat on the couch with her, "Is that a good thing?"

"Most definitely." She responded with a small smile.

"Good ... Is everything okay?" He asked carefully.

She chewed her lip for a moment, "Yes, I just needed some me time."

"Should I let you have some space?" She shook her head no. "It is a beautiful night isn't it?" He tore his eyes away from her and scanned the stars in the night sky, trying to calm his pounding heart. He had been able to keep his composure with her so far—had been able to hold some sort of boundary with her—but things just felt different after the last few days.

"Very and I have a thing for sitting by fires." Genevieve responded as she closed her book and tossed it on the end table next to her.

Kieron summoned a bottle of wine and two glasses, "Want some?" He offered.

"Always."

"Before you got here, I could not tell you the last time I just sat outside and enjoyed the night. It has been a good change." Kieron conceded as he poured a glass and handed it to Genevieve. He poured himself a glass as well, "Are you sure I am not interrupting your reading?"

"Interrupt away." Genevieve clinked her glass against Kieron's then took a sip and adjusted the way she was sitting so that she was facing him.

Kieron's eyes ran along her exposed shoulder. "It is nice to have good company too." He said softly.

She gave him a coy smile. "So, King Kieron, what did you want to be when you grew up?"

Kieron chuckled, "I never thought about what I wanted to be, but I did hope for a different life than the one I had."

"Tell me more."

"I built this home because it was my dream to have a lot of space and a quiet place to escape to. I hoped I would find someone worth sharing it with ... maybe have a few kids. And I just wanted to live a simple life and explore the Deserts and other kingdoms and worlds." He took a sip of his wine and averted his eyes. He had never said these hopes out loud. The way he was brought up did not leave room for hopes and dreams, but he had at least amassed enough wealth to build his dream home.

"Sounds a lot like what I hoped for. I had it for a minute too ..." Genevieve's voice trailed off and she cleared her throat, "I thought I wanted to be a doctor at one point. I think I just liked how impressed everybody was when I told them that was what I was going to do ... Oh well. I never thought I would grow up to be this—whatever this is."

"A traveler of worlds and multi-kingdom emissary?" Kieron offered.

Genevieve laughed, "Is that an official title?"

"Your official title needs to be more grand ... I will think of something." *The Queen of the Deserts* sounded right to him, but he was not ready to suggest it—and she was not ready to hear it.

"I will make a list with some suggestions." Genevieve teased.

"What is the first order of business once you are the official king?"

"I want to end all slavery in the Deserts. That means I will need to put people I trust in positions of power and obliterate the slave trade network." Kieron responded. It had been the plan in motion for centuries, now he would finally be able to see it through. "The only thing I have not figured out is what to do with the nearly one hundred thousand slaves that currently reside in the Deserts. Those that serve in the palace could stay on as paid help, but I imagine many will not even want to stay in the kingdom."

"One hundred thousand?" She breathed, her eyes wide.

Kieron nodded, "And every single one belongs to the crown."

Genevieve just stared at him for a few heartbeats, then a small shiver ran through her body as if she was trying to shake off the shock of what he had just said. "Well Ryett and Aveline already have systems in place to help the slaves build new lives in their kingdoms." Voss had not sent Kieron on a fool's errand after all. Genevieve continued, "Beck was willing to help with Ryett's plan to take down the slave trade, so both of them can help with that and I would imagine he has been putting resources in place to rehome slaves as well."

Kieron just stared at Genevieve in disbelief. Beck had offered assistance and he thought Ryett might be a future ally, but Genevieve just confirmed three kingdoms that could help. He had thought he would be doing it all on his own. He gave Genevieve a small teasing smile, "Well look at you Miss Multi-Kingdom Emissary. Sounds like we will need to have an inter-kingdom meeting."

"Will you let me be a part of it?" Genevieve asked cautiously.

"Of course. Why wouldn't I want you there?" Kieron asked, confused.

"I don't know, but I want to be a part of it. I want to help in any way I can. Staying busy ... it is just nice to be able to make a positive difference." Genevieve said.

"Then you are officially coming."

"Thank you." Genevieve looked down at her wine as if she had forgotten she was holding it. He wanted nothing more than for her to be part of it—all of it—but he realized he had been going about it all wrong. He had been trying to control her and she did not need controlling. She could not be controlled— "What would have happened had I not lost the baby?" Her voice broke as she said the words and her question jerked him from his thoughts.

Kieron's chest tightened. He took a deep breath before responding, "If she had been born, I would have torn every world I had to into pieces in order to keep you both safe."

Genevieve slowly raised her head and looked at Kieron. Tears gathered in the corners of her eyes. "She?"

Genevieve had not known. She would not have known the sex of the baby, "The seer told me our baby was a girl." Kieron said gently as he watched a tear fall down Genevieve's cheek.

"I am so sorry, Kieron." She breathed.

"There is nothing for you to be sorry about. Absolutely nothing. I am sorry I put you in that position and that you had to endure ... all of it." His hand found hers in her lap and he took it in his. She just looked back at him with sorrow and he watched her throat bob as she swallowed.

He lifted his hand. His fingers tracing up her bare shoulder, across her collarbone, and up until his hand tucked gently behind her neck under her hair. "I would really like to kiss you right now." He said, his voice soft.

"I think I would like that." Genevieve breathed back. She bit her lower lip as her eyes scanned Kieron's face. Kieron wanted to bite that lip and a whole lot more … but most of all, he wanted to erase all of her sadness.

Kieron dipped his head, skimming his lips against hers. They had kissed. But not like this. It had always been in the midst of pure physical passion. Caught up in the moment. Her lips parted slightly and he pressed his against hers.

The world around him disappeared and they were among the stars. He was back a moment later, Genevieve's tongue teased his mouth open. His tongue met hers as he tasted her. Then she gently pulled back and looked up into his eyes.

Whatever pieces of himself that were still whole shattered into a billion shards. He had only heard from others about finding their match and the pure physicality of it. The want and desire, the physical and magical connection. All of that was here too, but he never thought he could actually *like* another being so much. He loved just talking with her. Being with her. Every new piece of her that he learned made him want to be around her more.

And he had destroyed all of it. How could he ever come back from what he had done? She could say she forgave him again and again, but he could never forgive himself.

"What's wrong?" Genevieve whispered.

"I am trying to contain myself." He said gently and kissed her forehead. He had just lied to her. It was only one more addition to the very long list of terrible things he had done. Then he pulled back from her and withdrew his hand from behind her neck. He gave her leg a slight squeeze, "How about we get some sleep?"

Genevieve

I did not want to go to sleep and I definitely did not want Kieron to contain himself. I wanted him to kiss me again. To rip my clothes off and take me right here on the couches outside. To claim me as his and never let me go. But I could not bring myself to say it outloud.

"How about we take a late night dip in the pool first?" I suggested and stood, tugging on his hand for him to follow me. But he just let go of my hand and stayed seated. *Fine.* "I am going in, with or without you." I said with a teasing smile. Then I turned my back on him and walked towards the pool. I dropped my pants first, then my shirt, then I bent over as I slid my lacy underthings off—making a show of it. I chucked them over my shoulder and peaked in time to see them land right in Kieron's lap.

He set down his wine, then set my underthings next to the glass and stood. I watched him peel his shirt over his head before I turned and walked into the water. I waded all the way to the far side of the pool. Three quarters of the way there I heard Kieron's small splashes as he entered the water behind me. I waited for him as I looked out at the shadows of the dark cliffs and plateaus against a night sky that was brilliantly dotted with stars.

I pulled my hair over one shoulder and a moment later felt Kieron's hands on my waist. His breath caressed the skin between my shoulder and neck and I felt his teeth take a gentle bite. It sent a shiver of desire through my entire body. He moved around me and slid his back against the edge of the pool, sinking up to his neck in the warm water. Then he pulled me close, guiding my legs to wrap around his waist.

"The water is warmer tonight—" I started to say.

"I took a piss in it." Kieron teased with a smirk. I playfully pinched his arm, "I heated it as soon as I knew you were actually getting in."

"Teach me how to do things like that ... not just fighting, but heating pools, sending letters, everything. Will you teach me?" I asked, my voice a near whisper and my face only inches from his.

"I would love to." He responded and kissed me again.

Our last kiss had made my magic hum and pulse within me. This kiss must have sent me into a completely different universe. I had never asked Ryett why I saw mountain images when my magic reacted to his, but I saw all of that now too—I saw the same jagged mountains, bubbling streams, glaciers, and forest fires. I saw the soil rejuvenating with new growth among the fire's ashes, mountain meadows covered in wildflowers, and light snow catching on evergreen branches. But I also saw the desert sand crack in drought, the sun rise and set against a red rock plateau, bones whiten under the heat of the sun, and a desert storm flash lightning across the sky. Then I was pulled into a storm of stars and comets. Green and purple and blue light swirled around us with the stars.

I sucked in a surprised breath as our lips parted. Kieron's eyes must have been just as wide as mine. "Did you see that too?" He breathed.

"The mountains and deserts and stars?" I asked and his chin dipped in confirmation.

"The mountains must be you and the desert me, but I don't know about the stars—" His voice was soft as he spoke. I cut him off with another kiss, just so we could see it all again.

CHAPTER 26

Genevieve - A Few Years Ago.

I woke up feeling exhausted. I had not slept well again. I had not slept well since a letter from the Commanding Chief Chad Johnston had found its way to me while I was shopping in town. A stranger had handed me the letter. The note had been simple: *It's time to come home.* I knew exactly what it meant and knew Chad would destroy everything that got in the way of what he wanted.

Ever since I received the letter, Eli and I had been making plans to leave—to go deeper into the forest. I was not sure I would sleep better until I knew Chad was dead, but I did not know when or if that would happen. Many people had already attempted to kill him and none had succeeded. That was how he had continually moved up to the position of Commanding Chief—outliving everyone else.

Things had not been easy since Chad took over leadership in our territory. People were starving and unable to make ends meet. More and more of the males who had served in the military and held ranking positions were targeted and killed. It became clear that Eli might one day make that list and be targeted too. Over our years together, I gathered from the snippets of information Eli shared that he had been a commander of a special forces group who had done the darkest of work.

Eli told me they had spent much of their time navigating through abandoned mines. They used the tunnel systems to infiltrate enemy territories and execute morally questionable missions. He also told me there were things far worse than what we face in our territory every day. There were far worse things in this world our rulers did not want us to know about. He told me all of the fighting between territories might be nothing more than a distraction from the real problems our world faced. I did not press him on it. His eyes, which had slowly refilled with life, always seemed to die again when he mentioned anything to do with his time in the service.

Many of the groups who tried to remove Chad from power also sought Eli out to join them, but everyone who tried to take down Chad had been eliminated. Eli told me it was not worth the risk. At one point, things were looking so terrible for the people in our territory we had actually considered helping. I had provided as much information as I could on the way Chad operated, but when I finally became pregnant, Eli convinced me to move deeper into the wilderness to get away from it all. It had been the best decision.

I loved it out here. Eli loved it out here. We would take trips to town to get supplies when we needed them and check in on friends, but we mostly kept to ourselves. We told no one where exactly we lived and because the communication grids had been destroyed in the last war, it was extremely difficult for anyone to find us anyway.

I stretched my arms and pulled back the covers. Harlowe had slept through the night and Eli had hardly stirred either. I must have fallen back asleep in the early morning and slept in. Maybe that was why I felt so awful—oversleeping. I climbed out of bed and could hear giggling from the kitchen. When I poked my head out of the bedroom door I could see our dog, Rex, laying under the table half asleep and Eli dancing around the room with our son Harlowe in his arms. Harlowe was giggling as Eli spun in a circle and dipped him low.

"Good morning, babe!" Eli said when he saw me. He kept dancing as he continued, "We have already eaten, but I convinced Harlowe to save a few pancakes for you." Harlowe squealed as Eli buried his nose in Harlowe's neck and pretended to eat him. "Let's go give mama a kiss." Eli said and he set Harlowe on the floor.

Harlowe ran to me with his arms wide and I scooped him up. This would never get old. It did not matter how tired I felt or how bad of a day I had, seeing all of my boys made everything better. Eli wrapped us both in a hug and gave me a kiss before Harlowe grabbed my cheeks and planted a slobbery kiss of his own on my mouth. This really would never get old.

"I am sorry, I slept terribly last night. I hope I did not keep you up." I said to Eli.

"I know babe, that is why we let you sleep in. And why the three of us are going to run to town for some groceries and let you enjoy a quiet morning." Eli responded as he pulled a coffee mug from the cupboard and poured me a cup of steaming black liquid.

"Are you sure? We normally all go together …" I started as I set Harlowe down and accepted the mug. Harlowe crawled his way under the table and snuggled up to Rex. Rex lifted his head and grumbled at the intrusion before settling back down and resigning to let Harlowe lay against him.

"Of course. You need some mama alone time." I could only give him a smile of thanks as he gathered up his pack and grabbed Harlowe's shoes.

I gave them all kisses before I made myself comfortable in a chair on the front porch and watched Eli load the boys into the truck. "We will be back in about three hours. Enjoy yourself. Don't you dare clean anything! I love you!" Eli called as he hopped into the driver seat and started the truck.

"I love you more!" I yelled and Eli pretended he could not hear me as he put the truck in drive—pointing to his ear and mouthing *What? I can't hear you?* I yelled it to him again and waved. Then I watched them disappear down our dirt driveway as I sipped my coffee.

I had just started to think about those pancakes they had left me when I heard the explosion. I saw black smoke billowing up from the trees in the direction the road was. My entire body went cold and muscle memory had me shooting up from the chair and sprinting into the kitchen. I grabbed my go bag—the bag packed for emergencies only—and hurtled into the bedroom to grab Eli's gun from the safe next to the bed. I pulled out the black hand gun and an extra clip and found my boots by the door. I could only hear the roaring in my ears as I laced my boots with the speed and efficiency years of repetition brought.

Black smoke was filling the sky. The explosion was no more than a mile away. I sprinted from our home into the trees—praying my family was still alive.

I pressed myself against a tree and tried to breathe. Four males circled our burning truck and the bodies of my family lay burned and unmoving on the ground. *They were all dead.* Tears streamed down my face as I gasped for breath and tried to grab hold of any good sense I had left. It took everything in me not to hurtle down the hill and tear the males' heads off with my bare hands, but I knew I was overpowered and out gunned. I could not hear what they were saying, but I took in every detail of their features. One was obviously in charge as he pointed and shouted things to the others. Then I watched them get into their vehicle and speed off up the road towards our house. I stayed hidden, clutching Eli's gun.

I heard the explosions not long after and soon saw the smoke above the trees. Our house was gone too. I heard the vehicle approach and slow as it passed our burning truck. Then they sped off down the road back towards town.

I eventually found my way down the hill and to my family. I now sat on the ground in front of the fire that was turning them all to ashes. My throat and eyes burned. Everything else was numb. My body was empty. When the fire finally died out and the ashes had cooled, I pulled a small box from my pack and emptied the contents into another pocket. My hands shook as I gathered as many ashes as I could into the box. *I love you the most.* I whispered.

The sun had long since set by the time I wandered off into the forest. I could hear the wolves howling, but I only had one thing on my mind—how I was going to kill everyone responsible for the death of my family.

CHAPTER 27

Genevieve - Present Day.

"What does one wear to the Eastern Desert?" I asked Kieron as I flipped through my clothes. He was still laying in bed, the sheet barely covering one leg and his groin. I had to admit that he was extremely sexy with his arms resting behind his head and his body on display. His long hair was still messy from sleep and that beard —I wanted to tangle my fingers in that beard of his. Of course I knew that he knew exactly what he was doing to me—how he was taunting me by laying there naked and barely covered. It was why I had not bothered to put clothes on yet, hopefully I was taunting him just as much.

"We are packing light." He said from the bed, "Hopefully we will be in and out and onto Aridale in just a day or two. Might be a week. I suggest you leave your makeup and anything frilly at home."

Home. I swallowed down my reaction to the word. The warmth it sent through my body. The acknowledgement that Kieron and I had similar visions of what we wanted in our lives. That I truly wanted this to be my home. "So only one suitcase?" I joked as I turned and found a shirt from his side of the closet to slip over my head.

Kieron did not respond as I returned to the bed and sat down on the edge next to him. His eyes were just staring right through his shirt that I was wearing.

"Two suitcases then?" I teased. I had never packed two suitcases full of clothes in my life.

Finally the corner of his mouth twitched up, "There is a new pack for you on the floor in the closet. We can't summon anything into the Eastern Desert, so whatever fits in your pack, sweetheart. And keep in mind I will not be carrying it for you."

I allowed my eyes to drop from his face and scan along his torso. I bit my lip and restrained myself from reaching out to touch his toned naked body. He lifted his hand and brushed the back of his fingers down my arm. "I would not dream of asking." I replied under my breath and stood up to actually pack my bag this time. I did not know what was wrong with me. Our kisses last night had been ... I didn't even have words for how *magical* they were. But Kieron had somehow respectfully kept it to just kissing—even with my naked body wrapped around his.

I felt a tinge of disappointment. I liked how he had a hard time containing himself around me. How he looked at me with hungry eyes. How he handled me roughly and at any moment I felt like he would just rip my clothes off and take me for his. It did not frighten me. It excited me. I wanted it—I wanted *him*.

I pulled two pairs of pants, three plain shirts, and my leather jacket from the hangers. Then I pulled a few pairs of my more practical underthings from the drawer along with a few pairs of socks. I returned to the bedroom and tossed the clothes on the bed in a small pile. "How about this?"

I watched the shock cross Kieron's face as he looked over what I had selected, "You must be the world's lightest packer. I thought I would have to convince you to leave a few things behind."

I laughed, "I pretty much wore the same two sets of clothes for two years straight."

"Why would you do that?" He asked carefully.

I started to fold the extra clothing items, "I did not have a choice. This pile here has more clothes in it than I owned." He raised his eyebrows at me in question, "I was on the run and could not take many things with me. I opted for money and items I could trade for other necessities over clothing."

"Were you still on the run when we attacked you by the river ... with Sarla?"

I set the last pair of socks on top of my small stack of clothes and took a deep breath. "I had decided to stop running at that point. Apparently life was not done with me." I could not look at him as I spoke.

"I see." He responded softly. I finally forced myself to look back up at him. "I am glad you had a few more fights left in you." He said as his eyes scanned my face.

"I am still undecided on that topic." I breathed. Things had been a complete shit show since I arrived in this world. There were moments when I thought I was grateful, but overall I still was not sure.

"I am sorry you still feel that way." Kieron said as he finally sat up. One of his legs hung off the bed. "If there is ever anything I can do for you, if you want to talk about it, or need support in any way ... I just want you to know that I am here for you."

The sincerity in his voice caused my breath to catch. "Thank you, Kieron."

His hand wrapped around mine and gave a gentle squeeze. "And if you ever need reasons to keep fighting you come to me and I will start listing them for you."

I gave him a small smile and returned to the closet to retrieve the pack he had for me. I did not even let myself argue with him about bringing my own pack. It was not worth the energy. I slipped my clothes into the bag.

"I hope we will be able to return here soon, but in case we can't or we don't, maybe you should take these with you." Kieron was holding up a chain with two rings on it, "I got you a chain if you want to wear them around your neck instead of on your finger. I would suggest wearing them instead of keeping them in your pack."

They were my rings that had been hidden in my own pack. "How did you know about those?" I asked. I did not know if I was angry or not that he had been in my things.

"I found them when Voss first captured you. I know I invaded your space by taking them out, but I also know they are important to you. You should keep them with you." He said and held the chain out for me.

I carefully took the chain with the two rings from him. "I think I would like to leave them here ... if that is alright with you? These are just things and what is really important is already always with me." I tapped my chest over my heart. Kieron's home was safe and I wanted the memories of my husband and son to be somewhere safe and peaceful.

"Of course. Can I ask what their significance is? You do not have to tell me if you do not want to." Kieron asked, his voice gentle.

I sat down next to him to show him, "This is my wedding band," I said and showed him the smooth white gold band. Then I showed him the other band, also white gold, but hammered to create an uneven surface, "And this one, my husband got me after my son was born. I had another, it had a beautiful round diamond. My husband used that one to propose to me, but ... I sold it."

"Why would you sell it?" Kieron asked, his hand running down my back.

"Because I needed to buy the supplies I used to kill the people involved in murdering my family." I said quietly. It had been an extremely hard decision, but Chad's people had taken or destroyed everything else we owned. I would get my revenge, but I had not been willing to steal from innocent people to make it happen.

"I am so sorry." He murmured.

"Do people give rings here for unions?"

"Yes, they do. Typically the male presents the female with a ring when he asks her to join him in union, then they both exchange rings during the ceremony." He explained.

"That is how it typically worked in my world too." I said and gave Kieron a small smile. Then I stood and took the rings to the closet where I placed them carefully in the dresser drawer with my other things.

I stood next to Kieron in the courtyard of his home and looked around one last time, "Everything okay?" Kieron asked gently.

"Yes, I just … I hope I get to come back here. I really love your home, Kieron." I said.

He squeezed my hand, "Me too." Then the courtyard folded in and we were surrounded by red sand.

The arch that marked the entrance to the Eastern Desert was … horrifying. It would have been beautiful with the dead branches bound to create the almost delicate looking archway, but the partially rotted body and head attached on either side ruined its beauty. I looked from one to the other. The head was skewered through and so was the body. The worst part was they both were moving. The fingers flexed and wiggled and the body jerked occasionally. When I looked at the head, the mouth opened and closed, then turned into what I could only describe as a snarl. The eyes darted back and forth and would pause on us for heartbeats before darting around again.

Beyond the arch nothing looked different from where we were currently standing. Red sand dunes stretched away from us in every direction. Kieron had jumped us directly to the arch, explaining that once we crossed, we would have a day's walk through the desert to the Palace of the Undead.

"He is still … alive?" I breathed. I could feel my body tensing with fear.

"Yes." Kieron said flatly. "Let's go."

"But … shouldn't we put him out of his misery? Couldn't you end this for him?" I asked, placing my hand on Kieron's arm to stop him. He was not lying when he said that the Undead would keep living without their heads, but this was not what I imagined.

"I could, but I won't. He deserves to be here." Kieron responded, his voice hard. I looked up at him and saw the hate in his eyes as he looked at the body. I also saw the satisfaction.

If this male deserved to be here then I did not want to know what he had done. "Say less. Let's go."

Kieron's hand dropped to mine and he laced my fingers in his. He gave my hand a gentle and reassuring squeeze before guiding us through the archway. As we stepped through it felt like we were walking through a thin sheet of water—but we did not get wet. The entire landscape changed before my eyes. What was once red sand dunes stretching in every direction was now scattered with cliffs, plateaus, and rock formations. Sagebrush and other desert bushes and trees littered the landscape. For a place considered worse than the Wastelands, it was beautiful.

CHAPTER 28

Kieron - Months Ago.

Kieron lounged in the huge entry room attached to Voss's personal suite of rooms. This room had become their hang out—the place Voss's most trusted males drank and smoked together. Females weren't allowed in—unless it was a special occasion—and on those nights, Kieron always found somewhere else more important to be.

Kieron had returned to the palace after taking two personal days —two dangerous days to forward his plans of removing Voss from his throne. When he had returned, Kieron learned that Voss and Rook had taken it upon themselves to pay a visit to Beck. A terribly idiotic thing to do, but Voss and Rook tended to make ego-driven decisions—especially when left alone together.

Now Kieron sat on one of the couches and tried to calm himself as the time wore on. Clearly something had not gone to plan if they were all still gone. Maybe Beck had obliterated them. That was Kieron's hope at least.

The door banged open and Rook stormed in. His black clothes were covered in a slick of blood and partially dried blood still caked most of his head. "It looks like your adventure went well." Kieron teased from his seat on the couch.

"That fucking bitch shot me in the head." Rook seethed as he crossed the room to the bar and pulled out a glass. He slammed it on the bartop followed by a bottle of liquor before turning to look at Kieron. "I am going to cut her into tiny pieces when I get my hands on her."

Her. Shot me in the head. A female with a gun—it could only be Genevieve. *Why was Genevieve at Beck's?* "Where is Voss?" Kieron responded as coolly as he could. Inside he was screaming.

"Nash is dead by the way, not that you care, and when I woke up Voss was gone." Rook responded as he poured himself a drink and slammed back the entire contents of his glass before pouring another.

"Rook. Your king is missing." Kieron growled as he stood. He did not actually give two shits if Voss was missing. It was Genevieve he was worried about. "Tell me everything you know and then we are going to go look for him."

"Voss will fucking figure it out." Rook snapped back. "Maybe he will bring that bitch back with him too. Oh and apparently Ryett is not actually a business partner anymore ... some shit about what Voss let happen to her ... centuries of trusting him and one fucking female ruins a good relationship." Rook was far too okay with all of this. Or he wasn't. Kieron was never quite certain of what Rook was thinking—it was always something far darker and disgusting that Kieron wanted to admit.

"Nash is dead? Tell me what happened, Rook." Kieron pressed him.

"We thought we would go pay Beck another visit, see if he had changed his mind about partnering with us. And when we got there, we were surprised to find Zain and Alias there having a little meeting. Things ... escalated. Zain and Devron took the brunt of it and Zain somehow escaped Voss's containment spell. Then Ryett showed up. That is all I know because that bitch blew my brains all over the wall just as things were getting exciting." Rook downed another glass full of liquor.

This was bad. All of this was bad. "Where is Voss?"

"He wasn't there when I woke up. The asshole left me."

Kieron did not care if Voss had left Rook. He needed to know what had happened. "What else do you know?"

"Nothing. I didn't fucking stick around to ask questions, Kieron. I got my ass back here as fast as I could." Rook snapped. Then he paused for a moment, thinking. He chuckled to himself, "I did hear one of them say something about Voss taking her with him. Maybe he's just off enjoying himself right now."

Kieron ripped the bottle of liquor from Rook's hand before Rook could pour another glass. "Get out there and help me find our king before everyone else in this kingdom finds out he is missing." He said through his teeth. Rook glared at him for a moment before folding into the air. Kieron followed a heartbeat later.

Kieron was not actually looking for Voss—yet. It was a good excuse to keep Rook busy, but Kieron had some stops to make first. First, he jumped to the edge of the forest outside of Ryett's chateau. He knew he should not be here, but he had to see for himself who was still alive. It only took a moment before he felt her magic. *She was safe.* That was all he needed to know. Then he folded into the air before anyone had time to figure out he had been there. Next, he left a note just inside of the gate to the Eastern Desert. Orion or Zealand would receive it soon enough.

Kieron stood in the black and gray dust that coated the dead landscape. He looked down at a tiny green shoot that poked through the dust. Then he raised his eyes back to Vossarian's body. Voss's head still had a hole in it. It would be hours before Voss woke up again. Kieron bent down and picked up the gun that lay on top of Voss's body—Genevieve's gun. So Voss had taken her and she had shot him in the head. He smiled to himself as he folded into the air and left the twenty-sixth world. Voss would have to figure out how to get back on his own.

CHAPTER 29

Genevieve - Present Day.

I followed Kieron through red sand and rock as we made our way towards the cliff face of a large plateau. I could see the trail skirt up the side of the cliff as it zigzagged its way to the top. We reached the base of the plateau relatively quickly and I continued to follow Kieron as he made his way up the trail.

"You said the Eastern Desert was worse than the Wastes, but all I see is how beautiful it is out here." I panted as I climbed the path behind Kieron.

"There are a lot of things that will kill you out here. In the Wastelands it is just the beasts. What animals still find a way to survive out there will leave you alone. Out here, in the Eastern Desert, everything is trying to kill you. The heat, the storms, the animals, the beasts—and if none of those things succeed then there are still the Piraveh."

"The Piraveh?"

"They are worse than beasts—and worse than the esurimagicae. Esurim you can kill by chopping them into pieces. If they are outside of the Wastes, they will suck magic out of the air, but not all magic. You can kill esurim with dark magic, blood rain that is. But the Piraveh, some believe they were once beings like you or me, who committed acts of true evil in order to gain the powers of others. These acts usually involved eating another being." A shudder went down my spine. Kieron continued, "Some believe they are witches, some believe they are spirits or ghosts, but everyone agrees that they can shapeshift from looking like a male to any animal they desire—sometimes they only partially shift, keeping some of the male form and some of an animal form. If one catches you they will suck the magic out of you and then your life until your body is no more than a husk."

"Have you seen one?" I asked hesitantly.

Kieron paused and turned to look at me, "Yes."

I raised my eyebrows, "Care to elaborate?"

"I have been chased through these deserts by them more times than I care to remember." Kieron said.

"And what do we do if we encounter one?"

"We run."

"How do you kill them?"

"You don't." Then he turned to continue hiking.

I left it at that. Shapeshifting beings that wanted to suck us dry sounded like something I did not want to hear more about. Maybe when we were safely back in Kieron's home, but not while we were out here with the threat of them turning up at any moment.

We stopped under one of the few trees to get some relief from the scorching heat. It was brutal out here. Kieron pointed across the landscape towards red plateaus in the distance. "That is where we are headed."

It looked ridiculously far away. I sipped some water and put the canteen back in my pack. "And why can't we just jump there?"

"The Death Taker is the only one who can jump any distance within the Eastern Desert. Some can't jump at all and some of us can only jump ten feet or so. Other magic works here so I think it is The Death Taker's way to force those sentenced to life in the Eastern Desert to have to walk through the desert."

"I guess we should keep moving then." I said as I stood up, I was not one to complain about a long hike.

He gave me an amused grin, "I guess so."

We made our way along an animal trail that followed a cliff's edge. The brush and trees were taller here and provided some relief from the beating sun. I had to keep forcing my eyes back to the trail instead of looking out at the beautiful landscape. The drop from the edge was—far—and when I looked out at the landscape my eyes inevitably found their way back to staring over the edge. Nausea rolled in my stomach and I felt my hands start to tremble at the thought of being up so high—so close to the edge—it caused my breathing to become short and shallow.

I was so focused on trying to calm my nerves, I nearly walked right into Kieron when he stopped. I looked up at him and he held a finger over his lips. Then he pointed to his ear. I strained to listen. I could hear a faint clicking from over the cliff's edge. *Piraveh.* Kieron mouthed the word to me. The clicking grew louder and Kieron pushed me behind him as he backed away from the edge. A dirty hand with yellowing and cracked nails clawed its way over the edge, followed by another.

"Do not move, but be ready to run." Kieron said under his breath.

Leathery arms pulled the creature up and over the edge. Animal hides hung off of its boney body and a skull of a canine creature hid its face like a mask. It stayed squatted low to the ground as its head tilted from one side to the other. Black depthless eyes scanned us.

We stayed motionless. My heart was pounding in my chest and I forced myself to take slow deep breaths. Kieron's hand wrapped around mine and gave a reassuring squeeze. The clicking noise started again around ragged breathing. It was coming from where a mouth would be. Then an airy and gravelly voice leaked from the thing, "Powerful. So powerful. I have never tasted magic so powerful."

It cracked its neck and black smoke began leaking from its body. The animal hides seemed to fuse into place as arms and legs cracked and bent at odd angles as they transformed.

The air around us shimmered as Kieron let his power build. He gave my hand another squeeze and sent a spear of heat blasting towards the Piraveh. Then he was dragging me in the other direction as a blood curdling scream erupted behind us.

We sprinted across the sand and rocks along the cliff edge following a narrow trail. I willed myself to only look where Kieron's feet were falling—and not off the edge. Panic was rising in my chest and it could have been the steep drop to our right or the demonic being that was chasing us. Kieron skidded to a stop and I saw a rope fling out from his hand and wrap around one of the red stone arches that spanned between this plateau and another mesa. His other arm wrapped tightly around my waist. "I need you to trust me." He said gruffly.

I stared up into his eyes and gave a single nod. A moment later he hurled us off the cliff's edge and we plummeted towards the ground. I held on tightly as we fell and swallowed the scream that threatened to come out of my mouth. If this was how I died I was going to be really pissed. The ground was getting closer and closer and we were surely going to splat on it. There was no way that Kieron's hand on the rope was going to stop us from turning into splattered bugs on the desert floor—how did he even know if the rope was a safe length?

I buried my face in Kieron's shoulder—I could not watch. Then there was a violent jerk as our momentum stopped and I felt the familiar pressure of the world folding in before our bodies hit dirt and we tumbled along the ground. "Are you okay?" Kieron shouted from a few yards away.

I was laying on my back staring up at the bright blue sky between red cliffs. I lifted my hands to look at them and saw I was coated in red dirt. I was completely and utterly unharmed. I sat straight up and looked at him. He was also completely covered in red dirt. Then I turned and squinted up at the cliff edge we had just thrown ourselves off of—the shadow of a creature, half male and half animal paced the edge before disappearing.

"If you make me jump off of one more cliff … I swear …" I could not finish my thought as laughter erupted from me. I lay back down in the dirt and Kieron's shadow blocked out the sun as he leaned over me.

"Are you alright?" He asked again.

"Yes, I am fine. Are you alright?"

"Yes." He said and threw himself onto the dirt next to me.

"I mean it. No more jumping off of cliffs. You need to come up with a better escape plan next time."

He erupted into laughter next to me. "Sorry, sweetheart." He finally breathed. I reached my hand out between us until I felt his leg and gave him a few pats.

CHAPTER 30

Genevieve - A Few Years Ago.

I had completely run out of food. I was now standing on the edge of town and everything was quiet. Too quiet. I was going to starve to death if I did not buy more supplies. I guess I was going into town. I made my way down empty streets—the streets should not be empty—

"Psst!" I spun around at the sound, "Get in here now. Quickly!" It was Jacob, the sandwich shop owner. Eli and I had eaten together in Jacob's shop as our first unofficial date. We continued to frequent there as the years went on and Jacob had become a good friend and eventually a grandfather figure to Harlowe. He was older and had lost his family long before we met him. I hurried to his door and slipped in.

His eyes scanned me up and down then I saw the sorrow cross his face, "It's true then? The boys?" His voice broke as he asked the question. I could only nod as tears filled my eyes and his strong hands pulled me into an embrace. "I am so sorry, honey … You can not be seen here. The Commanding Chief has sent people looking for you. Your face is plastered all over the store fronts and they are questioning everybody. What happened? Did you do something?" His voice was low and hushed as he released me and ushered me towards the back of the store. He started pulling supplies from his shelves.

"They just ambushed Eli and the boys were with him." I managed to get out. Then I had to take a deep breath, "I should have gone back—the Commanding Chief—he summoned me and I didn't go."

"No. This is not your fault. Give me your pack." Jacob said. I slung my pack off of my shoulders and handed it to him. He began packing food into it.

"He said I had to go back if he ever summoned me. I didn't and now my boys are dead." I did not try to stop the tears that fell down my face.

"This is not your fault, do you hear me? You are a person. Not property. You never were and will never be anyone's property. This is not your fault." His strong wrinkled hands grasped my shoulders as he spoke to me. Then he lifted my now full pack and pressed it into my arms. "You need to get far away from here. Stick to the small caves, no mine tunnels and no cave systems, only the gods know what lives in those. Small caves only. Take the side road and look for the road marked zero two two seven."

"Jacob—"

"Honey, you need to stay alive. Come back only when things have settled down. Stay alive."

I nodded my head that I understood and Jacob showed me out the back door of his shop.

It was just so fucking cold. The snow was starting to fall as the sun dipped below the ridge and the temperature was dropping quickly. I was on a stretch of the road I had never been on. I had been hoping to find another town, one where the people did not know me, but now night was falling and I needed to find shelter—quickly.

I had passed a mining tunnel a few miles back, but Jacob had warned me months ago to stick to the small caves only. It was getting dark enough now that I could not wander far from the road to look for shelter without risking losing the road altogether. I might not have a choice. I started to jog down the road as I searched the hillside for boulders or down trees that I could quickly turn into shelter from the weather. Nothing. I could keep moving through the night, but I was getting too cold. I was also too low on food to expend that type of energy. Then I saw it—another mining tunnel.

I cautiously approached and shined my light into the tunnel. A warm breeze was blowing out of the tunnel. I swallowed—I guess I was going to go deeper and check it out. Hopefully it was not occupied already. I bent my knees as I ducked my head to move into the tunnel. My heart pounded in my chest. At least it was warm.

After a few hundred yards I had not encountered any signs of life. I turned and made my way back closer to the tunnel entrance

—to the edge of where the cold from the night air and the warmth from the tunnel met. I sat down with my back against the wall and looked around one more time before turning my headlamp off. I had to get some sleep.

I felt my boot move first, then I heard the breathing. I was not alone. What felt like a hand stroked down my shin. My foot jerked to the side as whatever it was pushed my boot again. I was holding my breath as one of my hands slowly and silently moved to my headlamp and the other to my knife. I flicked the headlamp switch and kicked my legs at the same time. The creature clawed at my legs and screamed—no, I was definitely the one screaming. A very pale and naked male was grabbing me. One arm blocked the light from his yellow eyes. His lips curled back and I saw his teeth were pointed and his gums black. I kicked hard and scrambled away across the dirt.

As soon as my light left his face he was on me again—tackling me to the ground. I rolled and shoved my knife into his body. It was his turn to scream. His nails dug into my arm and I slammed my fist into his face. I kicked again and broke free. Then I was sprinting down the tunnel—my hand skimmed the ceiling of the tunnel in front of my forehead as I ducked my head and ran as fast as I could. I could hear him behind me as I burst out of the tunnel and into the freezing night air.

Then I slammed into the dirt as he tackled me. We rolled through the brush. I felt his nails bite into my neck and I found myself staring up into his unseeing eyes—my headlamp blinding him. He held on as I thrashed and tried to buck him off of me. I stabbed my knife into his side again and again and he only screamed before releasing my throat and grabbing my head. I tucked my chin tightly to my chest and my hands clawed at his wrists. *Shit.* Shit. Shit. He was going to snap my neck.

A vicious growl ripped through the air and his body was torn off of mine. I rolled into a crouch and frantically whipped my headlamp towards the screaming. *Where was he?* Then it was silent. My lamp fell on a pale body—now covered in blood—with a giant white wolf pinning it to the ground. Blood dripped from the wolf's mouth. It turned its eyes towards me and I averted the headlamp so I was not blinding it. It was the biggest wolf I had ever seen and either this wolf had just saved me or I was about to be part of its next meal. I did not move as I watched it from the corner of my eye and I sucked in breaths trying to calm myself. The wolf just stayed staring at me. Then it simply turned away and padded off into the night. My body shuddered as tears of relief fell down my face.

CHAPTER 31

Genevieve - Present Day.

Jumping from the cliff had put us into the bottom of a canyon with a small stream that trickled down the middle. We had taken a few minutes to brush off as much dirt as we could, then we rinsed ourselves off in the stream before continuing to hike. There were a few trails that made their way up the steep cliff faces, but Kieron did not take any of them. At least down here we were in the shadows and it was much cooler.

"We won't be making it to the Palace of the Undead today. We are going to have to spend the night out here." Kieron said absently as we picked our way down the canyon following the direction of the stream.

Of course I did not want to stay out in the open in a land that Kieron had deemed 'worse than the Wastelands,' but I was used to sleeping under the stars in dangerous lands. "Did you bring any marshmallows?" I asked.

"What are marshmallows?"

I just chuckled and shook my head to myself, "Fluffy sticky sugar that you brown over a fire before eating. Best served with chocolate."

"You and your food." Kieron said under his breath as he finally pointed to a trail that headed up and out of the canyon.

Kieron

Dealing with Piraveh in the Eastern Desert was not new for Kieron. He had crossed the desert to the Palace of the Undead more times than he wished to remember and had crossed paths with Piraveh plenty of times. This encounter had been a relatively tame one. Normally the Piraveh did not stop to talk, they simply ambushed you. Regardless, his blood had never been pumping so hard after escaping from one of the Piraveh. He just kept thinking about how he had brought Genevieve into this danger—how he had been arrogant enough to think that bringing her here was a perfectly fine thing to do as long as she was with him. Some of the best equipped and most brutal males did not make it through these deserts and he had still brought her here. If they were lucky they would not encounter any more Piraveh.

At that moment, Kieron noticed the shadows that darkened the landscape around them. Then he heard it. The distant thunder.

They had to get to higher ground—any high ground. He pointed up one of the trails and Genevieve followed him closely without questioning him as he picked up his pace. This trail he realized led to a narrow slot between the rocks as it wove its way back into the plateau. *He had picked a bad trail.* Kieron's heart sank. He stopped and looked back at Genevieve. Thunder sounded again.

"What's wrong?" She asked.

"We might be about to get very wet." Kieron said flatly as he considered their options.

"I can survive a little rain, Kieron." Genevieve responded with a laugh.

"It is not the rain I am worried about."

He watched Genevieve look around—back down to the canyon floor and ahead on the trail where it snaked into the rocks. "Oh. Oh shit." She breathed. "Floods."

Before Kieron could respond, raindrops started pelting them. Water slowly started to trickle over the edge of the cliffs above them. Kieron grabbed Genevieve's hand and pulled her into the narrow slot—they had to keep moving and this was the only direction that continued to take them upwards.

They jogged at a steady pace as they wove through the narrow rock. At times they had to slow down and slip their packs off to squeeze through openings, but at least the trail kept a steady incline. Lightning flashed and lit the trail ahead of them. A heartbeat later thunder shook the entire plateau. Water from the rain and what was pouring over the cliff edges above them started to increase. Then it started flowing like a waterfall into a river. In seconds they were fighting against rushing water that was already up to their shins.

They rounded a bend and saw a long straight and wide stretch ahead of them. They started running up the slope. A huge wave crested the cliff edge above them and Kieron grabbed Genevieve's arm to pull her close. They were going to be swept away and he had to hold on to her. There was nothing for him to grab on to. Nowhere for them to climb to. He could not even jump far enough to get them somewhere higher. Water crashed into his body and slammed them against the rock wall.

Then Kieron felt nothing. They were not moving. They were not being pounded by water. Kieron looked around and saw a dark light enveloping them. Water rushed by outside of the light. He looked down at Genevieve—light was emitting from every pore in her body. She held onto him tightly, but her chin lifted as she looked up at him. "Thank you, my shield does not work like this." Kieron chuckled to her.

"Anytime." She said sarcastically and smiled back at him.

Genevieve

The sun was setting as we emerged from the canyon and moved towards another ridgeline. After Piraveh and floods and using my shield to keep us from being washed away, I was completely exhausted. At least the view was absolutely gorgeous—everything here might be trying to kill us—but it was still beautiful. Birds were singing their last light songs. I listened to them, admiring the way they sang back and forth. Trying to pick out how many different birds might be singing. Then an odd chirp sounded and I took a quick inhale. Another chirp sounded from the other direction. I silenced my breathing as I listened carefully for it to sound again. Nothing. My ears must be playing tricks on me.

Just when I had settled my beating heart, the odd chirp sounded again. It sent a chill down my neck. "I haven't figured out what bird makes that noise." Kieron said as we moved through the brush towards the ridge.

"That is not a bird." I said under my breath as I followed Kieron's steps along the rocks. There were not many animals that frightened me after surviving in the wilderness on my own, but this was one of the ones that did.

We crested the ridge and Kieron pointed to a rock outcropping that would provide us reasonable shelter, "Let's stay here for the night and continue on tomorrow."

We settled in against the stone and my eyes wandered from the shadowed ridgeline up to the stars. They were the brightest stars I had ever seen. The clear sky made the desert night even colder and the bright stars cast shadows that seemed to be alive. I was on edge after all that we had been through. Then screaming broke through the night air. A female screaming for dear life.

Kieron's hand shot out to my leg and he sat up alert. "There should not be a female out here—" he was interrupted as another scream cut through the night.

I gently placed my hand on top of his, "That bird you heard earlier has four big paws and fangs." His head whipped to look at me. I could only smile at his confused face, "Mountain lions, Kieron. The chirping and the screaming is one or more mountain lions."

"How do you know that? It sounds like someone is being eaten alive." He was still tense, his other hand hovered above the knife at his belt.

"I spent years living in the wilderness and then another two on my own in the wilderness. It is terrifying to hear, but those noises are mountain lions. I do not know what animals look like or how they behave here, but in my world those cats will hunt someone down if they are desperate enough."

"Let's hope they aren't desperate." Kieron breathed and he settled back against the rock, his hand still rested on my thigh. I felt a familiar warm pulse of magic. Then I realized Kieron had just created a bubble of warmth around us.

"Those pulses of warmth … it was always you?" I breathed. I had felt those same pulses of warmth wash through my body when I was in Vossarian's dungeons and at times when I had been emotionally unraveling. Those pulses of warmth had calmed and steadied me. In those moments I had never realized what they were —never realized they were from him.

"Yes." He said softly, "It tells your nervous system you are safe."

I leaned over and rested my head against his shoulder. I *was* safe with Kieron.

I woke up with my head in Kieron's lap and his hand resting on my shoulder. "Good morning." His deep warm voice whispered. The sun was barely starting to peek above the horizon, but it was already bathing the landscape in shades of pink and gold.

"Were you able to get any sleep?" I asked as I pushed myself up.

"Yes, some." Kieron responded with a small smile. It was so quiet. So peaceful. This land of death and demons was still unbelievably beautiful. "Are you ready to see what today has in store for us?"

CHAPTER 32

Genevieve

"We are here." Kieron said, his voice low. My eyes scanned along the cliffs until I saw it—an entire network of pathways, windows, and rooms were carved along the cliff face. "Stay close and ignore any crude comments, I would be surprised if you did not hear a few."

I followed Kieron closely as we made our way up a narrow path towards an arched doorway. The hair on the back of my neck prickled and I knew we were being watched. The door was ancient and wooden. Kieron did not hesitate as he raised his fist and banged on it. Just when I thought no one was going to answer, the door creaked open. No one was there. Kieron stepped into the darkness beyond the doorway and I followed him. Torches along the wall and down a hallway began to light, leading further into the earth.

My hand involuntarily grabbed Kieron's forearm, "It's a cave system?" I asked, my voice hushed and panicked.

He looked back at me and then down at my hand, "Yes. Everything alright?" He could probably feel my terror. I hid in too many caves and tunnels when I was running from Chad's people. I never wanted to go into another one, but here we were.

"Well fuck me." I breathed out, "Sorry, yes. Let's go." Kieron just looked me up and down again as I released his arm and I gestured with my hand for him to lead the way. I had promised myself I would never enter another cave system unless there was a damn good reason—I guess helping Kieron checked that box. I followed him down the now dimly lit hallway.

Eventually the hallway opened up to a much bigger hall and again into a gigantic underground cave. It was practically an entire underground city. I forced myself to swallow and take a deep breath as I looked around and saw males—each with varrying degrees of tattoos just like Orion's and Zealand's—moving about between the pathways, stairs, and doors. Many of them stopped when they saw us. "This way." Kieron said gruffly and I hurried closely behind him.

We made our way down the path and to another set of large wooden doors. Kieron pushed one open and held the door for me behind him as we entered.

"We were starting to wonder if you would ever come, Kieron." We had entered a throne room, long and narrow, and instead of a throne at one end, there was a large table with twelve males sitting at it. One of the males was standing. "Orion said you would be bringing company, a representative from the Mountains and the Lakes, but he did not warn us that it was a female. I am not sure a female has ever been in the Palace of the Undead."

"That detail was not your business, Cade, nor does it matter." I recognized Orion's voice. "Kieron, Genevieve, welcome."

We were now standing mere steps away from the table. I forced my back to stay straight and held my chin up as I sized up each of the males—all of them looked like hardened warriors and all of them had their faces tattooed with the image of the bones beneath. I notice that some of the tattoos continued down necks and even onto arms and hands. I kept my face neutral, even when I recognized Zealand among the group.

"Counsel, thank you for allowing us to come." Kieron greeted the males.

"Orion has filled us in on your proposal, Kieron. Or should I say King Kieron?" Cade drawled, "But perhaps you would like to take a rest after your journey? We can discuss business after you have freshened up and eaten some food. I am sure your ... companion would appreciate it." Cade's eyes fell on me with his last statement. I could not read his expression, but I met his stare with my jaw set and fire in my eyes.

"We would appreciate that, Cade." Kieron said as he took a subtle step closer to me.

"Great. Come with me." Orion stood up from his seat and made his way around the table. He grasped forearms with Kieron in greeting, then led us from the throne room.

"Here are your rooms." Orion said as he unlocked a door and

pushed it open for us. "I hope you will be comfortable here, I picked one for you that actually has a window. I also hope you will not have to stay long. I will let you get cleaned up and I will be back in a few hours. You will join us for dinner."

"Thank you, Orion." Kieron responded, "Any insight on how it is going to go."

"As we expected, Cade is causing some problems, but I do not think the others share his reservations." Orion replied. I could tell there was more to it that he was not going to share now.

"Right." Kieron said, "We will see you in a few hours."

Orion closed the door behind us and I turned to look at the room. In one corner was a small kitchenette. There were doorways on opposite sides of the room—they probably led to bedrooms. The rest of the room included a table for six, a couch and two chairs, and against the far wall was a window and a piano. I set my pack down next to the table and walked to the piano. I would never have imagined there would be a piano in a place like this. But here it was.

I sat down at the bench and opened the key lid. As I looked down at the beautiful white and black keys, Kieron slid onto the bench next to me. "Do you play?" He asked.

"Sort of." I replied. I had not touched Ryett's piano more than once and it was a long while before then that I had played. Kieron's fingers rested on the keys and he slowly started playing. I looked over at him in surprise. *Kieron played the piano.* "Well, I was not expecting that." I said as a smile crossed my face.

He laughed and stopped playing. "I used to leave sheet music I liked in the different worlds I world walked to. It kind of felt like I was sharing something I loved with the other worlds. Something good."

Then he started playing again. My eyes dropped back to his fingers on the keys. A familiar melody made my blood thrum inside of me. *I knew this piece.* I lifted my hands to the keys and started playing with him. My mother had brought this music home one day and it had become our favorite duet. I lifted my eyes back to Kieron's face. He was staring at me, his eyes wide. "Was this one of the pieces you left in my world?" I asked as his fingers stopped moving. I kept playing. The shock on his face only made my lips part into a huge grin. "This was one of my favorites. I had forgotten it until you started playing it ... Well, are you going to join me?"

Kieron's fingers resumed playing and we played out the finale. I banged down the final chords dramatically. When the notes stopped ringing I could not help but burst out laughing. "What's so funny?" Kieron asked, a small smile on his face.

"Do you realize how ridiculous it is that you left a piece of music in my world and somehow it made its way into my life and now we are sitting here playing it together? You could not make this shit up if you tried." I was nearly giggling as Kieron's large arm wrapped around me and pulled me close. He planted a kiss on my head.

"Play it with me again?" He asked, his mouth pressed against my hair. I nodded and gave his leg a squeeze before placing my fingers back on the keys.

Kieron

Playing the piano next to Genevieve might have been Kieron's most favorite thing he had ever done. He had been completely shocked when she had started playing the music with him. He had left that particular piece of music in the twenty-sixth world centuries ago. He was still in a daze as the two of them stepped into the shower to clean the red dirt from themselves. But he was not dazed enough to miss how comfortable Genevieve had become around him. Sure, there was a hint of fear that leaked from her, but there was something else. He had watched her as she had peeked into both bedrooms before declaring which one was better and placing both of their packs on the bench at the foot of the bed. Then she had simply dragged him into the bathroom and undressed before hopping into the shower and leaving the door open for him —as if she just expected him to follow her in.

"What is the deal with Cade?" Genevieve asked. Her question jerked Kieron back from his daze as he admired her under the stream of water.

"Cade is not my biggest fan. He is the one I will have to win over for things to go smoothly." Kieron answered. Not his biggest fan was an understatement. Cade and Kieron went way back to when Kieron was a child. The first chance Kieron got, he would end Cade. Becoming one of the Undead was a fitting punishment for what Cade had done, but Kieron would rather see him dead, or staked to the gates. Either would be fine with him.

"What's wrong? What aren't you telling me about him?"

Genevieve pressed.

"We have a history. I would rather he be dead than have to ask him to join me." Kieron replied tightly. Genevieve's hand reached up to rest on his chest. Kieron looked down at it. Then along her arm and over her naked body under the spray of water from the shower. That relentless urge to claim her and to protect her was still there, but there was something else too. He had known she was smart and thoughtful and knew those things were important to him. But as his eyes looked her over he realized that he respected her.

She had a presence that demanded she be treated equally. That demanded she be listened to and that she would not shrink in the presence of any male—even him.

Kieron took her hand in his and kissed her palm.

CHAPTER 33

Genevieve - A Few Years Ago.

I could not decide if this bar was classy or disgusting. Everyone was dressed nicely and the decor was tasteful, but there was just a reek of filth—and not the excrement kind. This filth was the filth of people who do terrible things and get away with it. The arrogance. The puffed chests and cocky exaggerated conversations. I would pity the females who were lounging in the laps of these males, but they all knew what they were getting themselves into.

I had come here a few nights now—never back to back—and had a good idea of how the nights normally progressed. Males came and pretended to be more important than they were and the females swooned over them until some of the more lucky males took a female or two home with them. I was only hoping to go home with one particular male. He had been here each night and I had figured out his type: tight dress, high heels, wavy hair, and enough makeup to hide what the female might actually look like. He just made it too easy.

I had slowly altered my appearance each night, moving closer to what it was he liked to take home. I had also made it clear that I had set eyes on him the last two nights I had been here. He had shown interest back, but had always given in to other females that came falling into his lap. Each time he had given me a final look before leaving. *Good.* It meant his eyes were on me too. I was his next conquest. Exactly like I wanted to be.

His apartment was cleaner than I thought it would be. I took a quick inventory as his hands ran along my body and he offered me another drink. I accepted of course—that is what the other females would do. Then the games began. He clearly was used to being in control as he tried to push me against the wall and pull my dress up. I scolded him and pulled him to the bedroom instead. His headboard was metal slats—this was going to be way too easy.

I continued to take control and pushed him on the bed. He chuckled and looked at me with hungry eyes. I straddled him and untied his tie, using it to tie his hands to the headboard. Then I slid off his shoes and pulled out his shoe strings. I used them to tie his ankles to the bed frame. He was enjoying this. Either I was doing a good job pretending he was about to get the best fuck of his life or he was too drunk to realize what an idiot he was.

Once he was secured I made a show of snooping around his

room, teasing him. Then I found exactly what I was hoping to find —his gun. *Game over.* I turned on the lights and sat in a chair.

He gave up his accomplices way too quickly. I would have thought a male who was so boastful down at the bar might actually have some balls or integrity. He had neither. I did not even have to torture him much before I killed him and I had exactly what I needed: All the names, confirming descriptions, and locations of everyone else involved in the death of my husband, son, and dog.

CHAPTER 34

Genevieve - Present Day.

I was sitting in one of the cushioned chairs while Kieron paced the room. Orion had not returned and it had been hours. I was trying to think of something encouraging to say, but before I could come up with anything there was a loud knock on the door. Kieron was there in a few strides and he cracked the door an inch before pulling it open.

Orion entered the room and slid out one of the chairs from the table before slumping into it. "I have a feeling this is not going to go as smoothly as we thought it would. Cade has amassed more support and refuses to discuss with the rest of the counsel his position. I am afraid we are going in blind to what he might demand from you, Kieron." Kieron swore under his breath, "The rest of the counsel supports you, so perhaps we do not need Cade."

"We might not, but I would rather not risk it. I do not need to be looking over my shoulder wondering if Cade and his followers will stab me in the back." Kieron said. He ran his hands through his long hair and then down his face and over his beard. "Well, if you do not have any advice, we better get on with it and see what he wants."

Orion sighed, "Do not give him too much, Kieron. We can do this without him and deal with him after if we need to. That is the only wisdom I have for you."

"Alright, let's go." Kieron said and he gestured for me to follow.

We followed Orion as he took us down yet another hallway and approached two large wooden doors. Orion paused before the doors. Kieron gave him a nod and Orion pushed them open. This was the room of males Kieron would have to convince.

"My offer is two fold. First, for those of you willing to help me take my throne, I will reinstate you as part of the forces who serve the crown. If any of you wish to live in peace and not in service, I will allow that as well within The Land of the Deserts. And the second part of my offer is that if any of you wish to pass on to the next life, I will assist you in doing so." Kieron explained to the counsel and the few handfuls of Undead who had joined us in the massive dining hall in the Palace of the Undead. He stood with his back straight and did not falter in his words. A room full of deadly assassins and warriors who had committed crimes did not frighten Kieron. I could see it in his eyes as he met the gazes of the males looking back at him.

From what I could gather, there was The Death Taker, who was the one who made the Undead the Undead. He had final say and complete authority over the Undead. He said who could leave the Eastern Desert and who could not. He also oversaw any punishment and sentencing for the crimes committed. The Death Taker was not present at this meeting.

Next in the chain of command was the counsel. They seemed to be made up of high ranking males who had won their seat through a democratic process. Each male of the counsel represented some portion of the Undead. The other males who had joined seemed to be other high standing and influential Undead. Those not in attendance were loyal to one or more of the high standing males or counsel members.

"How can we trust you Kieron?" Cade drawled, "You put many of us in here, either as punishment or because they took the fall for your own actions."

"Is my offer to end the lives of those who are ready to pass on and to allow the rest of you to leave the Eastern Desert to start fresh in my kingdom not enough?" Kieron countered. I could see the muscle in his jaw flicker slightly with his annoyance.

Cade tapped his fingers on the table, "Those who wish to die have already wandered deeper into the Eastern Desert. How can we trust that you really will let us live out our lives in your kingdom? That you will not just banish us back here?"

"I have given you my word." Kieron said through his teeth.

"The word of the right hand to the king who schemed behind the king's back for centuries. That is not worth very much now is it?" Cade smirked at us.

"Do you have a suggestion, Cade." Orion cut in.

"I am so glad you asked, Orion. Yes, I do have a suggestion." Cade said, his eyes gleaming. "Become one of us, Kieron."

"Absolutely not." Orion snapped. "How dare you—"

"It is my final offer. Become one of us and we will see to it that you sit on your rightful throne. I will give you until the morning to decide." Cade said as he stood up. A few others stood as well. They left the room. Then all but the counsel members stood and left too. The large hall was silent.

"I'll do it." Kieron breathed from beside me.

"No, you will not." Orion said sternly, "You will not toss away your life like this. We did not go through this for you to have to go through it too."

"That is the reason I will do it, Orion, *because* it should have been me. Not you. Not Zealand. Not the others. It should have been *me* who was marked and banished." Kieron stood suddenly.

"It is the worst thing you will ever go through, Kieron, and there are risks. Once you become Undead you cannot kill another Undead." Zealand cut in.

"I won't need to kill any of you." Kieron responded, "G, let's go. I have made up my mind."

Zealand stood and blocked Kieron's path to the door. I slowly stood up from my chair, "Hear them out Kieron. This is a big decision. Let's make sure you are going into it with every scenario considered."

Zealand noded to me in thanks before starting again, "I hope you will not have to kill any of us, but I do not trust Cade. Being able to turn any of us into blood rain is a good skill to have … to keep."

One of the other counsel members chimed in, "All of us in this room support you, Kieron. We do not require you to become one of us. With the others who are loyal to us, you will have an army big enough to take your throne."

"Cade will be a problem going forward. If he is not sworn to Kieron he is a risk to Kieron. At least if Kieron is one of the Undead, Cade cannot kill him." Another counsel member challenged.

"Are there other risks or consequences he needs to consider?" I asked. My head was spinning with the thought that Kieron would willingly become one of the Undead.

"Many. To become one of us, you will be forced to relive the worst things you have done and lived through. It is not only emotionally painful, but unbelievably physically painful as well. Once you have changed, it will take a day or so for your magic to come back to full strength, so you will be vulnerable during that time. You will lose the ability to turn another Undead into blood rain—which is actually quite brilliant or we would have figured out how to all kill each other long ago. However, as Zealand pointed out, you lose your ability to control any of the Undead by threat of ending them. You will be permanently marked. Perhaps we can request The Death Taker not mark your face, as you must be a king for all the people and the face markings were a specific request from Luther. And the obvious consequence is that you sign yourself up for a nearly endless life." Orion explained, his voice hard, "I am sure there are other details I am forgetting, but that covers most of it."

The room was silent as Kieron considered his options. "I'll do it." The counsel members all nodded. I scanned their faces and saw the respect and sorrow in them. "I will do it tomorrow morning.

Genevieve, with me." Then he strode towards the door and I gave Orion and Zealand a worried glance before hurrying after him.

I waited until he closed the door to our rooms before I said anything. "Kieron, are you sure? You can't come back from this."

"I have already decided. Do not question me." Kieron said through his teeth.

"And I will respect your decision, Kieron, but I do not think you have given yourself the time or space to think it through—" I started to argue with him, but before I could finish my thought he had me pinned face down, bent over the table.

"Do. Not. Question. Me." His voice was threatening, but he had not hit me yet.

I swallowed my shock and continued anyway, "You can do this without Cade and come back and remove him as a threat after you have taken your throne. From what Orion and Zealand said, you are putting yourself at risk by becoming one of the Undead. Sure, most of it might be temporary, but it is still a risk." I braced myself for him to hit me. He didn't. I kept going, "What if Cade allows you to be turned and then does not follow through on his end?"

"Then I will stake him to the walls of this palace." Kieron gritted out and his hand released me. I stayed bent over the table. My body was trembling. "Stand up. I am not going to spank you." Kieron said, his voice soft.

I slowly straightened up and turned to look at him. "I am not questioning your decision, Kieron. I am trying to be a sounding board for you. To be someone you can talk through things with." I forced myself to meet his gaze as I spoke to him, but my voice was shaking.

"I am already a monster, Genevieve. What difference does it make if I make it official by becoming one of the Undead? I need their support. I owe my life to many of them." Kieron crossed his arms and sat on the back of the couch.

"You are not a monster, Kieron." I argued back. We had this conversation before and he still did not get it.

"What is the difference between beating and raping you and the way I have punished you for breaking my rules? Not a damn thing." Kieron's voice was angry.

"Spanking me is not the same and I agreed to the damn rules." I said between my teeth. Even if they were dumb, I had *agreed*.

"And it was *wrong*. I was scared you would leave and I would lose you." He said, his voice breaking.

"Here I thought you just wanted to order me to have sex with you." I replied sarcastically.

"I told you I would not hurt you again. That I would never force you into it again." Kieron said with a bite to his voice. "I am not going to punish you. I am not going to touch you like that ever again without your consent."

We stood steps away from each other just staring. Heartbeats passed. "See. Not a monster." I finally said.

He let out a breath and his shoulders dropped. I took two steps to him and took his face in my hands, "You have to make the decision for yourself and for your kingdom, Kieron. I support you either way."

CHAPTER 35

Genevieve - A Few Years Ago.

The short blue dress I was wearing was exactly something Chad would have picked out for me and so were the strappy heels. This day had been over a year in the making and only one of us would survive it—or neither of us would. The others had died quickly. That was the problem with males. When they sought revenge it was always about who had the bigger dick. They want to talk or torture to show their dominance. They wanted to draw it out. I did not have a taste for that. If you had forfeited your right to live, why waste any more time? Bullets through the brain from a reasonable distance away took care of the three accomplices. They all deserved slower deaths than I gave them, but I needed them dead and I needed to stay alive to finish what I started.

I walked right in through the front doors of the capitol building. I knew where I was going, I had studied the blueprints of the building. The guard in the entryway just eyed me up and down before saying, "He's been expecting you." *Of course he has.*

I nodded and continued down the hall to the large double doors that marked the entrance to the Commanding Chief's section of the building. Offices flanked the large hallway down to the door that was Chad's office. I had not brought any weapons and it was obvious by the skimpy clothes I had on that I was not hiding a damn thing. Secretaries watched me silently as I walked down the long hallway and stopped outside of Chad's office.

"Is he in?" I asked his secretary. She nodded to me then looked at the young warrior who was guarding the door. He simply opened the door for me to enter.

There Chad was, standing looking out the window just like he had been the first day I was summoned to his office. It had been more than ten years since I had seen him and it was clear he still spent a lot of time looking at himself in the mirror. "I sent for you over a year ago." He said in greeting.

"Has it been that long?" I asked, faking boredom. I knew exactly how many days it had been.

I watched as he left the window and took a seat at his desk. "So you have finally come home then?" He asked.

"Depends. Are you going to tell me if you killed Eli because he was Eli or because I did not come when you summoned me?" I replied as I looked around his office, taking in every detail—the obvious wealth it took to buy all his furnishings and decorations. He had let his people starve and die all while spending their money on gaudy furniture and gold plated nick knacks.

"I thought I made myself very clear. When I summon you, you

come." He said as he laced his fingers through each other. He didn't answer my question.

"And what about my kid? Was that on purpose or an error?" For this question I stared him directly in the eyes.

"An unfortunate mistake." He stared back, his voice held no emotion. We stared at each other in silence. *An unfortunate mistake.* I was not sure what answer I expected, but I knew no matter what his answer was it would not fix anything. It would not tame the pure rage that pulsed in an eerie calm through my veins.

I broke his gaze and walked over to the bar cart next to the window. "I hope you weren't attached to any of the males you used." I picked up an expensive looking crystal decanter and poured myself two fingers of amber colored liquor. I replaced the stopper.

"They were all expendable. I had a feeling you would need to take some anger out afterwards." Chad replied coolly. I could feel his eyes watching me. I weighed the decanter of liquor in my hand. Then I smashed it against the wall, shards of crystal and liquor spraying across expensive paintings and rugs.

I silently picked up the glass of liquor and took a sip as I turned to meet Chad's eyes.

"Feel better?" He finally asked.

I chuckled and set the glass back on the bar cart, "Much."

"Good. Come here. Let me look at you." He commanded me.

I obeyed. I stepped around his desk as he pushed his chair back to make room for me to stand between him and his desk. I sat on the edge and leaned back. He was too busy looking at my legs and the short skirt to notice I slipped his bone handled gold plated letter opener into my hand. Chad always had a taste for extravagant things.

I lifted my foot and pushed his knee to the side so that he was sitting with his legs spread in front of me. My rage built in me as I saw him look at me with lust.

I pressed the ball of my shoe gently into his crotch and he groaned. I pressed a little harder. "Good girl. I knew you would come back to me." He said gruffly.

I removed my foot and hiked my skirt up with one hand before straddling his lap. His hands caressed my hips and I ran my fingers through his hair before grabbing a handful and yanking his head back. I felt his cock bulge beneath me as he groaned again. "I have missed you, Genevieve." *What a fucking idiot.* Chad had always been arrogant—arrogant enough to think I would never do anything to him. Arrogant enough to trust me—the killer he created—on his lap and think it was not a death wish in itself.

His fingers found their way under my skirt and traced the edge of my tiny underthings. I just stared down at him, schooling my face to show calm desire instead of the rage I felt. Then Chad licked his lip, "I killed Eli to remind you that you are *mine*. You seemed to have forgotten. You will never forget again. Have I made myself clear?"

Something deep within me rolled through my center and crashed against my skin as if threatening to break through and blow the entire world to pieces. *My family had died because of me.* I let my rage burn in my eyes as I spoke, "You made a very big mistake, Chad." His face flashed confusion at my response—at my sudden change, "You fucked with my family." I stabbed Chad's gaudy letter opener through his eye socket and stirred his brains quickly before pushing myself up and off of him.

I stared at Chad's dead body in his chair. *Fuck you, Chad.* I messed my hair and smeared my lipstick a little as I made a show of moaning and banging things like Chad was getting a good fuck in his office. I tossed things off of his desk as I fake moaned his name loudly. I ended it quickly though. No need to make them think Chad was any good in the sex department. I could give him that one last embarrassment. After another minute or two I slipped out of his office and closed the door quickly behind me. "You might want to give him a minute." I said shyly to his guard who only smirked back at me.

I headed straight for the exit.

CHAPTER 36

Genevieve - Present Day.

The stone table looked like a sacrificial altar. My blood had gone completely cold as we stood before hundreds of the Undead. The large cavern we were in was shaped somewhat like an amphitheater—and we were on the stage. I glanced at Kieron, he only gave me a strong stare and a subtle nod back.

"I am glad you agreed to my proposal, Kieron." Cade said with a smug sneer on his face.

"Let's get on with it." Kieron responded gruffly.

The entire cavern was nearly silent as an older male, his body completely covered head to toe in the bone tattoos, stepped forward—The Death Taker. "Remove your shirt, Kieron, then lay down on the table." His voice was gentler than I would have thought it would be for the male who had stolen death from hundreds of others and oversaw eternity of punishment for the worst kinds of traitors and criminals. No Undead could leave the Eastern Desert without his blessing and yet somehow Kieron had won his blessing to take hundreds of the Undead out of the Eastern Desert for good.

Orion and Zealand stood close on either side of me as Kieron removed his shirt and climbed onto the table to lay down. I winced as I watched The Death Taker pull out a long blade. It glinted in the light.

"He must first shave off Kieron's beard." Orion whispered. I let out a slow breath as I watched The Death Taker expertly shave the beard off of Kieron's face.

"Are you ready, Kieron?" The Death Taker then asked softly. Kieron nodded.

I felt Zealand's hand wrap around mine as the cavern darkened and The Death Taker bent over Kieron. His hands worked quickly as he used bone and a small hammer to tap the ink into Kieron's skin. The room shifted and my vision clouded. I could still feel Zealand's hand and he tightened his grip as I heard him urgently whisper something to Orion.

Then it happened. I was seeing through Kieron's eyes as he re-lived every horror he had experienced and committed. I saw his mother murdered. I felt rough hands holding his small body back and shielding in his magic as it erupted from him in anguish. I saw how Luther and Cade and another male, who I somehow recognized as his father, had broken him and beaten him. I saw the hundreds of prisoners and slaves Kieron had tortured and killed. I saw battles and death and the destruction of worlds. I saw myself. I felt his pain as his hand struck my face—

It was unending horror. Memory after memory of the brutal life Kieron had lived. The pain and darkness he had both endured and caused.

Then suddenly it was over. I was on my knees and Zealand was next to me with his arm around me, "Genevieve, you need to get up. I know you just saw everything, but you need to get up, right now." His voice was urgent and I forced myself to my feet as the giant room came back into focus. The first thing I saw was Kieron. His hands and arms and torso and neck, all the way up to his jaw, were covered with the image of the bones beneath. His body was trembling and Orion was stepping to the table to help him sit up.

"How long—" I started to ask Zealand quietly.

"It was not quick." He replied, his voice hushed. "Something is wrong."

My eyes instinctively flashed around the stage we were on. Something was definitely wrong. More Undead had moved onto the stage with us and their weapons were drawn. The others in the amphitheater were shifting and drawing their weapons also.

"Welcome to the Undead, Kieron." Cade's voice cut through the whispers. "Now that you have joined us, I have one more request." Zealand's weapon was out not a heartbeat later as warriors struck. My elbow connected with one male and I dodged another as I tried to pull my knife, but strong hands grabbed my arms. I was knocked to my knees between two males who held me firmly. Then the commotion stopped all at once.

"I will let all those who wish to join you leave, but I now rule the Palace of the Undead. Oh, and your pretty friend is going to stay here. A fair trade considering many of us have not enjoyed female company in quite some time." Cade sneered.

I looked at the Undead who were holding me, both males looked hungrily back at me. Then I scanned the room to Zealand, Orion, and Kieron. To the other Undead who I recognized as allies. They were all in compromising positions, but all still standing. Waiting. I could see them calculating their next moves.

"I did what you asked." Kieron gritted out as he struggled to stand up from the table. "Now hold up your end of the deal."

"Never make deals with criminals, Kieron. Perhaps this will be your first lesson as king." Cade gestured to the males holding me and they started dragging me across the dirt towards him. "I always knew you were a mommy's boy, Kieron, but I did not think you would find another weak whore from the Mountains to fall in love with. Maybe you won't cry as hard this time when we take her from you."

I saw red. Pure rage filled me as I realized it was Cade who had been holding Kieron as a child and forcing him to witness his mother's death. As I remembered Cade beating Kieron when Kieron was just a child. I could not control the blast of power that erupted from me. Dark light blasted from my pores and the Undead holding me fell back into the dirt. I saw the light still shining from the rims of my eyes as I stood slowly and laid my glare on Cade. Kieron was barely able to stand, but he had already taught me how to end this.

"You can insult me however you like, but there is no place in this kingdom for trash like you." My voice was low and hard and I took a breath—sending my magic to wrap around Cade and into his blood. I felt the steady rhythm of his heart.

Cade's magic pulsed and shimmered around him, "Oh I like a

female who is feisty. It is much more fun." He sneered at me and took a step towards me. His magic lashed out and broke against mine. Cade looked at me in shock at what had just happened.

"I am not here to have fun." I replied. Then I blew him into a billion pieces. Blood rained down and I heard the collective inhale from the other Undead.

I turned and faced the two males who had grabbed me. Both of their eyes were wide. Before their shock could subside, the other Undead moved into action and forced Cade's followers to their knees, blades at their throats.

"Who's next?" My voice echoed through the caverns. I counted three long and silent heartbeats. Undead just stared at me with shock and fear in their eyes. Then I let the light from my magic fade out around me.

"Kneel before your king." Orion's voice echoed around the cavern.

The hundreds of Undead dropped to their knees as one. I watched in awe as each one pulled out a knife and sliced their palm, holding out their fists and dripping their blood onto the earth. It sounded like rain. Then a booming voice I did not recognize cut the silence "Kieron, King of the Deserts, with this blood we are bound to you. May your reign be eternal, casting shadows that stretch across the worlds."

The army of the Undead stood as one.

Kieron's eyes met mine. It was as if the entire room disappeared again and it was just me and him.

"What do you want us to do with them?" Orion's voice interrupted the silence. They still had Cade's followers restrained.

Kieron crossed the space between us and stood over one of the males who had restrained me. He grabbed the male by his shirt and dragged him to his feet. Kieron glared into the male's eyes. Then one hand grabbed the male's neck and the other hooked under his chin before Kieron swiftly tore the male's head from his body. Kieron shoved the male's body to the ground and blood poured from the male's neck where his head had just been attached moments before. The male's hands patted and grasped the ground as they searched for the missing head. Kieron tossed the head out of reach. "Stake them to the palace walls." He commanded, his voice low and lethal.

CHAPTER 37

Genevieve

"Come back later." Kieron ordered Orion and Zealand as he closed the door to our rooms behind him.

"I know, I know. You said blood rain was to be used only as a last resort." I said exasperatedly, as I crossed the room. "I just completely lost it." My body had started shaking—the adrenaline must be wearing off.

"Genevieve." His voice was hard, he was only a step behind me.

I turned to him. "Punish me. Do whatever you have to."

"G. Shut up." Kieron commanded as he grabbed my face and pulled me to his lips.

His kiss had me swoon—nevermind, I was not swooning, I was just passing out. "Shit!" I heard Kieron's voice from far away, "Hang on baby, I've got you. You are just weak from depleting your magic. It is going to be okay, G. Stay with me."

I blinked my eyes over and over and tried to focus on Kieron's face as darkness started to cloud my vision.

"Stay with me, baby." Kieron whispered.

I felt warmth like the hot desert air wrap around my body and seep into my skin. The room became clearer and I realized Kieron was sitting on the ground holding me. "I'm okay." I breathed.

"Yes, you are. You are going to be okay." Kieron said and cradled me against him. "No more blood rain, baby. I should not have taught you—as much as I enjoyed that—no more."

"I'm sorry." I said.

Kieron chuckled, "Don't lie."

"Okay, I am not sorry for doing it, but I am sorry I just lost control. I had other options before I needed to splatter him into the dirt." I said and he pulled back and looked at me.

"Never again and I promise to never put you in a situation where you feel you have to do it again." He said as his eyes looked over me.

"You can't promise that." I responded and wiggled from his embrace, "And I can't promise that either, but I will avoid it at all costs."

He grabbed my hand before I could stand up, "Promise me."

I scanned his face and saw the pain in his eyes. "I promise." I breathed.

I stood and offered my hand to help him up. He took it and stood with me, his body inches from mine. "I felt you with me ... when I was being turned. You witnessed everything, didn't you?" I only nodded in confirmation. He continued, "I am so sorry you saw all of that."

"I'm not." I gave his hand a squeeze, "I am sorry you lived it, twice. And I am sorry if it was invasive, I do not know why I could ... I could not control it."

"I know you could not control it. I am guessing it is because you are my match ... but now you know who I really am ... what I have done ..." His voice caught and I saw the hurt in his eyes.

"I do not think less of you, Kieron." And I didn't. He had survived centuries of hell and somehow still saw the potential for good in his kingdom.

"I do not believe you. I told you before, I am a monster and now I am literally a monster, G." He tried to step back and away from me, but I refused to let go of his hand.

"And I told you, you are not the only one who is a monster, Kieron." I had to tell him. I had never told anyone—not even Eli had known the extent of what I had done. "You are going to want to sit down for this."

I watched his face turn from pain to confusion and I led him to the couch to sit. Then I told him everything. *Everything.* I watched his heart break for me. Watched the disbelief and horror cross his eyes. He never turned away from me. Never pulled away.

"That is why you ... I never could have imagined ... I am so sorry." Kieron said as he searched for the right words to say.

"I did not tell you for you to feel bad for me. I told you to show you that I am the last person who would ever judge you or think less of you for what you have done. I know who you really are inside and you are not defined by all of the terrible things you have had to do ... and even if you were, then I am too." His eyes just scanned my face as I spoke.

Finally he responded, "A letter opener, huh?" I just shrugged my shoulders and he chuckled.

"Do you believe me now when I tell you I do not think any less of you?" I asked. His chin dipped in confirmation. I could see his brain working, processing everything I had just told him. I did not care if it changed the way he thought about me. I only cared that he would stop thinking less of himself. That he would stop beating himself up over the things he had done. Punishing himself for them. "How are *you*? Did it hurt?" I ran my finger gently up his arm.

"It did hurt. A lot. I have never felt physical and emotional pain like that ... I am fine now. I can feel my magic is drained, but I am fine ..." His voice trailed off as his eyes dropped to his newly tattooed hands.

"Come on, let's go look at the whole thing in the mirror. It is beautiful." I said gently and tugged him towards the bathroom.

I woke up and realized Kieron was not in bed. It was still night and I found his shirt draped over a chair, but his pants were gone. I slipped into his shirt and opened the door to the bedroom. Kieron was sitting in a chair by the table. A single oil lamp cast shadows around the large living room.

"Hey." I said as I crossed the room towards him. His tattoos were even more beautiful in the shadows.

"Hey." He replied softly. I could see his eyes were brimmed with tears. He blinked a few times and the tears disappeared.

"What's going on? You weren't in bed—" I started, but Kieron interrupted me.

"When we leave here, you should go back to the Mountains. Ryett sent a message days ago that his mountain cabin is yours." He said, gravel in his voice.

"Kieron—"

"You are afraid of me, Genevieve. Your fear is so strong I can practically taste it. It has just been growing. I am not going to force you to stay. With the Undead behind me I will be able to take the throne. You do not need to stay." He would not even look at me as he spoke.

He had it all wrong. I had not been afraid of Kieron for a long time now. "Kieron, stop. I do not want to leave."

"Do not lie to me, Genevieve." He sounded so defeated. My strong, selfless king was breaking before my eyes.

"Kieron, you have it all wrong." I whispered as I slipped my leg over him and straddled his lap. I took his head in my hands and gently tilted it back so that he was forced to look at me. My thumb caresses his jaw line where his tattoo stopped. "Kieron, I am not afraid *of* you. I am afraid I am going to *lose* you."

I felt his hands gently run along my back. "What do you mean?" He breathed.

"Everything good seems to get taken away from me. I am terrified that if I choose you, then you will be taken away too." I could not take it if I lost him. After everything, I had fallen for him. He understood me and never asked me to change or hide any part of myself. He cared for me and for the people he loved and he would do anything necessary for them. We were two sides of the same coin.

"I am terrified I will lose you, too." He whispered.

Tears welled up in my eyes and a small smile crossed my face. I tilted my head and kissed his lips gently.

His arms wrapped around me as we kissed and I held him back. Finally, I pulled my lips away from his and ran my fingers through his hair, along his cheek, across his freshly shaved jawline, and down his neck. His hand wandered up my thigh and under his shirt that I was wearing.

"You are not allowed to leave me, okay?" I said as I stared deeply into his eyes. "When I am old and you are still young and sexy, then sure, I will let you move on to someone else, but no dying and no leaving me until then."

He only chuckled, "Good thing I am extra hard to kill now." Then his hand wrapped around the back of my neck and he pressed his lips to mine.

My lips parted and we tasted each other. Our hands felt each other's skin and mine made their way down to his pants. I undid the fastenings and pressed the palm of my hand along his cock. It hardened under my touch. His hands found the hem of his shirt that I was wearing and he pulled it up over my head between kisses. Then his head dropped to my breast, kissing and sucking my nipple into his mouth. He flicked it with his tongue then moved to my other breast. I could feel myself aching between my legs for him.

I pulled his head back from my breast and stood up between his legs. Then I slowly dropped to my knees. As I looked up at him I saw the pain in his eyes, the memories of the last times I was kneeling between his knees and how he had hurt me. But I did not fear him. I wanted to worship him—worship his body and show him that I was his.

I tugged the waistband of his pants and he lifted his hips as I pulled his pants down and off. I ran my hands along his thighs and looked up at him again, "I want this. I want you." I said softly. He could only nod in response.

I ran my hand up his hard cock and wrapped my fingers around its thickness. I ran my thumb across the tip before doing the same with my tongue. For all the sex we had had and teasing we had done, we had not done this, yet. Kieron groaned as I did it again. Then I dropped my tongue to the base of his shaft and licked all the way to his tip before sinking him into my mouth. I could hear his heavy breathing and felt his cock twitch in my mouth as I pumped him deeper and deeper. He was so big that I had to use my hands and mouth in tandem.

I could tell by his groans and the way his cock throbbed in my mouth that he liked a tight grip and when his tip hit the back of my throat. I gave him more of what he liked and I watched his face from beneath my lashes. His head tipped back in ecstasy as one of my hands cupped his balls and gently squeezed. He tasted so good and seeing him lose himself in the pleasure of it had wetness growing between my legs. But this was for him. All of it was for him.

"Oh baby, stop, I am going to come." He groaned as his hands pulled my face up and my mouth off of him.

"Good." I said back and sank his cock deep into my throat again. My hand continued to pump him and my other pressed his hip down as his muscles flexed.

His hand grabbed the back of my head and his hips pressed up, shoving his cock further into my mouth. I moaned around him and felt my inner muscles clench in response. He pounded up into my mouth again and again and I let him. I felt his cock twitch and he groaned as he erupted into my throat and I greedily swallowed and sucked until his body relaxed back into the chair. His cock was still in my mouth and I sucked it clean before flicking my tongue over his tip and looking back up at him.

His chest was heaving with his breaths. "Holy fuck, G." He panted as I stood back up and straddled his lap again.

His hands grabbed either side of my face and he kissed my lips. I took one of his hands and tugged on it, guiding it down between my legs and guiding his fingers to feel my wetness. "Do you feel what you do to me?" I asked against his lips. He groaned into my mouth as his fingers rubbed my center and circled my entrance. I moaned back at his touch, but quickly moved his hand off of me, "Tonight was for you." I said with a wink.

His gaze turned hungry, "Can that wet pussy be for me, too?" His hand slid back between my legs, but he paused, waiting for me to agree.

"Mmm, if that is what My King wants, that is what My King gets." I said with a teasing smile. His eyes scanned my face before he pulled my head close and kissed my lips. Then his finger slid deep into me and filled me with bliss.

I kissed him hungrily as he held me close and his finger stroked into me. My hips rocked against his hand and I felt electricity building under my skin. My climax was filling with magic. I pulled my lips back from his. "What if I break something?" I gasped out.

Kieron paused, his hand with his finger still inside of me stopped moving. "What are you talking about, baby?"

"My magic feels like it's going to release from my body and what if it destroys something?" There was no way I was telling him about what had happened when I had been with Ryett.

Kieron's thumb stroked my cheek, "No such thing is going to happen. I've got you, sweetheart. I will not let your magic destroy anything. Okay?"

"Okay." I breathed. His hand behind my neck pulled my lips back to his and he kissed me gently before fucking me hard with his finger. I could only gasp and hold on as he brought me back to my edge in an instant.

When my climax broke over me it was like the world was shattering into billions of pieces around us. I could only feel him —his body, his hand, his lips, his finger inside of me. My magic erupted from me and instead of being contained and held together it wove its way into Kieron's magic and raced outwards from us, pulling us into the stars.

PART 2: DARKNESS RISING

CHAPTER 38

Genevieve

The next morning we were eating breakfast in our rooms inside of the Palace of the Undead. My body was still warm and tingling with a desire I did not think would even leave me. Last night, Kieron and I had slid back into bed together and I had wrapped myself around his body. He was clearly still recovering from being turned and although I wanted nothing more than to feel his cock inside of me, I was just grateful to hear his deep breathing as he quickly fell asleep. He needed to rest and I had made my decision. I could wait. He had more important things to focus on today than slipping back into bed with me. He at least look rested this morning —

A knock at the door interrupted my thoughts. "Enter." Kieron called out. Orion opened the door and stood back for The Death Taker to enter. Then Orion followed him in.

"I expected them to follow you, Kieron, but I did not expect the blood oath." The Death Taker said smoothly as he slid into a chair at the table.

"I do not think that went as any of us expected it to." Kieron responded, "Do they still have your permission to leave?"

"Of course. And just like any blood oath, their immortal lives are bound to you and yet, you can end them if you see a need to. Quite a fitting plot-twist for The King of the Undead, if you ask me. It also appears you are already back to full strength this morning. Impressive." The Death Taker responded with a smile as his fingers drummed the table. After a few moments of silence, The Death Taker continued, "You know, many males have asked me to turn them, many kings have as well. I have never agreed."

"Then why did you agree to turn me?" Kieron asked, his head tilting slightly to the side. His head tilted like that when he was trying to read someone.

"They all wanted to be immortal. They all thought immortality was a blessing, not a punishment. But you, Kieron, you actually believe you deserve punishment for your crimes. This, however, is not a punishment for you and one day you will realize it." The Death Taker said. Then his attention shifted to me, "You were full of surprises as well, my dear." I forced my face to stay neutral as I gazed back at him, "Along with the current King of the Mountains, you might have the strongest mountain magic this world has seen in thousands of years. You might even rival Kieron's magic. Time will tell, but I have a feeling we will all find out sooner rather than later."

I swallowed and thankfully Kieron cut in, "You can leave Cade's followers staked as long as you deem necessary. I trust your decision on how best they should live out their banishments."

The Death Taker's head slowly turned back to look at Kieron again, "Very well. You will do great things for your kingdom, Kieron. The Deserts need a king like you. I will accompany you to the gates of the Eastern Desert when you leave." Then The Death Taker stood and Orion walked to the door with him before closing it behind him.

"The Undead are ready to move at your command, Kieron." Orion said. "We should be able to get to the gates in just over half a day and once we cross, we will move to the outskirts of Aridale in waves so that we do not attract attention."

"Good. We will leave at midday today and arrive outside of Aridale in the dark." Kieron responded. Then he dug back into his breakfast.

Our trip back to the gates of the Eastern Desert was nothing like our trip to the palace. With the army of the Undead with us, not a single living thing got in our way—no Piraveh did either. The Death Taker had insisted on accompanying us to the gates and said he would return to the palace after he had seen us through. Just like Orion had predicted, it took us just longer than half a day to reach the gates of the Eastern Desert. As we stepped through, the landscape changed—red sand stretched in every direction—and the only thing breaking the view was the silhouette of a male and a wolf against the setting sun.

"King. Genevieve." Zain greeted us as the Undead filed through the gates and took their place in a line behind us.

"Zain, what are you doing here? Did Ryett send you?" I asked before Kieron could say anything.

"Ryett does not know we are here." Zain replied and Mintaka stalked his way towards us. I stepped away from Kieron and met Mintaka half way. He gracefully lifted up on his hind legs and placed his paws on my shoulders as I scratched his ears and rubbed his head. With a lick to my face he hopped down and circled my legs, glaring towards the line of Undead behind me.

"I did not expect to see you at my gates so soon." The Death Taker said.

"Max." Zain greeted The Death Taker. *Max.* I would never have guessed The Death Taker's name to be *Max.* Everyone just called him The Death Taker.

"Prince." Max responded. *Prince? Had I heard that right?* Max just called Zain, *Prince.*

Zain and Max both took a few steps towards each other, "Do not worry, I am not here for you this time. Unfortunately, you still have work to do." Zain said calmly.

"Sadly, I do believe you are right." Max replied.

Zain turned to Kieron, "Kieron, King of the Deserts, we are here to help. I have served the Mountains for a very long time, but I am not bound to them. I go where I am needed and right now that is with you."

I turned and watched Kieron study Zain before he spoke, "Then welcome to the Deserts, Zain."

The Death Taker—Max—left us at the gates to the Eastern Desert. Before he had slipped back through he had looked over the body and head that was staked to the gates in disgust. Then he spat at the feet of the body and disappeared through the gates. Kieron gave the order and Orion and Zealand issued commands to various groups of Undead—each folded into the air moments later.

Zealand had disappeared with the first group and now reappeared. He nodded to Kieron and Kieron held out his hand to me, "It's our turn. Zain, you and Mintaka can come with us."

I took his hand and stepped in close. Then the red dunes folded in and we were standing at the edge of a plateau, overlooking a city that stretched through a valley and up the cliffside on the far side. I could see a red stone palace in the heart of the city. The streets and buildings seemed to fan out from the palace in the center in ever growing circles until they reached the city walls.

"I hope your visit to Aridale will be much more enjoyable this time around." Kieron said softly enough that only I could hear. I huffed a laugh under my breath. I did too.

Kieron led me away from the plateau's edge and into the quickly growing camp. There were few tents, but the Undead made themselves busy cleaning their weapons and preparing for the following morning. We would be entering the city at dawn.

We made ourselves comfortable around a fire pit in the center of the camp. Zain sat with us and Mintaka found a place at my feet to curl up. The Undead all watched Mintaka warily. *There are only three ways we know how to kill the Undead*—Kieron's lesson echoed in my head. One of those ways was death by a Great Wolf.

Kieron's arm found its way around my shoulders and I noticed Mintaka stir and turn to eye him. "Will you judge me if I am slightly terrified of him?" Kieron whispered in my ear.

I laughed, "Not at all, but I get the feeling he is not very concerned about you." Mintaka stood and stretched, then without warning, stepped close to Kieron and rested his head on Kieron's knee. I felt Kieron tense, "You should probably pet him. Here I thought you were a dog person." I teased.

"Mintaka is a Great Wolf, not a dog. It is not the same thing." Kieron replied softly. "And the two of us have already met." He slowly lifted his hand and rubbed Mintaka's head. Mintaka's eyes closed as Kieron's thumb stroked between his eyes. *They had already met?* I looked between the two of them. I had never seen Mintaka relax like this with anyone other than me.

"Mintaka is pretty picky, Kieron." Zain said from his seat a few paces away, "He is also a good judge of character."

I squeezed Kieron's leg in confirmation, but before I could say anything Orion was at Kieron's side and whispering something in his ear. "I will be back as soon as I can." Kieron said to me, "I need to make the rounds with Orion before we get some sleep."

I watched Kieron and Orion disappear into the night and Mintaka curled up at my feet again. I turned back to Zain. I had so many questions for him. "Zain, I am glad you are here, so please do not take this the wrong way, but *why* are you here? You said Ryett does not know where you are. What is going on?"

Zain sheathed the final knife he had been cleaning and settled back against the log he was leaning on. "A very long time ago I was told a key with magic from the Mountains would need my help. So I served the Mountains and waited for you, assuming if you had magic from the Mountains then I should clearly wait in the Mountains. Eventually, you did find your way there. But when Ryett came back without you, I knew my time there was over. I have been waiting in this world for you, Genevieve, for thousands of years."

My blood chilled as Zain spoke. "You have been waiting for me? Why?" I breathed.

"I imagine we will be finding out at some point." Zain said with a wink.

"And Ryett—" I started, but Zain cut me off.

"Ryett will be fine. I was rooting for you two, you know. At least that is how I thought this would play out, but it seems I was wrong. It all makes sense now why Kieron came to us when you were in Vossarian's dungeons." Zain said.

"What do you mean?"

Zain smiled, "Kieron is the one who told us where you were. Well not explicitly, but he was the one who made sure we found you. We were prepared to never set foot in Aridale again until Kieron came to me. He risked losing his head, or far worse, to ensure we found you."

I had always assumed Ryett had just figured it out or that it was pure luck he had come for a slave shipment while I was being held as a prisoner. But according to Zain, that was not what happened.

CHAPTER 39

Genevieve

The bone gates to Aridale, the capital city of The Land of the Deserts, creaked open in front of us. The hair on my arms prickled as I eyed the sun bleached male and female remains that made up the towering gate. The city was silent. "Only kill if absolutely necessary. Orion, take the city. Zealand, with me in the tunnels." Kieron commanded and the army of the Undead split in two.

Orion and his warriors filtered into the quiet city streets. Kieron led the rest of us through a wooden door. Zain and Mintaka flanked me as we found our place in the middle of the group. The tunnels were larger than I expected them to be. Eight warriors could walk side by side with room to spare and the ceiling was another two meters above our heads. Dim flames lit our path as we marched towards the palace.

Kieron stopped at a set of wide doors—the Undead readied

themselves—Kieron pulled the doors open and the first line of Undead slipped through. The clash of metal and yelling that erupted told me they had immediately hit resistance. Two more waves of Undead slipped through followed by Kieron.

"Stay close and do not engage unless you have to, Genevieve. Let the Undead do their jobs." Zain said flatly to me as we approached the doorway.

I had not been thinking about whether or not I would have to fight anyone, I was only thinking about Kieron and if he was okay. Of course he was okay. He was the most feared assassin across multiple worlds. I unsheathed two of my knives and we stepped through the doorway and into the chaos.

Blood already smeared the floor and walls of the hall. I stayed between Zain and Mintaka as we dodged our way through the few Undead who were still fighting warriors and assassins in this hallway. As we rounded a corner a palace assassin stepped out and swung his sword at Zain. Zain blocked it effortlessly and before I could blink Mintaka had ripped the male's throat out—blood sprayed across the three of us.

Zain grabbed my arm, "Keep moving." Then he shoved my head down as magic blasted above us. I felt the pulse of magic he sent back and heard the screams a moment later. "Shield us." He commanded and I let my mountain shield enveloped the three of us.

Weapons and magic bounced off as we rushed through the hallways and towards the throne room where the majority of the Undead warriors were also headed—where Kieron was headed.

I saw the tall doors to the throne room down the corridor. The last time I had been in that room I had been in golden handcuffs while I watched Ryett slit the throat of a slave. It all felt so long ago.

"Shield down and conserve your energy. Block and keep moving." Zain instructed. I let my shield dissipate and we wove through the bloody chaos. I watched an Undead get a sword straight through his middle. He only paused and yanked it out before reneging—blood dripping from his body. We ducked through the doors and into the throne room.

Zealand met us just inside the doorway and directed us up steps to the raised outskirts of the room and away from the fighting. I had never seen so much gore, but I guess it was to be expected when both sides were filled with immortal warriors.

I searched the room for Kieron. He was in the middle, working his way towards the throne, blood covered him as he gracefully and easily cut through bodies in his path.

"Rook!" Kieron's voice bellowed above the chaos. "This is between you and me." Kieron let a wave of his magic pulse and heat blasted the room. The Undead, warriors, and assassins all froze mid-battle.

"Here I thought you would just hide behind your army of the Undead rather than face me, Kieron." Rook's voice called out.

"No one is hiding." Kieron responded. "I will fight you for the throne. Let the others keep their lives."

Rook stepped out from wherever he had been and bodies parted to create a clear path between Kieron and Rook. "It must be easy to challenge someone when you know you can't die. How about we go until one of us loses his head. And no blood rain, Kieron, let's have a fair fight." Rook sneered.

"Until one of us loses his head." Kieron responded in agreement. "If you win, we will leave and let you rule as you see fit."

"*When* I win, your followers may leave, and you will stay staked to the city gates as long as I see fit." Rook countered.

"Deal." Kieron agreed. My stomach dropped. I would not let Kieron lose. I would tear the entire room to pieces before I let Rook stake Kieron to the gates.

I felt Zealand's hand on my shoulder, "I know what you are thinking and you cannot. You have to let him do this on his own. He will win."

I balled my hands into fists and let my nails bite into my skin. "He will never be staked to the gates." I whispered between my teeth. Zealand gave my shoulder a reassuring squeeze as Kieron and Rook approached each other and the others backed away, creating a ring for the two males to fight.

◆ ◆ ◆

Kieron

Kieron had sparred with Rook plenty of times over the centuries —he knew every move Rook had—then again, Rook knew every move Kieron had too. Kieron and Rook circled each other, getting a sense of the space the others had cleared for them. Kieron was already covered in blood, none of it his, but it looked as though none of the fighting had reached Rook.

Rook engaged first—the two male's swords clashing as they

connected. This would be a brutal dance and Kieron knew it. They danced the way they usually did, testing each of their movements, strikes, and blocks. Each advance was met with an ease that only centuries of training together would allow. Then a knife whizzed out of Rook's hand and embedded in Kieron's shoulder. Kieron took a few steps back, creating room between him and Rook. "Did not see that coming, did you?" Rook laughed.

Kieron reached up and pulled the knife out, blood dripped from the wound. He weighed the knife in his hand before settling back into his fighting stance. His magic quickly sealed the wound. Rook lunged and Kieron spun, blocking his blow and delivering Rook's knife back to him as he stabbed it into his gut. Rook staggered a few steps and glared at Kieron. "I thought you might need your knife back." Kieron replied.

Then all hell broke loose. Rook had never taken insults well and when his temper rose, he turned into a rabid animal. It was exactly what Kieron was counting on. Rook lunged and the two of them tumbled across the floor. Fists threw punches, knees slammed into bodies, and moments later both males were crouched feet apart and staring into each other's eyes. Then they were on their feet, blades swinging again.

In a fight like this, Kieron knew he had to conserve his magic. Sure the two of them could just blast away at each other until they depleted themselves and Kieron knew his magic would last longer, but this was not that kind of fight. This fight was one of honor and respect. That meant blades and fists. Magic would be reserved mostly for healing and the occasional attack or defense. He knew Rook knew all of this too.

A burning piercing pain followed by coldness washed through Kieron's side as Rook's sword sunk into him. He dropped his own blade and grabbed Rook's arm and shoulder. Kieron could smell Rook's hot breath and feel Rook's sweat under his hands as he pulled Rook closer—allowing the blade to sink deeper. His eyes locked with the blackness in Rook's and he felt the satisfaction leaking from Rook. *The asshole thought he might actually be winning.* Then Kieron cracked his forehead into Rook's face, extracting Rook's sword in one smooth sweeping motion. Then he buried Rook's own sword into Rook's back. Rook staggered away. Kieron watched Rook reach back and extract the sword from himself with a deep yell that echoed in the quiet throne room. Kieron extended his hand and his own sword returned to it.

Genevieve

Kieron and Rook moved so fast I could hardly see their limbs as their swords clashed and their bodies spun in a deadly dance. I watched as Kieron shoved Rook only to quickly turn and deliver a swift kick to Rook's already wounded back. Rook flew forward and crashed to the floor with the force of the blow, but was on his feet not a moment later. Kieron ducked as flames erupted from Rook and blasted over his right shoulder. The air rippled as Kieron sent a blast of his own magic back and Rook dove out of the way.

Rook tossed his sword to the ground and moved his knife to his dominant hand. "Come now, Kieron. I never knew you as one to shy away from close combat." Rook said as he circled in on Kieron. Kieron tossed his own sword to the ground and simply raised his weaponless hands, palms up, to Rook. With a small twitch of his fingers Kieron beckoned Rook to fight.

I watched in horror as the two males brawled. Fists connected and so did kicks. Rook's knife not only delivered wounds to Kieron, but Kieron used Rook's own knife against him too. I gasped as Rook connected with Kieron in a blast of magic and Kieron's body slammed against a pillar—the onlooking warriors barely stepping out of the way in time. Zealand squeezed my shoulder, either in reassurance or maybe to keep me from rushing into the fight, as Kieron slowly got back to his feet.

My eyes darted back to Rook, who although he had just delivered a terrifying blow, was slightly hunched, with one hand pressed against his ribs as if he was in pain. Kieron took his time approaching Rook. Both of them were breathing heavily. I turned to bury my head into Zealand's shoulder as Kieron and Rook took their fighting stances again. I could not keep watching.

Blood slicked the floor and it dripped off of both males. The fight had lasted far longer than I had expected and both males had received wounds that would have been fatal for anyone without immortality. It was obvious why Voss had chosen Kieron and Rook to be his top assassins—the fight had been brutal. I had to turn my head away multiple times, only to extract myself from Zealand's steady shoulder moments later to see what was happening. My hands were shaking from the stress of watching Kieron fight. I had witnessed battles and fights and far worse—I had even participated in worse—but this, this was something else entirely to watch the male I loved in a brutal battle for his life.

Kieron and Rook circled each other again. Rook struck next, but in a few quick movements, Kieron had Rook disarmed and on his knees with Rook's own knife blade pressed to his neck. Rook was absolutely still. In one movement Kieron could behead Rook, but they both were frozen. Kieron held Rook from behind with Rook's head cranked back and his neck exposed. The entire throne room was silent. All I could hear was the labored breathing from both Kieron and Rook. "Do it!" Rook yelled. It was the acceptance of his defeat. Kieron remained unmoving, but I saw his knuckles whiten as he squeezed the handle of the knife harder. "Do it." Rook gritted out again. Then Kieron sliced a small wound across Rook's throat and withdrew the blade, shoving Rook to the marble floor.

"I am the King of the Deserts." Kieron said as he walked a circle around Rook, his voice boomed and echoed in the silent throne room. He stopped in front of Rook. "And a better kingdom starts now. You will leave here and go to your home in the south to live out your miserable life, Rook. You are officially relieved of your duties to the crown. If I learn you are acting against my rule and law, I will end you."

Rook's eyes flashed with surprise as he looked up at Kieron. Kieron continued, "If any of you do not wish to serve under me, this is your chance to leave as well. As long as you live peacefully, you may keep your life." A few feet shifted, but no one left. Kieron turned his eyes back to Rook. "Get out." He commanded. Rook slowly stood. I saw his hesitation, but then he gave a small dip of his chin before folding into the air and disappearing. "Anyone else? This is the last chance I will give you." A handful of warriors disappeared a moment later. Kieron scanned the room. "Commanders, we will meet this afternoon. Get this place cleaned up."

CHAPTER 40

Genevieve

After we had all cleaned the blood off of ourselves—and I had anxiously watched Orion use his magic to heal Kieron's remaining wounds—we were settled back into the throne room. A large table had been brought in for the commanders to sit at, with Kieron at the head of the table.

Kieron had spent the better part of the afternoon and into the evening meeting with various people who ran the palace and the commanders for both the assassins and the warriors who chose to remain in the city and under his leadership.

I had watched quietly from a seat against the wall, Zain and Mintaka at my side. Most of the discussion was far over my head, mentioning names of people or places I had never heard of, but I could tell there was no resistance to Kieron's orders. It occurred to me that these males were used to following what Kieron ordered them to do—they respected him.

Through it all, one thing had been made very clear to them: The Deserts would be changing and they were to change with it. Kieron did not have to explicitly state what would happen if they did not follow his orders. They all knew the potential consequences.

As the last of the commanders shuffled out of the throne room, Kieron leaned back in his chair and let out a sigh. "That went well, Kieron." Orion said as he closed the door.

"It did." Kieron agreed. "Let's get everyone settled in and fed. Tomorrow we will celebrate, then we will get to work."

Orion nodded and Zealand joined him near the door.

As we all exited the room, a female waited for us in the hall. She was tall and her blonde hair hung down in waves past her shoulders. Her dark brows and lashes made her features striking. "Rooms and barracks have all been arranged and assigned, Kieron King of the Deserts."

"Thank you, Kamari." Kieron smiled at her.

"Of course," she responded, "What else can I do for you this evening?"

"Please take Zain to his rooms. Then you should rest. We have a lot of work ahead of us." She nodded at Kieron's reply. Then she gave me a smile before dipping her head to Zain. Zain and Mintaka followed her down the hallway and out of sight.

"We will see you in the morning, Kieron." Orion said and he and Zealand left as well.

I followed Kieron down hallways and corridors before he stopped at a doorway. "This room is yours." Kieron said as he opened a door to a massive bedroom.

I looked in at the beautiful white blankets, throws, and pillows that covered the grand four poster bed. The plush armchairs tucked in a corner that would be perfect for reading— "And what's wrong with your room? Is your bed too small?" I asked.

"You do not need to sleep with me anymore. You are safe here." Kieron responded.

"And if I want to sleep in your bed?" Kieron just stared at me, so I continued, "I thought I made it clear when we were in the Eastern Desert—"

"I did not want to assume you would continue staying with me. I wanted to give you a choice." Keiron cut me off.

"Do you not want me to sleep in your bed?" I asked, my voice breaking—my heart breaking. *Had Kieron changed his mind?*

Before I could spiral further, Kieron stepped close to me and wrapped his hand around the back of my neck. I looked up at him, my eyes threatening to water. "I am trying to be better, baby." He said and he dipped his head until his lips brushed my cheek. Then he whispered against my ear, "But you know exactly what I want."

"And if I want that too?"

The hall folded in and we were suddenly standing in a grand bedroom. There was a sitting area on one side and a massive bed on the other. Glass doors led to a huge balcony that looked out over the city. I looked around in awe before Kieron's hand guided my face back to his. "I have let you go twice before, I will not be letting you go again." He said, his voice low and serious.

"I do not want you to let me go." I breathed.

"You do not get to change your mind." It almost sounded threatening. His eyes were scanning over me, reading every reaction.

"I won't change my mind." I responded. I wouldn't change my mind. I had told Kieron the bar for my love was high, but he had surpassed any threshold I had set. He saw me exactly for who I was and showed me exactly who he was. I wasn't settling, I was choosing to be happy again.

"Forever is a very long time." He countered as his thumb gently stroked my cheek.

"I hope it is."

"And if I can't hold back? If I can't continue to contain myself with you?" He questioned.

"I do not want you to ever hold back." My breath caught as I said the words. My entire body tingled and hummed with energy.

His hands held my face and his eyes studied me before he gently kissed my lips. His tongue teased into my mouth and I stroked his tongue with my own. My body sunk against him and my hands grabbed his shirt at his waist.

He pulled my leather jacket off and lifted my shirt over my head. I laughed as we struggled to peel the tight bra I was wearing off. Then I returned the favor as I tugged his shirt up and off between our kisses. Kieron's hands ran over my body sending electricity through my skin. He squeezed my ass before he undid the fastenings on my pants and pulled them down and off of me along with my underthings.

Kieron pulled my naked body close as he kissed me deeply. His strong hands wrapped around the back of my neck and held my head as he kissed me. My entire body ached for him. I had been aching for him for weeks. Our hips pressed against each other's and the warmth from his body consumed me. My fingers dug desperately into his back as I kissed his lips. His lips pulled back from mine with a gentle bite to my lower lip and he looked me in the eyes.

"Do you trust me, baby?" Kieron asked, his voice low. Both of our breathing was ragged and laced with need. I dipped my chin, yes. "Will you do what I tell you to?" I gave him a questioning look, but nodded again. "I am going to tie your hands, legs, and ankles together, then I am going to make you come so many times you will not be able to stop trembling. So if you trust me and will do as I say, I need to hear you say yes."

My heart pounded in my chest. Warm electricity coursed through my entire body at his words. "Yes." I breathed.

"Thank you." He said with a hungry smile. Fire lit in his eyes as he took a step back from me and smooth black ropes appeared in his hands, "Now be a good girl and get on your knees."

My knees nearly gave out as my entire body pulsed with arousal at his command. I wanted his lips and mouth and tongue tasting me as I tasted him. I wanted his hands on me, his body pressed against mine. I wanted my legs wrapped around him as he buried himself inside of me. We both had waited too long for this and the pure desire in his eyes as he stared at me had my insides lighting on fire. I slowly dropped to my knees.

Kieron walked behind me and knelt down. Quickly and efficiently he tied my hands to my thighs and to my ankles. I could barely raise an inch. His fingers traced the lines of my body as he kissed up my shoulder and neck. I could feel my skin pebble under his warm touch and my aching need for him grew. My body arched and moved with his hands—begging him for more. Then he playfully gave my ass a spank. I wanted more. Needed more.

He rose and walked back around me so he was standing in front of me. My chest rose and fell as I looked up at him, my eyes begging him to touch me. I could see his cock bulging in his pants and it made my mouth water. He undid the fastenings and freed himself. I involuntarily licked my lips as I watched him stroking himself in slow long pumps. He stepped close and threaded his fingers into my hair, gently pulling my head back so that I was looking up at him.

"Open your mouth." Kieron instructed. It was that low coaxing tone of his that had me cursing under my breath at the almost intolerable wave of electricity it sent washing through my core. I opened my mouth. "Stick out your tongue." I did. He spit and it fell from his mouth onto my tongue. Before I could process what he had done, he rubbed the tip of his cock across my tongue where his spit had landed and pressed firmly on the back of my head. I opened my lips further to take his cock into my mouth. "Mmm that's it, sweetheart." Kieron groaned and he continued to stroke himself as he pressed his cock deeper into my throat.

I wanted to touch him, to stroke him myself, but I was completely at his mercy. It was driving me crazy that I could not touch him—that he was in complete control and that I would desperately do anything to meet his every desire. He slid his cock out of my mouth. I whimpered and opened my mouth for him. I wanted him to put it back in. He chuckled, "Do you want more?" Kieron's hand released my hair and firmly grasped my chin. His thumb teased into my mouth. I gently bit down on it as I nodded. He slowly pulled his thumb out, dragging it along my teeth and my lip. I was going to come right here, knelt on the ground with his cock in my face. His hand wrapped around the back of my head again as he slid his cock back into my mouth.

I moaned around him as he pumped into my mouth and throat. Between my legs ached for him—my whole body ached for him. I pulled against the restraints in my need for more of him, my fingers flexing then balling into fists. "You are sucking my cock so good, baby." He groaned out. My fingers splayed—now I was going to come from his cock in my mouth and looking up at his beautiful body. My back arched as my body begged for touch. "Relax now, sweetheart, I am going to pound your throat hard."

Kieron gave me a moment to process his words before both of his hands moved to the sides of my head and he pounded into my throat. Rope snapped tight on my wrists and ankles as I took it. And just when I thought I could not take anymore, he gave a final thrust and pulled out. I gasped for air as his hands pressed my head back and he dropped to his knees to kiss me. "You are being such a good girl for me, G." He whispered against my lips as his thumbs gently brushed away the tears that had involuntarily spilled from the corners of my eyes.

I was going to come completely undone. I had never willingly given up so much control and I loved it. I would let Kieron do whatever he wanted to do to me. I would submit completely to him. Surrender everything.

His strong arms scooped me up and laid me on my back on his bed. My wrists and thighs and ankles were still tightly secured. "Open your legs for me, baby." Kieron said in that low coaxing voice of his. I slowly let my knees fall open. "Yes, just like that. You are so fucking beautiful." He groaned and his head dropped between my legs, his tongue licking up my center. I let out a moan as my back arched and pleasure washed through me.

"I love how wet you are for me." Kieron breathed and his fingers rubbed circles on the bundle of nerves at the apex of my thighs.

"Mmm Kieron—" I moaned as my hips bucked.

He slid a finger into me and I felt my magic wash like a wave through me. "Yes, G. Let it out. I've got you." He coaxed as his finger curled and stroked firm long strokes inside of me. He brought me swiftly to my edge as I gasped and my eyes rolled back in pleasure. His mouth dipped to me again and his tongue flicked over me. I felt limitless as pleasure washed through my body, sending tingling electricity and warmth over my skin.

I cried out as his fingers and tongue took me over the edge. My body shook with my climax as Kieron's tongue firmly circled my clit. Kieron kissed and gently bit my inner thigh as I came down from my edge, warmth and electricity still tingling through my body as my breath calmed.

Then Kieron lifted me and flipped me over so I was on my knees with my chest and face pressed against the bed. My ass was in the air with my wrists and ankles still tied up tight. Kieron's hand stroked my ass then I felt the rope around one ankle release. Kieron guided my shin down to the bed before doing the same with the other.

I shifted onto one shoulder and twisted my head so I could look back and up at him. His eyes stared into mine as he rubbed the tip of his cock against my wetness. "I want you inside of me." I breathed— I begged—as I pressed my hips back into him.

A small smile crossed his lips and his eyes lit as he pressed the tip of his cock against my entrance. "Yes? Is this what my good girl wants?" He asked—teasing me like he might not actually give it. He *would* give it to me. I waited too long to feel him inside of me again.

"Mmm, yes. Fuck me, Kieron." I moaned up at him. His hand connected with my ass as he spanked me. A cry burst from my lips at the sting and his hand rubbed over the hurt. "Again." I breathed. He obliged and I gasped. I needed him in me. I needed him to fill me. Right. Now. "Kieron—" I begged.

"Say 'Yes, daddy.'" He commanded as he rubbed his tip over me. Then he slapped his cock against me. I could not wait any longer.

"Yes, daddy." I begged again.

His tip pressed into me and I whimpered at the stretch. "Breathe, baby." Kieron coaxed. He pressed further, "That's it. I know you can take it. That's my good girl." He slid back out to his tip before pressing further back in. I rocked my hips and he slid out a little before I pressed back into him. His hands grasped my hips and he groaned as I let him bury himself inside of me. He paused and let my body shudder as I relaxed around him. He slowly thrust in and out again and again—drawing it out and letting me feel every inch of him inside of me. It was bliss and I was lost in the pleasure he was giving me. Then he spanked my ass and pulled out. "Fuck G, you feel so good."

"Kieron, please—" I needed him back inside of me. He thrust back in and his hands tightened on my hips. His cock pounded into me and I cried out as he hit the perfect spot.

I felt his hand under my chest and he lifted me so that I was sitting back against him, his cock buried deep inside of me. "Look at how beautiful you are." He whispered against my ear. Through the light emitting from the rims of my eyes I saw there was a mirror in front of us. I was glowing a dark light and as it poured from my body it mixed with Kieron's shimmering desert magic that was emitting from him. Together the light and the shimmering heat made the entire room sparkle. I ran my eyes along his tattooed hands and arms that held me against his body and down to where his cock entered me. He pressed up into me and I slid further down onto him.

A knife appeared in one of his hands and he gently cut the rope that wrapped my wrist. I raised my hand to thread my fingers on top of his where he held me across my middle. Then he cut the rope that wrapped my other wrist. My hand found its way to the back of his head and I pulled his lips to mine. I gently bit his lower lip before slipping my tongue into his mouth. We *were* beautiful.

I rode his cock as he thrust into me and the room disappeared around us. I saw jagged mountains, bubbling streams, glaciers, and forest fires. I saw the soil rejuvenating with new growth among the fire's ashes, mountain meadows covered in wildflowers, and light snow catching on evergreen branches. I watched the desert sand crack in drought, the sun rise and set against a red rock plateau, bones whiten under the heat of the sun, and a desert storm flash lightning across the sky. Then I was pulled into a storm of stars and comets. Green and purple and blue light swirled around us with the stars. Then the stars faded and there was nothing and everything, the beginning and the end, and only the two of us.

Worlds stopped as our bodies became one—as we drew out the pleasure and ecstasy between us. Our magic was free and flowing.

And I could only feel him. I was safe and free. I was his and he was mine.

Kieron

Kieron already knew that sex with Genevieve was great—but this—this was something else entirely. Not only did he feel his own pleasure, but he could feel her pleasure as well. He held her trembling body against his as his room came back into focus from wherever their magic had just taken them.

"Kieron—" she breathed.

"I've got you, sweetheart." He said against her neck and she moaned for him as her body shuddered again. He had in fact kept his word of making her come so much she would be trembling. He guided her hips up and slid himself out of her as she let out a small whimper. Then he gently laid her on his bed.

She had given him everything—completely surrendered to him. Kieron could hardly believe this was happening. He had become king and his perfect female was here in his arms. He ran his fingers along her beautiful soft skin and turned her chin to him so he could kiss her lips. Genevieve was now his and he would never let her go. "Let's get you cleaned up, baby." He breathed.

"Mmm." She responded with a small satisfied smile, then she leaned in to kiss him again.

Kieron scooped her up and carried her to his bathroom. He had a large bath that looked out over the city—it was large enough to be a private pool. These rooms were Kieron's sacred space in the prison the palace had been to him for centuries. He had rarely shared his space with others, but he was beyond willing to share it with Genevieve.

"This bath is amazing." She said softly as he stepped down into it and dipped their bodies below the surface.

"I think my rooms are the only place in this palace I actually like." He said and wrapped her legs around his waist. He was not ready to stop touching her. She ground her hips against him and he chuckled, "Hey now, I want you to be able to walk tomorrow."

"Why would I need to be able to walk?" She asked and bit his lower lip.

Kieron let out a groan of desire and lifted her ass so he could slide his cock back inside of her. He could only gasp with the pleasure of being inside of her again. Her head tilted back as he filled her. She was going to ruin him. Kieron had held back for so long waiting and hoping she would choose him and when she had it had been better than he ever could have imagined.

After he had fucked her slow and deep in his bath, they crawled into bed together and he held her while she fell asleep. He was listening to her deep even breaths as he said a silent prayer asking that she never be taken away from him.

CHAPTER 41

Kieron

Kieron woke to someone banging on his bedroom door. With the wards he had in place only two other people could enter his rooms without his permission—Orion and Kamari. "Kieron, the boys were too scared to wake you two up, so I am here. Time to get up." Kamari called out.

Kieron chuckled and kissed Genevieve's head. "Sorry, baby." He whispered. Then he called back to Kamari, "Give us a few minutes, Kamari!"

"Yeah, yeah. I'll be here." She called back.

Genevieve stretched out her body then planted a kiss on Kieron's chest before she started to press herself up. Kieron could not help himself as his hand firmly grasped her neck and pulled her into a kiss. She let out a soft moan and melted into him. They were going to need more than a few minutes. He rolled on top of her and his eyes scanned her face, looking for any hint of regret after last night. Only a hungry desire met his gaze as she wrapped her legs around him.

"Unfortunately, I think I can still walk." She whispered.

Kieron smiled and kissed her again, "I guess we need to work on changing that."

It had definitely been more than a few minutes by the time Kieron and Genevieve had finally thrown on some clothes and ventured out of his bedroom. Kamari was sitting at his table waiting patiently for them. She gave them both a kind smile, "Good, you are finally up. Kieron you have business with the boys and while you take care of that, I am taking Genevieve for a spa day before the celebrations start this afternoon."

"Genevieve, meet Kamari, Zealand's sister and the best healer in all of Savengard." Kieron said as he took a few strides across the room and gave Kamari a big hug. Kamari was one of the healers in the palace who had been assigned to attend to the slaves. She had become an integral part of Kieron's small group of confidants. When Zealand had been banished to the Eastern Desert she had stepped up and made it her mission to do everything possible to help Kieron find a way to get Zealand back and end Vossarian's rule.

"It is nice to meet you, Kamari." Genevieve said.

"You too!" Kamari said brightly and gave Genevieve a big hug. "I hope you are ready for a relaxing morning at the spa because I asked them to pull out all the stops for us."

"I ..." Geneieve gave Kieron a helpless glance, "I have never been to a spa."

Kamari only smiled bigger, "You are going to love it. Come on, we will get you breakfast while we are there."

Kieron only gave Genevieve a wink as Kamari practically dragged her to the door, "Enjoy yourselves!" He called after them. Genevieve was in good hands with Kamari.

Before they closed the door, Orion and Zealand walked through with Hael—Kamari's partner and one of the commanders of the assassins.

"Hael." Kieron said as the two of them grasped forearms. "It is good to see you well."

"Kieron, we are glad to have you back." Hael said with a smile.

Genevieve

I followed Kamari down hallways and corridors and up sets of stairs until we emerged through a set of doors into an open air room with views overlooking the city. Creamy white curtains flowed gently in the breeze and plush chairs dotted the room while a small waterfall and stream cut through the middle. Arched hallways broke off from the main room and a female wearing flowing white clothes emerged from one of the hallways.

"Kamari, Genevieve, welcome." She said, her voice soft and

gentle. "I have set up the sky room for the two of you. There is food and drink waiting for you."

Then the female led us through one of the archways and down a hall. When she opened the next door, my breath caught. She led us onto a large balcony with creamy white drapes that provided shade and privacy. There was a large spread of fruit and eggs and pastries along one side of the balcony. Next to it sat a station with coffee, tea, juices, and sparkling wine. Two large cushioned lounges were placed so that while you sat in them you could look out at the view. I took a breath and smelled eucalyptus and lemongrass.

"Would you like a coffee? Or does this morning feel more like a mimosa morning?" Kamari asked as she floated over to the drinks. "I think it is a mimosa morning." She said—answering her own question—and poured two glasses of sparkling wine, then topped them off with juice.

"Thank you." I breathed as she handed me a glass. I was still taking in my surroundings.

She set her glass on the small table next to one of the lounges and picked up a white robe that had been folded neatly on the lounge. "Welcome to your first spa day. First we get naked. Then we just relax!" I laughed to myself and followed her lead as she slipped off her clothes and into the robe before settling onto the lounge. "First we are getting massages, then mud wraps, then facials, then we will finish with getting our nails done. I have also arranged for our hair and makeup to be done before the celebration starts this afternoon."

"What is this celebration? I know Kieron just became king, but how does all of this work?" I asked.

"For most in the palace and the city, the celebration today is just an excuse to party and celebrate the new king. Sort of a 'celebrate or pack your bags' kind of deal if you know what I mean." I winced. 'Accept the new king or die' was the translation she did not need to say out loud. "Some of us have been waiting centuries for Vossarian's family to no longer have the throne. When he died —thank you for that, by the way—and Rook took over, things were worse than before. Kieron let those of us he trusted know he intended to come take the throne. We knew Kieron was coming, but we have all been holding our breaths waiting for him. So today we celebrate. Then tomorrow we will start work. You know, all the boring stuff like Kieron setting his new rule and law."

I nodded, but my head was spinning. "I guess I need to find my place in all of this."

"Oh girl, you already have your place." Kamari smiled at me, "This is going to be your kingdom, too." The full weight of giving myself to Kieron hit me all at once. I was focused on just the two of us, but it would never just be the two of us. It would always be us and the kingdom. "Oh, no. No. Don't you dare freak out on me. You two are perfect together and you only need to be yourself." Kamari said as she sat up and faced me.

I was saved from whatever I was about to say by two females dressed in white flowing clothing. It was time for our massages.

◆ ◆ ◆

The morning had been absolutely bliss. I could definitely get used to more mornings like this. Talking with Kamari felt like talking with a friend I had known my entire life. "So what exactly have the boys been up to this morning?" I finally asked.

Kamari laughed, "Well I am sure they went and gave a big pep-talk to the Undead, assassins, and warriors. You know, one of those 'all hail your king' kind of things. Then I am sure they all beat their chests, did some sparring, and have already thrown back a few beers together. Hael, my partner, he was the one with Orion and Zealand this morning, said they would have their pre-party and wait for us in our rooms."

I laughed too, "Are you serious?"

"Completely. Real teenage male dick swinging veiled in a disguise of official business." Kamari said sarcastically. "I would not plan on them calming down for the celebration either. It will probably be rowdy, but all a good time. They all love and respect Kieron—even the ones who did not know he was working against Voss—they loved him more than they loved Voss."

"He doesn't act like everyone loves him." I ventured.

Kamari's face became serious, "He has been too busy hating himself to notice." My heart broke at her response, "He has had to do a lot of terrible things to be able to survive until now, but he is a good male. One of the best."

"I had the feeling he was." I said softly and she smiled at me.

"Oh good—" Kamari looked over my shoulder. "Time for hair and makeup and I hope you don't mind, but I selected something for you to wear."

"Okay, turn around." Kamari instructed. She had kept me from looking in the mirror since hair and makeup started. She had even asked me to close my eyes while she helped me slip into the dress she had picked out.

The black, semi-transparent lace and beaded dress hugged my body like it had been made specifically for me. A high slit reached nearly to the top of my left thigh and the heart-shaped bodice made my breasts look amazing. Thin straps grazed my shoulders and the back dipped low. Kamari had selected nude strappy heels to not distract from the gorgeous dress.

My hair hung in gentle waves down my back and was pinned out of my face. The makeup enhanced all of my natural features and made me glow.

"Shit, Kamari!" I breathed, "I look amazing!"

"Yes, you absolutely do! Kieron is going to fall over himself when he sees you." She smiled at me, then turned to grab her dress off of the hanger and started pulling it on.

As far as I knew Kieron had never seen me dressed up. He had seen me naked countless times, but he had never seen me in a dress with my hair and make up done.

"Let's go find the boys before the official celebration begins."

Kamari led us back through the palace to what she told me was her and Hael's rooms. The males would apparently be there between their pep-talk and the celebration. As we arrived we could hear laughter and voices through the door.

Kamari gave a sharp knock and then pushed the door open. The room had twenty or so males inside—they all turned to see who was joining them and the entire room fell silent.

Kieron stood as he saw me. His hand raised to cover his mouth and when it fell I had never seen such a big smile on his face. He crossed the room slowly and stopped in front of me. I admired the black suit he was wearing. The black shirt beneath and his freshly trimmed hair. His beard was already growing back and he had rough, but neatly trimmed stubble on his face. He looked unbelievably handsome. I realized I had never seen him dressed up either. I scanned up his body and I looked up at him as his hand gently grasped my chin. Then it slid behind my neck and his other around my waist as he pulled me into a kiss.

The room erupted in cheering. Kieron gently pulled back from me, "You look beautiful." He breathed.

"You look quite good yourself, My King." I said with a smile.

He laced his fingers with mine and turned back to the room, "Let's go join the celebration!"

CHAPTER 42

Kieron

The entire room had disappeared when Genevieve walked in. Barefoot and dancing in his kitchen with the hem of her pants cuffed up, her slouchy shirt exposing a single bare shoulder, and her hair messily tied up was still his favorite image of her, but this —this would bring him to his knees. With her by his side he felt like he could do anything.

Addressing his warriors, assassins, and the Undead earlier in the day had gone better than he had expected, but still a few heads had to be knocked together. They had let the males work out any disagreements and grudges in the training rings. Many of the Undead had scores they wanted to settle. Blood was spilled, but no one had lost their life. In the end they had all fallen in line and his commanders had laid out new assignments for the troops with only a little grumbling.

After they had gotten cleaned up, the commanders had joined him in Hael's rooms for drinks before the official party began. Everything felt unreal. He was used to the commanders following his orders—he had led them for centuries—but now they responded to him with even more respect. Like he was their king. He *was* their king. He had been lost in these thoughts when Kamari and Genevieve had arrived.

If the first time Kieron saw Genevieve made him lose his mind, this time separated his soul from his body. Not only was she gorgeous, but the way she carried herself and the power that hummed beneath her skin was magnetizing. He had completely forgotten he was in a room full of people until they all cheered when he had kissed her.

Kieron's hand now dropped to the small of Genevieve's back as he led her onto the rooftop of the palace. The rooftop held an expansive desert garden and the palace staff had transformed it into a beautiful space for dinner and celebrating this evening. Warm lights and creamy white linens made the place glow with welcoming warmth. Additional greenery had been brought in to soften the red stone and gray rock that dominated the garden space. Tables and chairs had been arranged for intimate conversations and allowed space for everyone to mingle. He watched Genevieve's face light up as she looked around in awe.

Genevieve

The evening felt like a dream. Everyone was so happy and kind and Kieron's attention was firmly planted on me. We ate and drank and danced. We sat and chatted with guests. We wandered the gardens and Kieron patiently let me fall over myself with delight as I took in the variety of plants.

Eventually we had ventured to a quiet corner of the rooftop and when I looked out over the city I saw that people were celebrating in the streets as well. "People are really happy you are king, Kieron." I said to him and squeezed his hand.

"People fear me, G. This is just an excuse to party." He replied solemnly.

I turned to him and his hand wrapped my waist as he stepped close to me, "Maybe they do not know it yet, but they are happy. You are going to do great things for this kingdom."

"We are." He corrected as he pressed a kiss to my forehead.

As the party slowed down and guests started to slowly disappear —probably heading off to bed—Kieron took my hand and led me back into the palace. "No one has given you a proper tour have they?" He asked.

"No they have not." I responded, then stopped Kieron so I could remove my heels. "Does that mean you are going to show me now?"

"I would love to." He said. Kieron's hand reached out and took my heels from me. Then the shoes disappeared from his hand.

The palace had four main wings. One was for official business and housed the throne room and various other rooms for entertaining and meetings. One wing was the private residences of the king and his leadership—Kieron's rooms were in this wing. One wing housed the palace staff and slaves, as well as, the facilities that kept the palace running—such as the kitchens and laundry.

The fourth wing was for training and health. It was where the spa was located on the top floors. The lower levels had multiple training facilities. The basement had a now abandoned dungeon and party room—it was where I had been kept the last time I was in Aridale. Thankfully, Kieron did not show me all of this, but gave me a brief tour and kept things focused on places in the palace that I might actually want to be. Most of the decor throughout the areas we walked was dark and stuffy. It looked expensive and that it was meant to look expensive. As we walked down a corridor with open arched windows overlooking the city Kieron took my hand in his.

"I would like to make a lot of changes to this place," Kieron began, "Mostly just rearranging what rooms and wings are used for and a lot of redecorating. What do you think about being in charge of that?"

I stopped walking and laughed, "I am completely the wrong person for that."

"No you are not. You would be good at it." He countered.

"What have we possibly done together that gives you the impression I would be good at redecorating anything let alone a palace?" This was hilarious. I watched Kieron shift on his feet, "Is it because I am a female?"

"No, G. That is not what I meant." He stumbled over his words.

I let him fumble for what to say next before I rescued him, "Kieron, I am only giving you a hard time. I have quite a variety of skills, but decorating is not one of them. Who did your private residence? Your home is gorgeous. Maybe you should have them do the palace too? I would be happy to oversee someone who knows what they are doing, but do not put me in charge of doing it."

He let out a breath, "I am sorry. That did come out very wrong."

"I had to make you squirm a little—" I teased, but before I could say anything else he quickly pinned me against the wall.

"Quite rude of you." He breathed against my neck as he slowly stretched my arms above my head, pinning my wrists against the stone, "I would love it if you would oversee someone. I need a fresh and clean slate here and I do not have the bandwidth to oversee it myself."

My body shuddered as his lips brushed my cheek, "Consider it handled, My King." I breathed.

"Good." He said deeply and released my wrists as he stepped back from me. "Shall we continue the tour?"

My chest heaved as I tried to calm myself. "I think your rooms should be next. I did not get a chance to look around."

He gave me a sly grin and pulled my hips close as the hallway folded in and we were suddenly standing in his rooms. It seemed private rooms across kingdoms had many things in common. Kieron's entry room had a kitchen in one corner with a stone topped island and a dining table. He had couches and chairs arranged into a cozy seating area in front of a fireplace and near the glass wall that led to the expansive balcony—which connected to his room and bathroom—was a grand piano. On one side were the large double doors that led to his bedroom and on the other side were four other doors—a bathroom, an office, a smaller bedroom suite, and Kieron's private armory.

Unlike his private residence, his rooms in the palace were decorated with a more dark and moody palette—browns, blacks, blues, and grays made up the color scheme. It was very chic and masculine, but he did have some plants strategically placed. I wandered towards his bedroom, I had been so busy looking at him that I had hardly looked around.

There was obviously the doorway that led to the bathroom, but there were also his and hers closets. I turned and smiled at Kieron when I saw he had already summoned some of my clothes to fill one of the closets. My heels from tonight sat neatly on one of the empty shoe shelves. "I thought you might need some clothes." He said as he shrugged.

I only chuckled and turned back to admire the large rug that his low bed sat on, the tall worn wooden framed mirror that leaned against the wall, and the blue gray drapes that gently flowed in the breeze from the balcony. "I don't think you should change your rooms. They are perfect." I finally said.

"Don't you want something that feels like you in here?" He asked as his hands caressed my shoulders.

"My clothes in the closet complete the whole vibe you have already got going on." I replied.

He kissed my shoulder, "These rooms are your home now too. I am open to any changes you want to make. We can even pick a completely different suite if you would like."

Your home too. The words made a lump form in my throat. I could not wrap my mind around feeling at home in a palace, but as long as it was with Kieron, my home could be anywhere.

CHAPTER 43

Genevieve

We had gathered in what Kieron called 'The War Room.' It was a large room with a balcony along one side. The room was big enough to fit a round table in the center that could seat twenty people. Today there were not that many people and we sat at a smaller live-edged wooden table that had been set off to the side. Kieron and I were joined by Orion, Zealand, Hael, Kamari, and Zain.

When we had all taken our seats, with Kieron at the head of the table and me to his right, Kieron began, "You all already know pieces of how I want to change this kingdom, but today I want to make some priorities and get your feedback on where we need to start and how best to approach some of these changes."

"I imagine it goes without saying, but some of these changes we will need to roll out lightly through the other commanders. We still do not have a full grasp on who can be fully trusted and who might cause problems if they do not like the changes." Hael said solemnly.

"The Undead do not have a choice, so if need be we can use them while we get a better read on the assassins and warriors." Orion offered. "Kieron, let's hear your plans so that we are all on the same page."

Kieron outlined his vision for the changes he wanted to make immediately. He planned to completely eliminate slavery in the Deserts. This included destroying the entire slave network Luther and Vossarian had created. Next, he wanted to change the laws that oppressed the females who lived in the Deserts—including, but certainly not limited to females who became pregnant outside of a union—and he wanted to restore the kingdom's heritage of healing and arts. He also explained how continuing to keep the kingdom's dominance when it came to armed forces and defense was crucial during this time of change. Unsurprisingly, the Deserts had many enemies and making these changes might only create more.

"I think we start by freeing the slaves. I cannot stomach another day knowing there are beings in my kingdom living in slavery." Kieron continued, a few heads around the table nodded in agreement. "Then we will take down the slave network."

"It would be nice to have both done before your birthday." Orion interjected.

My head jerked to look at Kieron, "When is your birthday?" I had never asked. I didn't even know how old Kieron actually was.

"The first of November." Kieron responded.

"You are kidding." I laughed. I glanced around the table and everyone was looking at me confused. "Is November first not a holiday here?"

"Besides my birthday, no." Kieron gave me an amused and questioning look.

I leaned back in my chair trying to hold back my excitement. "And how old will you be this year, Kieron?"

"Four hundred and twenty. Now what is this holiday you mentioned?" Kieron responded.

Four hundred and twenty years old. "Your birthday obviously." I was not about to spoil the completely epic birthday celebration I was already planning in my head for Kieron. In my world, the first of November was the day of the year when people celebrated their dead ancestors, family, and friends. Skeletons and bright colors along with candles and plenty of food and music was used to celebrate. It was undeniably fitting that The King of the Undead's birthday was on the day to celebrate the dead.

Kieron eyed me suspiciously before turning back to the group, "The first of November is a great target to have slavery abolished. Once that is done we focus on changing the laws for females. It will be easy to do, but more difficult to enforce the changes. We may need to assign an entire unit to ensure these changes happen. And finally, I would like to see if we can use some of the palace for training and education not only for vocational training, but to support the goal of restoring our reputation for having the greatest healers and the best artists."

"We can hand select a unit for law enforcement within Aridale and explore how to do this in the rest of the kingdom." Orion offered. "They can easily enforce no slavery, but the rights for females will surely prove to be more difficult."

Kieron nodded his approval, "Kamari, I believe you might be best to take lead on organizing healers who may be suited to train others and reestablish a healing center?"

"Of course, Kieron, I can do that." Kamari responded.

"I think we might be getting ahead of ourselves." I interrupted before Kieron could speak again. The room fell silent. "I agree these are all important changes that need to be made, but two of three of these priorities are very delicate topics and there will be a lot of resistance to change."

"And we have the best army in all of Savengard to enforce the new laws." Hael countered.

"I believe it. I just do not think that military enforcement is the way to go. I would propose we hold an inter-kingdom meeting with the Cliffs, Lakes, and Mountains before we break any news of ending slavery. From that meeting, we will hopefully have a plan for where slaves may go to start new lives if they do not wish to stay in the Deserts. We also should take down the entire slave network before slavery is ended here. If you end slavery first, it will only give the network a warning that you are coming for them. So step one is to have the inter-kingdom meeting. Step two is to wipe out the slave trading network. And step three would be to abolish slavery in the kingdom."

I paused to see if anyone had anything to say. Everyone just kept looking at me so I continued, "While steps one and two are taking place we can make plans for how to manage the slaves when they are freed—where they will live, how they will make money to begin supporting themselves, etcetera."

"And regarding rights for females and reestablishing our healing center and the arts?" Orion questioned.

"We need to prioritize the laws that need changing for female rights. Some, I imagine, will be pretty black and white, others will be much more delicate to handle. A good place to start would be finding more females who can contribute to the leadership of the city including within the palace, businesses, and any new programs that are being started—such as the healing center and arts and vocational training. Like you already said, Kieron, Kamari is the perfect person to lead that up and I imagine she can find a few other qualified females and males to assist her. The palace and this group advising the king needs to set a clear example of what equality for females will look like. It may take a longer time to make these changes, but the changes will hold if we do it properly."

I turned back from the others to look at Kieron. He was just staring at me. The room was silent for heartbeats. I had the sinking feeling that I should not have spoken up. That I had overstepped.

"Let's take an hour break and think over our options." Kieron said flatly, his eyes piercing into me. I heard chairs push back and a few confirming mumbles as the other stood to take their leave. I slowly stood up also. "Come with me." Kieron said gruffly and his hand grabbed my elbow. A moment later we appeared in Kieron's rooms near his kitchen island.

"Kieron, I am so sorry I should not have opposed your plans." I said as I turned to him. I had majorly fucked this up for him. "I should have kept my mouth shut or better yet, I should have supported the plan you were presenting."

He looked at me amused as he stepped close and pressed me against the edge of the counter. His hand raised to grasp my throat, "I would not have you in that room if I did not want you to share your opinion." He said and leaned in to bite my lower lip.

I was so confused. I thought he was angry with me. "Kieron—"

"I called a break because watching you school the rest of us on how to run a kingdom turned me on so much I could not think straight." His mouth hungrily kissed mine. Then he paused, "Now if you want something different, please speak up, because I am about to bend you over this counter and fuck you until I can focus again."

Oh. *Oh*. My body warmed and trembled at his statement. "The counter is just fine." I breathed. A heartbeat later he spun me around and yanked my pants down. He pressed my chest onto the cool stone and dropped to his knees behind me only to lick straight up my center.

If Kieron had fucked me until he could focus again, he had, at the same time, succeeded in fucking me until I could not think straight. We were now laying on our backs on his kitchen floor breathing heavily. "I like your plan better, by the way." Kieron finally said.

"I don't even remember what my plan was." I breathed.

He laughed and pulled me close so he could kiss my head. "I remember and it is good. We better get ourselves put back together so we can go tell the others what has been decided."

CHAPTER 44

Genevieve

We fell into a routine as we waited for news that the other kingdoms had accepted our invitation for an inter-kingdom meeting. Each morning Kieron and I would enjoy coffee and breakfast together on his balcony. Afterwards he would train with me—teaching me more combat skills and, of course, making me practice using my magic. Then we would find ourselves in The War Room discussing plans for freeing the slaves and changing laws. After lunch Kieron would show me some of the city or we would wander the rooftop garden—the latter had quickly become one of my favorite places. Then it was back to The War Room for more planning.

We would usually eat dinner late, sometimes with the others and sometimes alone. By the end of the day I was usually exhausted, but we always found time to sit together and enjoy time just the two of us before bed. Really the only surprises throughout the day were when and where Kieron would suddenly decide he wanted to fuck me.

Sex with Kieron was amazing. Whether it was quick or drawn out it did not matter. I completely surrendered myself to him and his desires. He made it easy to trust him and one thing was consistent—he always ensured I was willing and completely taken care of. It left me wholly satisfied and yet ravenous for more.

Today it was just Kieron and I in The War Room reviewing plans of the palace and trying to figure out how to rearrange the staff wing so that any slaves who wanted to stay on as paid staff would have reasonable accommodations. Kieron had found a professional decorator who would be meeting me today to walk through the palace and discuss ideas for changes.

"Kieron, I am not changing your rooms, they are perfect the way they are." I argued with him after he yet again told me I could change his space. "Do you want to move your things to a different set of rooms? I can take a look at some of the other suites if you would like me to."

"No, you just keep referring to things as mine. They aren't mine anymore, G. This is all *ours*." Kieron said as he gestured around the room and to the plans of the palace on the table in front of us. "And no, I like the suite we are currently in, but I also want you to feel like it is yours as well and if you keep referring to it as mine then I am going to question whether or not you feel at home here."

I let out a sigh, "I can't wrap my head around living in a palace, Kieron. You have lived here your whole life. It is going to take some time for me to feel comfortable with it."

"What can I do to help you feel comfortable with it?" Kieron pressed.

"Just accept that it is going to be a while. I do not mean anything by it when I refer to things as only yours. Also, they are not technically mine either. I just inherited the pleasure of using them by sleeping in your bed."

"You inherited nothing by sleeping in my bed." There was a stern bite to Kieron's voice. "This all became yours because I choose to be with you and you choose to be with me. Do you think I am comfortable being king? That this palace comes with the title? No. This palace has been a prison to me for centuries. Help me change that, G. Help me make it *ours* and something we both can love."

I could only swallow. He had a point. I nodded, "Yes, okay. Just please be patient with me."

"I can do that." He said gently then turned back to the palace plans, "What should we do with the dungeons and night club?"

I stared at the lines on the plans that showed the area I had been held captive. "Zain told me you were the reason Ryett came here when I was being kept in those dungeons." I finally said.

"Did he?" Kieron responded absently.

"Is it true?"

He turned to look at me, "Ryett was ready to completely cut ties with us. I thought you were either from the Mountains, or because you had helped Sarla, he was the best chance you had of getting out. So I arranged a meeting with Zain to convince them to come for one more slave shipment. Then I made sure they saw you. You know what happened next."

"Did you know he was a match to me?" I asked.

Kieron swallowed, "Not until he saw you. Then I knew."

"That must have been … difficult."

"Very." He breathed.

I scanned his face. He had been willing to let me go so that I could get out of this prison. I would do everything I could to make sure this place no longer felt like the prison it had been for both of us. "Thank you for being willing to lose me in order to save me."

We were interrupted by a knock at the door. One of the palace staff poked their head in to let us know the interior decorator had arrived. I gave Kieron's hand a squeeze and planted a kiss on his cheek before turning to go meet the interior decorator.

I was dragging by the time I had sent the interior decorator on their way and was able to make my way back towards our rooms. Redecorating an entire palace was going to be harder than I could have ever imagined and I was not even the one doing it. I could hardly answer any of the decorator's questions and I was starting to doubt myself—I had promised Kieron I would take care of it and now I was not so sure I could.

"Genevieve!" I heard Kamari call my name from behind me and turned around.

"Hey, Kamari. How are you doing?"

"Oh, girl. You look like you need some wine. What's on your mind?" She asked.

I could only laugh and shake my head. "Kieron asked me to

oversee getting the palace redecorated and I think I am in over my head."

"Ugh, this place is in serious need of a makeover. Let's go up to the gardens and have something to eat and you can tell me all about it." She suggested.

"Yes, please. I should probably tell Kieron where I am going."

"We will send one of the staff to let him know." She said simply. I turned and followed her as we headed for the stairwell that would take us to the roof.

We plopped down on lounges under one of the canopied nooks. The evening was still warm—it seemed like it was always warm in the desert—but a gentle breeze was blowing. A member of the staff arrived and summoned food and wine for us after Kamari had told her what she wanted. Then the female disappeared to go let Kieron know I would be with Kamari for the evening.

It had to have been hours. The stars were bright tonight. I never remembered stars in my world being as bright as they were in Savengard. One thing I appreciated about Aridale was, even at nighttime, the lights of the city were dim and engineered in such a way they did not disturb or drown out the stars. It made it seem like we were not in a city at all. We had long left the topic of decorating the palace—Kamari assured me I was capable of this responsibility and had some helpful insights I would be passing along to the interior decorator—and I was now laughing as Kamari told me about how Hael had convinced Zealand and Kieron to allow him to take her out on a date the first time.

"Well it seems like you two are having a good evening." Kieron's voice made me jump.

"Hey, Kieron, sorry I stole Genevieve from you this evening." Kamari responded calmly as she raised her glass in a salute.

"I'm sorry, it must be really late already." I said and started to gather my things.

Kieron just laughed, "Do not end your evening on my account. I just wanted to make sure you two were still awake up here." I relaxed back into the lounge and looked up at him. He took a step over to me and ran his fingers through my hair before planting a kiss on my head. "Stay out as long as you like. Stay out all night if you want to."

"We just might do that, Kieron." Kamari teased.

"Have fun you two." He said with a smile as he strode away towards the door.

After Kieron had disappeared from the roof, Kamari turned to me, "What was that about?"

"What do you mean?" I asked.

"The way you just about jumped up when you realized it was late. Like you were in trouble. Did you think Kieron was going to be upset? He is not like that, you know."

I let out a sigh. "I don't know what I thought. All of this is just really new between us."

Kamari nodded, "That is understandable. Just don't let him boss you around—he respects you, I can tell, but he can be a little protective of those he cares about."

I chuckled, "He is definitely bossy. I just ... we have just had some ups and downs since we ... first met—"

"Oh like you killing him and then everything he did to you in the dungeons here? I think 'ups and downs' might be under-selling it."

I looked at her in shock, "How much do you know?"

"I know almost all of it." I just stared at her in shock. She continued, "I was the one who gave Kieron the salve to heal your hand. He did not tell me everything, but I immediately knew something was wrong. I have never seen him so messed up." Kamari said gently, "The one thing he did tell me was he thought you must have been through worse. Was he right?"

I nodded in confirmation and looked down at my hands.

"Well, never again. This is a new chapter for all of us, Genevieve. I am glad you get to be part of it and to help us shape what things will look like going forward. I am glad to have you as a friend."

"I am glad to have you as a friend too, Kamari."

CHAPTER 45

Genevieve

"An inter-kingdom meeting is a big deal, Kieron. You will all need to present yourself a certain … way." Zain said carefully.

"And what way is that?" I asked as I raised my eyebrows at him. We had just received word the other kingdoms—Lakes, Mountains, and Cliffs—had agreed to the inter-kingdom meeting. It would be happening a week from today, in The Land of the Cliffs, and I was doing my best to completely ignore the fact that this meeting would put me in a room with three males I had slept with.

"There are customs and unspoken rules when it comes to these meetings. How you arrive matters. There will be a welcome dinner, where everyone will be expected to be dressed in their kingdom's best. The days of meetings do not require such formal attire, but what you wear—what you both wear—will send a message. We need to be sure it sends the right message." Zain said as he paced the room.

"What message are we sending?" Kieron asked between his teeth. I could tell he thought all of this was bullshit. He did not care about things as silly as what message clothing might send.

Zain paused and turned to him, "The message that reinforces the fact that you are the most powerful king Savengard has seen in thousands of years." We just sat silently at the statement, Zain continued, "We also must consider what message you two want to send. It is obvious you are together and do not insult me by arguing about it. Ryett and Beck may not like it or want to accept it."

"Do we need to keep it from them?" Kieron asked carefully as he shot an apologetic glance in my direction.

"You will not be able to hide it from them unless Genevieve does not go to the meeting and that would cause more problems if she stays here. The other option is Genevieve returns to either the Lakes or the Mountains before the meeting and then does not attend or attends with one of the other kingdoms. She can come back here after things are more settled." Zain said as he sat on the edge of the table and faced us.

"I do not feel the need to hide it. They will find out eventually and sooner is probably better than later." I said.

Zain stared at me, considering for a moment, "Okay then." He said finally. "I have just the person to help."

Zain escorted Belinda into the room we had set up with couches and changing areas for Kieron, Zealand, and me. The three of us, plus Zain, would be attending the meetings in The Land of the Cliffs to discuss the slaves. My face lit when I saw Belinda—we were definitely in good hands. "Belinda! Welcome to the Deserts!" I said as I crossed the room and she gave me a warm embrace.

"Thank you, Genevieve. It seems like I might need to update your wardrobe with some more climate appropriate items." She said with a smile.

"I would absolutely love that and you can send the bill to Kieron this time." I responded as I turned and gave Kieron a wink. He just chuckled and shook his head at me.

Zain introduced Balinda to Kieron and Zealand. I watched her closely and she did not even flinch as she looked at the tattoos and shook the hands of both males. "You have your work cut out for you Balinda," Zain started, "but I know you are the perfect person for this job. We have an inter-kingdom meeting approaching with the Lakes, Mountains, and Cliffs—we will be traveling to The Land of the Cliffs for it—and we need our attire to send a very specific message."

Balinda looked over all four of us, "Arrival outfits, formal dinner clothes, and meeting day attire?" She asked. She clearly knew the drill.

"Exactly." Zain responded, "I would expect a welcome dinner and then one more dinner. Two days of meetings."

"Excellent." Belinda said as she tapped her finger against her lips while she looked over the three of us. "And what message are you trying to send?"

"That The Land of the Deserts is strong, trustworthy, and

honorable." Zain said simply.

"Add 'completely badass' to that list too please." I added. Zain and Balinda both laughed.

"That I can do." Balinda responded. "The Deserts have traditionally worn black, is that something you plan to keep?" She looked at Kieron.

Kieron only looked at Zain and shrugged. "I am open to whatever you both think is best."

"Very well. And are we hiding that Genevieve and Kieron are together?" She asked casually. How she knew, I was not sure. Maybe it was just that obvious.

"No." Zain responded.

Belinda's eyes darted between all of us and a smirk crossed her face, "Well this could be an exciting meeting—"

"Belinda!" Zain cut her off.

"Right! Which one of you two is first, I need to get your measurements." Balinda stated as she wagged her finger between Kieron and Zealand. Zealand stepped up.

We received an entire lecture from Balinda and Zain as Balinda took Zealand and Kieron's measurements. She even took mine again, just in case things had changed since she measured me in Ryett's cabin after I had been a prisoner for two months in the dungeons below this palace. All of my clothes still fit, but I was pleasantly surprised to see a few measurements had increased—I had put on a little muscle and healthy weight.

Each kingdom had a traditional color they wore when inter-kingdom meetings were held. These colors went back millenia. Black for the Deserts, emerald green for the Mountains, a deep blue for the Lakes, and a silvery-white for the Cliffs. It was expected that each kingdom would wear these colors for the formal welcome dinner. Most kingdoms continued the color theme throughout their clothing choices for the entirety of their visits.

Just like that day in Ryett's cabin, Belinda summoned racks of clothing and inspected every item. She disappeared and then summoned new pieces. She held up items and glanced at Kieron or Zealand before nodding or shaking her head and putting the item back on the rack or summoning something else entirely. When she was finished, Zealand went first trying on all of his new clothes. Belinda had completely outdone herself. The biggest smile was plastered on Zealand's face as he admired himself in the full length mirrors that showed him every angle.

He tugged on the leather sleeves to the suit jacket he was wearing and inspected the zipper and silver button cuff. His button down black shirt was open a few buttons and tucked into his pants. The leather belt and silver buckle coordinated with the sleeves of his jacket as well as with the black dress boots he was wearing. Belinda had created this outfit for him to wear to the second dinner and he looked magnificent.

"I do not think I have ever had clothing this nice." Zealand said under his breath.

I glanced at Kieron who also had a big grin on his face as he watched Zealand. "Maybe I should commission Belinda to get you a few more things, Zealand. I imagine you will need them with your promotion to being my general." Kieron said casually. Zealand's head snapped up to look at Kieron in the reflection of the mirror. "That is if you accept the position."

"Of course, Kieron! It would be an honor." Zealand said as he turned around.

Kieron rose and the two grasped forearms before Kieron pulled Zealand into a big hug. "Good, because I am announcing it tonight and we will be celebrating."

We finished trying on our attire for the inter-kingdom meetings —Belinda had shooed Zealand and Kieron out before she allowed me to try on my welcome dinner dress. I was glad she did. Zain had proclaimed it was perfect before slipping out himself and telling Belinda where to find him when she was done. The dress was gorgeous and I could not wait to surprise Kieron with it. Then Belinda summoned me another rack of clothing to supplement my wardrobe and provide more desert climate appropriate options.

"I promised Zain I would not tell anyone I was here, but I know Sarla is beside herself and would like to hear you are okay." Belinda ventured quietly as she flipped through the rack of clothing.

I paused with the shirt I was looking at still in my hands and looked over at Belinda, "Well I would not want you upsetting Zain, but I do not mind if you report on me to Sarla. Hopefully, you feel you can tell her I am doing well."

"You do look like you are doing well, Genevieve. It appears to me Sarla has nothing to be worried about." Belinda responded with a smile. I returned her smile and nodded my head in confirmation.

CHAPTER 46

Genevieve

The ceremony to announce Zealand's appointment to general was ... boring. It was so official and stuffy, but I did my part and stood quietly off to the side as things proceeded. Afterwards the throne room erupted into chatter and celebratory cheers. Undead, assassins, and warriors grasped forearms with Zealand and thumped him on the back in congratulations. I did notice more than a few males glaring silently from the outskirts of the room —but there would always be sore losers and those who did not agree with new leadership appointments. I ignored them and stuck closely to Kamari.

"We are heading into the city for drinks." Zealand said as he and Kieron finally approached us. Hael slid next to Kamari and slung his arm over her shoulders.

"You all go ahead, I need to do a few things here first. Plus I don't think many of them will want their king tagging along for the entire night." Kieron said as he looked around the room. "G, you can go with them if you like. I will drop in later and join you all."

"We will look after her for you." Hael teased as he started to lead Kamari away. She grabbed my hand to take me with them.

See you later. I mouthed to Kieron as Kamari pulled me with the group. He just gave me a small smile and a nod.

We snaked through the city and eventually I found myself following Kamari and the others down a flight of stone stairs and through a doorway. The small dark hallway we entered suddenly opened up to a bar with blaring music. Magic must have been keeping the bar noise contained to the main room. The place was already filled with people—many I recognized from the ceremony. Zealand and Hael led us to the bar and a few males departed their barstools. Kamari hopped up on one and patted the seat next to her for me to join her.

It had been a long while since I had been in a bar. It made me smile as I looked around at everyone having a good time. Hael suddenly appeared with four bottles of beer and he shoved one into my hands before handing one to Kamari and one to Zealand. Kamari clinked her bottle with mine and I took sips as I tried to soak everything in—the rowdy males playing games across the room. The small groups that clustered together chatting. The dimly lit hallways that led out of the main bar area. The dark booths where males lounged and the luckier ones had their arms wrapped around females. It was just a normal bar.

I adjusted my shirt and I stepped into the dimly lit hallway as the bathroom door closed behind me. I swayed a little on my feet—apparently the beer was strong here. Water. No more beer. I needed water. "I knew I recognized you." A male voice said. My head snapped up and I saw the male who had spoken leaning against the wall. He pushed off and took two steps towards me, blocking my way back into the main room of the bar. It did not matter what world you were in, being approached by an unknown male in a dark hallway was never a good thing. "I thought Voss sold you and yet here you are at a bar in the Deserts. How about we take some pills and have a good night together, beautiful?"

"No thank you." I said firmly and tried to step to the side to move around him. He stepped with me and moved closer.

"That was not a question." He said as he stepped close to me. I backed away and he just kept coming.

"I said no. Now please move out of my way." Instead of continuing to back away I confidently stepped forward to push past him.

"I don't think I'm going to do that." His voice was low and his hand grabbed mine. I yanked my hand away. I could feel the fear inside of me washing through my veins and my head cleared from the haze the beer had put me under. "You can make this easy or hard. Either way I am getting what I want."

"Get away from me!" I shouted, hoping someone would hear me. Hoping someone else had been using the bathroom and would step into the hallway any second.

He only laughed. "No one can hear you."

I looked over his shoulder down the hallway. No one was there. The hallway was quiet except for the music playing—the sounds from the bar, where people were laughing and talking loudly, were separated by magic. No one could hear me. Then he grabbed for me again and without even thinking I threw a punch. It connected and the male staggered a few steps. I was not going to make this easy for him. I watched anger cross his face as he lunged at me and slammed me into the wall. *Shit. I was hoping he would back down.*

I shoved him back only to feel his hand connect with my cheek then his forearm slam across my throat as he pinned me against the wall. My eyes glared into his and a wicked smile crossed his lips. *Fuck him.* I took a breath reaching inside for my magic—*where the fuck was my magic?* The steady hum, the waves of electricity that normally washed through my body … none of it was there. I panicked and my hands grabbed at his arm that was pinning me. A low chuckle escaped his mouth as he leaned his head closer to mine. *I did not need magic.*

My knee slammed into his groin. His arm released me as he grunted and doubled over. I grabbed the back of his head and drove my knee straight up again as I pushed his head down. Pain shot through my knee as it connected. Then his arms wrapped my waist as he tackled me. My head cracked against the floor as he landed on top of me and I bucked my hips trying to loosen his hold. His hand wrapped my throat and my hand grabbed my other wrist as I drove my arms down against his arm, buckling it at the elbow and giving me a precious second to thrust up one hip and topple him off of me.

I tried to crawl away from him, but my head was spinning and he grabbed at my ankles. His hand found its hold and he yanked me backwards. My legs came out from under me and my body slammed to the floor. I rolled and kicked my free foot into his shoulder. His grip released and I scrambled away.

As I rose to my feet to run, I collided with another male. Hands grabbed my shoulders and I jerked back—"G, baby, it's me. It's me." Kieron's voice brought me instantly back from my panic. His hand grabbed my chin and he turned my head to the side as he looked at my face. I suddenly became aware of the sting from where the male had struck me—and the throbbing at the back of my head where it had connected with the floor. Kieron's hand gently caressed down my cheek and around the back of my neck as he looked over my shoulder and down the hallway. My body relaxed—*Kieron was here.* His hands slid off of me and he stalked down the hallway towards the male.

I watched Kieron yank the male up by the collar of his shirt and drag him from the hallway into the open room of the bar before throwing him to the floor. The crowd moved back as the male scrambled to his feet and turned to face Kieron. Blood was trickling from his nose—probably a courtesy of my knee to his face.

"We are all just here to have some fun, Kieron. I am actually surprised to see you out tonight as you have been avoiding most of us. Are you ever going to fill us in on your plans? Or do you think you are better than us? Do you think you can replace us, the loyal warriors and assassins, with the Undead. Maybe you are just weak. You did let Rook keep his life. Have you gone soft on us?" The male sneered as he thumbed under his nose, taking a moment to look at the blood on his finger before wiping the rest of the blood away with the back of his hand.

"I would think very carefully about what you say next to your king." Kieron leveled back at him in a cold calmness. The male glared back, the muscles in his jaw fluttering as he clenched his mouth shut at the clear threat from Kieron. Kieron continued, "Want to explain yourself and what you were doing in the hallway?"

The male laughed, almost sounding relieved. "What's got you so worked up over some slave whore?"

"You better correct yourself quickly, warrior. You touched the wrong *free* female."

The male glanced at me and then his eyes shifted back to Kieron. Panic crossed his face. "Had I known she belonged to you I would never have touched her."

"Apologize." Kieron growled.

"My deepest apologies, King Kieron. It will never happen again." The male stammered.

"To *her*." Kieron corrected, his voice murderous.

The male looked horrified, but he slowly turned his head to me, "I am so sorry. It will never happen again."

"You so much as look at her wrong, you die. You question my decisions as your king, you die. You break my rule and law, you die. Have I made myself clear?" The room was silent. "Have I made myself clear?" Kieron yelled.

"Yes, king." The male whispered and dropped his head.

Kieron slowly walked towards the male, a long knife appearing in his hand. He stopped only inches in front of him and put his hand on the male's shoulder. The male looked up and met Kieron's eyes. "Good." Kieron said flatly. Then he stabbed the knife into the male's gut and yanked it upwards. The male's hands clutched at the gaping wound in his abdomen as Kieron pulled the bloody knife from the male's sternum and turned his back on him as he walked away. The male fell to his knees and then face first to the floor. Blood pooled under his limp body.

"Don't let one asshole ruin the party!" Kieron shouted and the crowd cheered. Then everyone acted as if nothing happened. "Let's get a drink." Kieron said to me as his hand slid across my back and he pulled me close to his side. His fingers found my chin and turned my face up to him again as he looked over the mark that must have been on my face. I felt warmth like the desert sun warm my cheek and the sting from the hurt faded away.

I let Kieron guide me to the bar where Kamari was waiting, her eyes wide, but mouth firmly shut. I slid onto the stool next to her and she subtly leaned closer, "Are you okay?" She whispered. I only gave a shallow nod. *Was I okay?* I had been assaulted in a hallway after taking a pee and Kieron slaughtered the male in front of everyone. Maybe the male was immortal. Maybe he would come back from being carved open. I did not know how I felt about it all. The bartender slid two bottles of beer in front of Kieron and me.

Zealand appeared at the bar next to Kieron, "Sorry to ruin your celebration, Zealand." Kieron said quietly.

Zealand only took a swig from his beer and turned around to

look at the crowd, "Celebration not ruined." He patted Kieron's shoulder, "What's a party without a little fighting? And from where I stand, you did not start it."

Kieron only chuckled. I just stared at the beer in front of me.

Kieron

Kieron watched Genevieve pull a glass from the cabinet and fill it in the sink. She was staring off into nothing as she took a sip. "You have been quiet. Do you want to talk about what happened?" Kieron asked from across the kitchen island.

Genevieve's eyes slowly lifted to meet his, "My magic is gone." She whispered.

"What?" Kieron was not sure he had heard her correctly.

She looked back at her water and took another long sip, "I tried to use my magic when he attacked me and it ... it wasn't there."

Rage built under Kieron's skin. This was still a kingdom of drugs. Someone had targeted Genevieve and he had not been there to make sure it did not happen, "Who gave you your drinks?" He asked, his voice rough as he tried to force down his anger and think clearly.

"You think I was drugged?" She asked, her eyes darting back to Kieron's. Kieron gave a slow confirming nod. There was no way he would be able to rid the kingdom of all the drugs stashed away, but if he ever found out who had targeted Genevieve he would end them—slowly. "Hael brought the first round of beers, but I honestly did not pay attention to who brought drinks over after that. I don't know, I think it was the servers … I should have been paying attention." She sighed and rubbed her hands down her face.

She had not been paying attention? Kieron wanted to scream at her, but this was not her fault. Yes, she knew better, but this was in no way her fault. He was not mad at her, he was mad at himself. He should have just gone with them.

"Is he dead? Like dead dead?" She asked softly. Kieron just looked at her confused, "The male who attacked me near the bathroom." She clarified.

Kieron shook his head, no. Unfortunately, the warrior who had attacked Genevieve was not permanently dead. "I can make sure he is dead and does not come back from it if you would like me to. Had I known you were drugged I would have finished him off."

"No. We do not know if it was him who drugged me and I think he got the point." Genevieve responded then took another drink of water.

Kieron continued to watch her. Something else was wrong. Her emotions were flickering in and out like a sputtering candle. "What's wrong?" He asked.

Genevieve's shoulders lifted and fell as she let out a sigh, "That was horrible. All of it. Being attacked and now realizing I was drugged … But I cannot stop thinking about what that male said. That he questioned you."

"You do not need to worry about any of that." Kieron said sternly. She just tilted her head and gave him one of those looks back—the look that screamed *Are you serious? Of course I'm worried about it. Do not pretend it is not a problem.* "Okay. Okay. Yes, it is a problem. I have been keeping most of the warriors and assassins in the dark about our plans. I cannot trust all of them and I need our plan to work. I need to make these changes for the kingdom and if they have a problem with the changes I will deal with it then, but I will not let anyone stop us."

"Do you feel like your response might have been a little harsh?" She tentatively asked.

"No. He was trying to hurt you and I need all of them to see I am the king. I need them to see they cannot step out of line. Unfortunately, that means violence is sometimes necessary."

Kieron watched Genevieve take a deep breath, "Okay then." She said simply. He felt her emotions settle. "I imagine he is not the only one who remembers me as a slave whore from the dungeons."

Kieron walked around the kitchen island and took the glass from her hands. He set it on the counter and pulled her into a hug. "Probably not." He said gently, his lips pressed against her hair. He could not lie to her. He had heard the mutterings and murmurs. Maybe what had happened tonight would put a stop to it. Maybe what had happened would scare off anyone from trying to hurt her again.

Genevieve gently pulled back from his embrace, "Well that sucks." Then the corner of her mouth twitched up into a small smile. "At least I was memorable."

Kieron could only laugh.

CHAPTER 47

Genevieve

Kieron, Zealand, and I all stood in The War Room dressed in the attire Belinda and Zain had selected for us to arrive at the inter-kingdom meeting in. Kieron wore his leather pants and boots with a fitted black shirt and jacket that did nothing but show off the wealth of the Deserts and his undeniably impressive muscles. Zealand wore the black canvas combat pants that represented the highest level of leadership underneath the king. He also wore a long leather jacket and matching leather boots. I wore matching canvas pants to Zealand, but a fitted long sleeve top with a leather corset vest that made me look completely feminine and badass.

Zain was the only one of us not clothed in all black. He wore dark gray pants and a black button shirt. He was here to help us, but he also was not sworn to the Deserts. He was a more neutral party when it came to this meeting. "Are you all ready?" Zain asked as he looked at all of us.

"Yes." Kieron responded. Zain nodded, then the room folded in.

The sea breeze was cool against my skin. We had appeared on an open platform perched on the edge of a cliff. A long narrow path led towards a palace that sat on the edge of, and was nestled into, the cliff, overhanging the sea. "Welcome to The Land of the Cliffs." A female voice greeted us. "Follow me." The female wore a silvery white suit with matching pointed toe pumps. None of us spoke as we followed her towards the palace.

We entered a receiving room that was already filled with people. The Lakes and the Mountains were already here. "I can show the three of you to your suite." The female said looking at Kieron, Zealand, and Zain.

"And what about Genevieve?" Zain questioned as he put up a protective hand to stop all of us from proceeding.

"Genevieve is welcome to stay in one of the rooms in the suite Aveline has arranged for us, or Aveline has graciously provided an additional private suite for her to stay in." Beck said as he approached us. He stood with his shoulders back and glared directly at Kieron. "Either way, Esmay is here to take a look at her and make sure she is unharmed."

"None of that is necessary, Beck." Kieron countered. I could hear the subtle anger in his voice and feel his body tense besides me.

"Forgive us if we won't take your word for it, Kieron. This is not negotiable." Ryett chimed in. Rachel stood next to him and she averted her eyes, clearly uncomfortable with the entire situation. Sarla, Jax, and Devron all looked concerned, but none of them moved or said anything.

"Oh hi! It is so nice to see all of you again." I said sarcastically, breaking the silence. "Your little welcome argument is cute, but I am standing right here. So before any of you get too worked up let me remind you that even though I am female, I am completely capable of making my own decisions." All three males shifted their eyes to me. Before any of them could cut in, I continued, "If it will make you all feel better, I will happily agree to an examination from Esmay. And I will be staying in the suite arranged for the Deserts."

"I can move you all to a suite that has four bedrooms." A beautiful female who could only be Aveline chimed in. Her long brown hair hung nearly to her waist and her white pantsuit had an overlay of silver lace. A silver necklace draped her neck with a round coin like pendant that reflected the light and a silver tiara sat upon her head. She was definitely Aveline.

"Thank you, that is very kind, but it will not be necessary." I said, as I leveled a look at Ryett, then at Beck. Daring them to protest further.

"I insist that we have Esmay examine you immediately." Beck grit out between his teeth.

"That would be wonderful." I said and flashed an exaggerated fake smile. I turned to Kieron and to my surprise he only looked at me amused. I lifted my hand and gave his forearm a gentle squeeze as I winked at him. Then I turned to follow Beck to wherever I was to be examined by Esmay.

"Rachel, how about you come with me and the others while these three attend to their business." Aveline gracefully slid over to Rachel and linked her arm in Rachel's.

Beck led the way and Ryett followed us as we left the others in the receiving room and made our way to the suite that had been provided for the Lakes. None of us said a word.

Esmay stood as we entered to greet us. "Genevieve it is so wonderful to see you again. I thought we could do our examination in this room." She said as she gestured to an open door that led into one of the bedrooms off of the main living room of the suite.

"Esmay, it is always nice to see you." I responded and started to follow her. Beck and Ryett trailed behind.

Esmay stopped them, "If you boys think I am allowing either of you in here with us then you are delusional. Go find something else to do and we will be out when we are done." I could have laughed at the looks Beck and Ryett had on their faces as Esmay closed the door with a decisive click, but I pressed my lips together to hold it in. "They are seriously losing their minds." Esmay said almost to herself as she gestured to the small table and chairs for us to sit at. "So how are you, anything I should know about before we begin?"

"I am doing well. I have no concerns. I have been practicing using my magic a lot more so sometimes I get worn down from that." I said as I sat in the chair.

"Have you ever passed out from depleting your magic?" Esmay asked as she lifted her bag from the floor and set it on the table.

"Yes, one time." I responded, hoping she would not ask for details. I did not want to tell her I had turned a male into tiny droplets of blood.

"Okay, make sure to practice learning where that edge is for yourself. It can be extremely dangerous or deadly to pass that threshold. Unfortunately, you will just have to practice and test yourself to figure it out, but go carefully, little by little, and rest sufficiently in between. And I mean rest for days if you have to." She explained to me.

"I can do that. Thank you." I said.

"Alright, good. Well, I am going to check you all over and make sure those worry warts out there can get some peace of mind that you are okay." Esmay said brightly. I only nodded and she went to work examining me for who knows what.

Just as I expected, Esmay found nothing to be concerned about. I gave Ryett and Beck a smug smirk as they both listened to Esmay's report that I was indeed unharmed.

"Thank you, Esmay. I appreciate you taking the time to come with us." Beck said tightly. Esmay nodded and took her leave from the suite.

"Great. Are we done here? I would like to freshen up before dinner." I said as I slowly inched towards the door that led back to the hallway.

"No, we are not done." Beck said firmly. I froze. "We are prepared to arrest Kieron for his crimes. When we do, you will no longer be his possession and you can return to either the Lakes or the Mountains safely."

"How dare you! He called this meeting with the intention of building alliances and making Savengard better. How dare you—" The rage in me was building, I could not believe it. I could not believe the betrayal.

329

Ryett interrupted me, "We both sent letters demanding he let you leave in order for our alliance to hold. I should have never let you go with him to begin with and—"

"*Let* me leave? I did not want to leave the Deserts." I snapped back.

"Genevieve, he stole you away. He can not be trusted." Beck countered.

"He did no such thing. I asked him to take me with him."

"You did *what*?" Ryett bit out between his teeth.

"I asked Kieron to take me with him." I repeated.

"Why would you do that? After everything he did to you? He can not be trusted, Genevieve. I wrote to him over and over again asking him to let you leave. To show some good faith and let you leave." Ryett responded hotly.

"You wrote *him* letters? Did you think to write to me? To ask *me*?" I met his anger with my own.

"He can't be trusted." Ryett responded, completely ignoring my questions.

"Kieron *can* be trusted. He would have let me leave if I wanted to and I did not want to leave. I wanted to stay in the Deserts." I saw Ryett's anger building and I kept talking. "I could not stay in the Mountains and watch you be with Rachel. I could not do that to you. I could not do that to myself."

Ryett was going to explode. His chest heaved with his breaths and his hands clenched into fists—

"You trust him after everything he did to you?" Beck interjected, his voice laced with a lethal calm.

"With my life." I responded as I glared back.

"Beck, can you give us a moment alone?" Ryett gritted out between his teeth. I had never seen him look this angry.

Beck just looked at Ryett, then back at me, "Fine. I will be on the balcony."

Ryett exploded as soon as the balcony door closed, "What if I had chosen *you*?" He yelled at me.

I knew the conversation that was coming and that we needed to have it. I just did not want to have it. I took a deep breath and kept my voice as calm as I could. "You would not have chosen me, Ryett. Yes, we had a connection and we could have built it into something beautiful, but ... you never looked at me the way you looked at her. Our connection was not like the connection you have with Rachel and that is okay. I want you to be happy. You were always going to choose her—"

"You don't know that!"

"I do know that because I would have made the same decision if it was Eli."

His eyes searched my face and I watched the anger fizzle out of him. "Eli was your husband?" Ryett finally asked quietly.

I had forgotten I never even shared my husband's name with Ryett. I had not shared a lot of things with Ryett. Ryett still did not know who I was—the things I was capable of. I never felt I could show him that dark side of me. I nodded. "Ryett, you would not love me if you knew who I was. Who I am."

"That is not true. I *do* know you—"

I cut him off, "You only know part of me. I am not what you want, Ryett." Ryett would never love me if he knew what I had done. Ryett was *good*. He deserved someone who was good too.

"You don't get to choose for me. Show me then. Show me the other part. Give me a chance to get to know all of you." Ryett pleaded with me as he took a step forward. I took a step back.

"No, Ryett. We have both already chosen and we did not choose each other. We need to move forward." I said it as gently and firmly as I could. I had made up my mind. I would not settle for someone who was unsure. I would not settle for someone who when I needed them, they turned their back. I needed someone who would choose me first and always. That was Kieron. It was always Kieron. I chose Kieron.

"How do I move forward with her after ... us?" He whispered.

"You just continue to choose her day after day until you have no more days."

Ryett took another step towards me and reached out his hand. "But you are my soulmate, Genevieve ..."

I stepped back out of his reach. "'Soulmates' is just a word, Ryett. You still get to choose who you build a life with."

He let his hand drop and we just stared at each other for heartbeats. Finally, Ryett spoke, "I see. Then please forgive me for how I handled everything and I hope we can be allies and friends for a long time." It was a painfully diplomatic response, but his jaw was set, holding back emotion that threatened to spill out. "You will always have a home in the Mountains. Always."

"Allies and friends." I said in agreement. Then Ryett nodded and left me standing in the living room. I had a feeling this was not the last time we would have a conversation like this, but I wished it would be. He deserved to be happy. I had come back so he could be happy with Rachel—

"I will never understand why you would choose to go with Kieron." I almost jumped at Beck's voice.

"Good thing you don't need to understand it." I said stiffly as I turned to face Beck.

"I should probably let you know, I officially registered you as a member of The Land of the Lakes. You are welcome." He replied, nonchalantly.

"Why would you do that? How can you do that?"

"Because, Genevieve," Beck let my name roll off his tongue like he was tasting it. Like he was remembering tasting me. "I am the king and I can do what I want. Plus, you arrived in my lands first, you were mine first, and now you will always be a member of my kingdom."

If I had a weapon I would have hurled it at Beck. The way he was looking at me as he sauntered into the room made me want to break something. It took all of my willpower to simply respond to him, "I can't wait to figure out how to undo that mistake. I am certainly not part of *your* kingdom."

"Dressing in Desert black does not make you part of the Deserts. You know that right?" He said smugly.

"I believe I have the right to choose which kingdom I belong to and yes, in this case, dressing in Desert black to show I am part of the Deserts was exactly the intention."

Beck just looked me over like he was thinking hard about something. "You are a match to Kieron aren't you?" He finally asked. I did not respond. "Oh, I knew I sensed something different. His magic is stronger. Both of your magic is vibrating at the same frequency." Beck said as he plopped down onto one of the couches, "I knew you were different as soon as you showed up in my kingdom. That is why I want you for myself. Jokes on me that you matched both Ryett and Kieron. With Ryett it is clearly your magic from the Mountains, but with Kieron ... there is something else there ..." His voice trailed off, then he cleared his throat. "Do you really trust him after everything he has done? You should leave with Ryett, or better yet, come back to the Lakes with me, anything other than staying with that monster."

"Kieron is not a monster and I trust him with my life." I said again, keeping my voice as neutral as I could. I thought I could trust Beck after he helped us—helped all of us—but clearly I could not. The Beck I was seeing today was not a Beck to be trusted.

"Are you sure you want to gamble with your life?" Beck asked, his voice serious.

I ignored his question and continued before he could say more, "The Deserts asked for this meeting to strengthen alliances and make positive change. I hope you can drop whatever other issues you have and get on board with that agenda."

"So I do not have your approval to arrest him?" Beck asked as he spread himself out on the couch—his knees wide and both arms draped across the couch back.

"Don't you dare consider it." I said back between my teeth. Beck just looked me over head to toe with those deep blue eyes of his like he was undressing me and did not respond. *What an asshole.* I rolled my shoulders back and changed my tone, "Thank you for arranging this meeting. I think all of you have the same vision and goals for Savengard. I look forward to working with you, Your Grace."

He just gave me a sly grin, his eyes still piercing into me. "Oh, you are good. I look forward to working with you too, Genevieve."

Then it was my turn to leave the suite assigned to the Lakes.

CHAPTER 48

Genevieve

"Well I would pay big money to see the look on Ryett and Beck's faces again when you told them we did not need another bedroom." I found Kieron lounged on the balcony couches off of our suite.

"I am impressed by the way you handled yourself." I teased as I sat down next to him.

"Oh you clearly had it under control, sweetheart." He responded and threw his arm around my shoulders. "I am guessing Esmay gave her stamp of approval?"

"Obviously." I said as I looked out along the cliff's edge and out into the sea. "How long until we have dinner with everyone?"

"A few hours. Zealand is off doing who knows what and calling it security. Zain is probably with Ryett and company." His fingers idly stroked my shoulder.

"How are you feeling about all of this? Meeting with everyone?"

"Nervous. I have met with the worst kinds of beings, faced the worst beasts, but I have never had to negotiate with kings and queens."

"Understandable. You will be fine. You are a natural leader. Just show them who you really are." I responded. Then I adjusted the way I was sitting so that I could curl up and rest my head on Kieron's shoulder. "They wanted to arrest you." I whispered.

"I thought they might." Kieron responded calmly. "I am guessing they changed their minds."

"Something like that."

I looked at myself in the mirror one last time. The sheer black lace dress hugged my body perfectly. Delicate straps held up the plunging neckline and corset bodice. The billowing black satin over-skirt attached at one hip and wrapped around the back to attach to the other hip. It left the front of the lace dress beneath visible, but gave the illusion that I was wearing a ballgown. The black satin heels I wore were delicate and simple—the only thing simple about what I was wearing. A salt and pepper diamond hair comb pulled my hair neatly back on one side. This was the most beautiful gown I had ever worn and probably would ever wear. There was no way anything would ever top this.

I took one last deep breath and I opened the door to the living room of the suite. Zain had left earlier and would meet us at the dinner, but Zealand and Kieron were both waiting for me to finish getting dressed. Zealand was wearing head to toe black. His all black suit had all black buttons and a splash of finery with an embroidered vest underneath.

My breath caught as I saw Kieron. I had never seen him look so —*kingly*. His three piece black suit had satin lapels and the collar, cuff details, and pocket square all had embroidery that matched the lace pattern of my gown. Each button was crafted with a salt and pepper diamond. Instead of regular dress shoes, his pants were cuffed above shiny leather combat boots. His long hair was pulled back neatly and atop his head sat a white gold crown encrusted with salt and pepper diamonds.

Both males' jaws dropped as I stepped through the doorway. Zealand let out a low whistle and Kieron was completely speechless. "You both look handsome." I said with a teasing smile.

"You look absolutely incredible." Kieron breathed as he crossed the room and grabbed my hands—he held them up and admired me before walking around me in a slow circle. "You look incredible." Kieron repeated as he stopped in front of me.

"Thank you." I whispered and felt my cheeks heat as I blushed at his compliment.

Then Kieron smoothly slid next to me and offered his arm. "Shall we?"

◆ ◆ ◆

Sarla nearly knocked me over as she ran to me and threw her arms around me in an embrace. "Genevieve, I have missed you so much!" She whispered to me.

"I have missed you too." I said with a smile.

She pulled back and looked me up and down. "Damn. You look *good*." I only laughed in response, "Things have seriously not been the same, but clearly you both are doing well. Accomplished taking over your kingdom and all, Kieron." She said as she turned her attention to Kieron besides me.

"Sarla, I owe you an apology for trying to kill you. I am sorry." Kieron said.

She only waved a hand in dismissal and laughed, "It's cute you thought you might be able to." Kieron grinned back at her and she continued, "As long as you are taking good care of Genevieve we can call it even. It will make a good story at the next family reunion, anyway."

"It's cute you think Genevieve needs taking care of. I think she is taking care of me, Sarla." Kieron responded with a laugh.

"I knew I liked you." Sarla said with a wink. We all moved further into the room, accepting glasses of sparkling wine the servers offered us.

I stiffened as I saw Rachel heading straight towards us. I saw Ryett watching from across the room with an emptiness in his eyes. Those empty eyes caught mine for just a moment before I quickly turned mine away. "Kieron! Genevieve! I really need to properly thank you both for rescuing me." Rachel said as she stopped in front of us.

"You are welcome, Rachel. We are glad to see you are well." Kieron said as his hand raised to my lower back. I had never heard him sound so … formal.

"Ryett and I are planning our union ceremony and it would be so wonderful if you would both come. I promise it will be a good party and it would not be happening without you both." Rachel continued.

Sarla nearly choked on her wine and I felt Kieron's fingers tighten on my back as if to steady me. I was sure he could feel the wave of emotion that had hit me. I could not help it. Even if I had let Ryett go and understood his decision and chosen Kieron, I still did not want to be at Ryett's wedding. I was not ready for that.

"I look forward to seeing the invitation, Rachel." I said as calmly as I could and forced a smile.

The relief on her face was evident. "I just do not have anyone from my side to invite. My world is ... I guess you are the closest thing ..." Her voice trailed off as she realized she was blabbering.

My heart broke for her. Ryett's inner circle had not yet accepted her. She probably had not had the time to meet anyone in the last weeks and everyone from her world was dead. "I know the feeling, Rachel." I said gently. "My world is gone too."

Her eyes grew wide, "You are not from here either? Ryett would not tell me much about you other than you used to live in the Mountains. I guess I just assumed you were from the Mountains."

"No, I am not from here, my world was also destroyed by Vossarian." I was not going to touch the stuff about Ryett. I had never seen Sarla squirm under social pressure, but she was gulping her wine and giving me eyes that screamed how awkward all of this was.

"Oh look who has finally joined us." Sarla cut in and we turned to see Beck, Devron, and a female I had never seen before. Her eyes ...

they were Beck's eyes.

"Beck. Devron." Kieron said in greeting as they approached.

"Let me introduce you all to my daughter, Annistyn. She is extremely invested in the well being of others and will oversee any newcomers who will be making their home in The Land of the Lakes." Beck said.

"Nice to meet you." Sarla said and I only nodded.

"Kieron." Annistyn said with a small smile.

"Annistyn." Kieron replied. I think all of our eyes showed surprise at their greeting.

"I appreciated your warnings, but I am a little offended you did not tell me you were planning on becoming a king." Annistyn said with a light laugh.

"It was not exactly part of my plans, Annistyn." Kieron responded. Beck's eyes flashed between Kieron and his daughter.

"Oh, excuse me for being so rude. Kieron was sent to kidnap me this last year, but instead he provided a warning and assistance in avoiding Vossarian's schemes. I never got the chance to properly thank you, Kieron." Annistyn informed all of us. I could not believe it. Annistyn had been targeted by Voss—probably due to Ryett and Beck's meetings—and Kieron had found a way to keep her safe.

"You are very welcome." Kieron said and I saw his cheeks flush slightly. He was not used to people thanking him. He probably was not used to his good deeds even being known about.

We were interrupted from further explanation as Aveline in all her queenly glory swept in. She was flanked by two stunningly beautiful females who both carried long curved blades. "Welcome to the Cliffs." Aveline said as she gracefully moved to behind the seat at the head of the long table in the center of the room. Her white ball gown had shimmering sheer sleeves that hung off of her shoulders and large billowing skirts with shimmering beading. "Tonight let's celebrate new allies and friendships. But let's not have too much fun, for tomorrow we must do the hard work!" The servers motioned for us all to take our seats for dinner.

Kieron and I were guided to seats across the table from Beck, Devron, and Annistyn. Zain thankfully was seated on my other side, buffering me from Ryett, and Zealand was seated next to Kieron. Other members of Aveline's court joined us, but I missed any introductions. I was just trying to ignore how awkward this would be to eat dinner with Beck, Ryett, and Kieron all at the same table. Ryett was still looking anywhere other than at me and Beck was staring only at me. I let my eyes wander to the others across the table and noticed Annistyn's eyes catching on Zealand's tattooed face as well as glancing at Kieron's hands and neck. I also noticed Beck subtly refused the wine that was being offered by the serving staff. *Interesting.*

As we settled into our meals Annistyn finally spoke up, "I am sorry to stare, Zealand, your tattoos are just very beautiful. I have heard rumors of the Undead, but only thought it was a myth."

"We are not a myth and your apology is not necessary." Zealand responded with a small smile, his eyes lingering on Annistyn.

Beck shifted slightly in his seat. "Kieron, it appears you have new tattoos since the last time I saw you."

Kieron laughed, "It is hard to rule the Undead if you are not one of the Undead yourself. A somewhat unexpected side effect of taking my throne."

"And did you expose Genevieve to the dangers of the Eastern Desert, too?" Beck asked stiffly. I clenched my fork at his question. *He just could not help himself could he?*

"I think the Eastern Desert was exposed to the dangers of Genevieve, Your Grace." Zealand responded coolly.

I could see Beck's muscles tense, but his mouth stayed closed as he looked murderously between Kieron and Zealand. "And what does that mean?" Devron finally asked.

"The desert received some rain and the Palace of the Undead put up a few new decorations ... if you know what I mean." Zealand leaned back casually in his chair as he spoke.

I could not tear my eyes off of Beck. He slowly moved his gaze from Zealand to meet mine, "Very few beings have that ability. I assume Kieron taught you that skill as he is the only being in this room and maybe the only being still alive with that knowledge." Beck said finally.

I gave him a tight smile and shifted my attention back to my food without answering him. *Very few.* Kieron had told me very few beings had the ability to turn others into blood rain. I guess 'very few' meant only Kieron—and now me.

Zain rescued us all from awkward conversation for the remainder of dinner. As we stood to have cocktails outside on the balcony I found Annistyn slide into stride next to me.

"I believe I have you to thank for my father making an effort in my life." She said so only I could hear.

"What do you mean by that?" I asked.

"I am not sure if you noticed, but he has stopped drinking. He was quite fun when he drank, but it also brought out the worst in him. He reached out and asked for my help with these slave negotiations. When I asked him why I should help him, he told me about a female who had changed his perspective on things. He has been nothing but at the top of his game since. That is why I agreed and my relationship with him has never been better. So thank you." She whispered and gave my hand a squeeze as she gracefully slid off to chat with the others.

"Are you okay?" Kieron asked gently from behind me.

"Today has been full of surprises." I said and gave him a small smile.

Kieron

Kieron wanted nothing more than to just slink back to their rooms. He had never really enjoyed social gatherings and this one included too many people he did not know well. Sarla had dragged Genevieve off and he and Zealand were painfully making the rounds to make small talk with the others. As they moved towards another group, Kieron suddenly found Rachel stopping them.

"Hi, I'm Rachel." She said and stuck out her hand to Zealand. Zealand took it as he introduced himself back. "I do not think I ever saw you in the Deserts." She continued.

"I don't think you would have." Zealand said. "I was stationed in the capitol before being sent to the Eastern Desert."

"Oh, I see. Well it is nice to meet you." She resigned with a sigh.

344

"How are you doing, Rachel? Is freedom treating you well?" Kieron found himself asking.

"It is going fine. I don't think anyone likes me, though." She responded as she looked over the small crowd of people. Ryett was in a corner and deep in discussion with Aveline and none of the others from the Mountains were coming to rescue Rachel with conversation. "Please will you come to the union ceremony? I got the feeling Genevieve wasn't too excited by my invitation."

"I would imagine it is quite difficult for her to be around you, Rachel. Don't take it personally." Kieron said before he could stop himself.

"She hates me too?" Rachel asked, her shoulders sinking.

"No one hates you." Kieron tried to assure her.

"I would love to hear your story, Rachel. Before you came to the Deserts. I hear you and Ryett met in your world?" Zealand cut in.

At that moment, Ryett slid into place next to Rachel. "Kieron." He said tightly.

"Ryett, I hear your union ceremony plans are coming along." Kieron leveled back. Ryett just glared at him.

"Have a good rest of your evening." Ryett finally responded. "Rachel." He said firmly as he took her arm and guided her away.

Kieron let out a sigh of relief. Rachel had been the catalyst that started the chain of events that brought him Genevieve. That gave him a chance with Genevieve. He could not hate her, but he was growing rather annoyed with how Ryett handled everything. How he discarded Genevieve—it had worked out for Kieron, but it still bothered him—and now Ryett had been keeping Rachel in the dark about everything. Rachel deserved to know the truth, but it was not Kieron's place to tell her.

Fingers interlacing with his broke Kieron from his thoughts. "Hey. How about we sneak out of here?" Genevieve asked softly.

He wanted nothing more than to leave this party and slip into bed with Genevieve. To stroke his fingers along her skin. Kieron glanced around the room again and noticed both Beck and Ryett not so subtly glaring at them. "Zealand?" He asked, but Zealand just gave them a wave of his hand.

"I will be back soon. I have something to take care of first." Zealand responded as he gracefully turned and headed straight towards Devron and Annistyn. Kieron gave Genevieve's hand a gentle squeeze and they slipped back inside, heading for their suite of rooms.

CHAPTER 49

Genevieve

We had eaten breakfast in our suite and now we followed a female dressed in white down a long corridor. My black stilettos with their silver toes and heels clicked on the smooth stone as we walked. Kieron wrapped his tattooed hand around mine and I looked up into his eyes. His smart short sleeved shirt somehow both showed off his haunting tattoos and muscles while also succeeded in making him seem reasonably approachable. He gave me a small reassuring smile as we paused in front of a set of doors. The female pushed them in and stepped aside for us to enter.

A large round table with chairs for each of us was inside the meeting room. Aveline, along with the male and female who had been introduced as an advisor and her general the evening before, were already inside. Additional members of the Cliffs loitered near seats that had been placed along the wall. Beck, Devron, and

Annistyn were also already there. They turned to greet us and I watched Beck's eyes rake over my satin trimmed lace bustier top and highwaisted pants that gathered at my ankles above the stilettos. When his eyes met mine, I gave him a look that dared him to say something stupid. He didn't.

The doors opened again and Ryett, Rachel, Sarla, and Jax entered. "Good morning everyone. Take your seats." Aveline's voice rang out in the room. We did as requested and found our seats. "Thank you all for coming. Now Kieron, you called this meeting with two specific requests: for assistance in collapsing the slave trade network and finding homes for the slaves you plan to free from the Deserts. I will let you tell us in more detail." Aveline clearly knew how to get down to business and in a room with three other kings, she commanded everyone's attention.

"Thank you, Aveline. Thank you for hosting this meeting and thank you Beck and Ryett for coming. You are correct, Aveline. The first priority for the new Deserts is to eliminate slavery. We believe the best course of action is to first collapse the slave trade network and then to free the slaves within the Deserts. I am prepared to share every detail of the slave trade network along with my proposed plan for eliminating each piece simultaneously." Kieron spoke, his voice was calm and even as he addressed the other kingdoms. "Then I will free the slaves currently within the Deserts. I expect many of them will want to leave the Deserts. I will support this, but ask for your support and help in providing new homes, food, and any vocational training so they may be given every possible chance to become productive members of our kingdoms."

"How many slaves are currently in the Deserts?" Aveline asked.

Kieron turned his gaze to her, "Nearly one hundred thousands. All of them belong to the crown."

I glanced around the room and saw the shock on the faces of the others. One hundred thousand was an astonishing number. Especially because the previous rulers—Vossarian and Luther and Luther's father before him—had ensured the crown would be the only owner of slaves in the kingdom. I was speechless when I found out. It seemed the others were similarly shocked.

"And how do we fund the homes and food and vocational training for all of these newly freed slaves?" Ryett asked as he crossed his arms.

"I imagine the half a million coin you spent to free Genevieve will help. It is being returned to your accounts as we speak. I am also prepared to help subsidize the cost for the first five years, which hopefully will be enough time for the majority to get their feet under them." Kieron leveled back at him.

Half a million. Ryett had spent half a million coins on me when one hundred coins was considered a fortune and more than what ninety percent of residents in the Deserts had to their name. I could barely breathe at the thought. He had told me he would have paid whatever Vossarian had asked. I could not wrap my head around the extreme wealth these kings must have—and the fact Ryett had paid that ridiculous sum for me.

"Keep it." Ryett gritted out between his teeth.

"Too late." Kieron flashed a smile back.

Ryett's eyes glanced over at Sarla. She was scribbling on a piece of paper and then it disappeared. We all sat quietly. Rachel was staring intently down at her lap and Ryett's fingers tightened into a fist where his hand rested on the table. Then a piece of paper appeared in front of Sarla. She read it and then lifted her eyes to Ryett, "It has been confirmed. The funds are back in your account."

"Very well." Ryett said in a forced calm. "Where have you been keeping one hundred thousand slaves?"

"The palace and royal residences all use slave labor, but the vast majority of the slaves work in the three mines. The Salt Mine in the west, The Mineral Mine in the south, and The Diamond Mine in the north. We have been working on a plan to shift these mining operations from slave labor to paid employment for anyone who wishes to stay. As for the individuals currently in the palace and royal residences, they will also be offered paid positions." Kieron explained.

"I think we can all agree we like the idea of collapsing the slave network and we would not be here if we were not willing to take freed slaves from your kingdom, Kieron." Aveline said as if she was working through something in her mind. Beck and Ryett gave subtle nods of agreement. Aveline continued, "So do we start by determining how to handle the freed slaves or do we start with details on taking down the slave network?"

"I propose we start with discussing what to do with the freed slaves first." Beck suggested.

"Very well." Aveline gestured for Beck to continue.

"The Lakes could support up to three quarters of the freed slaves, but I would prefer to see the burden split more evenly." Beck said carefully.

"Likewise." Ryett chimed in. "If every slave chose to stay in the Deserts, would you be able to accommodate them?"

"Yes, we could accommodate all of them and would be happy to." Kieron responded, "Unfortunately, I believe many will choose to leave and I do not blame them. Conditions for the slaves have been very poor."

"Could each of us agree to support up to half of the freed slaves if needed? Perhaps that would give as many of them as possible a choice in where they go?" Aveline suggested. "The Cliffs could accommodate fifty thousand new residents and would not need additional financial support to do so."

Beck and Ryett were both quiet for a few heartbeats. Ryett spoke first, "I can agree to that and similarly would not need additional financial support."

"I can agree to it as well." Beck said.

It was Zain's turn to speak, "I believe we have all come to an agreement then."

Over the next few hours, Kieron and Zealand outlined our previously discussed proposal for the cataloging and transportation for the newly freed slaves along with our plans to provide protection for both the freed slaves and those who previously oversaw them. It would be a massive undertaking to ensure a peaceful transition for everyone. The other kingdoms had little to provide other than suggestions for the best process to transport the freed slaves to their new homes. By lunch time we had a solid plan in place.

Each of the kingdoms retreated to their suites for lunch. This was apparently customary for inter-kingdom meetings. Dinners were the only meals traditionally taken together, allowing the other mealtimes to decompress and regroup within our own kingdoms. I, for one, could appreciate the two hours of quiet. The time passed quickly and we were soon being escorted back down the corridor to the meeting room.

The room had been rearranged. A large board with a map of Savengard was at one side of the room and the tables and chairs were arranged in a semicircle facing the map. Red markers had already been placed on the map in three of the kingdoms. Everyone took their seats and Ryett stood with Jax near the map.

"Kieron. Zealand. We have already marked this map with the information we have on the locations and details for the network." Ryett began. "I spent the entire time I worked with Vossarian cataloging those involved and planning how we could eliminate them. Beck and Devron have already seen this plan and are prepared to help. This is the first time Aveline has seen it."

I watched Kieron lean back in his chair and cross his arms as he looked at the map. I had told him Ryett had a plan and that he was creating an alliance with Beck to help him execute it, but I had never seen the extent of what might be involved.

Finally Kieron spoke, "I am impressed, Ryett. I am also disappointed we did not know we were fighting for the same team until recently. Please, walk us through what you know and your plan."

We listened as Ryett explained each of the markers. Starting in The Land of the Plains there was a drug operation which used slave labor to grow the plants used to make the drugs. There were multiple growing sites and multiple processing plants. Two of the bigger cities were the distribution hubs for both the drug operation and slave trade. Next, Ryett outlined the logging operation that was a front for sex slave operations within The Land of the Giants. Then there was The Land of the Coasts. The Coasts had two portals that were used to import and export slaves to and from two other worlds—the twelfth world and world three. Ryett detailed the players in each cog of the operation. It was an impressive report and each of the details had been cataloged in writing on the map in the appropriate place.

Kieron slowly stood. "May I?" He asked as he gestured to the map. Ryett stepped to the side and Kieron approached the map. A pen appeared in his hand and he underlined a name in each of the pieces of the operation. "These males all work for me and are waiting for orders to collapse the network."

Beck, Devron, Aveline, and Aveline's general all stood and approached the map. "You have a sleeper spy in each piece of the network?" Beck asked in disbelief.

"I do. It took centuries to get the right people in place, but they are there and trustworthy." Kieron responded simply. "Your plan is good, Ryett, but I have plans of my own that I think will combine well with yours."

CHAPTER 50

Genevieve

We had somehow survived the first day of meetings. Thankfully everyone had been civil and what little tension there was between the groups was able to be worked through. I slipped my arms into the simple and extremely elegant black dress for dinner. Like many of my clothes, it had a deep plunging neckline. The dress also had long loose sleeves that gathered at my wrists and a high leg slit that nearly touched my underthings. I slipped into shimmering pointed toe ankle boots and stood back up to look myself over in the mirror.

"I am glad you are here with me." Kieron said from over my shoulder. I turned around and smiled as I saw Kieron with his hair tied back into a neat bun at the back of his head. He usually dressed so simply it was still shocking to see him dressed in finery. His clothes were elegant just like mine. Black dress boots. Black pants and belt. Black button shirt with a black vest and a tie that shimmered just like my boots.

"I am glad I am here with you too." I responded as I let myself admire him from head to toe again.

"I have something for you." He said and revealed a small box in his hands. He handed it to me and I cautiously took it.

"You got me something?" I asked as I slowly pulled off the lid. A silver lariat necklace with stacked onyx stones shimmered up at me.

"I know you do not wear jewelry much, but I saw this and thought of you. When you asked me if you could come to the Deserts and agreed to help me I had no idea how critical to our success you would become. You have given me unwavering support and I am just so grateful to have you here ... and I thought the necklace would look nice with your dress ..." He was slightly stumbling over his words and it made me smile more.

"I love it." I breathed. "It is beautiful." Then I draped it around my neck and turned to see how the stones dangled between my breasts. It was perfect with this dress. "Thank you." I turned and pulled Kieron's hips close to mine as I gave him a kiss. "Thank you." I whispered again against his lips before pulling back.

He smiled down at me and grasped the back of my neck before kissing me again.

Kieron

"Kieron, I am impressed with how much you were able to accomplish while living under Vossarian's thumb." Ryett said casually across the large dining table.

"I said it earlier and I will say it again, it is too bad we did not know we were on the same side until recently, Ryett." Kieron responded cooly. He did not know why he was so tense. Maybe it was the way Ryett looked at him, but Kieron just sensed Ryett still did not want to trust him.

"It is all working out now though." Aveline interjected, "With the insights from both of you we will be able to make massive positive change for the future of Savengard. I am pleased to have you as an ally, Kieron. You have exceeded my expectations. I know you will do great things for the Deserts in the coming centuries."

Kieron felt Genevieve's hand give his leg a small squeeze. *How was he so lucky?* Genevieve was beautiful and smart and believed in him more than he believed in himself. He could not do this without her beside him. "Thank you, Aveline. I am also pleased to have you and the Mountains and the Lakes as allies. I understand the other kingdoms might take some time to come around, but I think we have an opportunity to have a fully united Savengard again."

"I agree with you." Aveline responded with a smile. Servers appeared and cleared away the empty dinner plates in front of us. "Come. Let's move to the balcony to enjoy the rest of our evening."

The group rose from the table and filed out onto the balcony. Cushioned couches and chairs with low tables were scattered around. The males all seemed to move towards the balcony railing and Kieron glanced back to see Genevieve making herself comfortable with the other females at a cluster of couches. It was always amusing to Kieron how females seemed to flock together. There was just something about how they were able to connect to each other that completely mystified him.

"I do not know how you do it, Kieron." Beck said from his side as they looked out across the sea.

"Do what?" Kieron asked. It was an effort to be in the same room as Beck without tearing his head off let alone to collaborate with him. He had always disliked Beck. Beck was loved by everyone and had a reputation for great parties and a good time. Kieron always knew there was just a spoiled coward behind all the posturing. It was proven when Genevieve had shown up with bruises covering her body and a split lip.

"How you can handle knowing you will always come in second place to her dead husband." Beck said casually.

Kieron turned slowly to face Beck. He was deciding if he would toss Beck over the railing or simply knock him on his ass. Instead he turned his glare from hate and disgust to amusement. "That's your mistake, Beck, thinking her heart is not big enough to love Eli's memory as well as everyone else she cares about. I am not worried about being second. I am worried about not being on the list at all."

Genevieve

I watched Kieron blend into the group of kings and generals and commanders. If one did not know their histories, one would think they were all quite close friends as they lit cigars and stood at the balcony's edge chatting amongst themselves. Somehow the group had found itself split into males and females—I did not mind.

"How are the Deserts treating you, Genevieve?" Aveline's voice brought me back from admiring Kieron.

"I am sure you can imagine that it has been a little eventful, but I have been settling in." I responded with a smile.

"It appears you plan to stay?" Aveline pushed.

I could feel all the females watching me. "Yes. I have every intention of staying in the Deserts." I responded as casually as I could.

Aveline gave me a knowing smile, then turned to Rachel. "And how about you, Rachel? Are you enjoying freedom and the cooler weather of the Mountains?"

Rachel nodded, but she continued staring at her glass of wine in her hands. "Yes, I am." She said softly. Rachel had been mostly quiet the entire day. Then she lifted her gaze and looked straight at me. "Genevieve, you were a slave? Ryett ... bought your freedom?" My stomach dropped at her question.

I took a deep breath, "When I arrived in this world, I arrived through a portal in The Land of the Lakes. Beck was kind enough to let me stay while Sarla was healed. Unfortunately, I was kidnapped by Vossarian and put in his dungeons. Kieron was able to get word to Zain and Ryett that I was being held prisoner and Ryett bought my freedom. I stayed in the Mountains until … well until Vossarian died and you were found. Then I chose to go with Kieron to help him become The King of the Deserts."

"How did you get kidnapped out of the Lakes? My father has always had his estate locked down tightly." Annistyn cut in as she leaned forward in her seat.

I looked at Sarla for some help and she just slightly shrugged her shoulders and gave a subtle shake of her head. I was on my own for this one. "That is part of the story I do not need to share." I replied cautiously. Rachel was just staring at me. I could tell she had more questions and I was afraid of what she might ask next.

"And by 'until Vossarian died' you mean 'until you killed him?'" Aveline interjected.

"Yes." I replied and I turned my eyes to meet the gaze of the queen.

Aveline just stared back at me, contemplating. Then she finally spoke, "Good work. Apparently, we can't count on the males to get anything done correctly."

We all burst out laughing at her comment. "Aveline, you sure are being quite reserved these days." Sarla teased from beside me between her laughs.

Aveline winked at Sarla, "I was hoping to give those who have not met me a more professional impression, Sarla."

Sarla snorted, "Can we make bets on how long that will last?"

"If you bet longer than another ten minutes you will lose." Aveline saluted us with her glass before downing the rest of her wine in one swig.

We all laughed again. Then Annistyn spoke up, "It looks like the boys are getting along alright. Based on the pre-meeting briefing I received I imagined a few more fists flying."

"I would have bet on it as well." Sarla responded.

We all glanced over towards the railing. I caught Annistyn's eyes lingering as they made eye contact with Zealand's. "Annistyn, I would love to hear more about you. Beck only told me you existed, but I never had the chance to ask him more about you." I cautiously pressed, "Where in the Lakes do you live?"

She slowly pulled her eyes off of Zealand, "I have been living in a small town on the eastern edge of the kingdom. It is quiet and calm out there. I quite like it, but have agreed to move back to my father's lake estate temporarily. Until the slaves are settled."

"If you keep making eyes like that at Zealand, he might ask to move into the lake estate too." Aveline said quietly before sipping from her glass of wine.

Annistyn straightened and blushed, "I don't know what you are talking about, Aveline."

"We will need some help as we try to organize departures for anyone who wishes to leave the Deserts. Perhaps you could come stay in Aridale for a short while and lend a hand. You could help them decide which kingdom they want to leave to?" I offered. I did not know if we would actually need help, but the connection between Annistyn and Zealand was undeniable. I imagined Beck was nearly crawling out of his skin over it.

Annistyn blushed further, "Thank you for the invitation."

I gave her a smile and turned back to the others. I watched Aveline's fingers mindlessly play with the hammered coin shaped necklace around her neck. "Your necklace is very beautiful, Aveline." I found myself saying.

She smiled and looked down at it between her fingers. Then she let it rest back against her chest, placing a hand over it. "A friend of mine named Shadow gave it to me during the last war. He told me no matter how dark things may get in this world and between worlds, there are always those of us who are the light. He made me promise to keep being the light. I never saw him again after the war. I imagine he is back in his own world and hopefully is doing well."

We were all quiet. Then Sarla spoke up, "Was he *just* a friend?"

Aveline laughed and let her hand fall away from the necklace, "Yes, he was *just* a friend. Unfortunately for me, his heart already belonged to someone else."

"Well it is beautiful and he sounds like a good friend." I managed to say.

"Thank you ... he was." Aveline responded.

Then Sarla rescued us from the silence and began coaxing Aveline to share details about the more fun side of the Cliffs with Rachel and me.

As the night wore on we all mingled back together with the males. I found myself alone and requesting a glass of sparkling wine from the bar when Beck slid up next to me. "Should I be worried about her?" He asked. I looked at him then followed his eyes to where Annistyn and Zealand were standing close together at the balcony's railing and looking out at the sea.

"You will always be worried about her, Beck." I responded, "But you do not have to worry about her around Zealand."

He gave me a look, "He is an Undead, Genevieve. How can I not be worried about it? They are considered beasts—monsters."

"Just because they have been assigned the title of monsters does not mean they are or should be considered monsters. The Undead are still beings just like you and me. Zealand became an Undead for *this* cause. Because he was fighting for the freedom of all beings in Savengard. He is certainly not a monster."

Beck looked back at me. Then he stepped closer. His voice was low, "Kieron and Zealand were both monsters for centuries before they became Undead, Genevieve. You would be wise to remember that."

I let my eyes look Beck up and down like I was sizing him up. Beck shifted on his feet as I met his gaze. He was standing too close to me for it to be appropriate. I bit my lip, giving him the same bedroom eyes he had seduced me into giving him just days after we met. I watched the corner of his mouth twitch up—like he thought he was seducing me again. Like he thought his idiotic comments might be convincing me to return to the Lakes—return to *him*. "It sounds like I am in good company then." I leveled back at him. Shock flashed across his face at my response. Then I clinked my glass against his and walked away, leaving him at the bar, before he could say anything else.

I slipped out of my boots as we returned to the suite assigned to the Deserts. "Things are going well." Zain said absently as he loosened his dark gray tie and made his way over to the bar next to the small kitchen.

"I offered for Annistyn to join us in Aridale to help arrange any departures of freed slaves to the Lakes." I said as I eyed Zealand. I watched him straighten up slightly.

"I think that is a great idea." Kieron said and gave me a wink. He had noticed their connection too then.

"Tomorrow may still come with its challenges," Zain interrupted us, "Please continue to be on your best and most collaborative behavior. There is still time for them to back out. And Zealand, please give Annistyn some space tomorrow. We do not need Beck getting territorial over his daughter and acting irrationally. He has already been searching for excuses to end this alliance. Let's not give him any reason to."

"Oh I already tried to put in a good word for you with Beck." I teased.

"Is it that obvious?" Zealand asked as he plopped onto the couch.

"Yes!" We all responded in unison.

"I think it is great, Zealand. Let's just make sure we get through tomorrow." Kieron said as he sat on the couch across from him.

"You all have done a great job for this being your first inter-kingdom meeting." Zain continued. "The Deserts will be expected to take the majority of the effort and risk, so just be prepared that the others will ask more of you than they are willing to offer."

"I expected as much. We can manage it." Kieron said his face was calm and determined.

The meetings had gone exceedingly well. After the first day, there had been little tension with the group and impressive collaboration. It was now the afternoon on the second day and we had a nearly finalized plan. None of us had expected it to go so smoothly. Each kingdom knew exactly where, when, and what they needed to do so that we could collapse the slave network simultaneously. The Deserts were in fact expected to handle both the most and the riskiest portions of the plan, but Kieron and Zealand outlined exactly how we would manage it.

"Excellent. Is everyone satisfied with the plan?" Aveline questioned the group. Everyone was silent for heartbeats. This was it. We had nearly done it. Nearly finalized every last detail. Agreement from Aveline, Beck, and Ryett would mean we had solidified our alliances and would be ready to collapse the entire slave network—the first step to eliminating slavery in Savengard.

"I have one condition for my involvement." Beck spoke up. He then leveled a look at Kieron, "Genevieve does not participate in the collapsing of the slave network."

I saw red. *How many more times would Beck try to control my life?* "That is not your call." I said between my teeth.

Beck repeated himself slowly, "Genevieve does not participate."

Before I could spring across the table and punch Beck in the face, Kieron placed a firm hand on my leg. "You have my word." He said, his voice low. "She will stay in Aridale."

I bit the inside of my cheek so hard I tasted blood. Warmth radiated into my leg as Kieron sent a small pulse of his magic into me. I took a deep breath and just glared at Beck while I kept my mouth shut. I would have words with Kieron later, but I would not question him in front of the others. Beck nodded his approval and some of the others shifted in their seats.

"Okay then." Aveline started again, breaking the silence. "Anyone else have any final thoughts?" No one said anything. "Wonderful. It is all decided. Good luck to all of us."

The others pushed back their chairs to stand. I said my goodbyes under a haze of rage and followed Kieron, Zealand, and Zain back to our rooms. When Zain closed the door behind us I completely exploded.

"I don't get to *participate?*" I nearly yelled at Kieron's back. He stopped walking and slowly turned around. Zealand and Zain looked at each other and moved towards the door to leave, to give us some privacy. "You two can stay for this, I do not mind." I said through my teeth. They both froze.

"No, you do not get to participate, G." Kieron said calmly. "There are a lot of moving parts and I need to be focused on making sure it all works out. I cannot be distracted worrying about whether or not you are safe."

"I do not need to be looked after during a mission, Kieron." I countered.

"No, you absolutely do not. But if having you stay home gives peace of mind to me and any of the others, it is worth it."

"So you talk about equal treatment for females, but exclude me when there is an opportunity to treat me as an equal?"

"Males and females are not equal in all things, Genevieve." Zain interjected, "If any of us males are caught we will be tortured and eventually killed, but if you, a female is caught … there are far worse things they will do to you. I can assure you Sarla will not be joining Ryett either."

"Like Zain said, it is not equal danger. That does not mean females do not deserve equal say and rights in everyday life. It also does not mean I do not get to protect you. You will not be participating." Kieron said, his voice hard.

"If you think I should stay in Aridale, then I will stay in Aridale, but do you understand how demeaning it is to have you agree with Beck's condition? A condition that affects *me*. Not Sarla, not Aveline, not any other female. *Me*. And from *Beck*. You did not even stand up for me in front of him—in front of everyone. The way you both talked about me as if I was not there, as if I have no say … Don't you ever treat me like a piece of property in front of anyone ever again." With that I stormed into the bedroom and slammed the door behind myself.

Kieron

Kieron rubbed his hands down his face and looked at Zain and Zealand. "She has a point there, brother." Zealand said with a shrug.

"I royally fucked that up didn't I?" Kieron asked. Both males nodded agreement. "You two get ready to leave, I will go talk to her."

Kieron pushed open the door to the bedroom and found Genevieve with her arms crossed and staring out the window. She did not turn when he entered. "Genevieve." He said as he crossed the room to her. He placed his hands on her shoulders and she shrugged him off as she stepped away. When she turned to him she had tears in her eyes. Kieron had grown up in a kingdom where females *were* property and it sickened him. Now here he was perpetuating the problem.

"I am so sorry. I should not have yelled at you." Genevieve said quietly.

He reached for her again and she flinched—like she was expecting him to hit her. *What had he done?* "Baby, don't you ever—" She stepped another step back and averted her eyes as she wrapped her arms around herself, "Don't ever apologize for standing up for yourself." Kieron continued. Genevieve slowly raised her eyes to meet his. "I heard what you said and you are right. Regardless of if you were going to come on the mission or not I should have stood up for you. It should have been a discussion between us, not me making a unilateral decision. And it certainly should not have happened in front of the other kingdoms. I should have stood up for you. I am so sorry."

Genevieve's eyes scanned his face, "Thank you for apologizing." She finally breathed.

He stepped to her and she let him wrap her into his arms. "I am so sorry, baby." Then Kieron used his thumb and forefinger to raise her chin so he could give her a kiss. "Will you forgive me?" He asked. Genevieve nodded and he raised his eyebrows at her. "That easily?" Kieron teased.

Genevieve rolled her eyes and tried to push away, but he pulled her back and kissed her again. Kieron would never make this mistake again. "Are you ready to get out of here?" He asked. Genevieve nodded.

CHAPTER 51

Genevieve

I watched Kieron suit up with his weapons as I sat on the kitchen counter. I still hated that he was leaving me here, but I understood why. I just did not know what I was going to do with myself while he was gone—I knew I would be anxious to know what was happening, if the plan was working, and if he was safe.

"While I am gone, stay in our rooms. No person can enter these rooms without my permission except for Kamari and Orion. You will be safe here." Kieron said as he adjusted his leather wrist cuffs.

"Seriously? I have to stay in our rooms?" I questioned. That seemed a little extreme.

Kieron stepped over to me and took my face in his hands, "Yes, baby. Please stay in our rooms. I will be back no later than tomorrow morning. You can survive a single night without leaving our rooms."

"Of course I can." I responded and he scanned my face. Then he leaned down and kissed my lips.

"If things do not go as planned, Orion knows what to do. And that plan also includes you staying in here." Kieron said his voice hard.

"You do not have to worry about me, Kieron. Focus on what needs to be done and come back to me." I said as I ran my fingers through his long hair.

"I will." He breathed and stepped back from me. Then, with one final look, he closed the door behind himself as he left.

I felt my entire body tense with anxiety. I hated that he was going without me. I hopped off the counter and paced the room. I needed something to do. I sat at the piano and pressed keys down, hoping I would suddenly get the urge to actually play something. I didn't. I stood and paced our balcony overlooking the city.

Kieron, Zealand, Zain, and I—along with the trusted and participating commanders, assassins, warriors, and Undead—had run through the plans countless times. We had looked for any possible hole, any possible way a single piece of the plan could fail. We had found none, but I ran through the plans in my head again as I paced back and forth on the balcony.

The King of the Coasts was not aware the slave trade was operating through the two portals in his lands along with a handful of safehouses. The king's very own general led the operation and kept the king in the dark. Aveline and her forces would secure the portals, destroy the safehouses and deliver the general to the king along with the mountain of evidence Ryett, Kieron, and Kieron's inside guy had on him. Any slaves found in the process would be taken to the Cliffs.

In The Land of the Plains, The King of the Plains collected what was effectively a tax on the drug and slave trade. This kept the king rich and the drug and slave traders in business. The king however, still had a reputation of being a respectable and moral king in Savengard. Without his reputation, the other kingdoms would turn on him. Beck and Ryett would pay The King of the Plains a visit to remind him of what he has to lose while their forces along with Zealand and a group of the Undead destroyed the drug fields and processing plants as well as eliminated the entire chain of command in the drug and slave operations.

The third piece of the plan was Kieron and his forces secretly infiltrating The Land of the Giants to take out the logging and sex slave operation. Not only were the logging camps complete death traps, but The King of the Giants was known for eliminating anyone and everyone he found uninvited inside of his kingdom. Luther had decimated The Land of the Giants in the last war and since then The King of the Giants did not take trespassing lightly —apparently he was quick to kill and would not even bother to ask questions. The bodies of trespassers and enemies of the king were rumored to hang from trees in the forests until they rotted enough to fall to the ground and be consumed by the undergrowth.

None of our allies wanted to risk their people's lives by entering The Land of the Giants without an invitation. So clearly the burden fell on Kieron. The slaves Kieron was to free would then need to be transported to meet Zain and Ryett in the Wastelands. From there they would be brought to The Land of the Mountains. Ryett already had resources in place to care for slaves freed from the sex trade in his kingdom.

I ran the pieces, the timelines, and the players all through my head again and again until I realized even if I found a weak link, there was nothing I could do about it now. I stopped pacing and looked out across the city. The sun had fully set and the stars were out. I resigned to return inside. I would take a shower and go from there.

"How did you two get in here? Kieron said only Kamari and Orion would be able to enter these rooms." I asked from the doorway between the bedroom and living room. I had nearly jumped when I saw Zain lounging on our couches, Mintaka at his feet. I knew Zain would not be leaving until late, but I certainly had not expected to find him in our rooms.

"Remind me to talk to Kieron about updating his wards when he returns." Zain said, sounding bored. "It is nearly time for me to leave, but I thought you might need some company tonight." He gestured down to Mintaka who was curled on the floor next to him.

"Thank you, Zain." I sighed and crouched down to pet Mintaka's head.

Zain stood and straightened his leather jacket. "I do not want to frighten you, but something seems off tonight. Stay alert. We will all be back as soon as we can." I nodded and Zain folded into the air as he disappeared.

I threw myself down onto the couch where he had been sitting moments earlier and let my fingers mindlessly stroke Mintaka's head.

There was a banging on the door and Kamari burst through a heartbeat later. Mintaka was on his feet, the hair on his back standing straight up.

"It's okay, Mintaka." I said and patted his back. He stalked past Kamari and to the door where he paced back and forth.

Kamari's eyes were wide as she watched the Great Wolf walk past her. Then she shook her head and turned back to me, "There is a problem. One of the assassin commanders thinks he can take over the palace while Kieron is gone. Hael and Orion are there, but it is about to get bloody. This is the safest place for us."

"I cannot sit here while Kieron's throne is threatened." I said as I moved towards the door.

"What are you going to do?" Kamari tried to block my way to the door.

I paused and looked her dead in the eye, "Stop him."

Kamari stepped aside with a mischievous grin, "Then let's go. I am coming with you."

CHAPTER 52

Genevieve

As soon as we reached the wing the throne room occupied we heard the fighting. The rest of the palace had been eerily silent, but now ... The sounds of screams and moans of the wounded met us. The floors were slicked with blood and bodies slumped against walls. A few heads had been staked to the pillars that lined the hallways. The fighting was not in this hallway any longer and neither was anyone who was living. We raced on towards the commotion, turning down the gore filled hallways that would take us towards the back entrance to the throne room.

Mintaka cut us off at one corner and Kamari and I almost slammed into the wall as we came to a jolting stop. Mintaka stood still, blocking our path. The commotion we could hear was just out of sight. He gave us both a look as if asking if we were ready. "Let's kick some ass." Kamari breathed beside me. I gave a quick nod and

Mintaka turned, the three of us stepped around the corner.

I ran towards the fighting, bending down as I went to grab a knife off of a dead body. *How do we know who is good?* "Armbands!" Kamari called out as if she had read my mind. Some of the males had red arm bands. "Armbands are the bad guys!" She yelled again. I turned to see her crouched over a bleeding male who was clutching his abdomen. Light flowed from Kamari's hands and into the warrior—healing him. He did not have an armband.

The male looked up at me, "Get to the throne room." He gasped out. "They already breached the throne room."

"Go!" Kamari yelled, "I am more help to the wounded."

I kept running with Mintaka by my side and let my magic carry us. The hallway sped by as everything simultaneously turned into slow motion. Something inside of me seemed to awaken as we slipped between fighting males. I slashed and stabbed and blocked. I killed males with armbands and watched Mintaka not only keep up with me, but leave a trail of bodies in his wake as well. We skidded to a stop at the other end and took one last look at the hallway we had just crossed. Bodies littered the floor and assassins and warriors on our side of the fight looked around in shock as they quickly overwhelmed the few remaining attackers with armbands.

Then I felt the air move as if a strong wind blew and instinctively let my shield envelope us. Magic crashed and broke against it. I whirled around to see the blood covered warrior who had just sent the attack my way. The same warrior who I had met in a dark hallway at a bar weeks before. My eyes dropped to his armband. "Shall we try again, beautiful." He called out and he spun his sword arrogantly. I dropped my shield and faced him. Mintaka let out a low growl beside me. I did not have time for this bullshit. "Kieron is not here to stop me this time." He taunted.

"Who said I need Kieron to stop you." I called back. He sent more magic blasting my way. I easily blocked it with my shield as I stalked towards him. I yanked a sword from a body as I passed. "Leave or die." I yelled down the hall at him.

He only laughed, "Option C, turn you into my very own play thing."

"Die it is then." I responded coolly. Then with a quick skip I sent the sword I had just liberated flying across the hall and buried it through the warriors chest. I let my magic carry me as I sprinted towards him and slammed his back against the wall. "This time, you die for good." I whispered through my teeth as I glared into his eyes. Then I stepped back and let Mintaka rip his throat out. His body fell to the ground and with one more bite, Mintaka had removed the warrior's head from his body.

I gave Mintaka's shoulders a pat as we stood over the dead male. "Come on." I said, we had to get to the throne room.

There was already blood on the floor by the time Mintaka and I slipped in through one of the side doors near the throne. The two sides stood at a stalemate—both poised and ready to continue the fight. Orion and Hael stood in front of a small group of their males and between the traitorous assassin commander and the throne. The assassin commander had twice as many males behind him. "We don't like the direction things are going around here." He sneered. "Some of us aren't willing to give up our … lifestyle."

I walked through the males that protected the throne and made my way towards the front. "You are a coward, Nikolai, for waiting until Kieron was gone to make your move." Orion said through his teeth.

"Maybe I am just smart." Nikolai responded. Then he laughed as his eyes fell on me. "Looks like Kieron's whore wanted to come join the fun." His warriors and assassins behind him chuckled.

I stepped next to Orion and Hael, suddenly aware I had left my acquired weapon stuck in the body of a male in the hallway. I also had apparently not even put shoes on—the marble floor was cold on my bare feet. "Genevieve, you should not be here." Orion whispered to me. Then I watched Nikolai's eyes fall to Mintaka who had stepped next to me.

"What are two more?" Nikolai sneered. "Step aside or we will kill every single one of you and the ones who can't die, we will string up on the city walls like fucking decorations."

"I would like to see you try." I said and I stomped my foot down. My mountain shield erupted from me creating a solid, impenetrable wall between Nikolai and those protecting the throne.

"Genevieve!" I heard Orion's muffled yell. I had let my shield block everyone behind me and I now stood on the side with Nikolai and his assassins and warriors. *Shit*. Shit. Shit. Not exactly what I had planned, but impressive nonetheless.

"So you want to go first." Nikolai laughed wickedly.

"I guess I'm going first." I responded with a smile and took my fighting stance. This was not what I had planned, but I was going with it. Better to fake confidence than to show panic.

"Genevieve, drop your shield!" I heard Orion call out. I didn't drop my shield. Enough of Kieron's forces had been killed tonight. I would do what I could and when the time was right, I would drop my shield and let Orion and Hael finish the job. I had no intention of dying—and I was not delusional enough to think I would beat a room full of seasoned killers on my own—I was just tipping the scales in our favor. I was the distraction.

Mintaka stepped through my shield—I guess the laws of magic did not apply to Great Wolves. He circled my legs before taking his place next to me. An eerie calm settled within me as I watched Nikolai's eyes dart fearfully to the Great Wolf. "Kill her." Nikolia's order was nearly a whisper.

The front line of assassins and warriors all moved at once. With a quick movement of my hands I had used my shield to blast them all on their asses. The victory was short lived as more males appeared from the air near me, blades swinging. I barely gave it a thought and my hands now held long knives. I sliced and stabbed and blood sprayed as Mintaka and I cut down another wave of fighters. I did not think, I just moved. I let all of my training and all of my rage flow. It was easy—easy to move, easy to command my magic, easy to kill. My blade sliced the throat of a male as my shield blocked his blade from skewering me through my center. I pushed his body to the side and pointed my knife directly at Nikolai.

"You are just a fucking whore!" Nikolai yelled as he stalked towards me, "I will kill you myself."

A deafening crack split the air and Nikolai and his followers spun to the doorway of the throne room. "I suggest you set down your weapons and get the fuck out of my palace before my—what did you call her? Whore? Yes, I believe that is what you called her. Before my whore turns all of you into a bloody mist." Kieron's voice echoed in the silence. It was lethal and laced with boredom. No one moved. I let my shield that protected Orion, Hael, and the others dissipate. "What do you think, sweetheart? Should I let them live?" Kieron asked in a mocking tone.

"I think the Eastern Desert has a few vacancies." I responded flatly.

Nikolai started to protest, but before three words could come out of his mouth he and all the warriors and assassins with him folded into the air and disappeared. I looked around in surprise. Only Hael and his assassins were left. All of the Undead were gone, along with Kieron. Mintaka nuzzled his head under my hand and I stroked his head as I looked over him quickly. He was covered in blood—none of it was his. I let out a sigh of relief seeing he was unharmed.

A moment later Kieron reappeared in front of me, "And what are you doing out of our rooms, baby?"

I shrugged my shoulders, "I couldn't let the boys have all the fun. What happened to them?"

"We took them to the Eastern Desert." He said simply as Orion and the Undead reappeared in the throne room. "If they make it to the Palace of the Undead then they might get the opportunity to live."

"So how was the rest of your evening?" I asked as if this was just a normal day. As if I had not just been facing a group of assassins and warriors who promised to kill us. As if Kieron had not just suddenly returned from hopefully destroying the portion of the slave network he was assigned to dismantle.

Kieron looked down at my bare feet and then back up at my face with raised eyebrows, "Successful, but it looks like your evening was also exciting." He stepped close to me and lifted my chin to give me a kiss. Then he whispered so only I could hear him, "I will only ask you one more time. What happened to staying in our rooms?"

I bit my lip and looked into his eyes, "I will take my spanking whenever you see fit to give it."

His eyes lit with amusement and hunger. True to his word he had stopped enforcing his rules after that night in the Eastern Desert, but that did not mean I didn't let him spank me. "It is going to be much more than a spanking." He said, his voice low.

"Good." I breathed as my heart skipped a beat.

CHAPTER 53

Genevieve

"Did you have any surprises?" I asked as Kieron and I finally slipped back into our rooms. Kieron had spent the last hours ensuring everything was safe in the palace and the city—as well as making sure the blood was cleaned up from the palace and the injured and dead were taken care of appropriately. I had mostly just tagged along and watched in awe as Kieron gave orders. Assassins and warriors dropped their eyes and dipped their chins to me. Kieron explained it was a gesture of respect—apparently word had gotten around that I was not just a slave whore from the dungeons.

I was walking across the living room towards the bedroom when I felt Kieron's hand slip into mine and pull me to a stop. "I thought I was going to lose you." Kieron said as he stared into my eyes. "I have never been so afraid in my entire life, G." He whispered. I could see the pain behind his beautiful hazel eyes—the fear.

"We had it under control." I managed to say softly back.

His hands brushed my hair back from my face as he stepped close to me. He tilted my head so he could kiss my forehead. "Maybe." He breathed and wrapped his arms around me. The warmth from his embrace washed through my body as I sunk into his arms.

We stood embracing each other for heartbeats. "Hey now, I thought you were going to give me a spanking." I finally teased.

He pulled back and looked at me, "I am serious, G. Please do not ever scare me like that again."

"I did what—"

"I told you to stay in our rooms." There was a slight bite to his voice.

"I was not just going to sit here and do nothing—"

"Baby! What if they had killed you? Or worse?"

"This was not my first fight and you trained me better than that." I countered.

"It was an entire group of assassins and warriors, G. Some of the most deadly males in all of Savengard and you locked Orion and Hael out from helping you. What were you thinking?" Kieron said sternly as he held my shoulders and stared into my eyes. It felt like I was being scolded.

"If they were some of the most deadly males in all of Savengard, then you boys need to step up your training because I held them off just fine." I stepped back from him and crossed my arms over my chest. "You can thank me whenever you feel like it."

Kieron rolled his eyes and shook his head as a small smile crossed his mouth. "Okay, it was pretty badass. *You* were pretty badass."

"Thank you." I said matter of factly. "Now I would like to receive my spanking." I could not even keep a straight face as I said it.

Kieron chuckled and scooped me up, wrapping my legs around his waist and his hands squeezed my ass. His lips pressed against mine and he playfully bit my bottom lip. My hands held his face as I kissed him back. *He had made it back safely.* All of the tension I had been holding on to finally released from my body as I kissed him. Desire and warmth rushed in to take its place. It did not matter that we were both exhausted. I wanted him. I needed him right now. He swept us into the bedroom and closed the door before pressing my back against it.

My entire body heated as we tasted each other and Kieron's hands expertly roamed my body feeling every curve and corner. He set my feet down on the floor only to remove his jacket and shirt. He dropped them in a pile on the floor. Then he pulled my shirt over my head and my pants down and off. His lips trailed kisses up my body as he returned to standing. "I thought I was going to lose you." He breathed again as his nose brushed mine.

"You didn't lose me." I whispered back against his lips. My hands found the fastenings on his pants and I undid them. I stroked the thick hard length of him with my hand and his body shuddered.

Then his hands gripped my ass as he lifted me again. I let my legs wrap around his waist as he pressed my back against the door and guided himself to my entrance. I gasped at the stretch as he pressed into me. "That's it, baby." Kieron coaxed and he slid slightly out before pressing himself back in deeper. I could not help the whimper that escaped my lips as I rocked my hips to take him fully inside of me. This was a craving I could never satiate. I would never get enough of him. One of his hands raised to my face as he kissed me and let my body relax around him. We had sex almost every day—and sometimes multiple times in a single day—but each time Kieron made sure to let me adjust to his size.

The wooden door bit into my spine and shoulder blades as Kieron slowly began to thrust into me. I clung to him as pleasure filled my body and warmth tingled through all of my limbs. My hips rocked as I moved with him, taking him deeper. Then Kieron pulled me from the door and carried me, with himself still inside of me, to the bed. He lay me on my back and slowly pulled out. I watched him pull his pants fully off and opened my legs for him expectantly. Instead of kneeling between my legs, Kieron dropped to his knees and pulled my hips to the side of the bed, guiding my legs back so that I was completely open to him. His head dipped to me and he licked up my center. I moaned in pleasure as he did it again before his mouth closed around my bundle of nerves as he kissed and teased me with his tongue.

Kieron drew my pleasure from my body and through his mouth as he feasted on me. His hands roamed and rubbed and teased. When I had climaxed for the third time he gently guided my legs around him as he kissed and licked and tasted his way up my body. I pulled his mouth to mine and he slid himself inside of me. I dug my fingers into his back and he groaned against my mouth as our bodies moved together.

I did not feel our magic taking us anywhere tonight. Instead I felt it holding us right here in this moment—in this world. In the beauty of the sweat mixing between our bodies. In the pleasure of where our bodies joined and became one. In the pure raw emotion of love that we both had not yet spoken, but clearly worshiped each other with through our touch.

Kieron pulled my body as he rolled to his back and positioned me on top of him. I let his hands guide my hips as I rode him. I let my eyes close and my head tilt back in the ecstasy of it. "No, baby. I want you to look me in the eyes while I fuck you." Kieron groaned as his hand reached up and he laced his fingers into my hair behind my head. I did exactly as he asked and turned my face to stare directly into his hungry eyes. Just seeing the way he looked at me while he was inside of me had me almost at my edge again. "That's my good girl." He whispered and another climax tore through my body, sending warmth and electricity washing through my skin.

"Oh fuck, Kieron." I moaned as he pulled my body down on top of his. His tongue slid into my mouth and I sucked it as he thrust into me. He gently tugged my hair to pull my face away from his. "You fuck me so good." I gasped between my whimpers. "I want you to come inside of me."

◆ ◆ ◆

Kieron

Kieron's eyes rolled back as electricity washed through him with what Genevieve had just said. It had almost sent him over the edge, but he forced himself to return his eyes to meet hers. His hand tightened in Genevieve's hair and his other hand lifted her ass and held firm. "Tell me to come inside of you again, baby." Kieron groaned out.

"Come inside of me." Genevieve gasped as he pounded hard into her. It did not matter if it was slow or fast or in their bed or against the wall or across a table—Kieron loved fucking Genevieve. He loved her taste, her smell, the way her skin felt. He would never get enough of her. She let out a moan and her voice begged him again, "Come in me. Oh fuck, come in—I'm going to come, I'm going—oh yes!" Kieron's cock was ready to explode and watching the pleasure on Genevieve's face as she stared into his eyes and came for him made him that much closer. Her inner muscles tightened around him and he could not contain it any longer. Kieron grunted as he pounded three last thrusts deep into her and her body shuddered in his grip. Kieron groaned in ecstasy as he pulled her body close to his. He held her firmly as he pressed deep inside of her, filling her with his seed.

Their breathing was synced as Genevieve lay on top of him. Kieron gently untangled his fingers from her hair before stroking them down the back of her head. "You are so fucking beautiful." Kieron whispered quietly between his deep breaths. She was. She was magnificent. She was *his.* Genevieve lifted her head to look at him and Kieron brushed her hair out of her face before kissing her again. *Genevieve was his.*

CHAPTER 54

Genevieve

We received word the following day from our allies that each portion of the slave network had in fact been destroyed. Everything had gone as close as you could get to exactly as planned when it comes to missions with multiple moving pieces. Between our four kingdoms, we had enough forces to execute each portion with minimal casualties. I could tell Kieron's mind was wandering and in complete shock as we continued to receive the good news. He had tossed and turned all night and now came the next huge step in changing his kingdom: Today he would announce the end of slavery in the Deserts.

I had given him a few words of support and encouragement over breakfast and before we entered the throne room for the announcement. The room was filled with leadership from the palace and city. Leadership from other cities in Deserts were also present. I stood off to the side with Zealand and Orion as Kieron took a seat in his throne. The steady buzz of chatter from the full room quieted as Kieron sat.

"First, I would like to announce the formation of formal alliances with The Land of the Mountains, The Land of the Lakes, and The Land of the Cliffs. These three kingdoms have offered their support and resources to The Land of the Deserts. The new Deserts. For in the coming days, months, and years, we will be making changes not only to the laws that govern this kingdom, but to the way we choose to live our lives in this kingdom." Kieron's voice was strong and even as he addressed the crowded court within the throne room. He paused and there were only small murmurs among the crowd.

Kieron continued, "Effective immediately, there will be no more slavery within The Land of the Deserts and the Deserts will no longer support any other kingdom or individual who wishes to keep slaves." The room fell completely silent. "Starting today, the slaves within the royal residences will be met with and given their freedom. Next, we will be visiting the Diamond, Mineral, and Salt mines to arrange for a pause in the mining operations as the slaves are given their freedom and assisted in creating their new lives either here or in one of our allies' kingdoms. All members of the royal service in the positions of overseers will be reassigned with their preferences taken into account. Any disturbances to the process of welcoming new members to our kingdom or relocating them to another kingdom will not be tolerated."

Kieron stood from his throne, "The court is dismissed." The room erupted in chatter as we left through the side door. Orion and

Zealand flanked us and Zain waited for us in the hallway. Hael and his guards remained in the throne room.

"Well done, Kieron." Orion said as we walked, "Now to the mess hall to share the good news with the new members of our kingdom."

It had all been arranged, small groups of the slaves would be filtered through the slave dining hall and given the news. Kamari and the other volunteers were already set up to provide each one with their information packet and next steps as they exited. Over the coming week they would be able to decide if they wanted to leave or if they would stay. And if they were staying, they could then choose between continuing to work within the palace, taking vocational training, or seeking employment outside of the palace. We had people in place to help them on their journey whichever way they chose.

We entered the dining hall to a room full of people. Most of them kept their heads down and all seemed highly anxious. Never had a king summoned a gathering of his slaves and never had a king come to their dining hall to address them.

The afternoon was a blur. I sat at the long table with Kamari and the other volunteers as we provided information and next step directions to the newly freed slaves. They all waited patiently and quietly in line to reach the table. Many had tears streaming down their faces as they accepted their packets and returned to their quarters. I watched as the palace guards, now under Hael's command, compassionately assisted the new members of the Desert kingdom in gathering their items and navigating where they were to go next.

It was nearly midnight by the time we were able to abandon our posts and head back to bed. I knew the next day would be more of the same. And the day after would be too. We had just begun the huge undertaking of helping these people join regular society. I found Kieron awake in our kitchen sipping a glass of amber liquor and staring blankly into nothing when I returned to our rooms.

"Hey." I said as I slid up against the counter next to him. I summoned a glass and poured myself a splash of liquor too.

"Hey." He whispered back.

"Everything okay?" I asked.

He finally turned his head slowly and looked over at me. "We are doing it. The slave network is gone. We are freeing the slaves. We are doing it. I have been planning this for nearly four hundred years and it is finally happening. I am so afraid I am going to go to sleep and wake up to find out this is all just a dream."

I slid my arm around his waist and rested my head on his shoulder. "It's not a dream."

"I just can't stop thinking about what bad things might be coming next. Nothing this good ever happens to me. You are here. We are ending slavery and transforming the Deserts into a better place than it has been in thousands of years ... What terrible thing is going to happen to balance all of this out?"

I felt the same. I was not used to having good things stay around. With every good thing I saw, my brain offered me an equal and opposite tragic scenario of how this would all come crashing down around me. I was haunted by these thoughts. We were silent for heartbeats, then I finally spoke, "I have one rule: Don't die. Outside of that, whatever happens we can handle it. We will face it together, Kieron."

He huffed a small laugh. "I don't like that I am leaving you here when I go to the mines tomorrow." He replied.

"I don't like it either." I chuckled.

"I mean it. I know it makes the most sense for you to stay and continue to help here, but I do not want to be away from you after this."

I gave him a squeeze, "Then let's not be apart after this. Maybe in like a hundred years when you are sick of me you can take a solo vacation, but you are stuck with me until then."

"Deal." He breathed and kissed my forehead. "Let's get some sleep."

Zealand met Kieron at our rooms the next morning. He was in charge of the forces that would be accompanying Kieron to the mines. I knew this might be the most dangerous part of freeing the slaves—when you had nearly thirty thousand people who had been forced into slave labor for centuries in a brutal work camp there was always the possibility of something going wrong.

"We will be back in three days." Kieron told me as he gathered his things. "Please let Orion and Hael watch over you, I know it is a little over protective, but if someone wants to get at me they are going to target you."

"I know, Kieron. I promise to let them watch over me. I won't slip the guards they assign to me either." I gave him a wink.

"You better not." He laughed.

Then I turned to Zealand, "Zealand, I am sorry, but I got word that Annistyn is unable to come. I will continue to find reasons to invite her if you want me to."

Zealand blushed a little, "Thanks, Genevieve. Maybe after all of this is sorted ..."

"Of course." I smiled at him. "Now you two, please stay out of trouble."

"What? We never get into trouble." Zealand said, faking that he was offended by my comment.

I rolled my eyes at them and gave Kieron a hug. He squeezed me tightly before kissing me on the lips, "I will see you soon." He whispered. Then the two males left our rooms as they headed to join the warriors who would accompany them.

It was lunch and Kamari and I were organizing packets and flipping through records to see how things were progressing. The other volunteers were off enjoying a break.

"Hey, Kamari. I know this is probably not the right time or place to be asking you, but how might I get myself a contraceptive? What I have is almost empty." I asked as I filed papers away.

She simply summoned a small bottle and held it out to me, "You asked the right person."

I took it from her and disappeared it—sending it to our bathroom. "Thanks."

"You know ... both of you don't need to take a contraceptive." She said casually. I stopped what I was doing and looked at her. She glanced up, "Kieron has been taking one for months."

"How long ... he got me ..." My mind was spinning. *How long had he been on a contraceptive? Was he on one when he had gotten me pregnant?*

Kamari's eyes widened, "Oh shit. That's ... He got you pregnant while you were in the dungeons." She breathed. She looked completely horrified. I nodded slowly. "After you were gone from here he came back one day freaking out and asked me about missing a dose and if that could allow him to get a female pregnant ... I did not know he was asking because he ..." Her voice trailed off as her wide eyes searched my face.

I sat down in a chair. "Obviously I lost the baby." I whispered.

"I am so sorry, Genevieve." Kamari said as she sat next to me. "All of that must have been completely awful." I gave her a small nod of confirmation. Her hand found mine and she sat quietly with me until I shook off my thoughts and stood to get back to work.

CHAPTER 55

Kieron

They arrive at The Diamond Mine in the north of his kingdom first. Next would be The Salt Mine in the west, then The Mineral Mine in the south. The mines had always haunted Kieron. He had sent many slaves to their death by sentencing them to work in the mines. The Diamond Mine was the worst—by far. It had small tunnels that were dangerous and prone to cave-ins. In the winter months it could be brutally cold at night and it was not unheard of for slaves to freeze to death from exposure with the poor excuse for clothing and shelter they were provided.

Not only did he need to eliminate the slave labor in this mine, but it needed a complete overhaul. Maybe it just needed to be closed. Either way, he could not deny that the stones pulled from this mine were beautiful. They were known for their extremes—either clear as glass or flecked a beautiful salt and pepper. The salt and pepper diamonds were his favorite. Each one was unique. The clear diamonds all looked the same once they were cut.

The overseers from the mines took their leave as Zealand gave directions to the new forces who would stay at the mine while the slaves transitioned to freedom. After all the overseers had left, Kieron and Zealand made their way to the building that housed the management for the mining operations.

"King. General." The mine's chief operator greeted them. "The leadership of the slaves have gathered and are waiting for you."

The announcement had gone well. The slaves were now being processed and many were already on their way to Aridale to heal from the horrors they had endured and to choose what would come next for them. There was one group of newly freed members of his kingdom who had asked to remain at the mines to work—with the condition they could improve the mine's operations and more appropriate living quarters would be arranged for them. It had been an easy ask to agree to.

The leader from that group—who currently oversaw the sorting of the diamonds pulled from the mine—now tentatively approached Kieron. "King of the Deserts. I would like to give you something." He said nervously. Then he stuck out his hand. Kieron lifted his palm and the male dropped a single salt and pepper diamond into Kieron's hand. "This stone is the last stone to be mined under slave labor. It represents an end to a horrible and dark time and the beginning of something new. Something better. Thank you. Thank you for granting us freedom."

Kieron, in his shock, just looked down at the large stone. When he looked back up the male bowed his head and hurried away. Kieron's fingers wrapped around the beautiful diamond before he slipped it into his pocket.

Kieron stood in the ginormous Salt Mine tunnels. He knew Genevieve had an aversion to tunnels and caverns, but this was something he would need to take her to see. It was impressive to say the least. The Salt Mine was the most prosperous mine of the three—and the safest.

When Kieron had shared his proposal for wages and upgraded housing, many of the new members of the kingdom had requested to stay and continue working the mine. Kieron had been shocked. That shock still had not worn off as he now stood at one of the mine's main tunnel intersections with Zealand beside him. They stared into the dark tunnels that stretched out in multiple directions in front of them. The mine had levels upon levels and tunnels that traveled for miles. "Have you heard the rumors about this place?" Zealand said quietly.

"Which one?" Kieron asked. He had heard countless tales about each of the three mines—all of them were dark and twisted and made of nightmares.

"That no one has been to the bottom of this thing in thousands of years. They say there is something lurking down there." Zealand said as a visible shiver ran through his body.

Kieron just glanced over at his friend. He had not heard that rumor. "So the safest mine of the three mines in the Deserts is the home of some unknown ... *thing?*"

Zealand patted Kieron on the back, "Well I sure as shit am not going to go down there to find out." Kieron laughed and they both turned back towards the entrance to the vast tunnel system.

Kieron woke on the third day away from Aridale with a strong ache in his body. Everything inside of him was pulling him to return to the city—to return to Genevieve. It was not because he felt she was in any danger. He just no longer felt ... *whole*. He had waited centuries for a fraction of the good he currently had—for a fraction of the happiness he felt—but it still felt like a dream. Like it was not real. He rolled out of bed and slipped into his clothes. One more day and he would be back with her. He had lived his entire life without her, he could get through one more day.

Kieron heard a knock at his door and Zealand cracked it open a moment later. "They are ready for you, Kieron." He said simply. Kieron nodded and took a deep breath. This was the final piece of freeing every slave in the Deserts and it was just the beginning of the work that needed to be done to ensure his kingdom changed for the better. He had never wanted to be a king. Never wanted this responsibility. Never wanted the attention. But since he was here, he was going to make sure he did everything in his power to create lasting change for his kingdom.

CHAPTER 56

Genevieve

The last few weeks had been a blur. Surprisingly everything had been going quite smoothly with the relocation and redistribution of the new members of the kingdom. There had of course been a few disruptions, but Orion, Zealand, and Hael's forces had been prepared to diffuse each situation—or end it quickly. Many of the previous overseers took to their new assignments well and were even glad to no longer be running slaves. If anyone was having a hard time with the changes, they were doing a good job keeping their mouths shut.

Word had gotten around quickly that Nikolai and his followers had been banished to the Eastern Desert and it appeared no one else wanted to meet the same fate. The greed and hunger for complete domination from Vossarian and his forefathers was a blessing we did not know we had. Most of the new members of the kingdom as well as those who served the crown saw slaves as things belonging to the king. Most of those who served the crown had stayed clear of the slaves for fear that they would be punished for using something that was not theirs to use.

I kept busy checking in with each of the groups to make sure things were still going smoothly. I also spent too much time with the palace designers arranging and rearranging rooms for new employees, as well as classrooms and meeting rooms for the vocational training that would happen at the palace. At least most of the stuffy and dark decor had been removed from the palace and what replaced it gave new life and color to the halls.

I was on my way to The War Room to find Kieron and hopefully sneak him away for a quiet dinner just the two of us. I knew we both needed the quiet. Watching Kieron rule his people was amazing to see—being deep into helping reshape this kingdom was amazing to be a part of—but when it was just the two of us we both admitted we missed the quiet. That we would not choose this chaos or this responsibility. However, we both believed so much in what we were doing that we would see it through.

◆ ◆ ◆

Kieron

"The gates are still up, but we have lost our trace on Rook." Zealand informed Kieron.

"What do you mean you have lost Rook?" Kieron's head snapped up.

Zealand pulled a map from the air and unrolled it across the table of The War Room. Kieron stood up to look at the map with Zealand, "Rook has been keeping to his home in the south—rarely leaving and he has only had a few visitors. Three days ago he went out and never came back. We tracked him through the dunes and into The Land of the Plains. That is where we lost him. We have also seen odd movement of the beasts in the Wastelands near gates six and twenty." Zealand's hand skimmed along the map pointing to the different areas he had described.

Kieron's fingers tightened on the table, he had taken a huge risk letting Rook leave with his head, and now they were going to learn how big of a mistake it had actually been. Gate six was the king gate that bordered The Land of the Mountains and gate twenty bordered The Land of the Giants. "We have to find him." Kieron said, his voice low. "If he has left the Deserts and entered the Wastes then he is probably heading to—"

Genevieve pushed in the door. "Well you two look serious. What am I interrupting?"

"Rook is missing and probably up to no good." Kieron said as he straightened up from the table.

"We will obviously keep looking, Kieron. I will assign a group to head into the Wastes now." Zealand said. Then he nodded to Genevieve and left the war room.

Kieron should have killed Rook when he had the chance. Rook was a rabid animal and would do everything he could to regain power and status. He did not even want to think about what would happen if Rook was behind whatever strange thing was happening with the beasts in the Wastelands.

"Are you able to have dinner with just me tonight?" Genevieve asked as she slid next to Kieron where he stood at the table.

He wrapped his arm around her shoulder and kissed her hair, "Of course, baby. Let's get out of here."

As Genevieve and Kieron settled into dinner, Kieron's brain was wandering elsewhere. If Rook was heading into the Wastes it was quite possible he was heading to the tombs—

"What's on your mind?" Genevieve asked gently. Kieron glanced up and saw her looking at him, her head slightly tilted to the side.

"I'm sorry, baby. I am thinking about what Rook might be getting himself into ... getting all of us into." Kieron responded as he set down his fork.

"What do you think he is doing?" She asked.

"I think he is heading to the tombs." Genevieve only raised her eyebrows in question. "In the middle of the Wastelands is The Lands of the Mother. Just south from there are the tombs. No one is quite sure who is buried there. It is heavily guarded by the beasts of the Wastes, but some of the legends allude to dark gods who fought in the war that resulted in the fracturing of our world into the twenty-seven worlds being entombed there. These dark gods do not have life and death like other beings, so it is more of a prison than a tomb, but these are just stories and hypotheses." Kieron explained.

"Why would Rook be going there?" Genevieve asked carefully.

"To free them." Kieron said simply, "It was part of Vossarian's plan to gain access to The Lands of the Mother. Free the dark gods and use their power to destroy the gates … or destroy enough of the worlds that the gates would fall. If Rook is sneaking his way into the Wastelands I would not put it past him to give it a try himself."

"Maybe—"

"I know. I should have just killed him." Kieron resigned. He should have. He had been trying to be better—to be an example for a better kingdom—but he had put worlds at risk if this was really what Rook was up to.

"That was not what I was going to say." Genevieve said sternly.

"Well I should have at least sent him to one of the destroyed worlds and made him work his ass off to get back here."

Genevieve just studied him for heartbeats before asking, "What world is Savengard?"

"Everyone thinks Savengard is World One. The Original World." Kieron took a swig of the amber liquor in front of him.

Genevieve snorted, "Of course they do. Doesn't every world think they are The One, The Only, The Original?"

Kieron had to laugh at that, she was right. He stroked his beard, "You are very right, sweetheart. What is even more interesting is that we are missing a world. From the Tenth World to the Twenty-Sixth World we know which is which. We even know that magic fades and life spans decrease as the world number increases. Obviously there is some debate about the Twenty-Seventh World, if it exists, but you know it does. However, World One through World Nine, no one can agree which world is which. We have assigned World Three to the world with a portal into the Coasts and World One to Savengard, but there are only eight worlds catelogged."

Genevieve leaned back in her chair and stared at him. This issue was the weirdest thing to Kieron. It bugged him greatly. He had researched it for centuries. World Walkers had been traveling between worlds for tens of thousands of years and still did not have an answer. Kieron had also not been able to figure out an answer in all the time he spent exploring the corridor between the worlds.

"That is … very odd." Genevieve finally said. Then she shook her head, "What I was trying to find out was how many worlds have been destroyed and how weak would that make the gates to The Lands of the Mother."

"Again another discrepancy. I know of six destroyed worlds … most believe there are only three destroyed … plus yours would make seven." Kieron explained. Only the destruction of three of the worlds had been publicly announced. The other three had been secretly torn into little pieces until they no longer existed. Word had not gotten out about the fate of the twenty-sixth world. There were few enough remaining active World Walkers that they still had not figured out which worlds were gone.

"So if Rook frees these dark gods—" Genevieve started.

"We are all fucked." Kieron finished for her.

CHAPTER 57

Genevieve

I took a deep breath and let my magic wrap around my body, pulling me back and the world around me closed. I gasped as I smacked into our couch across the room.

"Yes!" Kieron yelled, "You did it!"

"I did it!" I screamed back in excitement and spun around in time for Kieron to tackle me onto the couch. "I jumped!" I said between the kisses Kieron was planting on my lips.

"Yes you did, baby!" He said with a huge grin. Then he pushed himself up from the couch and pulled me with him, "Now do it again."

Kieron had continued to train me each day and we were able to dedicate more time to it as things settled down with helping the new members of the kingdom figure out where they wanted to be and what they wanted to do. My fighting had continued to improve and my strength and control over my magic was growing as well. Today was the first day I had actually accomplished jumping.

In my excitement I wrapped my magic and the world around me again and appeared in the kitchen. Then again and appeared on the balcony. Then again and appeared right back at Kieron's feet, where I slung my arms around his neck and gave him a kiss. "I did it!"

He was grinning ear to ear as he lifted me up and spun me around. "Now that you know how it feels to do it yourself, there is something I want to show you if you are up for it?"

"Of course!" I beamed back at him.

His hand wrapped mine and the world folded in. For a split second I felt the crushing pressure I had felt when I had traveled between worlds—then there was just … nothing.

I looked around. It wasn't light. It wasn't dark. There was just … nothing—and it echoed like an empty hallway. "Where are we?" I breathed.

"Between worlds." Kieron replied. "I did not go to world walker school. Luther and Orion taught me themselves. Both of them went and they taught me the same way—use your strength to tear through the worlds. It seems that everyone who can world walk just forces their way through from world to world. I used to world walk just to escape the Deserts. When I was pushed past my limits I would just disappear into other worlds for a while. Then one day I found this." He gestured to the nothingness around us, "As best as I can figure out, this is almost like a corridor that stretches between all of the worlds. You won't find mention of it in any of the books about the worlds either. I have looked. And from this corridor, we can simply pick which world we want to go to … and more or less when as well."

I took a careful step forward. I could feel solid ground beneath my feet, but I could not see it, there was just nothing. I took another step and shimmering rectangular—what I could only describe as windows—emerged from the nothingness. Countless windows stretched in every direction. "What are those?" I asked.

Kieron took my hand, "Those are gates to the other worlds. On the floor in front of each gate you will see the world number and sometimes other numbers inscribed. Those other numbers tell you the when. Some gates are missing, or at least I have not found them yet." I looked up at Kieron in shock. This corridor was a catalog —a master gate—for every world and every point in time. Kieron continued, "I have never gone through a gate for another time, only the gates for the present. That was the one thing Orion continually and painfully lectured me on, 'Don't fuck with time, Kieron.'" Kieron chuckled as he said it.

I was speechless and my mouth hung open in awe. Kieron tugged on my hand and he playfully hopped a few steps backwards, dragging me with him. Then he took me in both hands and pulled me into a waltz. Dancing with Kieron was never a performance. It was never for onlookers or to show status. When Kieron danced with me, he was solely focused on me. It was a way to connect with each other. A way to share joy. A way to show he cared about me.

A giggle erupted from my lips as he spun me out and back into his arms. He planted a kiss on my mouth, "Come on, I have somewhere in particular I am taking you." He nearly whispered. Then he led me by my hand as he jogged into the nothingness.

Windows into worlds flashed by. The scenery changed with

every one. It was like window shopping down a main street full of shops—but the shops were worlds. Then Kieron stopped in front of a dark window. He reached his hand out and it disappeared as it crossed the plane of the window. I followed next to him as we stepped through.

The land around us was covered in black and gray dust. The shell of a few trees remained. "Welcome back to your world." Kieron said softly. I looked around. It was just like the last time I had seen it. "I thought we could finish restoring it together. Help life begin again."

I looked up into his golden hazel eyes. "I don't know how." I breathed.

"I do." He said gently. "Look at this." He bent down and brushed dust back from a single green sprout. "You said you sent pulses of your magic out into this world when Vossarian took you here. When you did that, you already started the process. Since you were here, it has not deteriorated further, but it also has not changed. It is like it is paused. Waiting. The land just needs more of your magic poured into it."

I looked around again. The people of this world had been destroying it—we had been destroying it. Slowly killing the land. And for what? Power? Money? Some people were trying to save it. Trying to make changes for the better. There were good people who were killed when Vossarian destroyed this place. Maybe it could give life to good people again. "Show me how." I said to Kieron.

Kieron

Kieron stepped behind Genevieve and gave her a hug before guiding her hands out in front of her with her palms facing up. "Just let your magic flow out of you and wrap it into the land. Let it flow like a trickle of water. I will be right here with you and I will not let anything happen to you."

Kieron had helped Vossarian destroy worlds—sucked the life right out of them—but he had never restored one. In theory, the only world he would be able to restore was Savengard. He was not even sure he would be able to do that. Genevieve had magic that matched his—dark and powerful—and he had only learned to use his as a weapon, but when he was with her, when their magic was together, it felt like he could *create* worlds.

Genevieve took a deep breath and as she let it out, Kieron could feel her magic slowly pour out through the palms of her hands. "That's it, baby. You are doing it." He breathed against her hair. Dark light wove itself into the dust and spread out from them. As he watched it, he had the urge to let his magic flow as well. He raised his palms next to hers and shimmering heat wove its way into her magic and out into the dust. The air and the ground sparkled around them as their magic mixed and flowed out into the twenty-sixth world. He felt Genevieve's body relax back against his and he dropped his hands to wrap them around her.

He did not know how long they stayed like this, but he eventually felt Genevieve's magic start to weaken. The stream that poured from her was smaller now. He raised his hands and wrapped her hands closed in his. "That is enough, sweetheart. You did it."

Green shoots now peeked their way up through the dust all around them. The gray of the sky had lightened and a soft breeze was blowing. "Thank you, Kieron. Thank you for bringing me here so we could restore my world." She whispered.

"You're welcome, baby. Now let's get you home so you can rest." He said and kissed her hair. She nodded and he pulled them back into the corridor that spanned between the worlds.

CHAPTER 58

Genevieve

I opened my eyes and looked at Kieron breathing heavily next to me. He was still asleep and the sun had just started to rise. Today was his birthday. His four hundred and twentieth birthday. Somehow between everything that had been going on, Kamari, Hael, Orion, Zealand, and I had found the time to recruit some of the staff from the palace to plan a party Kieron would never forget.

When we had approached many of the restaurants and the shops in the city with requests to commission them to participate, they all waved away our money and told us it would be an honor to celebrate their king. Somehow, as word and plans spread, Kieron seemed completely oblivious to the fact that anything was going to happen. Probably because he was so completely engulfed in running his kingdom and managing all of the changes—it was easy for any one of us to distract him with some urgent need if he almost stumbled upon our birthday planning for him.

I slipped out of bed quietly and got dressed in the bathroom before jumping from there to the doors of Kamari and Hael's rooms. I knocked and a few moments later Kamari opened the door.

"Good morning!" She said brightly, a grin plastered to her face. She stepped back and let me inside.

"You are way too perky at this time of the morning, Kamari." I responded with a laugh.

"How can I *not* be? Today is going to be such a good day. We have never thrown a party like this and everything is ready to go."

I gave a sigh of relief. That was exactly what I needed to hear. "Thank you, Kamari! I am still planning for us to exit the front doors midmorning."

"We will all be ready." She said with a smile.

"Perfect. I will see you then." I responded, then with a wink I folded into the air and reappeared in our rooms near the glass doors that led to the balcony.

I listened for a moment and did not hear that Kieron had woken up yet. I let myself stare out over the city. In my world, this day was to celebrate all who had passed on from this life to the next life. I knew too many people who had. I had sent too many people into the next life. I took a moment to send my love out to everyone I had lost—and to three in particular. It was an ache—a hole—that could never be filled, but I could still find joy in this life. I could still find more love. I still had love to give. I took a deep breath. The rest of today was for Kieron.

I slipped back into our bedroom and dropped my clothes before climbing back into bed and wrapping my body against Kieron's. He groaned gently and wrapped his arm around me, pulling me closer.

"Good morning, birthday boy." I whispered against his skin before planting a kiss on his chest. His hand stroked my back.

"Good morning, sweetheart." He whispered back.

As Kieron had requested, we ate breakfast together in bed. Naked. Then we retreated to our massive bath. While we were in the bath I summoned a small black box and held it out to Kieron. He gave me a questioning look, "What is this?"

"I got you a present." I said with a small smile.

He took it from me without dropping his eyes from mine. Then he looked down and slowly pulled the ends of the leather strap I had used as a bow. He opened the box and pulled out the braided metal bracelet I had gotten him. I watched his throat bob as he swallowed. "Thank you, baby." He whispered as he gently set the box on the side of the tub and slipped the bracelet on his wrist.

"Do you like it?" I asked carefully. He was just staring at it. I really hoped he liked it.

He nodded and then raised his head and reached out to pull my body close to his. "I love it. No one has ever gotten me a gift on my birthday and this one is extra special. Thank you." His hands found the sides of my face as he stared deep into my eyes before kissing me.

Finally, midmorning was approaching and we had somehow found a way to extract ourselves from each other and from the bath. "I have somewhere in the city I would like to take you this morning." I said to him as we slipped into our clothes.

He looked at me suspiciously, "Really?"

"Yes! So if you can be ready to leave in another fifteen minutes that would be fantastic." I teased.

He only laughed, "Okay. Okay."

I held tightly to Kieron's hand as I led him out of the palace's grand front door and into the streets of Aridale. Decorations had been hung between the buildings and twinkling lights floated above the streets to illuminate them when the sun eventually set. Vendors had set up with food and drink and restaurants had opened their doors and patios to the streets as well. We were met with a deafening cheer from the people who waited for us.

People hung out from their windows waving brightly colored

cloth and they lined the streets as well. Many had painted their faces to look like skulls. They all wore Desert black with a variety of bright colored accent pieces. Kamari, Hael, Orion, and Zealand, along with many of the commanders and members of Kieron's forces, stood lining the street. "Happy Birthday!" The crowd yelled in unison. It was more grand than I could have even imagined.

Kieron took a step backwards and I turned to look at him, praying he was okay. His hand covered his mouth and I saw water glisten in the corners of his eyes. His hand dropped and a huge smile plastered his face. He waved to the crowd and they cheered again. Then he pulled me in and gave me a crushing hug, "You did all of this? For me?" He whispered against my ear.

"I had help." I said as I squeezed him back.

"Thank you, baby." He said with a huge smile as he released me and nearly dragged me with him as he stepped into the streets to explore.

Kamari, Hael, Orion, and Zealand joined us as we wove our way through street vendors and people. The pure joy that bathed the streets from everyone who was out today was undeniable. Zealand waved us over to one of the nearby restaurants where he had already commandeered a table. When we had all gathered around it, a server appeared with a large tote bag of items and a tray of tiny glasses. Kamari handed me a tiny glass as the others all took theirs.

"Kieron! Happy Birthday brother." Zealand started, then his eyes teared, "I am so proud to be a member of your kingdom." He had to pause and wipe his eyes. "Let's fucking celebrate!" He managed to yell and everyone cheered before they swallowed the contents of their tiny glasses—alcohol. It was straight alcohol and it burned going down. I coughed and Kamari just winked at me as she pulled the tiny glass from my hand.

Next Orion pulled out an extremely gaudy and clearly fake crown from the large bag and placed it on Kieron's head, followed by an assortment of beaded necklaces to place around his neck. Kieron looked highly amused and slightly embarrassed by the accessories. "Shall we continue on?" Orion asked as he gave Kieron a strong pat on the back.

"Let's go!" Kieron agreed and he wrapped his arm around my shoulders as we followed our friends.

We played games and drank and danced and drank and ate and drank more as we played more games in the streets. The street games were my favorite. People would join in playing with us or they would simply stand by and cheer for whomever they had decided they were rooting for at that moment. Everyone had a great sense of humor as we tried new games and usually were completely terrible at them. It did not matter though. Everyone had huge smiles plastered to their faces and they were clearly enjoying themselves—Kieron most of all. He had even given his crown away to a young boy who he had let beat us in one of the street games—"The winner's prize!" Kieron had said as he dramatically placed the crown on the small child's head. The grin on the boy's face was something I would never forget.

In the late afternoon we stopped at a particular restaurant to have a proper meal. When we had finished eating, the owner brought out a huge cake with small burning candles. Kieron had immediately whipped his head to look at me, "Cake! You got me a cake for my birthday? Why is it on fire?"

Laughter erupted out of me, "You blow out the candles and make a wish."

The cake was placed in front of Kieron and he slowly turned his head back to look at his cake with the candles. Then in one big breath he blew out the candles.

CHAPTER 59

Genevieve

We spent all day in the city and by the time the sun was setting we were pleasantly overfilled with food, drink, and fun. Everyone we had met was beyond thrilled to be celebrating—and even more thrilled to be celebrating with Kieron. Kamari had been right. The people loved him. They respected him. He might have once been the most feared and brutal assassin, but it was clear his people were glad to have him as their king. Since we had returned to Aridale, and removed Rook from the city, the city had slowly started to clean up. It was as if life was breathed back into the streets. Into the people.

The twinkling lights lit the streets as Kieron and I said goodnight to our friends and strolled together, hand in hand, back towards the palace doors. People were still celebrating around us as we walked. "Today was amazing. Thank you." Kieron said softly.

I gave his hand a squeeze, "You are welcome."

"So what is this holiday that falls on my birthday?"

"The Day of the Dead." He stopped walking and turned to look at me—the look he gave me screamed 'Are you serious?' I laughed and continued, "In my world, some people believe those who have passed on to the next life come and visit on this day. Others just use it as a day to remember those who have left us. The holiday was celebrated in a variety of different ways depending on where you were from. In my territory, everyone would dress up with bright colors and decorate with skeletons and celebrate with food and drinking and dancing. Mostly it was just a good excuse to party. Anyway, this seemed like a rather fitting way to celebrate The King of the Undead's birthday, don't you think?"

"So that is why you looked so shocked when I told you my birth date?" He asked with a laugh.

"Yeah, you seriously can not make this shit up, Kieron." He laughed with me and slung his arm around my shoulder.

We pushed open the front doors to the palace and entered. Kieron stopped me in the grand marble entryway. Then the room folded in and we were standing on the rooftop. No one else was up here. I walked to the edge and looked out across the city—the beautiful sparkling city full of life and laughter.

"Did you have a good day?" I asked and turned to him.

"The best." He breathed as his hand wrapped around the back of my neck. "Now I am hoping you will give me one more present." I could only laugh. "That came out rather cheesy didn't it?" Kieron chuckled.

I nodded my head in agreement. "But I will happily give you one more present … Whatever you want." I said as I let my eyes devour him. We certainly had too much to drink and all I wanted at this point in the night was for him to be buried inside of me.

"Whatever I want?" Kieron asked and licked his lip.

"Whatever you want." I said again. My breath caught as he gently brushed my hair behind my shoulders.

His eyes raked over me. "I want to do terribly dirty things to you." He breathed, his voice gravelly. I swallowed. I would let him. I would let him do anything he wanted. "I am afraid you won't like it." He whispered as his hand caressed my cheek and then wrapped my throat. "I am afraid it will bring up bad memories for you and you won't like it."

"It is your present … I don't have to like it." I countered quietly. When I said whatever he wanted, I meant it.

His hand tightened slightly around my throat as he pulled me closer to him and kissed my lips. "I want to be completely selfish."

"Good." I whispered back.

Kieron looked deep into my eyes. Both of our breaths shuddered with the desire that laced the air between us. "I will not hit you." I blinked in surprise. I was not expecting *that* to come out of his mouth. My eyes searched his face. He continued, "But this still might hurt you."

"What—" I began, but his thumb pressed over my lips, silencing me.

"I want to fuck you very roughly. I will not hit you, but I will spank you and I will choke you and I will probably restrain you." His thumb pressed between my lips and into my mouth. "I am going to find your edge." I looked at him in confusion and a small wicked smile crossed his lips, "Yes, baby, I want to find out exactly how hard I can fuck you. I want you to allow me to do anything I want ... And I am warning you, this will not be gentle." My eyes widened and my breath caught. I did not know if I was frightened or extremely aroused. And I did not know what to say as Kieron slowly drug his thumb out of my mouth. "Now is your chance to refuse ... but I am hoping you will be a good girl for me and agree."

I slowly nodded my head, yes.

"I need to hear you say it, baby." He said softly.

I looked at him for heartbeats. I would sell my entire soul for Kieron. I would give up *everything* for him. I trusted him completely and I respected him. I had already committed to living my now very long life beside him—I didn't even need a union. I did not need anything from him. I was willing to give myself to him unconditionally until he was done with me.

Kieron's eyes just burned into mine and his thumb stroked across my lower lip again. He was waiting. Waiting patiently for my answer. "Yes." I whispered.

◆ ◆ ◆

Kieron

"Thank you." Kieron said quietly. His heart pounded in his chest. He had wanted to take Genevieve like this since the moment he saw her in the twenty-sixth world, but things had gotten … complicated. Maybe it was because they had a little too much to drink today. Maybe it was because he had been holding back all these weeks to ensure she really would not change her mind when she saw this side of him. Maybe he was just done waiting. Either way, he was going to fuck her so hard it was possible she would not enjoy it.

Kieron pulled Genevieve away from the edge of the roof and to one of the large four poster lounges. He pushed her up against one of the smooth wooden posts and ran his hands along her body. Her body opened for him as it responded involuntarily to his firm touch. He kissed her forcefully, pressing her head back against the wood, and bit her lower lip—hard. A small cry released from her mouth and Kieron felt the hardness of his cock already bulging against the fastenings of his pants.

Genevieve's hand reached out to touch him and he grabbed her wrists, pulling them up and pinning them above her head. "You are going to do exactly as I tell you to." He whispered as his nose brushed hers. He could feel her arousal and anticipation building—and there was the slightest most delicious bit of fear leaking from her too. She gave a subtle nod of agreement. "That's my good girl." He responded and basked in the wave of her arousal that met him.

Kieron slowly brought Genevieve's hands down from above her head and turned. He sat on the lounge and positioned Genevieve in front of him between his legs. "Take off your clothes ... Slowly." He commanded.

Genevieve stared at him for a moment before she slowly lifted her shirt up over her head and dropped it on the ground next to her. She was not even trying to be sexy—no teasing, no exaggeration, just following his command—and it was the hottest thing he had ever seen. "Keep going." He whispered as he leaned back to enjoy the show. Desire pulsed through his entire body. He was going to get everything he wanted tonight and he could hardly stand the anticipation. Her fingers undid the fastenings on her pants, then she pulled off her boots and socks before sliding her pants down and off and adding them to the pile of her clothes on the ground.

He took his time admiring her standing there between his legs in nothing but her black lace underthings. "Your bra." He finally said as his eyes lingered on her breasts. They were rising and falling with her breath.

Genevieve unclasped the hooks and let her bra fall to the ground. "Your underthings." He continued. She slipped them off and dropped them on the top of the pile. Genevieve just stood there, looking down at him, waiting. "Turn around." Kieron said. She slowly turned and Kieron raised his hands to stroke down her hips and over her ass. He was going to absolutely destroy her tonight.

Kieron stood behind her then guided her to put her hands against the wooden beam of the four poster lounge and to bend over slightly. "Don't move your hands. You hold right here until I tell you otherwise." Kieron whispered against her ear. He felt her body shudder and saw her skin pebble.

He stepped back and spanked her with a force he had never spanked her with before. She flinched and cried out at the pain of it. Then Kieron slid his finger deep into her from behind. His other hand wrapped her throat and he watched her fingers dig into the beam as she held on while he fucked her with his finger. But she didn't pull away from him—she moaned and pressed her ass back into him. The way she just let him handle her—the way she submitted to him and surrendered herself—it only made Kieron's desire grow.

Kieron felt her magic rising within her and used his own magic to tamp hers down as he leaned over her. "No magic." He growled into her ear as he squeezed her throat tighter, "Tonight I want to feel your body here in this world only." She only gasped beneath his grip on her throat and dipped her chin in acknowledgement of his request.

Kieron let go of her throat and pressed her against the post as he pounded into her with his finger. Just when she was about to cry out with her climax he pulled his hand away and slapped her ass. She gasped, then whimpered and arched her back, offering herself to him again. "That's my good girl." Kieron said with a smile. He was going to completely lose his mind with her.

Kieron summoned a rope and, in a few swift motions, he tied her hands to the post in front of her. Genevieve gasped as he pulled the rope tight and he saw it bite into the soft skin of her wrists. She only watched him with her eyes wide and her breath heaving in her chest. She didn't even struggle.

He guided her around so that she was kneeling on the large lounge bed, Genevieve's hands and wrists tied tightly to the post in front of her. Kieron tore off his own clothes and knelt on the lounge behind her. He pushed her knees apart further and guided himself to her entrance. His hand gripped her hip as he thrust himself into her with one stroke. He did not even wait for her to adjust to his size before his other hand found her hair and tugged her head back as he began pounding into her. "Oh fuck!" She yelled out and her body arched.

Being blown into another universe and drawing out their pleasure together was beautiful and unreal—but feeling his cock inside of Genevieve and her smooth skin under his hands while they stayed in this world was even more pleasurable. It was real and raw and primal and completely transcended the fact the universe had—for some reason—chosen them to be a match. It proved to Kieron that even without their souls intertwined he would still desire her. He would still believe their bodies becoming one was the most beautiful things that could happen in any world. He would still love every piece of her.

Kieron felt his climax building and with one final thrust, pulled himself out. He dropped his mouth to her and slid his tongue into her. She moaned and her body shuddered as he feasted on her. When she had come on his tongue he moved up to taste every part of her. Kieron bit Genevieve's ass hard only so that he could hear her cry out before he marked a trail of gentle kisses up her spine. Her body shook with her heavy breaths and her hands clutched the post they were tied to.

He was not gentle when he grabbed her chin and turned her head so that he could kiss her lips. Genevieve kissed him back hungrily and Kieron slid himself back inside of her. He held her there as he pounded into her again, tasting every moan and whimper and small cry that left her lips.

Then Kieron summoned a knife and cut her hands free from the post before pushing her body back onto the lounge. He straddled her chest and pinned her arms at her side and her wrists beneath his shins. He stroked himself above her as Genevieve looked up into his eyes. Kieron did not even have to ask for Genevieve to lift her head and open her mouth for him. He squeezed his shaft tight at the sight of it, he was going to come all over her beautiful face if he wasn't careful.

Genevieve licked the tip of his cock before taking him into her mouth. She continued to look up at him as she sucked him. His hand slid into her hair at the back of her head as he began to guide her. "I fucking love watching you suck my cock." Kieron groaned. He felt her body tighten beneath him as her hips rocked. She was taking his cock so good and she still wanted and needed something inside of her. Kieron reached back and rubbed his fingers over her bundle of nerves. Genevieve moaned around his cock in her mouth and her eyes rolled back for a moment.

He plunged his finger into her then quickly added a second. A muffled cry escaped her lips followed by another moan as she rocked her hips into his hand and shoved his cock deeper into her own throat. Kieron could not stop himself as his hand tightened in her hair and he pounded into her mouth. He grunted and let out a groan as he watched her take him in her mouth and tears began to fall from the corners of her eyes. He pulled her head back for a moment so she could gasp for breath, but then he pressed himself back against her lips. She opened her mouth for him again and he pounded into her throat harder. Her body convulsed as she gagged on him. "That's it baby, gag on my cock." Kieron gasped as pleasure washed through his entire body.

Genevieve's makeup was smeared and tears were streaming down her face as she gagged and choked again. He fucking loved watching her—loved ruining her makeup and loved pushing her to her edge. Kieron quickly pulled himself out as she coughed and gasped for breath. "That's it. Breathe baby, you were such a good girl, breathe."

Kieron lifted himself from sitting on top of her and gently stroked his hand down her body as he moved between her legs. He kissed her cheek and neck before gently biting down. Her body was heaving and trembling as she tried to catch her breath and her hand darted up to wipe away some of the tears still on her face. His hand caught hers and gently pinned it down against the lounge they were laying on. She looked at him through wet eyes as he playfully kissed and bit her lip. "I want to hear you screaming for me baby." Kieron whispered. He could hear her take a nervous swallow, but she only kissed him back in response.

Kieron pushed himself up and lifted Genevieve's legs over one of his shoulders. Then he slid his cock back into her and leaned over her so he could grab her jaw as he kissed her. He wanted to stare into her beautiful eyes as he fucked her. He wanted to see the pleasure on her face as she came for him. He wanted to watch her dance with consciousness as he choked her. Genevieve's eyes met his with a look that begged him for more.

◆ ◆ ◆

Genevieve

The gentle stroke of Kieron's fingers down the side of my body sent a shiver through me. I was curled on my side on one of the massive lounges on the rooftop. My body was trembling. Then I felt the familiar warmth of Kieron's magic pulse through my body. Everything in me relaxed a little. "Are you okay, sweetheart?" He asked in a warm whisper against the back of my neck.

He had indeed fucked me roughly. Very roughly. I was not sure where the pleasure stopped and the pain began. The only thing I knew was that I was completely spent and some parts of me hurt more than others.

"Mhmm." I managed to whimper.

"Will you turn and look at me?" His voice was low and gentle—like he hadn't just had me screaming for him as he ravished me. Like he hadn't just teased and tasted and pounded every part of me until I came for him over and over again. When I thought there was no way I could climax one more time he had found new ways to coax another one out of me—commanding me not to come until exactly when he wanted me to. I slowly turned my head and let my body roll to my back on the lounge. Kieron's hand stroked my cheek as his eyes looked over me. My chest heaved with my heavy shuddering breaths. "Are you sure you are okay?"

I nodded and raised my hand to stroke down his face—my hand trembled as I did. His hand wrapped mine and held it against his cheek. He moved my hand to his lips and gently kissed my palm. Then he kissed my wrist where the burns from the rope he had tied me with still stung. "Let's go back to our rooms." He said softly. I nodded. His arms scooped under me and he lifted my limp body off of the lounge. As he stood, the rooftop folded in and we were suddenly in our bathroom.

Kieron stepped into our huge pool-like bath and lowered us both into the warm water. My body went weightless in the water and I turned to wrap my arms around his neck and my legs around his waist. He pulled me close and his hands caressed my ass. I winced slightly. It was still tender from him spanking me. Still tender from where his teeth had bit into me. His eyes searched my face and he looked concerned.

"Well ... was it good for you?" I managed to whisper, my throat was sore and raw. I had moaned and screamed and gasped for breath as pleasure had torn through my body while he choked me until I nearly passed out.

His body shook with his quiet laugh. "Most definitely ... Was it good for you?" He ventured carefully.

It had been fucking amazing. I was completely obliterated and I loved every second of him taking me. Claiming me. I loved feeling his powerful body completely controlling every drop of pleasure it drew from mine. I loved seeing the look in his eyes as he dominated me and made me come for him.

"I loved it." I breathed.

An amused smile turned up the corners of his mouth, "Oh really?"

"Mhmm." Kieron's still hungry eyes dropped to scan over my lips. "You said I would like giving away my control and I ..." My voice trailed off as Kieron started to chuckle. I scrunched my brows at him in confusion.

"No, baby. Don't you see?" He leaned in and started trailing warm kisses up my neck, each one filling me with more desire, "*You* controlled your magic to release or stay within you. *You* let me keep going when you could have simply asked me to stop at any time." His lips caressed my ear as his voice deepened, "I might have been leading the fun tonight, but *you*, baby, you had *all* of the control."

My breath caught as my need for more of him suddenly sent an ache through my body. I rolled my hips, rubbing myself against him —*Kieron owned all of me.*

CHAPTER 60

Genevieve

It was one week after Kieron's birthday and we were in The War Room reviewing laws that affected the female residents of the Deserts. I felt like my eyes were bleeding from reading through all of the documents. I also felt a persistent nausea from the disgusting way females were talked about throughout the pages and pages of laws. Sarla had once told me The Land of the Deserts and The Land of the Giants were the worst when it came to laws that affected females—she undersold it. It was completely sickening.

The only thing that made it slightly better was although many of these laws were written, many seemed to no longer be enforced —and soon they would be wiped from the written law altogether. I had just come across one particularly nauseating law. Without warning I started to read it aloud for Kieron, Orion, and Zealand,

"'Any female on her cycle may be bartered or sold for temporary usage, at the discretion of her guardian or proprietor. Should the female in question exhibit unwillingness or defiance in her participation, her guardian is hereby vested with the authority to administer any punishment they deem fitting and appropriate, without restriction or limitation.'"

I looked up from the documents and saw all three males looking at me. I could not tell if it was sadness, disgust, or simple resignation on their faces. "Did you all know this was still a law?"

"Yes." Kieron said simply.

I was going to throw up. "Is this still practiced? Kieron you told me …" My voice trailed off. Kieron had told me a female on her cycle was celebrated, not *sold for temporary usage.*

"It is still practiced." Zealand answered my question. My eyes darted from male to male trying to read their expressions.

"We will put it on the list to be changed with the first batch of laws, G." Kieron said gently.

I did not know how to respond. *This law was still practiced.* Any and all females in the Deserts were at risk of this happening to them. Their guardian only needed to decide they wanted to barter or sell her for use. *How many females had actually been subjected to this?* I felt completely murderous. "We will change it immediately." Kieron said again. His tone made me realize he indeed felt I was about to kill someone. *Good.*

"Who is my guardian … my proprietor?" My question was almost a whisper.

"Technically, me." Kieron responded gently. *Of course.*

I was almost scared to ask my next question, but I had to know.

"Have any of you—" I started, the words said through my teeth.

At that moment, Zain burst in through the doors to The War Room. Mintaka was on his heels. "Montvera is under attack." He said, there was panic in his voice. I had never seen Zain shaken like this.

Kieron's head turned quickly to Zain. "Who is attacking them?"

"An army of beasts and some of the defectors from this and the other kingdoms." Zain said hurriedly. I jumped to my feet and my hands pressed into the table to steady myself as I processed what Zain was saying. Before Kieron or I could respond, Zain continued. "I am leaving immediately to help."

"We will come too." Kieron said without hesitation. "Orion, Zealand, gather the Undead and meet us there." The commander and general disappeared a heartbeat later.

"It is Ryett and Rachel's union ceremony today." I breathed. We had received the invitation weeks ago. Kieron had found a way to politely decline and send a gift in our stead.

"I imagine that is why they chose today. Ryett would have been distracted and the whole kingdom celebrating." Zain said, flatly. I could read the guilt on his face. That he felt he should have been there to stop this somehow. I had not pressed Zain when he had told me he was not attending.

"I am coming with you." I stated.

Kieron only summoned a belt of knives and tossed it to me, "Of course you are, sweetheart."

Kieron

Kieron, Zain, and Genevieve appeared at the edge of the forest overlooking Ryett's chateau. It was chaos. Magic swirled in the air along with the roars and screeches and screaming of beasts and beings. The lawns were already covered in blood and bodies.

Kieron had centuries of battle training—centuries of experience with killing and war and destruction. This was not a battle or a fight or an ambush—this was a massacre. His entire body went cold as he felt the terror and horror that bathed the chateau's grounds. His eyes darted to the wall of magic that separated the city from the chateau. They had cut the chateau off from any outside help—but if they had, how had Zain gotten them inside?

Kieron quickly let the thought go. He had to break the wall so the Undead and reinforcements from the Mountains could get in too. Without giving it another thought, Kieron's magic ripped the wall to pieces and across the chateau grounds he saw warriors from the city charging into the fight.

"Thank you, Kieron. I am glad to see I didn't even have to ask you to take care of that for us." Zain said flatly beside him. Then Zain continued, "You two get inside the chateau and help fight from the inside out. We will provide cover for you to get to the tunnel entrances and then help with the fight out here." As the words came out of his mouth wolves came lurking out from the forest. There had to be fifty of them.

"Prince." Kieron breathed. Max had called Zain, *Prince*. And Great Wolves did not follow the orders of anyone but their own kind. The

Princes of the Great Wolves had long been feared and worshiped, but no one had reported seeing one in millenia ... And that was how they had passed through the wall of magic—Great Wolves did not abide by the same laws of magic as other beings. "Zain, you are a Prince of the Great Wolves." It explained why Kieron had never been able to get a read on Zain. Why he had always had a deep unexplainable fear of him.

Zain only winked back at Kieron, "Ready?"

"Ready." Genevieve said as she touched Kieron's arm to make sure he was ready to follow her. He nodded to Zain.

The Prince of the Great Wolves turned back to the battle field and as he stepped from the woods his body transformed. The silver gray wolf, larger than the others, let out a howl that sent a shiver down Kieron's spine.

They ran for the nearest cottage with the wolves leading the way as beasts turned their attention to the new threat.

CHAPTER 61

Genevieve

"Why does there always have to be fucking spiders?" I cursed as I led Kieron through the maze of tunnels underneath the chateau's lawns. Tiny balls of light lit the tunnels as we hurried in the direction of the chateau's main building. The small lights extinguished as soon as we passed, leaving Kieron and I only able to see a few paces in front of us at a time. I remembered the maps Ryett had shown me. If I was counting my strides correctly, we only had another hundred paces before this tunnel would put us into a small storeroom near the weapons room. I pushed down my fear of tunnels and small spaces. And stupid spiders. I shook off the shiver that ran down my neck and spine thinking about all the fucking spiders in here.

Kieron chuckled and I felt a small pulse of his magic. "Now they are all dead spiders." He said.

"Remind me to properly thank you for that when we get home." I laughed as I realized not only had his magic wiped out the spiders, but it had also cleared the cobwebs from our path.

Just as I expected we reached the cool metal door quickly. I tugged it open a crack and peaked through. The hallway was clear, but I could hear commotion and glass breaking further inside of the chateau.

"I will go first." Kieron said and he put his hand on the door. His eyes locked with mine as he paused. "Kick some ass okay, baby? Just do not do anything stupid."

"Who me? Do something stupid? I would never." I teased and he gave me an amused smile before pulling the door open for us to step through.

We hurried down the hall towards the main rooms of the chateau and I spotted Sarla rushing from one side of the chateau to the other. "Sarla!" I called out. She slid to a stop.

"Genevieve, Kieron, thank the Mother." She breathed and hurried towards us. Her beautiful emerald green dress had dirt and blood sprayed across the skirts. Her hair, which had clearly once been pinned neatly up, had fallen down in places. She had a belt of knives slung over her shoulder and the curved sword in her hand was slick with blood. "This wasn't your surprise was it?"

"No! Of course not. I sent a huge chocolate dick, not beasts." I replied quickly.

Sarla choked on her laugh, "Oh, that's good—"

"Zain and a group of Great Wolves are here already fighting and the Undead will be here any moment to help." Kieron interrupted, "Tell us what to do."

Sarla's face switched back from amusement to complete focus, "We have to get Ryett and Rachel out of here. We are going to lose the chateau and Ryett will not leave. They are here for him, please help me convince him to leave." Sarla spoke quickly and motioned for us to follow her. We rushed down the hall into the main entry.

"Genevieve?" Ryett's voice cut through the commotion outside. "Kieron? What are you doing here?"

"We are here to help, Ryett." I said. "But you have to leave. The army of the Undead will be here any moment and will help end this, but you have to leave."

"I am not leaving my people. I should be out there fighting alongside them, not hiding in here." Ryett gritted out.

"Ryett—" Rachel pleaded.

"Get Rachel out of here." Ryett cut her off. I turned to Rachel. She looked absolutely stunning in her ceremony dress—just like weddings in my world, it was white and extravagant. Her dress had a fitted bodice with billowing skirts of tule and shimmering beads. A huge emerald set in a rose gold and diamond studded band wrapped her ring finger. A rose gold tiara was woven into her hair. She looked like a queen.

"Genevieve, sneak Rachel out through the tunnels. When you get out, you have to get to the edge of the forest before you will be able to jump back to Aridale. I will stay to fight with Ryett." Kieron said, his voice was authoritative and left no room for questions. I had never jumped so far, but just hearing Kieron say it like I could do it gave me hope I could actually do it. Or at least jump us far enough from here to get Rachel to safety.

"Okay. Okay, Rachel, come with me." I motioned for Rachel to follow me and she hesitated, "They cannot focus on what they need to focus on if we are here, Rachel. We are a liability."

Ryett grabbed her hand and gave her cheek a quick kiss, "Go with Genevieve. I will see you soon."

"Better go fast!" Sarla called out, "They are breaching!"

I turned to look at Kieron as we both stepped away—me towards Rachel and him towards the battle. *I love you.* Kieron mouthed to me. It was the first time either of us had said those three words to each other. My heart skipped a beat. *I love you.* I mouthed back. I meant it. I meant it with every fiber of my being. Then I grabbed Rachel's hand and drug her towards the tunnels. The screeches and bellowing of beasts echoed through the chateau.

Kieron

The chaos of fighting around Kieron completely faded away as he watched Genevieve's lips mouth those three beautiful words back to him. *I love you.* He wanted to say it properly. To say it out loud while she was in his arms, but he could not go another second without telling her. He almost did not expect her to say it back.

Focus. He blinked and the chaos and commotion from the fighting—from the massacre happening on the lawns of the chateau—came rushing back to his ears. Genevieve and Rachel disappeared around a corner and he turned back to face the windows that had just been shattered and now allowed beasts and warriors to pour through. A quick burst of his magic took out the front line of intruders as he unsheathed his axe from his back.

"Thanks for coming." Ryett said calmly from beside him.

Kieron turned his head to glance at his fellow king. "Ryett, if things go bad here, you get out. Make sure they are safe." *Make sure Genevieve is safe.* Were the words he meant, but did not say. If things went badly, Kieron would be trapped on the chateau grounds. Only Ryett and the members of his inner circle could jump in and out of this place. One of them would have to take Kieron with them or he would have to fight his way out.

"We are all getting out of here, Kieron. I won't leave you." Ryett responded quietly.

There was no more time for talking as Kieron swung his axe and severed a limb from a charging beast. Magic and blood and the clash of weapons filled the chateau a heartbeat later.

CHAPTER 62

Genevieve

I swung the cool metal door closed behind us and pushed my way past Rachel's billowing skirts. We started down the dark tunnels, the lights flickering on as we went, barely lighting the path. I took a deep breath and stuffed down the tightness in my chest. *I had just been through these tunnels, it was safe in here.* I reminded myself. I heard Rachel struggling and cursing behind me.

"You have to cut these skirts off, I can hardly move." Rachel said as I turned to see what was wrong. Her hands were fumbling as she tried to gather her skirts.

"Rachel, it's your wedding dress—"

"It is just a dress. Give me a knife and I will do it myself." She cut me off. *Okay then.* I pulled out a knife and knelt. "Cut it here and here." She instructed. I did and she tore the top layers of her billowing skirts off and tossed them to the dirt behind her. *I might actually get along with this female.* I thought to myself. "Much better, let's go." She said, I could hear the determination in her voice.

We hurried down the tunnel and I tried not to think about what was happening above us. Tried not to think about the beasts that Kieron was facing—that my friends were facing. I tried not to think about whether any of them were already hurt. With any luck, the Undead would already be here and decisively ending this thing.

"You were with Ryett, weren't you?" Rachel's voice cut into my thoughts.

"Sorry, what?" I said absently as I peeked down one fork of the tunnel before deciding to turn down the other. I had the maps of these tunnels burned into my memory, but I had never actually been in them.

"Before I came back, you and Ryett were together. You freed me and you knew it might end the two of you. Why?" Rachel asked.

I stopped walking and took a deep breath. "Yes, Ryett and I had just gotten together when everything happened."

"Then why did you free me?" Her voice was hard. Emotionless.

I just looked at her. "Because Ryett deserved his happily ever after and you did too."

"Not good enough." Rachel responded. "I cannot just believe you were willing to walk away from your soulmate like that."

She knew. "So he finally told you?" I asked quietly.

"No, I figured it out. I cannot believe everyone just kept that from me. He lied to me. They all lied to me. They should have told me immediately. Instead I was just walking around in a haze of love like a complete idiot." I could hear the frustration in her voice, "No wonder everyone hates me. They wanted *you.*"

"Rachel—" I began gently.

"How could you just walk away?" She pressed again. There was anger in her voice.

I closed my eyes and pinched the bridge of my nose. This was not the time or place to be having this conversation. I let out a sigh. Rachel needed to hear the truth. "He chose you, Rachel. He chose you as soon as he saw you again and he broke the bond between the two of us. I knew it was going to happen—I was shown it was going to happen when I was in the twenty-seventh world—and when it actually came true I left because I wanted to let him have happiness. I could not stay and watch you two be together, so I left."

"I ruined it for both of you ..." Rachel whispered sadly.

"No, Rachel. You ruined nothing. I barely knew him. And I would have made the same choice he did if my dead husband magically came back." I said to her sternly. Her wedding day had just been ruined by a complete blood bath of an ambush. We did not even know if our loved ones and friends would survive the fighting. I was not going to let her feel bad about being with the male she loved.

We just looked at each other for heartbeats. "Is there a chance your husband could come back?" Rachel finally breathed.

"No, Rachel. He is gone."

"But Ryett thought I was gone—" She pressed.

"I burned his dead body to ashes along with the bodies of my son and my dog."

She just stared at me, her eyes wide. "I had no idea ... I am so sorry." Her voice was barely a whisper.

I reached out and took her hand. "You and Ryett were meant to be together. He chose you and there is nothing to be sorry about. There is nothing to feel bad about. I think I was always meant to find Kieron. And right now, we both need to get the fuck out of here so that we can live long enough to see both of them again."

Her eyes searched my face as she blinked back tears. "Okay." She finally said and she gave my hand a squeeze.

◆ ◆ ◆

Kieron

The beasts did not stop coming. Sarla had slipped through one of the windows to fight on the patio outside. Kieron and Ryett, along with a few others from Ryett's court, still fought the beasts that flowed into the chateau. Bodies and limbs and blood covered the floors. From the quick glances Kieron was able to take, the battle on the lawn was not going much better. He could see the Undead had arrived and were doing their share to eliminate the enemy, but there was no end in sight.

Rachel and Genevieve should be through the tunnels by now. Hopefully they were crossing the lawns and into the forest where they would be able to jump to safety. Then the rest of them would have to abandon Montvera. They were going to lose this fight. Unless another thousand warriors from the Mountains or the Deserts or one of their allies miraculously showed up, they were going to lose.

Maybe Orion or Zealand had already sent word to bring more forces—both of them would have seen immediately this was a losing battle, but it would take time for any reinforcements to arrive. Kieron needed to know Genevieve had gotten to safety, then he would get Ryett and his court out. They would have to reclaim Montvera later, but they would not be able to do that if the King of the Mountains was dead. It was better to live to fight another day than to be slaughtered by beasts in your own home.

He fought his way across the room to Ryett. "Ryett, we need to be prepared to leave." He yelled over the noise.

"Not yet!" Ryett replied as he cleaved the head of an enemy warrior from his body. "I can't let my city fall." Then with a blast of magic Ryett cleared the room of their opponents.

Even with Kieron and Ryett's magic combined there were too many enemy combatants for them to win. As an Undead, Kieron knew he could now completely expend his magic without dying, but he did not know if it would be enough to save all of them. He also knew he would be rendered completely useless if he tried it and it did not work.

"We need to decide soon, Ryett. Whether it is today or any other day, I swear to you I will help you get Montvera back." Kieron knew Ryett hated him, but he did not want bad blood between them any longer. Ryett was one of the good ones and there were few enough of them already. They would need each other in the coming centuries, and today was a good day to start.

Ryett's eyes pierced into Kieron's and he gave a quick nod of acknowledgement. Then the two kings turned back to the fighting that continued to overrun the chateau.

CHAPTER 63

Genevieve

Rachel and I emerged into one of the cottages. I peeked out the window to confirm this was indeed the cottage closest to the edge of the forest. It was. I then turned my eyes to the chateau lawns and saw the carnage. We were losing. Badly. My skin prickled and I swallowed down the sick that threatened to come up.

This beautiful home was now a graveyard. If anyone survived, how would they ever be able to rebuild the beauty and safety this place once held? I blinked back tears as I remembered finally feeling at home here. Feeling like I had found friends and family—and now it was all being destroyed.

The army of the Undead had arrived, but so had more beasts and enemy warriors to fight against them. We were greatly outnumbered and unless one of the Undead had already returned to Aridale to get more help, no one else was coming. We had to make a run for the forest where I would be able to jump us out of here. I had promised I would get Rachel to safety—and then I would get more help.

"Stay close." I said to Rachel as we moved to the back door of the cottage. "We are going to make a run for the forest. There is enough chaos that hopefully no one will see us."

"Okay." She breathed behind me.

I inched the door open slowly and we stepped out. I looked around and reached back to grab Rachel's hand, "Let's go." I whispered.

We started to run. The forest was not far, but it seemed too far with the battle raging nearby. The chaos was deafening. The smell of blood filled the air and the screaming and moaning of the injured made my stomach twist into knots. A moment later I felt something tear into my side and my feet lost the ground. I heard Rachel scream and a screech shook my bones as I slammed into the grass. I was up a heartbeat later, standing over Rachel with a knife drawn and my mountain shield around us.

Kieron

Kieron had fought his way to one of the blown out windows. Esurim had now begun to take over the battle. More of them had somehow arrived. He watched the other beasts wait in anticipation as the esurim sucked the magic from the air. As he scanned the battlefield, his eyes caught on Jax. He was engaged with a beast and an esurim was approaching quickly from behind. Kieron obliterated it moments before it slashed through Jax's middle—blood rained down on Jax. Jax quickly wiped the blood from his eyes with his sleeve before engaging with another beast. *They were losing.*

The screech that echoed through the chateau made Kieron duck his head in pain as he whirled around to see the largest esurim he had ever encountered climb through one of the shattered windows and into the chateau. Beasts climbed through behind it. They needed to leave. Now.

◆ ◆ ◆

Genevieve

The beast stood back on two of its legs and let out another screech—esurim. The two slits for its nostrils flickered as it sniffed the air. Its long claws flexed and glinted in the light from the setting sun. *It was a fucking esurim.* I raised my hand to feel my side and dared a quick glance down. My hand was wet with blood. Then my shield flickered and died—like the air had been sucked out of it. *Esurim will suck magic out of the air.* The esurim landed back on all fours and stalked around us revealing three males behind it.

"Did you really think you could escape all of this?" One of the males chuckled. "No, Rook thought you might be here. He planned on it really. So can you tell me, what is better than killing two kings?" I recognized this male. That snickering laugh. That scar on his face. Byron. He had come drunk to my cell with Rook when I was being held captive by Vossarian. Kieron had snapped his neck. "No guesses? Shame. Clearly it is capturing two queens." He sneered as he flipped a knife in his hand.

"Byron, good to see your head on straight again." I spat back at him. I had to keep him talking. These males were all the same—they always wanted to talk talk talk. They would share everything if they thought they were winning. If he was talking it would give me time to figure out what to do. How to get us past him. Past the esurim.

He gave me a tight lipped smile. "Where is your king anyway? Not here to save you this time?" He took a step towards us. There was nowhere to go with the esurim behind us. "That's it, take a look. All of your friends and your kings, if they are lucky, will die today."

I did look. We were still losing. I watched beasts circle one of the wolves. I watched a male in a suit be tossed to the side like a rag doll. I watched blood spray and swords clash. I forced my eyes back to Byron. "Then what? What's the plan, Byron?"

"Oh, Rook has many plans. First it was to take down Ryett. Today seemed like the perfect opportunity. It just worked out in his favor that Kieron did indeed show up for the fun too. Next comes Beck and Aveline. Then the other kings will have no choice but to kneel to Rook."

"And where is Rook now? Is he too scared to get his hands dirty?"

"Rook is busy in the Wastes. I am sure he will be ecstatic to see you again." Byron continued as he stepped closer to us.

Rachel slowly stood up from the ground behind me and I could feel her trembling. "I am sure he will be." I said. *Shit*. Shit. Shit. I had to get her out of here. I had to do something. Distract. Fight. Run. I moved before I could question myself further.

I sent one knife into Byron's chest and whirled around to send another into the skull of the esurim behind us. The esurim only let out a roar and reared back to pluck the knife out with its clawed fingers.

I spun back to unleash my magic, but nothing happened. *Fucking esurim.* I quickly pulled another knife and sunk it into the shoulder of the warrior who rushed me. I pushed him aside and sent a kick into another warrior's stomach. I felt a body crash into my back and I used the momentum to roll as I was taken to the ground. I popped up to one knee ready to slash the assailant with my knife when I heard Rachel scream again. "One more move and she dies." Byron barked at me. I froze.

Not a heartbeat later I was enveloped in strong arms and felt cold steel at my throat. I turned my head sharply and felt the steel slice into my skin, but now I could see Rachel. She was restrained in the arms of another warrior. "Did no one teach you about esurimagicae, Genevieve? And did you also forget that I am immortal? What a shame." Byron whispered against my ear. His fingers fumbled and tugged on the buckle for my belt of knives as he tore it away from my body and tossed it onto the grass far out of my reach. I was now weaponless.

Byron then jerked me around to face the chaos of the battle. He grabbed my jaw and forced my head to stare straight into the carnage. "Look at them. Take one last look and say goodbye to your friends."

Rage filled me. There was no room for panic or fear or sadness as my rage rushed through my blood. I would not let these awful beings and beasts kill another good person. I would not just give up. I would not say goodbye. Not today.

Esurim ate magic—but they could not stop *all* magic. They could not stop dark magic. I closed my eyes as I sucked in a breath and cast my magic out like a wave across the chateaus grounds— wrapping it around every beast and being who was bringing harm to us. I willed my magic to spill into the chateau, through every room and hallway. I could see it all. Every blow and block. Every blade swinging and every claw connecting with flesh. I could feel their heartbeats. The blood pulsing in their veins. *You can't bring someone back from this.* Kieron's voice echoed in my head.

Kieron. The male who had taunted and teased me. Who had pushed me to keep fighting. Who had unrelenting belief in me. Who had brought me back from a place so unbelievably dark and lonely. Who never asked me to change even when he saw me for exactly who I was. Who was the only one who would truly understand the monster this rage brought out in me. Kieron the male who understood this monster would do terrible things if it had to—if *I* had to.

I breathed in one more deep breath and felt in my magic that I was only touching those who fought against us. That it was only the beasts and beings who had hate and evil within their blood. I opened my eyes and saw dark light emitting from me—from the rims of my eyes. Byron's hands still tightly held my body. Still held my face. I heard words of shock spilling from his mouth, but I did not listen. I pursed my lips and emitted a single puff of air—blowing the world into a billion pieces.

CHAPTER 64

Kieron

Kieron's axe connected with nothing but air and mist as he swung. The beast that had been in front of him was suddenly gone. He did not know if he had stopped hearing or if everything was suddenly quiet. His eyes locked with Ryett's across the now empty room. Then he heard it. The pattering of rain. Blood rain.

His eyes dropped to the floor and he watched as blood splattered down upon the stone. Billions and billions of drops of blood rained down around them. Then it stopped. "Kieron, what—" Ryett started.

"Genevieve." Kieron's throat tightened as he said her name. He had not done this and he knew of no one else here who had the dark magic to do this. If she had killed all of them ... Panic set in, "Where is Genevieve?"

"Help! Somebody help us!" The screaming female voice cut

through the eerie silence. Ryett was across the room, his hand wrapping around Kieron's forearm before Kieron could protest. The room folded in around him.

Rachel was holding Genevieve as she knelt on the blood soaked lawn. Kieron fell to his knees across from her and gathered Genevieve into his arms. Ryett was beside him a moment later, a dark light pouring from him and into Genevieve. "Genevieve! Come on baby, wake up!" Kieron shouted at her as his hand pushed her hair back and caressed the side of her face.

He sent a pulse of his own magic into her. Nothing. He wrapped his magic around her and into her—her heart was still beating. She was still breathing. He sent another pulse of magic. Genevieve took a gasping breath and her eyes fluttered open. "It's okay, G, I've got you. It's over. I've got you." Tears were streaming down Kieron's face.

"I am so sorry." She whispered, "I broke rule three."

"What are you talking about, baby?" Kieron cradled her close to his chest, his hand stroking her hair.

"You told me not to do anything stupid and I think this counts as pretty stupid. I also promised—" Her voice was so soft, so weak.

"No, baby, it's okay. It's okay." Kieron reassured her as Sarla flung herself onto the grass on the other side of Genevieve and golden light flowed from her hands into Genevieve's body.

Kieron looked up at Sarla. Sarla's face paled, "Ryett, it's not enough …" She whispered.

More magic flowed from Ryett. "Tell us what to do, Sarla." Ryett commanded.

Sarla swallowed, "If we stop, she will die. She must have created a hole when she released her magic. It is like a hole in the bottom of a glass, her magic is draining out and when it's gone, she is gone. I can't plug the hole. Pouring our magic in is only prolonging ..." Sarla's voice trailed off.

Kieron felt like he had stopped breathing. Like a fist was squeezing his chest so tight it would crush him. This was it. This was the thing that would balance out all of the good that had been happening. He could not take it.

He looked down at Genevieve in his arms. He could not let her be taken away from him. She had seen him for everything he was and still somehow loved him. He was a better male when he was with her—he was a better male because of her. This world was a better world because of her.

"She needs the Death Taker." Zain spoke from behind them. "Kieron, you must take her to Max and turn her." There was no air left for Kieron to breathe as heard Zain's words. *There had to be another way.*

"Make her Undead?" Sarla asked, "That ... that would work, but —"

"No." Kieron said forcefully, "There has to be another way." He could not do that to her. Not only was becoming an Undead the worst possible thing he had ever gone through, but it would sentence her to immortality. As much as he could not lose her, Kieron could not do that to her. He could not take her death from her. There had to be another way.

Sarla's hand gently touched Kieron's forearm. He raised his eyes to meet hers. "Kieron, it is the only way for her to live." Sarla said. There was sadness that leaked from her. Everyone knew what turning someone Undead meant—even in a kingdom ruled by an Undead king, with an Undead army—becoming one of the Undead was still sentencing someone to the prison of a nearly eternal life. It was still sentencing someone to being seen as no more than a monster.

Kieron looked back down at Genevieve in his arms and pushed her hair back again, "Baby, tell us what you want us to do." He could not stop his tears. He could not let her go, but he also could not imagine turning her into one of the Undead. Both options were bad.

Her eyelids fluttered open as she looked up at him again. Those beautiful golden brown eyes rimmed with blue gray steel. "It's okay, Kieron—" She breathed. Then her eyes closed as she went unconscious in his arms.

It was not an answer. Kieron lifted his head and looked at the others through his tears. He would have to choose for her.

ACKNOWLEDGEMENT

A huge thank you to Kari Francisco for reading my early drafts, sharing your insights, spending countless hours discussing and rereading, and for always being my ultimate hype girl.

To Samantha Najer, thank you for being the friend I can unapologetically share everything with—whether it's venting about the little things, celebrating my biggest wins, or talking endlessly about my books on repeat. You're always there, and I'm so grateful.

Elyse Conroy, thank you for helping me fully embrace the woman I'm becoming, including the part of me that writes the spicy, smutty stuff. You are a true force of empowerment.

To my husband, Taylor—thank you for always believing in me and encouraging me to keep pushing forward.

Dad (Brian Anderson), thank you for helping bring my vision of Savengard to life, and for never shying away from asking the tough questions as I navigate these new challenges.

And finally, thank you to every single one of you early readers who took a chance on my first book. Your support means everything.

ABOUT THE AUTHOR

The Journey Behind The Seventh King Series

It is December of 2023, and if you had told me then that I would be a published author by the summer of 2024, I probably would have laughed. I did not have any grand designs to become an author. In fact, my entrance into the world of writing was entirely unplanned. I simply started feeling creative and daydreaming about a storyline, and the thought struck me: "Why not give it a try?"

At the time, my only goal was to enjoy myself. I had no particular plan in place—no desire to publish, no burning ambition to craft a literary masterpiece. But as I began writing, I found the process so enjoyable that I decided to challenge myself. Could I actually finish a book? The answer turned out to be a resounding "yes." Fast forward a few months, and I had completed The Seventh King, the first book in what has now evolved into an entire fantasy romance series.

The first book was officially published on June 3, 2024, and to my own surprise, I didn't stop there. The joy of creation was too addictive, and so I moved straight into the second book, Crown of Shadows, which was published on November 1, 2024. What began as a casual project has now blossomed into a full-fledged series, with plans for five main books and a standalone spin-off.

A Romantasy World Built On Imagination And Magic

The world I have created for this series is a vast, complex tapestry of magic, politics, love, and betrayal. Much of the landscape in my books was inspired by Montana's majestic mountains, wide-open spaces, and serene natural beauty. There are scenes, towns, and chapters that reflect areas I love in Montana, which served as a perfect backdrop for the magical expansiveness I wanted to create. In The Seventh King, readers are introduced to Genevieve, a woman in her thirties who is thrust into a new world where magic pulses in the very air she breathes. Genevieve's journey isn't just one of self-discovery—it's one filled with intrigue, danger, and deep emotional stakes.

Caught between the politics of multiple kingdoms, Genevieve's story is one of survival, growth, and mastery of her own power. Many of my main characters embody the rugged independence and resourcefulness I see in the people of Montana. This lifestyle, deeply rooted in self-reliance, mirrors the challenges my characters face as they navigate treacherous landscapes and complex relationships. The romantic entanglements Genevieve finds herself in are as complex as the magic she is learning to control, creating an electrifying story that is both spicy and emotional.

From Cellphone To Self-Publishing

One of the funnier parts of my writing journey is how much of The Seventh King was written, believe it or not, on my cellphone. Between managing the chaos of a toddler and squeezing in time during naps, writing on my phone became my go-to method for getting words down. When I eventually transitioned to my computer, I realized how determined I had become to make this story happen, no matter the hurdles.

What is even more interesting is how this process evolved into self-publishing. Once I finished The Seventh King, I realized I wanted to share this story with the world, but I also wanted control over every aspect of the publishing process. So I took on the challenge of self-publishing. From editing to cover design to managing the actual publishing and marketing of the book, I have done it all myself. While it is an enormous amount of work, it is also incredibly fulfilling to have ownership over every detail of my books.

Of course, I am not entirely on my own—I have a strong support system of close friends who beta-read for me and provide invaluable feedback. The world map found in The Seventh King and Crown of Shadows was designed by my father, whose artistry added an extra layer of depth and richness to the world I had envisioned.

Balancing Life As A Stay-At-Home Mom And Author

One of the questions I get asked most frequently is how I balance writing with being a stay-at-home mom to a toddler. The answer? Nap time is sacred. Those few hours of quiet during the day are my most productive writing times. Being a full-time mom while also trying to write and promote a fantasy series isn't easy, but it's become a rhythm that works for me. I have learned to work in bursts of creative energy, often finding inspiration in the most unexpected moments.

When my family and I moved to Bozeman in 2020, I never anticipated that I would spend my days alternating between mom duties and creating an expansive magical world in my spare time. Living in Bozeman has given me a peaceful, creative environment to write in, and when I hit a wall, stepping outside into Montana's natural beauty always helps me clear my mind. A hike, a picnic, or even just time outdoors usually brings new ideas, or helps me untangle tricky plot or character issues.

A Journey I Never Expected

What continues to surprise me is how much joy I have found in writing. I never set out with the goal of becoming an author, but as I have immersed myself in this creative process, I have realized just how deeply I love storytelling. The more I write, the more stories I want to tell. I have a clear roadmap for my current series—five books, with an additional standalone spin-off—but as long as I continue having fun, I will keep writing. Who knows what other worlds or stories I will stumble upon along the way?

Looking Forward: Beyond Crown Of Shadows

With the release of Crown of Shadows on November 1, 2024, I am eager to share the next chapter of Genevieve's journey. The stakes are higher, the magic more powerful, and the relationships more complicated (and dare I say, spicy). Readers will see Genevieve evolve as she navigates the shadowy undercurrents of not only this new world, but of herself.

In many ways, this second book is even more exciting for me, because I have grown more confident in my storytelling abilities and my understanding of the world I have built. The complexities of the characters and their relationships deepen, and the magic system I have created becomes richer and more intricate.

Final Thoughts

Looking back, what began as a simple desire to try something new has transformed into a true project of passion. Writing this series has taught me so much—not just about the craft of storytelling, but about myself. I never expected to become an author, but now that I am, I can't imagine doing anything else.

As I continue to explore Genevieve's world and delve deeper into the intricacies of magic, love, and power, I'm reminded that the best journeys are often the ones we never plan for. And for that, I am endlessly grateful.

BOOKS IN THIS SERIES

The Seventh King Series

The Seventh King

Crown Of Shadows

Made in United States
Cleveland, OH
08 January 2025

13227703R00277